SOMETHING WYVERIAN THIS WAY COMES

JEFFREY POOLE

Jeffrey Poole's Epic Fantasy Books
Bakkian Chronicles:
The Prophecy
Insurrection
Amulet of Aria
Disneyland Debacle (short story)
Winter Wonderland (short story)

Tales of Lentari
Lost City
Something Wyverian This Way Comes
A Portal for Your Thoughts
Thoughts for a Portal
Wizard in the Woods
Close Encounters of the Magical Kind
The Hunt for Red Oskorlisk (short story)
May the Fang be With You (Pirates trilogy #1)
The Hammer is Strong with This One (Pirates #2)
These are Not the Stones You're Looking For (Pirates #3)
Blast from the Past

Dragons of Andela
Harness the Fire
Strike the Spark
Clear the Water

Mysteries by J.M. Poole
The Corgi Case Files Series
18 delightful cozy mystery novels featuring corgi
sleuths, Sherlock and Watson

SOMETHING WYVERIAN THIS WAY COMES

Tales of Lentari, Book 2

JEFFREY POOLE

Secret Staircase Books

Something Wyverian This Way Comes
Published by Secret Staircase Books, an imprint of
Columbine Publishing Group, LLC
PO Box 416, Angel Fire, NM 87710

Book layout and design by Secret Staircase Books
Interior illustration created by Brett Gable, used with permission.
First Secret Staircase paperback edition: July, 2023

First Secret Staircase e-book edition: July, 2023

* * *

Publisher's Cataloging-in-Publication Data

Poole, Jeffrey.
Something Wyverian This Way Comes / by Jeffrey Poole.
p. cm.
ISBN 978-1649141347 (paperback)
ISBN 978-1649141354 (e-book)

1. Lentari (Fictitious location)—Fiction. 2. Epic fantasy fiction 3.
Dragons and mythical creatures—Fiction. I. Title

Tales of Lentari : Book 2.
Something Wyverian This Way Comes
Poole, Jeffrey, Bakkian Chronicles epic fantasy series.

BISAC : FICTION / Fantasy/Epic.

813/.54

For Grandma Bonnie —
(1926-2014)

This book is dedicated to a sweet lady who has been there for me all of my life. You may be gone, grandma, but you will never be forgotten.

I promise you, we will see each other again!

Acknowledgments

I'm quickly becoming dependent upon quite a few people helping me out whenever I'm ready to release one of my books. Here we go…

Providing the illustration of the dragon egg is Honorary Citizen of Lentari, Brett Gable. You might remember Brett as being the person responsible for drawing the wonderful Questor's Mark from Lost City, as well as everyone's favorite tool, the Narian power hammer.

Chief among the list of people to thank are my beta readers. You guys are awesome! There isn't one group of people who make me feel like a dunce more than these guys. To all those many errors everyone found, I'll just blame the keyboard for not being able to keep up with my typing skills. Hmmm. Anyone buying it? :) Giliane (my wife), Diane (my mother), Jamie, (Lia), Brett Gable (Tristofer), Derek Pritchard, Laura Mathews, Debra Shapiro, Jeryme Hunter, Caroline Craven and Scott Poe. Then, I have to thank my second set of beta readers: Susan Gross, Sandra Anderson, and Paula Webb.

Finally, I have to thank *you*. The fans. I can't say this enough: THANK YOU! It's been an absolute blast keeping Lentari alive when I was originally planning on ending it after Amulet of Aria. You asked to keep the series going, so thanks to all of your support, there are more stories on the way!

Thanks again & happy reading!

J.

Table of Contents

"He believes the time of the wyverian is over."
— *Kahvel*

Prologue

How many have fallen now, beloved? How many more must fall before he will do something? Surely he will seek help from our allies, or perhaps —"

"He will not seek help. You know him as well as I."

"What are we to do? We must do something. There is too much at stake!"

The huge golden dragon angled his long serpentine neck to look back at their nest. After a few moments, his mate came up next to him and gently twined her green neck with his. Together, they gazed into the dark recess of their cave.

"I cannot believe Rinbok will sit idly by while the rest of us suffer."

"Rinbok has become stricken."

Pryllan's eyes widened with surprise. This was not news she wanted to hear. She clicked her fangs together, worried.

"How long has he had it?"

"At least a month," her mate told her.

"We have allies! Why will he not prevail upon them for help? They will come to our aid. I know it!"

"He believes the time of the wyverian is over," Kahvel said softly.

Anger flared. Pryllan bared her fangs and growled. "Do you believe that?"

Kahvel's neck untwined itself from hers. His large golden head turned to regard her. "I want to believe he's wrong. So many of our brethren have succumbed, my love. So many! I begin to wonder if perhaps he's right."

Pryllan wrapped her long tail around her mate's body and shook him. "You cannot think like that. I do not agree with Rinbok Intherer about this. Neither should you."

Kahvel was silent for a few minutes before he responded. "No. For Pravara's sake, I refuse to."

"How strong is your resolve?"

"Why do you ask that?"

Pryllan's green slitted eyes narrowed. "Would you disobey Rinbok's orders?"

Kahvel looked back at the dark opening of their cave and sighed.

"Aye, I would. Now explain yourself."

"We must consult the humans. They have a wizard. A wizard and his jhorun could help us."

Kahvel shook his head. "There's no way we can ask the human wizard for advice without word reaching their king. The human king would have to inform Rinbok for fear of jeopardizing the wyverian-human pact."

"What about Steve?"

Her mate's surprise was evident by the way his body gave a slight jerk and then froze. Slowly Kahvel's head turned to face her.

"That human is in another world. Besides, he is but one human man. What could he possibly do?"

"Whether he would be able to help us remains to be seen. However, if there is a chance that he might be able to do something, do you not want to try?"

Kahvel was silent for a full five minutes before answering.

"Very well, I am tired. I will stand watch. I know not how

to initiate contact with a being in another world so I cannot offer any guidance on how to proceed."

Pryllan unfolded her wings from her back and stretched them out to their fullest potential. "Perhaps a dwarf would know. I remember hearing somewhere that one of the dwarves has contacted him before. I must find out which one."

"Be discreet," Kahvel warned. "Remember, we must not arouse Rinbok Intherer's suspicions. Confide in only those that you trust."

Pryllan nodded. Beating her wings, she lifted off the ground and ascended into the air. Gaining altitude, she dipped her right wing and started to turn east. Looking down at the rapidly passing grasslands of the valley, she briefly wondered how she should make contact with the dwarves. She knew of five entrances scattered throughout the valley. She knew there were more subterranean entrances hidden within the forest, but since she could not reasonably move her bulk in such close proximity to the heavy concentration of trees, she ignored them and instead focused on those that were more readily accessible.

As a member of the largest species of winged creatures that called Lentari home, she was more at peace in the wide-open skies with the wind under her wings than being stuck on the ground for an indeterminable amount of time. She couldn't imagine a worse fate for a dragon, than being grounded. That was why she must prevail. That was why she had to find the only human she had ever allowed to ride on her back. The problem was this particular human was in another world.

She knew of the portals, which, if the right portal key were used, would create a doorway to allow travel between the two worlds. She knew that the key to activate Steve's portal was kept in his world and since he and his mate had been responsible for the well-being of the young human prince, contact between the worlds was strictly monitored. Any contact with the other foreign world would have to be from their end, not from Lentari. Now with the threat to the human prince neutralized, both the human king and Steve kept keys so either side could initiate contact with the other. The problem with the portals, unfortunately, was that only a human would be able to fit through. There was no way a creature her size would be able to use it.

There was that instance last year when Sarah, Steve's wife, had accidentally teleported her, and her rider, back to his world. She had seen firsthand what Steve's home world looked like and quite frankly, he could have it. There were small metallic bugs scooting along the ground and loud speeding monsters flying through the air faster than she could go; none of it appealed to her. But, it was Steve's world, and he was her friend. She knew if she could just make contact with him, he'd be willing to help.

Choosing the most frequently used dwarven entrance, Pryllan landed quietly beside the large boulders and camouflaged herself. The last thing she needed was to have it look as though she was lying in ambush for a dwarf to go in or out of the hidden tunnel. Her mate had said she'd need to be discreet, so discreet she'd be.

Invoking her species natural ability to protect itself, her skin took on the coloring of the surrounding environment. In this manner, she could choose to look like either an enormous mound of grass, or she could become a group of the huge stones. She opted for the latter. Now, all an outsider would see would be a large jumble of stones sitting near the individual rock that hid the door leading down. All she had to do now was to wait.

Nearly an hour later she felt several tremors in the earth. Cracking open an eye to investigate her surroundings, she saw that the dwarf door was opening. The large boulder lifted easily off the ground and swung up into the air. A group of three dwarves, chatting merrily, emerged from the depths of the earth and started north while the door noiselessly swung back down and clicked into place.

"Pardon me."

All three dwarves whirled around and stared, disbelievingly, as a pile of nearby boulders sprouted eyes. Two green reptilian eyes blinked a few times as if they had just awoken after a long nap. Both eyes swiveled as they locked onto the dwarf that was nervously edging out in front.

"Who are you, dragon?" the lead dwarf exclaimed. "Why do you lie in wait for us? I thought there was a pact in place which prevented such atrocities from happening again."

"Be at ease," Pryllan told the dwarf as gently as she could. She let her camouflage drop and presented herself before the dwarf in her true form. "I come in peace. I'm looking for a dwarf."

Relaxing somewhat, the lead dwarf narrowed his eyes as he stared at the enormous green dragon.

"Who is it then? Who are you searching for?"

"I'm looking for, er, for…"

Pryllan hesitated as she realized she had completely forgotten the dwarf's name. Suddenly, and without explanation, it came to her.

"Breslin. I'm searching for Breslin. Do you know where I can find him?"

"How do you know Breslin?" one of the other two dwarves suspiciously asked.

Facts started falling into place. Pryllan smiled. "We fought together during the battle with the human sorceress."

The dwarves' demeanor instantly reversed. Gone were the skeptical frowns and scowls.

"Why the ruddy hell didn't you say so before? Any friend of Breslin is a friend of ours! I am Loken. That's Argus on my left and on my right is Xaj."

"I am Pryllan."

"I thought as much," Loken nodded. "You're looking for Breslin? Well, if you're willing to wait, he's due Topside in just a few hours."

"That is acceptable," Pryllan told them.

Several hours later Pryllan was flying back to their nest. The news Breslin had given her hadn't been very encouraging. Apparently, there was a way to communicate with Steve in his home world, but that would work only if Steve was holding a special sword, while Breslin maintained physical contact with his own weapon. Holders of the Mythra weapons could then communicate telepathically; otherwise, someone would have to journey to Steve's world and ask him directly. Since she couldn't fit through the portal and didn't know who to trust when it came to her family, she hesitated in confiding with the dwarf. She liked Breslin well enough, but not enough to relay her concerns about her fellow dragons.

Returning to her nest, she approached Kahvel, who had encircled the nest with his body and had clamped his tail with his teeth. With as much stealth as she could afford, she crept over Kahvel's resting body and carefully curled up in their nest. She thought again of the importance of protecting those she cared about. Pryllan vowed to find a cure for whatever was plaguing her fellow dragons. She would not allow those under her care to come to harm.

Snuggling up next to Kahvel, basking in the warmth his body was generating, she fell asleep, pondering how to best contact her human friend.

Chapter 1 — Do Dragons Dream?

The treetops were passing swiftly by him far below. Faster and faster he beat his wings, as though one of the dreaded mechanical devices that had attacked his brethren years ago was somehow on his tail again.

He dipped his wings and banked to the right, inhaling deeply as he did so. He could detect the fragrant scent of pine trees intermingled with the aromatic scents of blooming pontal, mixed in with the unmistakable trace of water. Without looking about, he knew that the lake lay directly behind him.

He dipped his left wing this time and brought himself completely around so that he was now flying north. There, just as he expected, was the huge freshwater lake he had flown over countless other times. Gliding low, he lazily dropped a foreleg down so that his claw gently broke the surface of the water.

Several hundred feet from the northern shore a strong breeze kicked up, threatening to send the strongest of fliers off course and possibly down into the water. Not him. He was a dragon. He was simply too massive to be bothered by a breeze that could barely be felt under his wings. Nevertheless, he shifted his wings up and angled the tips so that he was now using this new wind to gain altitude. Higher and higher he rose, until the large body of water looked like the smallest of ponds.

A strange feeling of uneasiness came over him. He was worried about something, but he didn't know what. What did he have to be worried about? Nothing in the air, or on the ground for that matter, could threaten him, so what did he have to fear? He was at the top of the food chain. Nothing preyed on a dragon. However, the more he dwelled on the foreign sensations, the more worried he became.

Something wasn't right.

He turned his heavily armored neck to look to his left, then his right. Bending his neck back until he was looking directly behind him, he looked for signs of danger. Nothing presented itself. Huffing irritably, he returned his gaze to the north and again scanned the environment for potential hazards.

Nothing.

The air turned thin. His wings began to lose purchase and he fell from the sky. What was going on? Why couldn't he remain airborne? No matter how hard he flapped his wings he couldn't seem to slow his rapid descent. He was plummeting dangerously fast and there wasn't anything he could do about it.

He roared in frustration, but then his mouth snapped closed. His flames hadn't appeared. Had he lost the ability to spit fire, too? He inhaled, pumping much-needed oxygen into his internal furnace to fuel his flames. He had intended to let out a blast of fire to alert any other wyverians in the vicinity that he was in trouble. The blast would have melted the strongest suit of armor in less than a second; however, nothing happened when he finally let his breath whoosh out. No smoke, no searing hot flames.

Alarmed, he looked down at the rapidly approaching lake. He was going to strike the lake almost dead center. As he watched the water loom closer and closer, his befuddled mind kept asking why this was happening to him. What had he done to deserve this treatment? He was no water dragon. He didn't even know how to swim.

Resigned to his fate, he closed his eyes and waited for the impact.

Cold water splashed his face, going promptly up his nose. He leapt out of bed with a curse and struggled to come to his senses. Directly across from him, laughing hysterically, was his wife. She was twirling the empty bucket around on her finger.

"Why you... you..."

"What?" Sarah asked playfully, even innocently. "Didn't I warn you I was going to get you back when you threw that water on me in the shower yesterday?"

Steve slid a hand down his face to push the excess water onto the floor. He stood, dripping wet, as he glared at his wife.

"I said it before, and I'll say it again: it was an *accident*. I don't know why there was a cup in the shower. It filled up on its own accord. You're the one that tipped that thing over on yourself. I had nothing to do with it!"

"So you're saying that I dumped that glass of cold water on myself? Is that the story you're sticking with?"

"Revenge will be mine, lady," Steve vowed with a grin. "You have to fall asleep sometime."

"I'd rephrase that if I were you," Sarah warned with a laugh. "You're a heavier sleeper than I am."

Steve's smug smile disappeared in the blink of an eye.

"There's never a dull moment around here, that's for sure," Steve chuckled as he pulled the sopping wet sheets from the bed.

"It'd be too boring otherwise," Sarah agreed, lending a hand in changing the bedding.

An hour and a half later they were inside Sarah's store, Cookbook Nook. Since he didn't have any computer repair calls to attend to today, Steve decided to hang around the store and help Sarah out. He was given a stack of internet orders and tasked with collecting all the necessary books so that they could go out when the shipping service came at eleven o'clock.

"I don't suppose there's a map of this place, is there? I don't know how you can find anything in here."

Sarah looked down at him from the second story balcony. "Look at the size of this place. It's not that big, dear. We don't need a map. What are you looking for?"

"Some cookbook called *Duckberry Patch* something or other."

"That's a very popular line of cookbooks. It's over there, on that spinning display rack. See that metal thing next to the tray of cookies?"

Steve's head jerked up. "Cookies? You have cookies here? What kind are they? Better yet, where are they?"

Sarah sighed and shook her head. "Fill the orders and you can have as many cookies as you'd like."

"Hunk oo berry ucchh."

"You already ate one, didn't you?"

Steve spun away from his wife and hastily swallowed. "Did not."

"Yeah, right. Sure you didn't. Just fill those orders, please. Lia isn't in until ten."

"You got it."

Sarah's manager, Lia, arrived just in time to start a cake decorating class, held upstairs in the small commercial kitchen. While Lia showed another batch of hopefuls the intricacies of creating delicate gum paste flowers, Steve sidled up to Sarah and tapped the small shoebox on the counter.

"What's this?"

"It's the box of recipes I borrowed from your mother. I was planning on returning them this afternoon after I have lunch with my mom."

Steve nodded. "I thought that box looked familiar. I didn't even know you had it. When did she give it to you?"

"Last month."

Steve nodded again. There weren't many people, he thought with amusement, who could carry out an afternoon like the one his wife had planned. Lunch in Sacramento, California, with a stopover in Phoenix, Arizona. Unless you had your own private jet, that sort of thing wasn't typically possible. Not unless you happened to be one of two humans on the face of the planet who could actually perform magic. Not the fake magic which involved sleight of hand, or mirrors, but actual science-cannot-explain-it magic. Sarah could teleport. Distance was irrelevant as long as she could picture where she was going.

Therefore, an out-of-state journey to see her family in northern California was literally accomplished in the blink of an eye. Steve wondered again how many people would love to do that. Then again, he was the other person who could perform magic, so he really didn't have any grounds for complaint. His magical ability allowed him to summon and control fire.

His magic wasn't very useful in his everyday life, especially in a store full of books, but in the magical Kingdom of Lentari, where both of them had received their gifts, they were a force to be reckoned with. No one wanted to cross a fire thrower, especially one of his caliber, nor would they want to anger the teleporter who could not only protect herself, but was married to the aforementioned fire thrower.

However, their fighting days were over. Steve hadn't had to use his flames to do anything, besides lighting their barbecue or their fire pit, in well over a year. And if he were asked, he'd say that's how he preferred it.

"Sure you don't want to come with me?" Sarah asked, looking up from her stack of unfiled books.

Steve shook his head. "Hmm, as appealing as that is, I have to take the truck in to get the brakes checked. Damn things have started squealing on me."

"Want to meet at the Hacienda for dinner tonight?" Sarah asked hopefully.

"Absolutely. It's Friday, which means it's date night. You're not getting out of date night."

Sarah giggled. "You're on. See you at five."

A few hours later, Steve strolled in to Hacienda, their favorite restaurant. He presented Sarah with a bouquet of flowers and settled into the booth. Sarah's eyes opened wide with excitement, as they always did, whenever he brought her flowers.

"Aww! Carnations! How pretty! Thank you!"

"Yeah, that was a real hoot, standing in the checkout line holding a bunch of pink carnations. I think the cashier was laughing at me."

Sarah grinned. "She's just jealous."

While eating their dinner and chatting amicably back and forth over the day's events, Steve's nostrils flared as he picked up the scent from Sarah's flowers. He gently picked them up and lightly sniffed.

"Smell great, don't they?" Sarah beamed.

"They sure do," Steve agreed. "Reminds me of the dream I had last night."

"You dreamt about pink flowers?"

"Hardy har-har. Of course not. Well, no, that's not true. There were flowers there, although I didn't see any. But I could smell them."

"What were you dreaming about that involved flowers?" Sarah wanted to know.

"It was a very vivid dream. Very realistic. I can usually tell when I'm dreaming, only this time I couldn't. It felt so real."

Intrigued, Sarah leaned closer. She rested her elbows on the table and gazed at her husband.

"Well, tell me about it. What can you remember?"

"Everything," Steve told her. "I remember it like it just happened to me. I was flying through the air. I remember flying out over a sea of treetops; clearly, I was high up in the air."

"Lentari," Sarah guessed correctly. "You were dreaming about Lentari. That isn't surprising. You've told me that you do that all the time."

"Yeah, I know, but this was different," Steve insisted. "This dream had me convinced I was there. Sights. Sounds. Smells. Everything was perfectly done."

"You've been to Lentari before," Sarah pointed out. "Several times. Of course, your dream is going to get it right. In fact, I dreamt about Lentari last night, too."

Surprised, Steve lowered his glass of soda and stared at his wife.

"Don't look so shocked," Sarah scolded. "I can have the crazy fantasy dreams like you have every once in a while."

"What was yours about?"

"I was looking through the eyes of a dragon," Sarah recalled. She sat back in her chair and smiled. "We were up high in the sky, flying back and forth, as if we were looking for something."

"Next you'll tell me that you started smelling water."

Sarah tilted her head and was silent as she regarded her husband.

"Well?"

"How did you know that?"

"And once you were over the water," Steve continued, "you started feeling uneasy. A wind appeared over the water and it pushed you up."

"Way up," Sarah whispered quietly, properly spooked.

"Once you were up there, your wings lost the ability to hold the air and you plummeted straight down."

"How are you doing this?" Sarah asked, shock evident on her face and in her voice.

"I had the same dream, babe."

"You did? How's that possible? What does it mean?"

Steve shrugged. "I'm not sure. Think something is wrong in Lentari?"

"It couldn't hurt to check, could it?"

"Meaning you'd like me to check the sword or do you want to use the portal?"

Their waitress, pausing only long enough to drop the check on their table, regarded them with a suspicious look.

"It's this new video game we're playing," Steve explained with a smile. "It's easy to get caught up in it."

The waitress gave the two of them a patronizing smile and moved to the next table.

"Okay, it's time to go."

Returning to the mansion the two of them inherited after Steve's grandparents had passed away several years ago, Sarah headed straight to her husband's office on the main floor.

Living in Coeur d'Alene, Idaho, had become an absolute dream. Living in an area which saw nearly six feet of annual snowfall had been a challenge at first. But, then again, when you're married to a walking, talking, human flame thrower, snow removal had become a thing of the past.

Steve followed her into the office. He took down a two-handed broadsword that was hanging from a solid oak display on the west wall. Also on the wall were several other swords. One had a golden dragon on the hilt. Next to it were several axes. Sliding the scabbard off his sword revealed a dark green blade. He gripped the piece in both hands and waited. Quieting his mind, not thinking of anything else, Steve strained his senses to see if he could hear any voices in his head.

Nothing.

He waited a few moments longer before he hung the Lentarian sword back on the wall.

"There's nothing there," Steve reported to his wife. "I couldn't hear anything. If someone from Lentari was trying to contact me, then you'd think that'd be the way they'd do it."

"They could have used the portal," Sarah reminded him. "It'd be much easier to do."

"What do you want to do?" Steve asked. He was starting to get concerned. Something just didn't feel right.

Sarah turned to look at a statue of a griffin standing majestically on a large pedestal in the far corner of the office. "I think we should go take a look. Just to see for ourselves that everything is okay. Besides, we have a house there now. We have permission to come and go as we please. What do you think?"

Steve had already made up his mind and was thankful he wouldn't have to convince Sarah to go. "I think we should go pack a bag."

Less than an hour later, husband and wife were standing before the griffin safe. A soft musical chiming started up as Steve approached the statue. As soon as he was standing directly in front of the mythological creature, the griffin raised a foreleg, revealing a button that had been hidden from sight. Steve pushed the button and waited for the safe's door to open.

There was a loud click as the front of the pedestal swung outward a few inches. Steve pulled open the door and reached inside, extracting a small pewter box. He handed the box to Sarah, who opened it to find a green crystal key nestled within. She took the green key and hesitated. She looked up at her husband.

"I could just teleport us all the way there. We don't really need to use the key."

Steve nodded. "I know, but if there is something going on, don't you think you'll want to save your jhorun for any emergency jumps?"

Sarah thought back to the last time she teleported from one world to the other. Ordinarily, it should be unheard of for a human to teleport that great a distance. However, her jhorun, her magic, was stronger than most as it was bestowed on her by a powerful sorceress who had lived hundreds of years ago. As powerful as her jhorun was, a single jump from their world to Lentari would more than likely deplete it. While her natural reserves would recharge by the following day, Steve was right. It was an unnecessary risk. It would be better to use their portal and save her powers.

"You're right. Let's use the portal. Better safe than sorry."

Steve noticed Sarah was still staring at the open safe and glanced down at the pedestal. Sitting in a tray, on the one and only shelf in the safe, were two pieces of a broken amulet. Husband and wife eyed each other.

"Absolutely not," Sarah declared.

Steve slammed the safe closed. "Couldn't agree more."

He took the key from Sarah and led them to the top floor of their manor. He closed the large master bedroom doors and stared again at the fascinating carving that had been revealed once the doors were closed. It was a carved representation of Lentari, displaying the mountains to the north and southeast as well as the major rivers bisecting the country from the east coast to the west. Also visible, in the top right corner of the carving, was a multi-turreted castle. One of the castle's windows was shaped like a keyhole. Sarah inserted the key and twisted.

Within moments the manor's two master bedroom doors fused together and they were looking at a forest path.

"Brings back memories, doesn't it?" Steve remarked.

"It sure does," Sarah agreed. She nudged her husband in the ribs. "Come on, let's go."

Steve felt mildly ridiculous as he picked up their suitcase and stepped through the portal. Both of them turned to look at the rectangular opening showing them an image of their house back in Coeur d'Alene, Idaho. Within moments the portal had vanished and they were alone in the middle of a forest. Sarah took his hand. The forest winked out and was immediately replaced by a quiet, dark living room in a small two-bedroom house.

Humming merrily, Sarah walked around the house and verified all was well. Steve wheeled the heavy suitcase into the larger of the two bedrooms and set their luggage up on the bed. He walked over to a large wardrobe and opened it to reveal a selection of tunics, trousers, gowns, footwear, and essentially anything else it would take for the two of them to blend in with the rest of the villagers.

"Tell me again why you had to pack so much when all of our Lentarian clothes are still here?"

Sarah smiled. She reached into the open suitcase and pulled out a small bag. She held it up so that Steve could see it. "See any electrical outlets around here? I'm not going anywhere without my curling iron. Do you know how difficult it was to find one that runs on batteries?"

Steve chuckled and wisely decided to keep his comments to himself.

Once they were properly attired, Steve strapped Mythrin, his special green-bladed broadsword, to his hip.

"You'd think there'd be a better way to communicate than having this thing strapped to your belt," Steve complained. "If Rhenyon or Breslin don't have their weapons handy, then they wouldn't even know if we encountered trouble."

"You love having that thing on your hip and you know it," Sarah countered.

Steve grinned. "True."

Steve? Is that you? Are you really back in Lentari?

Steve jumped and dropped a bottle of water he had been about to open. Alarmed, Sarah rushed to his side.

"What's wrong? What's the matter?"

"It's Pryllan. Hang on; let me see what she wants."

Hi, Pryllan. It's me. Is everything okay?

Is Sarah with you? Will you meet me at the valley?

The valley south of Lake Raehón? Sure. When?

Now.

Okay, I'll have Sarah take us there. Do you know where those large boulders are near the southern edge of the valley?

I do.

One of them is a dwarf door. We'll meet you there. Whoops, don't tell them I told you that.

Agreed.

"We need to head north. I don't know what the problem is, but Pryllan sounded worried. Remember that large boulder? That's where she's going to meet us."

Sarah nodded. "No problem. Ready?"

Steve tossed his water bottle back on the bed.

"Ready."

In the blink of an eye, the stuffy air of their cottage in the Lentarian capital of R'Tal was replaced with a cool mountain breeze wafting gently from the north. They could smell the nearby pine trees; they could detect traces of moisture coming from the large freshwater lake sitting off in the distance; as well, they picked up the fragrant scent of numerous wildflowers all scattered about. They both inhaled deeply. Even though they lived in the northern Idaho panhandle, and Coeur d'Alene sat in the middle of a forest bearing its name, the scents assailing them now were nothing like back home. Perhaps it was the lack of industrialization?

"I'll never grow tired of this," Sarah observed as she shielded her eyes and looked around at the quiet, serene valley. "So, where is she?"

"I'm here," a voice said from directly behind them.

Steve and Sarah both jumped and whirled around. Pryllan was there. How dragons could move with such stealth, Steve would never know. He was glad, though, to see his friend.

"Pryllan! It's good to see you again!"

"And you."

"Is everything alright?" Sarah asked, concerned. "Steve seemed to think you sounded worried."

"I am worried."

Steve shared a look with Sarah. What could possibly worry a dragon? Before he could ask, a memory from last night's painfully vivid dream flashed before his eyes. He swallowed nervously.

"Can you tell us what's going on?"

Pryllan cast an anxious look around the valley.

"Not here." Pryllan opened one of her mighty claws. "If you will allow me."

Not showing the slightest bit of hesitation, both Steve and his wife sat companionably in the open palm.

Pryllan gently cupped her two claws together. Both humans felt the huge dragon bunch her muscles and then they were launched straight up. Extending her wings as soon as she hit the peak of her jump, Pryllan banked to the right. Once the western Bohanis were before them, she leveled off and started flapping her wings to gain altitude. Higher and higher she rose, as they flew out over the western shores of Lake Raehón.

The valley fell behind them, replaced by numerous mountains, some covered with nothing but rock and others covered by trees. One barren peak, completely devoid of greenery, appeared farther west. Pryllan dipped her wings and angled herself toward the mountain.

As they neared, they could see a black dot high up the southeastern side, facing the distant valley. Also visible was enough room immediately outside the cave entrance for a dragon to bask in the sun, as Kahvel, Pryllan's mate, was doing. The golden dragon's head jerked up and he watched them approach.

Landing softly next to her mate, Pryllan waited for the two humans to reach the ground before straightening back up.

"Hello, Kahvel." Sarah smiled up at the imposing figure of the golden dragon. "It's nice to see you again."

Kahvel nodded at her. "Sarah." His golden eyes fixed on Steve. "Good day to you, Steve."

Steve was silent as he studied Kahvel. This was the first dragon he had ever met and was still the largest, provided Steve didn't include the king of sourpusses, Rinbok Intherer, Dragon Lord. Granted, it had been a while since he had spent any time amongst the wyverians, but he could still see that something was bothering the powerful dragon.

"What's gotten into you?" Steve inquired. He ignited his hand and generated a chaser, which he spun on his index finger. "Who's ticked you off? Let's go kick their butt together. What do you say?"

The tiniest trace of a smile appeared on Kahvel's reptilian face before the dragon was able to compose himself.

"If only it were that simple," Kahvel's deep voice rumbled.

"What's going on? Why have you brought us here?"

Kahvel shook his head.

"I did not bring you here." The golden dragon nodded his head toward his mate. "She did."

"How did you manage to give us both the same dream?" Sarah wanted to know. "That was both creepy and impressive at the same time."

Pryllan smiled cryptically, but remained silent.

"So what's going on?" Steve asked again.

Kahvel finally stirred. He lifted his neck up and swung his head to the left to look east. "I believe we are under an attack."

"Excuse me?" Steve stammered.

He stared in shock at the golden dragon. Steve and Sarah eyed each other nervously. What creature in their right mind would dare to take on the dragons? Steve noticed that Pryllan had bared her fangs. Clearly this must be a sore subject for her.

"You don't know that for certain," Pryllan growled.

"How many have we lost now?"

"Excuse me?" Steve repeated, raising a hand. "Lost? You lost some dragons? As in some dragons have lost their lives?"

Sarah clapped her hands over her mouth in horror.

"They have not succumbed," Pryllan told Steve, glancing briefly down at the human. "Not yet."

"But they will," Kahvel spat. "You have not seen what they've become. Listless. Lifeless. They wait to die."

"This is more serious than we thought," Steve whispered to Sarah.

"I will NOT allow Pravara to suffer the same fate!" Kahvel roared. Steve and Sarah inadvertently took several steps back. "This must be stopped and must be done NOW! We need to act before it's too late!"

"Um, who's Pravara?" Sarah asked in a quiet voice.

Pryllan stared at Kahvel a few moments longer, as if daring him to lose his temper once more. When Kahvel finally looked away, Pryllan's demeanor softened. She nodded toward the cave.

"She's there. She *was* sleeping, but I'm sure she's awake now."

Sure enough, they could hear something stirring in the far recesses of the dark cave. The noises grew louder as whatever was in the cave headed toward them. They heard a soft rasping sound and then the creature moved into the sunlight.

Sarah went all mushy. It was a baby dragon.

Chapter 2 — Family Values

The young dragon was five feet tall at the shoulder, and from snout to tail, was nearly fifteen feet long. The baby's thin, leathery wings were folded flat against its back, and as far as her mass, Steve estimated her to be twice the size of a baby elephant. The scales were the darkest, deepest forest green color either of them had ever seen. As soon as the sun hit the creature, it sparkled with radiance. Steve saw that each of the baby dragon's dark green scales was edged with a thin line of gold, no doubt due to Kahvel's golden coloring. The dragonlet sniffed the air and then turned to look pointedly at the visitors, noticing for the first time that a couple of non-wyverian beings were present.

"Aww! That has to be the cutest thing I've ever seen!" Sarah wanted desperately to go over to the baby and cuddle it, but was unsure how docile a baby dragon would be.

Pryllan looked with undisguised pride down at her offspring. She clicked her fangs together to get the baby's attention. Once she had it, Pryllan inclined her neck toward the humans.

"Pravara, we have guests. These are…"

"Humans!" Pravara finished for her mother. As soon as she noticed that she had become the center of attention, the dragonlet frantically rushed to her mother and hid behind several coils of Pryllan's green tail. Pravara peered suspiciously at them from the safety of her mother's side.

"Pravara, don't be rude. This is Steve, and the female is his mate, Sarah."

Pravara inched away from her mother and gradually approached the two newcomers. The dragonlet sniffed cautiously, familiarizing herself with their scents. Once that dangerous task had been successfully accomplished, she turned tail and fled back to the safety of her mother. Two large golden eyes watched the proceedings from a much safer distance.

"She's adorable," Sarah told the two dragons. "How old is she?"

"She hatched almost ten months ago," Pryllan answered.

"Wow. Is she big for her age?" Steve stared with fascination at the strikingly dark green creature before them. He smiled up at the dragon baby who was staring at him with equal curiosity. "Do young dragons grow quickly?"

Pryllan nodded. "Kahvel disagrees, but I maintain if you watch her long enough, then she will grow right before your eyes."

Sarah smiled. "All parents say that, Pryllan."

"Wyverians will generally reach their adult size in a few years," Kahvel informed them. "Pravara is actually small for her age. She must take after her mother."

Pryllan's head jerked up. She stared at her mate.

"It's just my own opinion," Kahvel hastily added.

Steve held out a hand, as though he was facing a stray dog.

"Hi there! I won't hurt you. Neither of us will. Look at those pretty golden eyes. I'll bet you get into all kinds of trouble, don't you?"

Pravara blinked her eyes a few times as she studied him.

"Lots of trouble," Pryllan agreed.

Pravara glanced up at her mother before returning her gaze to Steve. It was as if the little dragon was unable to look away. Her large golden eyes glanced briefly at Sarah before returning to Steve.

"Dr. Dolittle strikes again," Sarah murmured as she also noticed the young dragon's fascination with her husband.

"What is doctor dolittle?" Kahvel asked.

"It's just something I always say," Sarah explained. "It means Steve can make friends with just about any creature out there. Dogs, cats, birds, and apparently dragons."

"Where is the peanut?" Pryllan suddenly asked. "It has been some time since I've seen the little creature. Is it well?"

"Are you asking about Peanut, our corgi?" Steve asked the dragon. "I'm sure she'd love to see you again. Better yet, I'm sure she'd love to meet Pravara. As luck would have it, Peanut is here in Lentari at the moment. She's been with Mikal in the castle for the past couple of weeks. You'll have to stop by and say hello!"

"Or we could bring Peanut here," Sarah suggested. "It'd probably be easier."

"Okay, sure, go for the easy way out," Steve laughed. "We'll have to find a way to introduce Peanut and Pravara. That's something I just *have* to see!"

"At what age does a dragon begin to speak?" Sarah asked, curious.

"Usually around four months of age," Pryllan answered. "Once a dragonlet is eight months old then they begin to make their wants and needs known. Pravara began speaking at three months, and was forming complete sentences by six months of age."

Becoming bolder by the second, Pravara eased away from her mother and approached Steve.

"Where are you from?" the tiny dragon inquired.

"Our home is a long way from here," Steve informed the dragonlet. "Farther than a dragon can fly."

Pravara shook her head. "That's not possible, is it? Father?"

Kahvel stared down at his young offspring and hesitated.

"In this case, it is, young one. Their home is so far away

that they must use a portal."

"A portal?" Pravara paused a few seconds to think about the unfamiliar word.

"It's an aperture, typically jhorun in nature, which leads from one location to the next, regardless of distance," Kahvel answered, giving his offspring what sounded like a text book definition of a portal.

Pravara's golden eyes blinked rapidly while she thought about her sire's answer.

"She doesn't understand," Pryllan said to Kahvel. "She's too young."

"I am not!" Pravara declared, baring her tiny fangs in an incredibly realistic impersonation of her mother. "I know what it means!"

"Have you met many humans?" Steve good-naturedly asked the baby dragon.

Pravara emphatically nodded her head yes.

"Would you be referring to the two of us?" Sarah asked, with a twinkle in her eye.

The young dragon sheepishly nodded her head. A few moments later Pravara's innocent gaze locked onto Steve once more.

"What type of jhorun do you have?"

"Pravara!" Kahvel snapped.

The young dragon whipped her head around to stare at her sire.

"We do not ask questions like that. Most humans do not like informing others of the nature of their jhorun."

Crestfallen, Pravara dropped as low as she could to the ground.

"It's okay," Sarah quickly said; Pravara's head perked up at this. "We don't mind. We're not from Lentari, so we don't have the typical misgivings most humans who live here have."

Thankful for the swift intervention, Pravara timidly approached Sarah and stopped at a comfortable distance from both of her parents.

"What is your jhorun?" Pravara asked again.

"I can teleport," Sarah told the young dragon. "Watch this!"

Sarah disappeared. Startled, Pravara looked right, then left.

"Where did she go?"

Both adult dragons sniffed the air.

"She's nearby," Kahvel reported. "Somewhere south and at a lower elevation."

Pryllan looked over the side of the nest and down at the distant ground.

"She's there. She's waving to me."

Pravara hurried to the edge of the nest and looked at the ground far below, but was unable to see anything. The dragonlet's visual acuities, while impressive, were nowhere near her mother's. Not yet, anyway.

"I don't see her."

"Your sight and smell won't advance until your first year," Pryllan told her. "You must be patient."

Sarah appeared back at Steve's side, which was behind Pryllan and Pravara. Both mother and offspring were still looking over the edge of the nest.

"I'm back!"

Pravara jerked her head to look back at her. The little dragon trotted over to Sarah's side and sat down.

"You can move without moving!"

Sarah smiled and nodded.

Pravara sighed wistfully. "I wish I could do that."

Sarah touched Pravara's wings. "Oh, yeah? You have wings! You can fly! Or will, someday. I'd love to be able to fly!"

"I can fly now!" Pravara proudly declared. "Do you want to see? Look!"

Pravara leapt into the air and spread her small wings. Hovering unsteadily in the air, the little green dragon was flying, albeit a little on the wobbly side.

"You should show her your nose wiggle thing," Steve joked, referring to Sarah's ability to teleport objects without having the object vanish. It meant she could move objects about, as though they were guided by an invisible hand.

"I don't want to frighten her," Sarah told her husband. "Maybe later."

Pravara plopped back to the ground and folded her wings. She turned to Steve.

"What kind of jhorun do you have?"

"Hoo boy," Sarah mumbled under her breath. "Here we go."

Ignoring his wife, Steve faced the little dragon and ignited a hand.

"Your hand is on fire," Pravara helpfully informed him.

Nodding, Steve ignited his other hand.

"You're burning," Pravara told him again.

"On purpose," Steve remarked. He generated a basketball-sized fireball and spun it on his finger.

"Your jhorun is fire?" Pravara asked, amazed that the human could generate fire, let alone not be burned by it.

"Yep. Watch this, squirt!"

Steve created another dozen or so fireballs and let them hang suspended in the air next to the spinning chaser on his finger. He let the extra fireballs float harmlessly for a few moments before he sent them zipping around the perimeter of the nest. Kahvel and Pryllan watched the fireballs fly into their nest, prompting Pravara to hurry over to their cave to see what they were doing. Doubling back, the train of fireballs sped by her and back out into the open air before being called to Steve's open palm. The last fireball didn't make it; Pravara had snapped it up as it flew by.

Chewing thoughtfully, the dragonlet looked at her mother with a surprised look on her face.

"I can't taste anything."

"Because nothing is there," Pryllan informed her.

"Yes, there is," Pravara argued. "I saw it burning. Something was burning."

"He made a fireball," Pryllan tried to explain. "Steve doesn't need any material to make one."

"Then how does it burn?"

Exasperated, Pryllan looked at Kahvel, who shook his head. "Don't look at me. If you want a detailed explanation, then I'd say you should consult the one who made the fireball."

Steve looked up at the huge golden dragon.

"Excuse me?"

"That fireball was of your doing," Kahvel told him. "You've confused Pravara. It's up to you to explain it in such a way that she'll understand."

"Umm, okay. Pravara, look." Steve sat down on a nearby rock and lit his right hand. "Ordinarily this would hurt like ... well, it would hurt. My jhorun prevents my hand from burning. I can choose whether or not to let something burn. Since I don't want to be in pain, my hand isn't burning. Do you understand?"

Pravara was silent as she studied Steve's burning hand.

"Without jhorun," Steve continued, "if I were to thrust my hand into a roaring fire, I'd hurt myself. Same thing with Sarah. Her jhorun will move her around all without her moving, like you noticed before. With me so far?"

The young dragon nodded.

"Just like Sarah's jhorun, my own will allow me to burn something, regardless of whether or not there's anything there to burn."

"Can you make something burn that isn't supposed to burn?" Pravara thoughtfully asked.

"You mean like a rock?" Steve picked up a small rock from the ground and held it in his hand. "I can make the rock burn, but as soon as I pull my jhorun away from it the flames would disappear. Watch."

The small rock was suddenly engulfed in flames. Pravara watched, fascinated, as the rock appeared to burn like a dry piece of timber.

"As soon as I extinguish my flames," Steve told the dragon, "this is what happens."

The flames poofed out, which left a red-hot stone lying in Steve's unscathed hand.

"Is the stone warm?" Pravara inquired.

Sarah gently held her hand over her husband's.

"Yes, it's warm," Sarah agreed. "If that were sitting in my hand right now, I'd be badly burned."

Steve pulled the warmth away from the rock until it was cool to the touch once more. He dropped the now harmless stone to the ground.

Anxious to impress the visitors, Pravara reared up and

started taking deep gulps of air.

"I can make fire, too! Watch!"

Giving little consideration to what she was aiming at, Pravara let loose a single jet of flames. Tiny for a dragon, but still more than adequate to inflict damage if one didn't have heavy scales to protect them. Unfortunately, Pravara's flames were headed straight toward Sarah.

Sarah gasped with alarm and darted behind Steve, hoping he'd be able to shield her from the sudden onslaught of fire. Steve brought up an arm and instructed his jhorun to absorb all the incoming flames, regardless of source. Pravara hiccupped with surprise as she felt her flames being sucked out of her mouth at a high speed.

Absorbing the last of the little dragon's fiery breath, Steve visibly sighed. He glanced behind him to verify Sarah was okay; she nodded that she was.

Kahvel was outraged. "Pravara! What have I told you about spitting fire at your age? You don't have enough control yet! Apologize to Steve and Sarah. Now."

Properly cowed by her sire's glare, Pravara whispered an apology and retreated into the darkness of the cave.

"Are you two injured?" Kahvel asked, concern evident in his voice.

"No harm done," Steve assured the golden dragon. "Had that been you or Pryllan's flames my response would be different, I'm sure. As it is, it's just a harmless mistake."

Sarah nudged her husband and whispered a few words in his ear. Steve nodded as he turned to face the wyverian couple.

"Both Sarah and I are in agreement here. Whatever has you spooked, Kahvel, you can count on us to help. Whatever it takes, you have a fire thrower and a teleporter in your corner."

Kahvel nodded while Pryllan bowed her head.

"You have our thanks," the emerald dragon responded.

Steve asked. "What's going on that's bothering you enough to contact us? You mentioned before that several dragons had been lost. What did you mean?"

"There's some type of malady spreading throughout

the wyverian population," Kahvel informed them. "Large numbers of our brethren have reported they are at the first stage."

"The first stage of what?" Sarah wanted to know.

"This malady comes in three stages," Pryllan explained.

"So far as we know," Kahvel added darkly.

"The first stage happens once a dragon has become infected. After a few days, the victim loses the ability to spit fire."

"That's horrible!" Sarah exclaimed.

"The second stage," Pryllan continued, "is the loss of the Collective. For a dragon, that's detrimental to our wellbeing."

"The Collective?" Steve repeated, puzzled. "What's that? After all this time I thought I knew everything there was to know about dragons, but it turns out that I really don't know anything. Not a word, dear."

Sarah managed to keep her face neutral.

"The Collective is a telepathic connection to other dragons," Pryllan told them. "The voices of our brethren are there whenever we need them, whether to call for help, or to communicate with the Dragon Lord, or to ask a simple question. The Collective is the embodiment of everything that it is to be a wyverian."

"So this second stage cuts you off from other dragons?" Steve asked.

Kahvel nodded. "Correct. If you become hurt, or if you need to alert your brethren of a threat, you'd be unable to do so."

"What does the third stage do?" Sarah whispered, not really wanting to hear the answer.

"Loss of flight," Kahvel angrily informed her.

Steve held up his hands. "Wait just a moment. You're telling me that this wyverian malady results in a dragon becoming defenseless? What if they need to call for help? What about getting away?"

Kahvel and Pryllan both nodded.

"So that's why you're so concerned," Steve observed, looking at Pryllan, "and why you're angry," he finished, looking at Kahvel. "You two are new parents. You want to protect Pravara."

"We do," Kahvel agreed.

"How do you contract this malady?" Sarah asked. "Does anyone know?"

"How long ago did it first show up?" Steve asked.

"Who got it first?"

"How did it spread?"

Kahvel looked at his mate. Pryllan gave him the approximation of a shrug.

Kahvel suddenly looked off to the east.

"What is it?" Pryllan asked.

"I have been summoned."

"Does he know about the involvement of the humans?" Pryllan asked worriedly.

"No. If Rinbok Intherer did, he would have voiced his displeasure by now."

Steve held up a hand.

"I thought you guys were always talking with this Collective in your head? Wouldn't he already know we're here since the two of you obviously know?"

Both dragons shook their heads.

"The Collective doesn't work that way," Pryllan gently told him. "We use the Collective only when we need to. The Collective is never invasive. When we require access, we share our minds." Pryllan looked pointedly at Steve. "You should know what that is like, correct?"

Steve nodded. "Gotcha."

"Is she talking about the connection the two of you share?" Sarah softly asked, bending close to his ear to keep from being overheard.

Steve nodded again. "Right."

Kahvel extended his great golden wings and within moments he was gone, having disappeared high into the sky.

"I hope everything is alright with Rinbok," Sarah remarked, still staring at the large cloud Kahvel had just flown through.

"Rinbok has become infected," Pryllan softly said. "So has Kahvel. He hasn't said anything to me but I can tell."

Both Steve and Sarah gasped with shock.

"Are you sure?" Steve asked.

Pryllan nodded. "Kahvel informed me about the Dragon Lord a few days ago."

"And Kahvel?" Sarah gently inquired.

"I believe he has recently contracted this malady. His body is cool to the touch. His body is never cool unless he suffers from an ailment."

"What stage are they?" Sarah wanted to know.

"Providing Kahvel's condition has not worsened, the first stage. However, from what I've been told, Rinbok has been at the second stage for over a week. He will lose the ability to fly any day now."

Steve huffed out an irritated breath and began to pace. "We have to figure out what's going on and we need to do that now. The question is, how?"

"Like any other problem," Sarah told him. "We need more information. We can't make an informed decision until we know what we're dealing with."

Steve looked up at Pryllan's large form. "I'd say there's only one way to do that."

Sarah turned to her husband. "How?"

"We get Pryllan to snoop around. Ask some questions. The more we can find out, the better we can pinpoint what to do next."

Two slitted green eyes stared down at him as Pryllan's elegant green nose lifted higher into the air.

"Excuse me? I'll have you know I have never snooped a day in my life."

Steve smiled up at the large dragon.

"Maybe it's time you learned how. For Pravara's sake."

"Speaking of which, what am I to do about Pravara? She can fly, yes, but not with much stealth."

It was Sarah's turn to smile. "I guess we'll have to watch her for you."

Surprised, Steve turned to his wife. "Babysitting? We're babysitters again? Are you sure?"

"It's only for a little while, dear," Sarah complacently told him. "If we want to know more about what's been affecting the dragons, Pryllan will have to be the one to do it. The least we can do is watch Pravara for her."

"She's asleep in the nest," Pryllan told Steve, sensing his reluctance. "She shouldn't be a bother to you."

"Babysitting a dragon," Steve repeated as he started to smile. "I don't suppose you have a bottle of some sort should she wake up, do you?"

Pryllan blinked with surprise.

"A bottle? Of what?"

"Forget it," Sarah told Pryllan. "He's joking. We'll be fine. Go. See what you can find out. Just be careful and avoid contact as much as possible. I don't want you catching whatever it is they have."

"Agreed," Pryllan agreed.

Pryllan took off in her trademark fashion, which was leaping over a hundred feet straight up and extending her wings only at the apex of her jump. They watched Pryllan's retreating form until she vanished from sight high in the sky.

"Where did she go?" a quiet, timid voice asked.

"Son of a biscuit eater," Steve swore softly.

Together, he and Sarah turned to the mouth of the cave and saw Pravara sitting on her haunches. Wide awake, Steve noticed. He glanced nervously at his wife.

"Your mother, um, had some errands to run," Steve lamely told the young dragon. "She'll be back in a little while."

If Pravara was concerned, she didn't show it. Instead, she looked back at her nest, then up at the sky, and finally back at her two babysitters.

Steve clapped his hands together and rubbed them rapidly back and forth. "So, Pravara, what would you like to do now? Umm, what does a baby dragon like to do for fun?"

"I'm no baby!" Pravara growled. "Babies can't spit fire, or fly! I can do both!"

Pravara leapt into the air, much like her mother would, and flew out over the nest and started toward the ground far below. At least she would have if Sarah hadn't caught the young dragon with her own jhorun and began pulling her back to the nest much like a fisherman would do after hooking a fish.

"What's going on?" the young dragon demanded. "How

are you doing this? Let me go!"

Pravara flapped her wings harder in an effort to break Sarah's grasp.

"Don't just stand there grinning at me!" Sarah scolded her husband. "She's strong. I'm not going to be able to hold her there forever!"

"And what exactly am I supposed to do?" Steve asked.

"I don't know. I don't care! Distract her!"

Steve looked at the struggling dragonlet and smiled. He ignited three chasers and began juggling the fireballs, throwing them higher and higher in an attempt to get the dragon's attention. It worked. Pravara was still flapping her wings in an effort to escape, but now it was only a half-hearted attempt.

Steve added a fourth and a fifth fireball. As he juggled, he noticed a large flat surface to the immediate left of the cave entrance. Inspiration struck.

He let the fireballs extinguish, one after the other, and then walked over to the left of the cave entrance. He drew a large six-foot diameter circle of fire and instructed his jhorun to keep the circle lit. Then he drew a couple of concentric rings inside the large circle and also kept the rings burning.

"What are you doing?" Sarah demanded, somewhat crossly.

"Drawing a bullseye."

"I can see that. Why? Why did you stop juggling?"

"I have an idea. I'm going to work with Pravara on her aim."

"Good luck with that."

Steve adopted his smug smirk and mimicked his favorite old west movie star. "Just you watch and learn, little lady. Hey Pravara!"

The dragonlet finally ceased her flapping and hung, motionless, in the air. She turned to look at Steve, who pointed at the bullseye.

"I'll bet I can hit the center more times than you can."

Pravara was silent as she was slowly lowered to the ground. Once Sarah had deposited her safely in front of her nest, she relinquished her grip on the small dragon and waited to see what Pravara would do.

"What is that?" the dragonlet asked, curious.

"It's a target. Come here, I'll show you."

Forgetting that she had just tried to escape her nest, Pravara obediently joined Steve and together they stared at the target.

"Here's what you do. See the dot in the middle of all those rings?"

Pravara nodded her head.

"See if you can do this!"

Steve ignited a chaser and threw it at the target, decreasing the intensity and strength of the fireball as much as he was able. Deliberately aiming a few feet to the left, the chaser impacted the outermost ring of his target and glowed brightly a few seconds before disappearing.

"Oh, darn. I was so close. It's your turn. Think you can hit it?"

A grim look of determination appeared on the young dragon's face. Standing as still as she was able, she stared at the center of the target for a few moments before whipping back her head, like Steve had seen Sarah do when trying to swallow vitamins, and then snapped her head forward. The resulting fireball spun off to the right and threatened to fly into the nest before Steve was able to stop the ball of fire and have his jhorun absorb its energy.

"The sun was in your eyes," Steve told the forlorn little dragon. "I do believe you get another shot."

Pravara's ears perked up. Once more she sighted the target and was ready to snap back her neck again when Steve gently placed a hand on her long-scaled neck, drawing her attention.

"Try this. Instead of whipping your neck back, which takes your eyes of your target, try to keep your head level. Don't move your neck. There, that's good. Now, with the target still in your sights, inhale as much air as you need and once you're ready, release your breath in a fast whoosh, like you're forcing yourself to sneeze. Can you do that?"

Pravara did as she was told and when she released her breath, as fast as she was able to exhale, she was startled to discover the resulting fireball was larger than her normal shots but also had much more power behind it. Pravara's shot ended up flying a little bit straighter. She missed the outer ring of the target, but only by a few inches.

Excited, Pravara turned to Steve to ask his permission to go again, but Steve was already waving her on for another shot. As Pravara practiced, her accuracy improving with each of her shots, Steve wandered over to where Sarah was sitting on an outcropping of rock.

"You do realize you're never, ever, going to rid yourself of your Doctor Dolittle moniker if you keep doing stuff like this, don't you?"

"What's the problem? I'm just helping her work on her aim."

"Look at her! It's been, what, ten minutes and she's doting on every little thing you say. You certainly don't need me here."

"Steve! Look! Look! I hit the target!"

Steve and Sarah rose to their feet and walked over to the side of the cave with the burning rings still visible. Inside the outermost ring, but fading fast, was the strike from Pravara. They turned to face the little dragon who was practically bouncing up and down on all four legs.

"Nicely done!" Steve praised, giving Pravara a pat on her shoulder. "Not bad at all!"

"I got closer to the center than you did!" Pravara declared proudly. "Let's see you beat that!"

"Ah! I see! The challenge is back on! You got it, squirt."

Steve ignited a chaser and spun it on his finger as he pretended to aim for the target. Once he had put on a little show, he flung his chaser out, but not before Sarah appeared behind him and kissed his neck just as he threw the fireball.

His chaser spun out of control and impacted the mountainside nearly twenty feet away.

"You need to practice," Pravara helpfully told him.

"Mmm-hmmm," Steve grumbled, casting a look over his shoulder at Sarah, who was practically in tears from laughing so hard. "Let's try that again, shall we?"

Steve ignited another chaser and lined up his shot for real this time, all while keeping an eye on Sarah, who was inching closer and closer.

"Keep your distance, lady."

Sarah backed a dozen feet away and held both arms out, palms facing up, as if to say, 'who, me?'

Just as Steve threw the chaser, Sarah vanished and appeared right next to him and blew softly in his ear. This chaser struck the mountain even farther away than the previous one.

"You helped me practice," Pravara informed him. "I'll do the same for you."

"Aren't you a barrel of laughs?" Steve chuckled as he frowned at his wife.

Sarah put both hands on her hips. "I *know* you didn't just scowl at me."

Steve wiped his defiant expression from his face and started backpedaling. Rapidly. "Nope. Of course not."

Sarah gave her husband a smug smile. "Good answer, Paco."

"I'm hungry."

Together, husband and wife turned to look at the dragonlet. Sarah helplessly looked at Steve.

"What do we do?"

"Don't look at me. I don't seem to be lactating right now."

Suddenly Pravara looked up at the distant clouds, causing Steve and Sarah to mimic her. A tiny speck had appeared and grew steadily larger. Pryllan had returned. Hanging limply from her mouth was some sort of dead animal. Apparently Pryllan had returned with lunch.

"How long does it take her to eat?" Steve asked, swallowing noisily. The last thing he wanted to witness was a dragon feeding, let alone two.

"No more than a few minutes," Pryllan told them. "She's a very fast eater. I keep telling her to slow down, but it falls on deaf ears."

Sarah pointed at Steve, but he interrupted her first. "Nope. Put that finger down. Don't even say it."

Confused, Pryllan's gaze darted between man and woman and then back again.

"How was Pravara? I see that she awakened."

"Almost as soon as you left," Sarah admitted.

"And you kept her entertained?" Pryllan asked, incredulous. "I am impressed. You have my thanks."

"Don't thank me," Sarah informed her. "You can thank Steve. He even worked with her on improving her aim."

Shocked, Pryllan stared at the fire thrower. However, at that moment, the first sickening crunch of bones sounded as Pravara took her first bite of lunch.

"We'll be back in about five minutes," Sarah assured Pryllan. She took her husband's arm and teleported them down to the base of the mountain where she had gone earlier that day. After waiting close to ten minutes, to make sure all traces of the kill had been removed, Sarah returned them to the nest to find Pravara excitedly demonstrating her new skills for her mother.

"Most impressive, Pravara. Your aim has improved significantly. Your sire will be very proud."

Pravara's scales sparkled in the sun as she beamed with joy.

"I assume Kahvel has not returned?" Pryllan asked, once she had spotted the two of them.

"We haven't seen him since he left," Sarah answered.

"What did you find out?" Steve and Sarah sat down on the nearby rocks. "Were you able to find out anything useful?"

Pryllan nodded. "Indeed. I must say I rather enjoy snooping."

Both Steve and Sarah laughed out loud.

"It's more fun than you realize." Steve looked at his wife. "Some of us are better at it than others."

Sarah elbowed him in the ribs. "What's *that* supposed to mean?"

"Your jhorun is more suited to snooping around than mine is."

"Oh."

"What'd you think I meant? You know what? Don't answer that. I don't want to know."

"What I have learned," Pryllan began, "is that the symptoms first appeared about three fortnights ago."

"Roughly a month and a half ago," Steve translated for

Sarah's benefit.

Sarah playfully smacked his arm. "I know what a fortnight is, thank you very much."

Pryllan waited a few moments to make sure she could continue.

"Three dragons became infected after returning from a hunt in the far north. Within several days it had spread to five of us. Unfortunately, the infection rate has been steadily increasing ever since."

"Do we know what these three dragons did to become infected?" Steve asked. "Did they all eat part of the same animal?"

"Unknown," Pryllan answered.

"So is this a disease?" Sarah asked. "It's sure sounding like it right about now."

"If this is a malady, then it has been previously unreported until now."

Steve raised a hand. "What about when they lose the Collective? Would it, or someone on it, inform you if someone else had been kicked off?"

Pryllan shook her massive head. "It doesn't work that way. The Collective is a mental gathering of wyverian minds. If you choose to use the Collective then you open your senses and quiet your mind so that you can hear the voices of the others. If one voice is silent, we would be unable to determine which voice that is."

"Have you noticed anyone disappearing from the Collective?" Sarah asked. "For example, can you tell how long it's been since you've last contacted so-and-so?"

"What I have noticed," Pryllan admitted, "is that the number of voices in the Collective has dropped. It is possible for the Collective to become all but silent, provided every dragon chose to shun contact with the others; however, no one has ever noticed it this quiet for this long. This malady is definitely affecting the Collective, as more and more voices are going silent."

Kahvel swooped in from the east, circling about overhead to give everyone time to make enough room for him to land. Folding his wings and laying them flat against his back, he regarded his mate with a troubled look.

"What is it?" Pryllan asked. "What has happened?"

"Rinbok Intherer believes he has just reached stage two."

"Didn't he just use the Collective to summon you?" Steve asked, confused. "Stage two is the loss of the Collective, right?"

Kahvel nodded. "It is. He progressed to stage two in my presence. I could see it in his eyes."

"Don't you guys have some sort of a doctor you can go to if you have any type of medical problems?" Sarah asked, exasperated. "I can't believe there's no one you can turn to for help in a situation such as this."

"We dragons are naturally resilient to medical ailments," Kahvel proudly informed them. "The services of a healer are rarely needed."

"What about now?" Steve asked, raising an eyebrow.

Kahvel grunted but didn't say anything.

"There is someone we might be able to turn to for help." Pryllan turned to look at her mate. "Do you think Sciathan could shed any additional light on the matter?"

Kahvel was silent for a few moments. "If ever there were anyone that could, aye, I believe he would. Provided you can find him."

"Who's Sciathan?" Steve asked.

"One of us who has lived for many centuries," Pryllan answered.

"So he's an elder dragon," Sarah observed. "He'd be perfect."

"Ascertaining his location will be a problem," Pryllan admitted.

Steve scratched his head. "Why? Oh, let me guess. Because no one who goes to see him ever comes back alive?"

Pryllan and Kahvel both stared at Steve as though he had just belched up a fireball.

Steve grinned at the two adult dragons. "Okay, that's a little inappropriate. Sorry."

"Can you ask this elder dragon what his present location is?" Sarah inquired as she mentally crossed her fingers.

Pryllan shook her head. "His voice has been absent from

the Collective for some time."

Steve sighed. He stretched his back and turned to look southeast, back toward the distant lake.

"Do we have an idea where to look?"

Kahvel approached Steve on his right and looked northeast. "Do you see the three peaks to the north?"

"I see a peak off by itself and two others a little farther away on its left. Is that what you're talking about?"

Kahvel shook his head.

"Not even close. You need to look further north. The three peaks sit side by side."

Steve squinted at the distant mountains and then held a hand over his eyes to shade them. Sarah tapped Kahvel's foreleg to get his attention.

"I see what you're referring to. Is that where we have to go?"

"Aye. That was his last known location. I'm not sure Pravara would be able to —"

Pryllan thumped the ground with her tail to get Kahvel's attention. "Pravara will remain here. With *you*."

Kahvel, noting the hostile tone emanating from his mate, swiveled his head to look at her. "Caring for offspring is the duty of the female."

Sarah rapped Kahvel's closest foreleg and then rubbed her stinging knuckles.

"Excuse me? What did you just say?"

Pryllan stepped up to Sarah's side and together the females glared at the two males.

Steve held up his hands and backed away. With a smile, he looked up at the towering golden dragon.

"What was it that you once told me before? Oh, yes, I have it. 'Your female, your problem.' You're not dragging me into this, buddy."

Kahvel looked down at Sarah and then up at his mate. Both were still scowling at him. Well, Sarah was scowling; Pryllan was growling. Sarah wagged her finger at Kahvel.

"If we weren't going to go find this elder dragon, we'd be continuing this right now. Consider yourself lucky."

Kahvel snorted; a thin line of smoke escaped from each

nostril. He withdrew from the debate and retreated inside the cave.

Chapter 3 — Flying the Friendly Skies

So how are we going to do this?" Steve asked as he turned to his wife. "I mean, I'm allowed to ride on Pryllan's back but you're not."

"I would say she's going to have to carry me. But are you really going to make me sit in her hand by myself?"

"Of course not."

Sarah nodded. "Good. Thank you."

"Just this once," Kahvel's deep voice rumbled, surprising them all as he poked his head out of the cave, "I believe it wouldn't hurt to have you both on her back."

Steve turned incredulously to the mouth of the cave. "Aren't you the one who once threatened me…"

"He *advised* you," Sarah interrupted. "He didn't threaten."

"Whatever. He was steadfastly against anyone riding on a dragon's back."

"And yet you've done it before," Sarah reminded him.

"Besides, he isn't talking about you, he's talking about me. Kahvel, thank you for the offer, and your blessing, but I was there when Rinbok granted Steve permission. He didn't say anything about me. Unless he personally gives me his blessing, I wouldn't feel comfortable doing it."

Kahvel briefly glanced east before returning his attention to Sarah. "I certainly would not tell him, nor would Pryllan. He'd never know."

"But I would know," Sarah insisted. "I'm sorry, but I just can't do that." She turned to Steve. "Are you saying that you want me up there with you?"

Steve hesitated so long that Sarah had to nudge him on the shoulder. "As much as I would like to have you riding behind me, I gave Rinbok Intherer my word. I'll ride with you in Pryllan's hand."

He looked over at Pryllan, who had been watching him intently. "If I were to ride in your hand, could we still share senses, like we have before?"

Pryllan reacted with surprise as she stared down at him. "Obviously. We have communicated over large distances before. Before the battle with the human sorceress Celestia, I shared your senses when you were discussing plans with the king. Do you not remember this?"

Sarah tapped Pryllan's leg. Once the green dragon was looking down at her, Sarah pointed at her husband. "His memory is going downhill. Fast. It's not his fault, he just can't help it."

Steve stared at his wife as though he was regarding a stranger. "I'm standing right here. You do see me, right?"

Ignoring him, Sarah turned to look northeast at the distant mountains Kahvel had singled out earlier.

"How long will it take you to fly all the way there?"

Pryllan narrowed her eyes as she studied the distant peaks. "Several hours, depending upon the velocity with which I choose to fly."

"Can you make it there and back before sunset?" Steve asked.

"Provided Sciathan is there and we do not have to search the nearby peaks? Easily."

"Then you three had better depart," Kahvel told them. "The sooner you leave the sooner you return."

"You and Pravara will be fine," Pryllan assured her mate. "Have her show you how well her aim has improved."

Curious, Kahvel turned to look back at their dragonlet, who was sitting complacently by Steve's side. "Indeed? How has she managed to accomplish that?"

"With help," Pryllan told him.

She opened her right front claw and waited for the two humans to jump on. Once they were situated, she partially closed her claw and prepared to depart. Just as she was about to leap straight up, her mate's thought sounded in her mind.

Keep yourself safe. For Pravara's sake. The humans are formidable and I am glad they accompany you. Do not be ashamed to ask their help should the need arise.

Surprised, Pryllan glanced at Kahvel, who was watching her. She nodded her head. Looking down at Pravara, Pryllan saw her offspring staring uncertainly up at her sire. She sent a reassuring thought to her family and then, without warning, leapt into the air, eliciting a scream of surprise from Sarah, who hadn't expected the abrupt departure.

Rapidly gaining altitude, Pryllan dipped her left wing, turning to the north. Leveling off, as she lined up the three peaks off in the distance, she found a suitable air current and adjusted the angle of her wings so that she barely had to use them to stay aloft.

Pryllan, can you hear me?

Pryllan bent her neck down low and glanced at her claw.

As we are communicating telepathically, and not using our own voices, I would have to answer no, I cannot hear you.

Ha, ha. You know what I mean. Can you bring Sarah into the loop?

I'm already here, Sarah's thought came back at him, loud and clear. *And I'd have to agree with Pryllan. I can't hear you, either.*

Aren't you two a kick in the pants? Steve shook his head and grinned at his wife. *You have to admit, this is pretty cool, right?*

Sarah stared back at him. *You had just better be careful with your thoughts. They're going to get you into trouble.*

Why do you say that?

I didn't say that. I thought it.

You know what I mean.

Weren't you just thinking about that time we were laying poolside at that resort in Hawaii?

Steve mentally choked. The tips of his ears turned bright red as he blushed furiously.

What is a 'bikini'?

Now look what you've done, Sarah mentally scolded him. *You're going to make Pryllan blush, too, if you explain yourself to her.*

Damndamndamn, Steve swore to himself.

There's no 'to yourself' here, Sarah reminded him. *Everything you're thinking is being broadcast to the two of us.*

Steve gave himself a few moments to compose himself. How would he ever be able to explain to a dragon how fetching he thought Sarah looked in a bikini?

So I assume a bikini is a piece of apparel?

Crap. I did it again.

You really enjoyed that trip, didn't you? Sarah playfully poked her embarrassed husband in the ribs. *Maybe we'll make a return trip once everything has settled down here.*

Can we change the subject please?

Steve fidgeted uncomfortably in Pryllan's palm as he heard both Sarah and Pryllan laughing at him.

What would you like to talk about?

Steve raised himself to one knee and peered through the gaps in Pryllan's claws at the passing mountains far below.

Are we still over the Bohanis?

Aye.

Are we close to Ylani? Sarah asked.

Are we close? Aye, you could say that. We have been in Ylani ever since we crossed the lake.

Surprised, Steve looked up at Pryllan's head. *I thought all dragons lived in Lentari.*

Lentari, Ylani, it matters not to dragons. We live where we choose.

Yet the vast majority of you all choose to live around Lake Raehón. Why is that? Sarah inquired. *Why not someplace else? Down south in the Selekais, for example. What makes the Bohanis more appealing?*

Both husband and wife felt the dragon's hesitation in answering the question. The two humans looked at one another. What was she not telling them?

You do remember that I can still sense your thoughts?
Steve shook his head. *Sorry. I keep forgetting that.*
The lake is home to Rinbok Intherer.
And he makes all the dragons live nearby?
Again, they felt Pryllan's hesitation. Both husband and wife tried to keep their minds empty. However, before they could still their own minds, thoughts of an enormous subterranean cavern flashed through Pryllan's.

Steve jerked his head up. Sarah clutched at her husband's hand in an attempt to get his attention before he could say/think anything, but she was too late.

What cavern?

Pryllan gave a visible jerk, lurching to the left. After a few moments of turbulence, the dragon was able to get her flight back under control.

As they would say in my world, the jig is up, my friend. Steve grinned up at the dragon. *What can you tell us about this cavern?*

Sarah punched him on his arm. *Did you ever stop to think that maybe she shouldn't be telling us about the cavern?* Sarah shook her head and looked annoyed. *Don't press her for information if she's not allowed to tell.*

There is no harm done. As Kahvel reminded us, the Dragon Lord has progressed to the second stage. He is unable to use the Collective, so we have nothing to fear from him. The cavern I am referring to is located deep beneath the lake. It is home to not only Rinbok Intherer but is also the final resting place for all the great wyverian rulers.

Steve looked at Sarah, unsure if he had heard that right.
Rinbok lives in a mausoleum?
I am unfamiliar with that word.
It's a place where dead people are buried.
Then aye, you would be correct.
Does he like living there? Sarah asked. *Or is that something he was forced to do when he became the Dragon Lord?*
It's an honor every wyverian strives for.

Oh.

The location of the cavern is a closely guarded secret, revealed only to a select few.

Do you know where it is?

Aye.

How?

Pryllan was silent. This time she was able to get her mind under control so she wouldn't disclose any additional details.

Steve tapped his wife on her shoulder to get her attention.

It's because of Kahvel. He knows, and since he knows, Pryllan knows. Am I right?

A sense of guilt washed over Pryllan as she realized she had inadvertently acknowledged how she had come to learn of the cavern's location.

Sarah put her hand on one of Pryllan's massive claws.

Don't worry, Pryllan. Your secret is safe with us.

You have my thanks.

So how old is this elder dragon? Steve asked, changing the subject. He looked at Sarah and then up at Pryllan. *Does anyone know? And what did you say his name was again?*

We are seeking Sciathan. He was hatched nearly three millennia ago.

Steve blinked with surprise. *Three thousand years old? Wow!* Steve tried to whistle but was unable to hear anything. If Pryllan were to share her sight and aural abilities, then they would be able to converse normally, but apparently the dragon was reluctant to connect with more than one human at a time.

Precisely, Pryllan agreed.

How much of these mountains have been charted? Sarah wanted to know.

Sarah stuck her head through a gap between Pryllan's claws and looked down at the miles and miles of pristine forest covering the rugged peaks. Every so often they'd pass over a small lake and she would catch a glimpse of Pryllan's massive body as viewed from down below.

I don't see any roads, Sarah thought. She turned to look back the direction they had come from. *No structures or signs of civilization. There's nothing but mountains and trees. Is this why the dragons choose to live around here? They prefer their privacy?*

Aye. Wyverians are typically solitary creatures, preferring isolation to companionship.

Clearly not all dragons feel that way, Steve argued. *Take you and Kahvel, for example. He's liaison to the humans. He must like a little company now and then.*

Pryllan gave a small shake of her head.

He used to. Now he has become a traditionalist. He would be content to live on the most remote mountain he could find. And we would, if not for the fact that he knows I crave companionship, which is what brought the two of us together. And, he knows I prefer to fly with a rider, which puzzles him to this day. Thankfully he supports me and my decision.

You can have the best of both worlds, you know, Sarah told the dragon. *Have Kahvel find his ideal setting for your nest. Then all I'd have to do is see it once and then Steve and I could visit whenever you wanted.*

Pryllan glanced briefly down at Sarah, who winked up at her. Sarah's desire for her happiness and safety were easily read in her thoughts, and that made Pryllan determined to do whatever was necessary to assure the safety of her family. If she had to fly halfway around the world then she would do so without thinking twice about it.

And we'd be there every step of the way.

For the second time that day, Pryllan was surprised. She had temporarily forgotten that two humans were listening to her thoughts.

Takes some getting used to, doesn't it?

It does.

Two hours later Pryllan was flying in slow circles around one of the three peaks. The center peak, a barren mountain devoid of trees, shrubs, or greenery, rose sharply into the sky, culminating in a jagged point thousands of feet off the ground. Neither Steve nor Sarah could see any caves on the mountain's surface. After they started circling around for the fourth time, Steve looked up at Pryllan.

What exactly are you doing? We've been going around and around this mountain for close to fifteen minutes. I don't see any caves. Should we try another mountain? Looks like that one to the east has caves all

over it.
No. He's here. I can smell him.
Where? There's no place for him to hide.
I don't understand.
What's not to understand? If you can smell him, and since we don't see him, then he has to be hiding somewhere. The question is, where?

Sarah laid a hand on her husband's arm and indicated she wanted to ask a question. *Pryllan, do you see his cave?*
Aye.
Steve was surprised. *Where?*
Pryllan swooped low and circled back around to the eastern side of the crag.
Do you see the split in the rock? High up the mountainside, perhaps several hundred feet from the summit?

Steve had seen the crack but hadn't figured a dragon could have made it into an opening so tiny. *That? You can't be serious. There's no way a dragon could fit into that. I don't even think Pravara could slip in there.*

That crack runs mostly vertical, Sarah observed. *Although near the top it does level off a bit. That's where I can see a slight bulge, as though a piece of the mountainside is ready to break off and fall to the ground. There's a ledge there. A small dragon might be able to use that as a cave.*

I certainly cannot fit through there. I will have to drop you two off and wait up here.

Husband and wife eyed each other uneasily.
Is that the only way? Steve asked.
Aye.
Are you absolutely sure? Sarah asked. *Are you sure there's a cave behind that crack?*

Aye. My gaze has been able to penetrate a dozen feet or so into the cave as I fly by. How much the cave widens I am not certain, only that it does.
You sure we have the right dragon?
I have not detected any other wyverian activity in the area. This is the location Kahvel indicated. It must be him. Besides, he knows we're here.

Steve sat upright and automatically glanced down at his

clenched fists. His hands had turned red and were ready to ignite should the situation call for it.

How do you know?

I can hear him growling. Something isn't right. I do not recall hearing a growl like this before. It is deeper than most growls, even deeper than Kahvel's. Additionally, it sounds muted. We must be ready to depart at a moment's notice.

Steve pointed at the nearest neighboring mountain which was wearing a blanket of thick pine trees.

Look at that one. It has trees everywhere. It's the perfect place for a dragon to hide. Are you sure you don't want to check it out first before we place ourselves in danger?

A tree-covered mountain most assuredly guarantees you will find no dragons nearby.

Why?

Trees will burn, Pryllan explained. **Dragons are territorial. No dragon would choose a setting where they could be driven out by a rival. While not impossible, it is highly unlikely you will find a dragon nest on any other type of mountain besides a barren one. Observe the other two peaks. Both are covered with trees. Thus, this is the correct mountain, provided Sciathan has not moved on.**

You can smell him, Sarah remembered, *so…*

Sciathan is nearby, somewhere on this mountain. The only cave I can see is the one behind the split in the rock.

Pryllan flew close to the massive crack on the eastern face of the mountain and hovered there. The amount of air being displaced by her immense leathery wings would have ripped the trees out of the ground had there been any nearby. As loud as the howling winds were, they could all hear the growls emanating from deep within the hidden cave. If the elder dragon was holed up in the cave, he was giving every indication that he wanted to be left alone.

We have no choice here. We must make contact with Sciathan. Steve, be ready to protect Sarah. Sarah, be ready to teleport the two of you to safety.

I'll take us back to your nest if I have to, Sarah promised her.

Excellent. Are you ready?

Steve took his wife's hand and held it tight. *We're ready here. Don't worry about trying to get us down there. Sarah can just teleport us down there.*

Acknowledged. Whenever you're ready.

Sarah closed her eyes and brought up a mental picture of the small ledge in front of the somewhat horizontal section of the large crack. Once she was certain she had the image safely centered in her mind, she ordered her jhorun to move the two of them to the mountain. Their perch on Pryllan's claw was replaced by a narrow expanse of rock that was only ten feet wide at its widest point, and stretched south for about fifty feet before it eventually tapered away and disappeared into the sheer walls of the mountain. Instantly apparent were the vicious growls coming from within the depths of the cave. Pryllan was right. Another dragon was here and it certainly wasn't happy to see them.

I will be in touch.

Steve turned to look up at Pryllan, who was circling high overhead. *Trust me, it's appreciated. Here we go.*

Still holding on to Sarah's hand, they turned to face the split wall of rock. Steve nervously cleared his throat.

"Umm, hello? Is anyone there? We're no threat to you. You don't need to keep growling at us. We're friends to the wyverians."

The growls didn't cease. If anything, they increased in volume. Steve paled. He let go of Sarah's hand and stepped in front of her, igniting both of his hands as he did so. He decided to try again and this time he dropped a name he hoped the dragon would recognize.

"We're friends! My name is Steve and this is Sarah. We know Rinbok Intherer. Surely you've heard of him?"

Something stirred deep within the darkness of the crevasse. A creature was pulling itself along the ground. Both humans quickly glanced up to make sure Pryllan was still nearby, which she was. When the creature finally emerged into the daylight Sarah went instantly sympathetic. It was a dragon, but the poor creature was in bad condition.

He was thin, weak, and very sickly in appearance. Pulling himself out onto the ledge, he collapsed. The growls they had heard were coming from his stomach. The dragon was starving.

Forgetting that this was an unknown dragon, Sarah rushed to the sickly wyverian's side. "Are you Sciathan?"

The feeble dragon nodded. He focused his bleary eyes on Sarah and blinked with surprise. "A human. What is a human doing here?"

"At the moment I'm helping you. Pryllan! We need you to go hunting! Quickly! Find food for him. Anything!"

High above, Pryllan banked sharply left and headed toward the closest source of water. Every dragon knew that locating a watering hole would be the quickest and easiest way to find game.

Steve approached the small black dragon and squatted down low. "Are you hurt? No offense, man, but that right wing of yours doesn't look right."

"That's because I broke it several weeks ago when I discovered I couldn't fly," the dragon softly told him.

Husband and wife shared a look. Sarah nodded and patted her shirt, verifying her medallion, a gift from Shardwyn years ago, was still there. She pulled the medallion up from beneath her clothes and activated the hidden compartment, revealing a tiny vial. She uncorked her precious elixir and applied a tiny drop to the dragon's crippled wing. In just a few seconds the bones rearranged themselves and healed back together. The dragon nodded appreciatively but was still too weak to move. The elixir could heal all manner of wounds and injuries, but it couldn't cure starvation. Sarah returned the vial to her medallion and slipped it back under her shirt. She looked compassionately down at the helpless dragon.

Steve nodded. "You've contracted this malady that's spreading around, haven't you? Have you lost your ability to spit fire, too?"

Sciathan weakly nodded. "Aye. Let me tell you, it came as a surprise to me."

"The loss of flight is stage three," Sarah recalled. She put a friendly hand on the dragon's shoulder. "Without the

Collective, you wouldn't have been able to call for help."

"Aye. I've been stranded here without any way to hunt. Complicating matters is my lack of strength to climb down."

"How long has it been since you've eaten?"

"I do not remember."

"How long do you typically go between meals?" Steve wanted to know.

"A wyverian in his prime can go without sustenance for weeks at a time. The older a wyverian gets, the more frequently they need to feed."

"So we're standing in the presence of a super hungry dragon," Steve concluded. "That's just great."

"Fear not, human," Sciathan told him. "I haven't fallen so low that I'd resort to eating a human. Besides, they taste terrible."

"Tell me you're joking."

Sciathan eyed him and said nothing.

Steve took Sarah's hand and pulled her away from the thin dragon. "Uh huh. We'll wait over here, thank you very much."

"Your escort has left. You are over a thousand feet from solid ground. What exactly do you think you could do to prevent me from attacking you? I won't, but I could."

"Your bedside manner sucks for someone who needs our help," Steve said as he adopted a neutral tone of voice. He ignited both hands and faced the dragon. "Unlike you, my fires haven't gone out."

Sciathan visibly recoiled backward a few feet as he eyed Steve's flaming hands. Sarah laid a hand on her husband's shoulder.

"Don't worry, honey. I've got this one." Sarah turned to face the elder dragon. "First, it's rude to get all snotty with us when we're here to try and help you. Second, you have no idea who we are so you don't know what we're capable of doing. And third…"

Sciathan suddenly rose several feet off the ground and swung out over open air.

"And third," Sarah continued, "if you so much as threaten myself or my husband, I'll drop your sorry hide off this cliff.

But, I'm sure we won't have to resort to anything like that now, will we?"

The small black dragon looked down at the distant ground and swallowed nervously. It nodded. Sciathan was returned to the rocky ledge and lowered back to the ground in front of a very smug Sarah.

Sciathan regarded Steve for a few moments before he returned his attention to Sarah. Finally, he lowered his head in a tiny bow.

"Nohrin. I have heard of you. Never would I have believed that it'd be the two of you who have come to my aid."

"It's the two of us and Pryllan," Steve corrected. He had relaxed somewhat but his hands were still that ugly shade of red which usually signified a blast of fire would be following shortly.

"Ah. Kahvel's mate."

"Do you know her?" Sarah asked.

"Not personally, no," Sciathan admitted.

"Don't worry. Pryllan will return shortly. I'm sure she'll have no problem finding some game."

Sciathan sighed and sank down to the ground in an effort to conserve his limited energy. He angled his head to watch the two of them.

"What do you know about this bug you've caught?" Steve asked. His hands had finally returned to a healthy pink color.

Sciathan blinked his large silver eyes uncomprehendingly at him.

"Your disease," Steve clarified. "Whatever it is you caught. What can you tell us about it?"

Sciathan gave a tiny nod. "Quite a bit. When I realized that I had become confined to my cave, I began to think about my predicament. When that's the only thing you're able to do, then you do a lot of it."

"That means you know something about what's going on, don't you?" Steve said excitedly.

Sciathan nodded.

I will be there momentarily. I have found the partially dismembered carcass of a bolger. Please make sure

there is room for me to drop it next to Sciathan.

"Oh, gross," Steve muttered to himself.

"What?" Sarah asked.

"Pryllan must have temporarily cut you out of the loop. Trust me, that's a good thing. She found a partially eaten bolger. She's bringing it here for him."

"Partially eaten? Couldn't she have found something better?"

Steve nudged Sarah and looked at Sciathan. The black dragon was drooling so much that a small pool had formed under his head.

Pryllan arrived and plopped down her grisly find on the ledge. She retreated into the air and resumed circling Sciathan's peak. The elder dragon's eyes went wide with excitement.

"I think we should wait elsewhere," Sarah suggested. She had promptly turned around so she wouldn't have to look at a half-eaten animal.

Sciathan shook his head. "No, Nohrin, stay. You must hear this. It's essential that I impart what I've learned to someone who is capable of helping."

Sarah started to turn back around when she heard the first crunch of bones snapping. Sciathan was tearing into his meal and enjoying every second of it. Steve caught Sarah's arm and rotated her so she was facing away from the mouth of the cave.

After hearing Sciathan take the third or fourth bite, Steve had to turn and face the same direction as Sarah. Swallowing nervously to try and clear the queasy sensations running rampant throughout his stomach, Steve began humming.

"I have figured — *crunch* — out quite a bit about this ailment," Sciathan was saying, between bites. "Turns out it's not — *crunch* — an ailment after all, nor is it — *crunch* — a disease. It's a curse."

Steve and Sarah looked at each other at the same time they heard Pryllan's shocked reaction in their mind:

A curse? Who would want to curse the dragons?

"Are you sure?" Steve asked. "Who'd want to curse you dragons?"

"Ask yourselves who — *crunch* — would want to curse us? Who has — *crunch* — the motivation to do so? By the way, I'm finished, so you may turn around now."

Steve and Sarah turned around and stared in wonder at the transformation happening before their eyes. Sciathan's scales were becoming shinier. His eyes had cleared and he was now able to hold himself up off the ground. Becoming stronger by the second, Sciathan turned back to the spot where Pryllan had dropped the carcass and gave a final lick to the dark stain on the rocks.

"Pardon me. I do love the taste of decaying flesh. So many flavors running rampant over your tongue. How could you not enjoy that?"

Properly grossed out, Steve's eyes shot skyward. "Ewww. Dude, you said you were done."

Sciathan flicked his tongue and ran it through several of his larger fangs.

"Focus," Sarah reminded the black dragon. "What were you saying about the person who had the motivation to curse the dragons?"

Sciathan nodded. He arched his back and stretched his muscles.

"The answer to that question is simple. We wyverians have no natural enemies. Nothing has threatened us since that fiasco several years ago with the human sorceress. By the way, I hear you played a part in that."

Both husband and wife nodded.

"As I was saying, there are no known enemies of the dragons, yet last year we picked up three."

The two humans stared at Sciathan; shock was evident on their faces.

"What three enemies? What happened last year, anyway?"

"I know the dwarves finally discovered that city they had been searching for," Sarah mentioned. "Kri'Entu was telling us about it. It's their version of Atlantis. Is that what you're referring to?"

Sciathan nodded.

"The dwarves had apparently lost a city. How someone is able to lose a city, I'm not sure. It was during this excursion that our diminutive allies stumbled across the lair of a creature that would play a significant role in this curse. Tell me, famous Nohrin, what do you know about zweigelans?"

Chapter 4 — A Double Dose of Revenge

Steve looked at his wife and shook his head. She mimicked him. Neither one knew what a zweigelan was. Sciathan had said 'lair', so Steve figured it must be some type of monster. Sarah wasn't so sure.

"Never heard of 'em. Since we haven't, would you care to tell us what a zweigelan is?"

Sciathan nodded. "A two-headed dragon."

Sarah was shocked. "A two-headed dragon? Really?"

Focusing his clear silver eyes on the two humans, Sciathan nodded. "Indeed. They are a rare cousin to the wyverians. Smaller, leaner, and much more confrontational, a zweigelan is an elusive creature that thrives on creating chaos whenever and wherever it can."

"Why would Rinbok Intherer tolerate that?" Sarah asked. "He doesn't really strike me as the type of dragon who'd allow any sort of dissent."

Steve smiled at his wife. "Dissent? Nice word!"

Sarah returned his smile. "Thanks! It was on my word-a-day calendar last week."

Sciathan's expression was grave. "He doesn't, which is the whole point."

Steve nodded, understanding.

"Oh. That makes sense now. You said three. There are three zweigelans? What happened last year to make these three two-headed dragons hate you guys?"

"One zweigelan was located and forced to swear allegiance to Rinbok Intherer and join the Collective."

"And that's a bad thing?" Steve asked.

If you believe yourself to be superior to everyone around you and therefore be exempt to anyone's rule, don't you think you'd view your subjugation as a negative experience?

Steve and Sarah looked up at Pryllan flying in circles high in the sky. Even Sciathan was watching her, whether jealous that she could still fly and he couldn't, no one could say.

"Once the zweigelan had joined the Collective, everyone could see that perhaps this wasn't Rinbok Intherer's wisest move," the elder continued. "The creature's thoughts were dark and full of anger. We wyverians made a dangerous enemy that day. However, the Dragon Lord determined the problem was resolved and dwelt no more on the matter."

Steve raised a hand. "I have a question. Have you ever encountered a zweigelan before?"

Sciathan nodded. "Once, many years ago. Believe me when I say they are cunning and not to be trusted. Ever."

Surprised that a dragon would refer to another dragon with such distaste, no matter how distantly related they were, Steve shared a look with Sarah.

"They are an unpleasant bunch," Sciathan continued, noting the surprised look the two humans had shared. "I recall it being resentful that there weren't more of their kind, although why this would bother them remains a mystery to me."

"Why?" Steve prompted.

"Because they do not tolerate other wyverians, especially

their own kind."

"Why'd they wait so long?" Sarah wanted to know.

Twin silver orbs focused on her as Sciathan cocked his head slightly to his left. If a dragon could have raised an eyebrow, it would have done so then.

"If they were that distrusting and resentful of their dragon brothers..."

"Cousins," Sciathan corrected. He briefly flicked his long forked black tongue and looked longingly at the dark stain on the rocks.

"Fine. They're your cousins. Whatever." Sarah took a deep breath. "If they didn't like their cousins that much then why would they resort to such a devious scheme to harm the dragons? Why would they wait so long? If they are as long-lived as the other wyverians, why now? Why not go on the attack centuries ago?"

"Because the first zweigelan was forced to surrender the locations of the other two."

Steve nodded. "I bet that ticked the other two off."

"One was located," Sciathan told them. "It was forced to join the Collective as well."

"What about the third?" Sarah asked. "I take it that one was forced to join, too?"

Sciathan's black tongue snaked out of his mouth several times in rapid succession. "The third remains at large."

"And you suspect number three is the culprit?" Steve asked.

Sciathan nodded. "I do."

"How would a dragon, even one with two-heads, be able to create a curse such as this?" Sarah wondered aloud. "As far as I'm aware, dragons don't have jhorun, do they?"

Sciathan shook his head. "They do not."

"Then how could they cast the spell necessary to create this curse?" Sarah demanded. "Something doesn't add up."

Sciathan easily lifted himself off the ground and approached Sarah. "Do you not think the renegade zweigelan has the motivation to find someone that could?"

Steve choked. "Could what? Create a curse? Correct me if I'm wrong, but there's only one wizard in Lentari, and that's

Shardwyn. I doubt very much his services are for hire like that. There's no way he'd be involved with a scheme like this."

"Thaden wouldn't be able to do it," Sarah reminded her husband. "Not only was he a poor excuse for a wizard, he had his jhorun stripped from him. So the Ylanian wizard is out."

"There might be another Ylanian wizard," Steve suggested. "I remember Ylani's capital, Zaran, had a resident wizard, too. What about him?"

Sarah stared at Steve with a look of pity on her face. "Have you forgotten when we went undercover with Rhenyon up there? We were able to find out that everyone in that neighboring kingdom had subpar jhoruns when compared to the people of Lentari. There's no one there powerful enough to do this. Trust me. Ylani is out."

Steve nodded, pleased. "Then that leaves Lentari, and since we know Shardwyn wouldn't do anything like that, it couldn't possibly be a wizard's doing. Everyone is spoken for."

Are you sure about that?

Both humans looked up as Pryllan's shadow passed over them.

"Don't even go there," Steve warned. "You're suggesting there's another wizard out there and his services are for hire. That's not even funny."

I did not mean to offend. I merely offer it as a suggestion.

"No one is offended," Sarah assured the dragon. She frowned at her husband. "She's only trying to help. Now apologize."

Steve sighed. "Sorry, Pryllan. Didn't mean to bite your head off."

Bite my head off? That is physiologically impossible.

"It's a figure of speech. It means I shouldn't have been rude."

I see. Your apology is accepted.

Steve smiled. "Thanks."

"It's an interesting suggestion, though," Sarah conceded. "What if there is a second wizard hiding in Lentari?"

Steve held up his hands. "Wait. Just wait a minute. Let's

say for the sake of argument that there is another wizard out there and he's the one who cursed the dragons. What ties would he have to the wyverians? I mean, what's his motivation? I thought we were talking about these two-headed suckers?"

"We are," Sciathan confirmed. "We have identified the motivation behind this curse. Now we're attempting to discover how the curse was created so that we might better understand how to neutralize it."

"So you're suggesting that this third zweigelan is the one responsible for bringing about this curse?" Steve shook his head. "I find that hard to believe. Even if there were renegade wizards lurking about in Lentari, and I'm not saying there are, how would a completely conspicuous two-headed dragon manage to contact one? I don't care how small this dragon is. Can you just imagine a zweigelan trying to sneak in to Donlari?"

"What I can imagine," Sciathan countered as he fixed his silvery eyes on Steve, "is that if this zweigelan was *half* as active as the first, then it's highly possible that it could have learned about the existence of someone, anyone, who might be able to help it exact revenge."

"What does that mean?" Steve asked, puzzled. "Half as active as the first? What is it that these zweigelans do?"

"The Lentarian zweigelan accosted travelers and asked them riddles," Sciathan told them.

"That doesn't sound so bad," Steve said as he turned to Sarah. "Sounds like the Egyptian sphinxes."

"I'm not familiar with that word," Sciathan admitted.

Nor am I.

"It doesn't matter," Steve told Sciathan, briefly glancing up at Pryllan. He looked back at the small black dragon and shrugged. "I'll be quiet now."

Sarah stifled a laugh.

"If the traveler answered the riddle correctly," Sciathan continued, "then they would be free to go about their business."

"And if they didn't?" Steve prompted, already guessing what the answer would be.

"They'd lose everything they were carrying."

"That's *so* not what I thought you were going to say."

"What does the zweigelan do with its winnings?" Sarah asked.

Sciathan gave the approximation of a shrug. "Unknown. It was reported that its nest was extensive. My guess would be that it keeps its victims' possessions as a type of trophy."

"Suggesting that it was a hoarder," Sarah deduced. "Got it."

"So what now?" Steve wanted to know. "Where do we go from here? If we are to assume everything Sciathan said is right…"

"If you are to assume what I said was right?" Sciathan repeated, incredulous.

"It's a figure of speech. Relax. Now, where do we go from here?"

"I think the first thing we should do is check in with Kri'Entu and Shardwyn. They need to know what's going on."

"Knowing Rinbok Intherer as well as I do," Sciathan began, "he won't want our troubles publicly announced to any other species, including the humans."

"Not even if the humans offer their help?" Sarah asked, annoyed.

"Have you not met the Dragon Lord?" Sciathan countered.

Sarah nodded. "Good point. Tell you what. We'll promise not to let the king know what's going on, only that we're helping Pryllan and Kahvel with a personal problem. That way Rinbok would be able to keep as much dignity as possible. Would that suffice?"

It would.

"It would," Sciathan echoed, mirroring Pryllan's sentiments.

"Are you going to be alright up here by yourself?" Sarah asked the elder black dragon. "Would you like me to lower you to the ground? At least you'd be able to find some food."

"There will be no hunting for me." Sciathan shook his head. "I am too old to try and sneak up on unsuspecting prey and if I were to find game, without my flames, I might as well ask my prey to smash themselves over the head with a rock."

I will find more game which will hold him until this infernal curse is broken.

Steve relayed Pryllan's thought to Sciathan, who nodded his appreciation. The elder dragon looked forlornly up at the sky.

"Don't worry," Steve assured the small dragon. "We'll break this curse and get you back in the air before you know it."

"You cannot guarantee that with any certainty," Sciathan argued. "That being said, thank you for trying."

After Pryllan had deposited several more hapless victims onto the ledge next to Sciathan's cave, Steve and Sarah bade farewell to the elder dragon and returned to Pryllan's open palm. Together they retreated into the sky and vanished among the clouds.

We go to R'Tal?

Yes, Steve nodded. *We need to check with Shardwyn to see about the possibility of any other wizards being in Lentari. Maybe there's some type of test he can do to check for unregistered wizards.*

Unregistered wizards? Sarah repeated, laughing. *Is that a technical term?*

Steve shrugged. *For now. Pryllan, how long will it take for you to get there?*

Perhaps two hours.

Steve turned to his wife. *Couldn't you teleport her there?*

I would rather fly, as teleportation is an unpleasant sensation.

It does take some getting used to, Steve agreed. *Alright, we fly.*

Two hours later, Pryllan silently dipped below the heavy clouds that blanketed R'Tal castle and the surrounding orchards. Not one human noticed their approach.

Landing quietly at the base of the large grassy mound with fruit trees all around them, Pryllan hurried into the mouth of the large, dark cave, which had been constructed by the human king for any dragon in the area. The unprecedented gesture on the humans' part was largely responsible for an invitation to open negotiations between Rinbok Intherer and the human king, Kri'Entu. That historic meeting had culminated with the first ever wyverian-human pact.

Steve's thought suddenly appeared in the midst of hers.

Rinbok agreed to meet with Kri'Entu because of this cavern?

Pryllan jumped with surprise. Once again, she had forgotten that her thoughts were being broadcast to two human listeners.

Sorry. We've landed. Usually you turn off the telepathy and resume normal talking.

Withdrawing her senses, Pryllan nodded. With her thoughts once more accessible to her and her alone, she took stock of their situation. The total absence of light in the huge cavern didn't disturb her in the slightest. As with Sciathan, she preferred the dark and actively sought out caves that were buried deep within mountains.

Closing her eyes, she switched her vision to her parietal eye. This organ was concealed beneath a flap of her skin directly between her two primary eyes and could be detected by observing a patch of skin that was slightly duller than her typical emerald green color.

The confines of the cave leapt into focus for her and she glanced down at the two humans. Sarah was clutching one of her mate's hands and whispering in Steve's ear. Finished with whatever she had to say, Sarah blindly cast her eyes about the cavern.

"There is nothing to see, Sarah," Pryllan gently told her. "Do not look so alarmed."

Pryllan's gaze shifted to Steve, who was subtly gesturing with his right hand. Knowing what was coming, Pryllan quickly switched back to her primary vision and kept her eyes closed. Several seconds later a huge fireball appeared and zoomed around the cavern to light the torches placed at twenty-foot intervals on the walls.

Sighing inwardly, Pryllan opened her eyes and looked back at the two humans. She blinked her eyes with surprise. Sarah had vanished.

"Has Sarah gone to ask about the renegade wizard?"

Steve nodded. "Yes. She told me that she's going to give the Kri'yans a friendly hello and then see about talking to

Shardwyn."

"And you did not go with her?"

Steve shrugged. "I offered, but she doesn't want to leave you alone in here, so I'm to keep you company."

"Appreciated, but unnecessary."

Steve smiled. "Trust me, I know." He slowly sank down to the floor and rested his back against the closest wall.

Pryllan settled herself to the ground as well. "What will you do if the wizard knows naught of a renegade sorcerer?"

"I don't know," Steve admitted. "The way I see it we have two possible avenues to explore. First, find whoever is responsible for creating the curse. And second, even if the existence of another wizard is confirmed, we still need to interrogate the mastermind of this whole nasty affair."

Pryllan nodded. "The third zweigelan."

"Exactly. If we can find him and make him talk, we'll find out how to break the curse."

"And if the renegade does not cooperate?"

Steve gave her a speculative stare. "I assume you dragons have ways to make other dragons talk?"

Saying nothing, Pryllan nodded. She was well aware of Rinbok Intherer's methods of coercion, and while she didn't approve of most of them, she was willing to look the other way if the welfare of her species was at stake.

Thinking of her nest back in the safety of the mountains, she decided to check in to see how Kahvel was faring. Making certain she wasn't sharing her thoughts with Steve, she mentally sought out her mate's mind and initiated contact.

What is taking so long? Kahvel's irritated thought bombarded her the moment she felt his presence. *I must be off. I have been summoned by the Dragon Lord.*

Again? Why does he need to speak with you so often?
I am sure he has his reasons.

If you must go then take Pravara with you, Pryllan gently suggested. **I know he doesn't care for young dragonlets in his presence, but if he wants to see you that badly then he'll have to tolerate her for a little while.**

I cannot. I will not take her there.

Pryllan hesitated. **Where is 'there'?**

The caverns.

Pryllan growled. She had no desire to let her offspring anywhere near that foreboding place.

You are not taking her there.

I agree, which is why I am stalling for time, awaiting your return.

Steve rose to his feet.

"You're growling an awful lot. Is everything okay? What's the matter?"

"A moment, if you please," she gently told her rider. She returned her attention to her distant mate.

Why does the Dragon Lord wish to meet with you in the caverns?

I do not know.

You're hiding something, Pryllan thought crossly. **I can feel it. You're trying to conceal something.**

She felt her mate grow uneasy.

Kahvel sighed. *You are correct. There is a reason I am being summoned there, but I have been forbidden from disclosing the details.*

Will you ever be able to tell me?

If things progress quickly, I should be able to tell you within the week. Maybe even in a day or two. So, have you met with Sciathan yet? What have you learned?

We are dealing with a curse, more than likely brought on by one of the zweigelans.

Pryllan's eyes widened with shock and disbelief as Kahvel's angry profanity-laced tirade echoed loudly in her mind. She decided to let Kahvel vent his frustration in private.

I'll be in touch, my love. Fear not. We will put an end to this.

Not wanting to wait for her mate to calm down, she broke contact and sighed.

"Were you just talking with Kahvel?" Steve asked.

Pryllan nodded. She sighed again.

"I thought Kahvel couldn't use the Collective? How is it you're still able to talk to him?"

"The Collective is a joining of multiple minds," Pryllan explained. "If you choose to be mated with another, then a bond is created that allows mental contact regardless of distance."

"So two acquaintances would be unable to converse mentally?"

Pryllan nodded. "A private conversation would be impossible on the Collective. A wyverian can only speak privately with its mate. We dragons mate for life."

"Humans do, too," Steve told the dragon. "Well, most do. So is all not well on the home front?"

Confused, Pryllan looked down at the human.

"By that do you mean is all well between Kahvel and myself? Aye. I just informed him of our suspicions."

"And?"

"I had to break contact. He was a little angry."

"I'll bet. Something startled you. What was it?"

Before Pryllan could respond, Sarah appeared a few feet away. The stern look on her face wasn't encouraging. She walked over to her husband and embraced him. Pryllan saw that Steve was instantly worried and tried to console Sarah, a trait she loved about her own mate.

Steve finally broke their embrace and looked into her eyes. "What is it? What happened? Better yet, what took so long?"

Sarah turned to look up at Pryllan. "Let me start by saying I didn't tell the king anything about the curse."

Pryllan nodded.

"I told him what we had agreed upon, that Steve and I are helping you and Kahvel with a delicate situation. The king guessed that I wasn't telling the whole truth, but to his credit, he didn't press for details. What he did do, though, was promise his help if we were to ever ask for anything. No questions asked."

"Your king is very trusting," Pryllan observed quietly. "He has my thanks."

"So is there another wizard that Shardwyn hasn't told us about?" Steve asked, hoping there was. At least they'd have a clear idea what to do next.

Sarah shook her head no. "He's not aware of any others. He says he has ways to tell, but he made the mistake of saying that in the presence of the king. The king took one look at Shardwyn, then back at me, and then ordered him to do a scan of the kingdom. Apparently, it's something they do once every ten years, like a census for us. He told him to be as thorough as possible. Kri'Entu didn't like the possibility of another wizard who was free to do as he wanted, hiding somewhere in Lentari."

"I can believe that. How long will that take?"

"I asked. He said it could be anywhere from a few days to as long as three months. The only thing the king could tell me is that he'd let us know once Shardwyn had finished and had reported the final tally to him. Let's just say Shardwyn was less than thrilled."

Steve eyed Pryllan. "So, option one is out. We won't know anything definitive about the existence of another wizard for a while. We should just assume, until we're told otherwise, that there's another one hiding around here somewhere. Since we don't know where to find him, we go to option two."

"What's option two?" Sarah wanted to know. She looked up at Pryllan, who had anticipated this very question.

"We find a zweigelan," the dragon answered.

"Is everything alright?" Sarah asked, noticing something was troubling their friend.

"I have reason to be concerned," Pryllan told her.

Sarah looked questioningly at Steve, who held up his hands in an 'I don't know' gesture.

"Have we heard from Mikal yet?" Steve asked as he took Sarah's. "He's gotta be around here somewhere."

"I actually asked the king that," Sarah told him. "He went camping with several of his friends. I'm told he'll be back in a few days."

They bade goodbye to Pryllan and walked toward their home in the city.

Pryllan came within sight of her nest as the sun was preparing to set for the night. Pravara, ignoring the indignant outburst from her sire, flew up to meet her, as Pryllan beat her powerful wings to slow her descent. She touched down next to Kahvel and nuzzled her long neck with his.

Beloved.

Pryllan closed her eyes and rested her head against Kahvel's golden neck. **My love. Do you have time or must you leave this instant?**

Kahvel growled. ***I am sorry, beloved. I must go. A fourth messenger departed just before you arrived. Several other dragons have also been summoned. Something is amiss; more than I originally thought.***

Go then. Do what you must. Include me when you can.

I will.

Kahvel's situation worried her. She was due to fly the humans south to the Selekai Mountains tomorrow. What if Rinbok Intherer's business with Kahvel wasn't concluded by tomorrow morning? How could she travel that far away without anyone to look after Pravara? What was she supposed to do?

There was only one thing she could do. Pravara would have to come along with them. There was no way she would typically fly that great a distance with such a young dragon, but since the alternative was to leave her only offspring in the care of another dragon, exceptions would have to be made. Therefore, the young dragonlet would have to accompany them.

The following morning, once Steve and Sarah had returned to the nest, Pryllan broke the news to Pravara. The young dragon's bright golden eyes sparkled with wonder as she listened to her mother give her the wonderful news.

"I'm accompanying you? Now? Today? With the humans?"

"Yes, young one. It's a long flight. Eat. You'll need your strength."

"So, does anyone know where we can find this zweigelan?" Steve asked. Pravara had locked her gaze on him the moment he arrived and she continued to follow him around their nest. Steve smiled at the dragonlet.

"I asked Kahvel that question last night," Pryllan informed them.

"And?" Steve prompted.

"The lair of this zweigelan, provided he hasn't relocated his nest, is in the southeastern part of the kingdom."

"Do we have something more tangible than that?"

"I have been checking the Collective but no one has answered me yet."

"We can at least get going in the right direction," Sarah pointed out. "Hopefully someone will answer you soon. However, I just thought of a question. What if we do get directions to its nest and it has since relocated. What then?"

Pryllan shook her head.

"Unlikely. I'm told its nest is quite extensive and would be too cumbersome to effectively move. He should still be there."

"What can you tell us about this zweigelan?" Steve asked as he tightened Mythrin's strap along his chest for the third time. "What were your opinions about this two-headed dragon? Better yet, did you ever meet it?"

Pryllan shook her head. "I did not. Kahvel did, as he was part of the team that assimilated him into the Collective."

"What was his impression?" Sarah asked. "Did he say?"

"Arrogance," Pryllan answered. "Defiance. The zweigelan had no desire to join the Collective and acted as though it would prefer death. Rinbok Intherer gave it that option, but the zweigelan had a change of heart. I believe it has a strong desire to live. As you can imagine, it was not an easy assimilation."

"How does a dragon become assimilated and join your Collective?"

"By swearing allegiance to Rinbok Intherer."

"That's it?"

Pryllan nodded. "Once allegiance has been sworn, there is no further need for hostility. We become his brethren just as he becomes ours."

Sarah frowned. "So, it's the wyverian way or the highway?"

Pryllan blinked her eyes a few times in rapid succession. "I do not understand."

"Essentially you give the zweigelan one choice if he wants to live? Join the Collective?"

"You may think it harsh, Sarah, but it is our way."

"Don't you think that maybe this is why the zweigelans targeted you dragons? No wonder they're so angry."

"Your objection is duly noted, Sarah," Pryllan patiently told her. "I cannot say that I fully agree with everything the Dragon Lord does. Nevertheless, it is our way."

Filing her annoyance into a growing pile of arguments she wished to have with Rinbok Intherer, Sarah plastered a smile on her face and let the matter drop.

Recognizing Sarah's ire, Steve wisely changed the subject. "So, umm, who do we know that would know where to find this zweigelan?"

What was that?

Steve looked at his wife. "What?"

They exchanged a puzzled glance before the voice came again. Steve noticed Mythrin, his special broadsword strapped across his back, had grown heavier.

Breslin?

Obviously. Good to hear from you, Sir Steve.

"What's going on?" Sarah asked.

Steve hooked a thumb at the large sword on his back.

"The voice I heard in my head was Breslin's. Let me see what he wants."

You, too, Breslin. Is there something I can do for you?

You contacted me, something about a zweigelan?

Oh, I didn't realize … Do you know where it is?

I should say so, lad. I was a member of the team who found it. What do you need to find it for?

We just need to ask it a few questions.

Oh. No worries, then. Now, here's what you do. Get yourself a map of the Selekais and I will tell you exactly where to look.

An hour later they were ready. Pryllan had stalled long enough, hoping against hope that Kahvel would return. He hadn't. Sarah had returned to R'Tal for a map which included detailed sketches of the Selekai Mountains, which the king gave her. True to his word, he hadn't asked any questions. Once Breslin told Steve where to find the zweigelan's peak, Steve located the nest on the supplied map. Pryllan committed the map to memory and was ready to depart. Pravara was more than ready.

Pryllan had to practically hold Pravara down on the ground as she was very eager to get started on their journey. She listened with the patience only a mother could possess as her offspring prattled on and on about their upcoming adventure. What were they going to see? Who were they going to meet? Why were they going to the Selekais? Why were there bad dragons in the world? Were they going to try and talk some sense into it?

"All in good time, young one. Are you ready?"

Pravara vehemently nodded her head yes.

Promise me you will stay safe, Pryllan thought to her mate, knowing full well he wouldn't answer while occupied with whatever he was doing for the Dragon Lord. Surprisingly, a response came back.

I will, beloved. Be safe.

And you.

Cradling the two humans within her talons, she leapt straight up and snapped her wings open. Pravara mimicked her as much as she was able. Pryllan turned to look at her offspring as she rose higher into the air.

"This will be the longest flight you have ever been on, Pravara. If you tire, do not hesitate to tell me."

"I will be fine," the young dragon assured her. "You won't need to worry about me. You'll see!"

Chapter 5 — Cantankerous Companion

Leagues of forests, mountains, and prairies passed beneath the two dragons. Pryllan turned to look behind her, seeing that Pravara had started to fall behind.

"Don't fight the air currents, little one. Use them. Keep your head and wing tips up or you'll be driven into the ground. You want to soar, rather than using your energy to flap your wings."

The small green dragon struggled a few more minutes before she got the hang of it.

"You've done remarkably well, and I can see you are tired. We will find a place to rest."

Pryllan directed her thoughts to the two humans nestled in her talons. **We are descending so I can find us a suitable place to rest.**

That's fine by us; Sarah's thought came back to her. *Mister Narcolepsy here fell asleep an hour or two ago.*

Narcolepsy?

It's a word used to describe a condition where uncontrollable periods of deep sleep can happen to someone under any circumstances. That about sums up my husband. Steve can fall asleep anywhere and anytime. I don't know how he does it. Just do me a favor.

Yes?

When you land, don't try to land all soft and gentle. Feel free to shake things up a bit.

Sensing the mischievous nature of her intent, Pryllan nodded.

Selecting a tiny lake—for a dragon—nestled in the thick of the forest, Pryllan guided Pravara down to the eastern shore. Once the young dragon had touched the ground, Pryllan landed unceremoniously next to her. A few dead trees crashed noisily to the ground.

Steve practically leapt out of Pryllan's open claw and adopted a combative stance, both hands ignited. "What the hell!"

"Good morning, sunshine!" Sarah cheerfully told him as she merrily hopped to the ground.

"What … where … what's going on?"

"You were snoring."

"I was not."

Pryllan turned her head to look down at the two humans. She focused on Steve. "How Sarah manages to sleep through that ruckus eludes me."

Steve gave the dragon a neutral stare.

"Aren't you a barrel of laughs? What was with that landing? You could've woken the dead."

Sarah cleared her throat. "Well, seeing how it woke you up, I would say that's an accurate—"

Steve held up both hands in an I-surrender gesture.

"Fine, you two win. Why'd we stop?"

"Pravara is tired."

"Oh. Poor thing. Anything we can do to help?"

Pryllan gently walked over to her now-sleeping offspring and curled her body around Pravara's.

"I thank you for your concern, but no. She just needs to rest."

Pryllan took the tip of her tail in her teeth and extended a wing to drape it over Pravara's still form.

Sarah nudged her husband's shoulder and pointed back toward the small lake.

"Come on; let's give them some peace and quiet."

Together husband and wife approached the lake's edge and turned right to follow the perimeter of the small lake. Looking back at the sleeping dragons, Steve was surprised to see a large grassy knoll where Pryllan had been curled up. Impressed, he whistled softly. The ability of a dragon to camouflage itself was still something that took his breath away regardless of how many times he witnessed it. One would never know that the grassy hill contained a sleeping mother dragon and her baby.

"I love how she does that," Sarah whispered. She stepped next to her husband and slipped her hand into his.

"That's just so cool!" Steve echoed, giving his wife's hand a kiss. "So, what are we supposed to do now? How long are we going to be here?"

"I'd say until they wake up."

"Thank you. That was incredibly helpful."

"Come on," Sarah urged as she pulled her husband away from the camouflaged dragons. "We can go for a walk around the lake. It isn't that big."

As the two of them walked hand in hand around the circumference of the tiny lake, Sarah pulled them to a stop on the western shore directly across from Pryllan's sleeping form.

"What's the matter?" Steve asked as he looked around.

Sarah let go of his hand and walked over to the closest tree. The pine tree, as with the others in the vicinity, didn't have any branches on its eastern side, from trunk to top. From a distance they all looked like half-trees.

Steve stared silently at the tree. He slowly looked around the small glade and noticed the deformed trees were only on the western shore of the lake. Everywhere else were green, healthy trees. A closer inspection of the tree nearest him revealed a number of old scars scattered all around the trunk. The sight triggered a memory.

"Is this the lake we found after we escaped from the mugger's house?" Steve asked, looking south for a decrepit, run-down cottage.

"I think it is," Sarah agreed as she nodded.

"If this is the same lake, then our captor's cottage should be over there."

Steve followed her gaze south and remained silent. Sarah gave him a gentle nudge in his ribs.

"That was a joke. Don't even think about trying to find him again."

"I would love to say hello."

"Yeah, right. I'm sure that's the only thing you'd say. Come on, let's keep going. It's not worth it."

They completed their trek around the lake in just under an hour, with Steve remaining on high alert the whole time. What they saw when they arrived drew them up short.

Half a dozen griffins were milling about on the ground, sniffing around the base of the grassy knoll that concealed both dragons. One large adult griffin had even alighted on the top of the small hill. Curved beaks lifted high into the air as clearly the griffins could detect something in the vicinity but were unable to fathom what it was.

Six avian heads jerked up, eyes landing squarely on Steve and Sarah. Several griffins squawked out warnings, daring the two of them to come any closer.

Steve pointed at the large lump the griffin was perched on. "You might want to come down from there," he began. He could only hope Pryllan was asleep and didn't know a griffin was perched on her head. "It would perhaps be best if you guys went about your business."

One griffin, with more red in his wings than his companions—indicating its young age—let out a series of squawks and chirps that required no translation; it wanted the two humans to move off.

Steve pointed at the mound. "Trust me on this. You're going to want to move away. I say this not because I want the hill for myself but rather for your safety."

All six griffins puffed out their chests and tried to look intimidating, which wasn't saying much as each of the griffins, now that Steve looked, had a fair amount of red coloring in their wings. Steve shook his head. Apparently, teenagers in any species would always think they knew what was best.

The griffin perched on Pryllan's head dug in its claws and issued a challenging squawk, daring him or the other griffins to make him move. The young griffin pawed the grass-covered hill, daring anyone to dethrone him as king of the hill.

Two narrow slits appeared in the grass and blasted smoke. The griffins beat a hasty retreat, squawking as they took to the sky.

Pryllan stirred. The grassy knoll disappeared and once more Steve and Sarah found themselves standing before the dragon's massive form. The emerald dragon twisted her neck so she could peer into the sky.

"What happened?"

Steve stared at the befuddled dragon.

"You mean you don't know? Did you doze off?"

Pryllan turned to look at Sarah with a confused expression on her face.

"He's asking if you fell asleep," Sarah translated.

Pryllan nodded. "Apparently I was more tired than I thought."

"How's Pravara?" Sarah inquired.

Pryllan rose to her feet and folded her wing against her back. Pravara's dark green form was stirring. The young dragonlet stretched her back, then her wings, and then finally opened her eyes and looked around.

"Where are we?"

"En route to the Selekai Mountains," Pryllan told her.

Pravara moved into a beam of sunlight. Her scales sparkled with radiance, a dark green dragon with a soft golden glow. Pravara extended her wings for a few more stretches before finally joining her mother in the air.

Several hours later they were flying over a vast open plain. To their right, in the distance, were the snow-capped mountains of the Selekais. On the left they could see the edge of the forest, visible as a thick green blanket covering much of the land in the north.

Steve was sitting back against the curve of Pryllan's huge

palm. Sarah was nestled against him. Both had their eyes closed; only Steve could still see everything happening around him. While Pryllan shared her senses with him he could see everything she saw, smell everything she smelled, and could hear everything she could.

It still doesn't make any sense.

Would you like me to explain it again?

Please do.

The word is 'vegetarian'.

Many animals only eat plants. That's not the part I'm confused about.

I figured. What's the confusing part? Why someone would choose to forgo meat?

Correct. Why plants? They do not taste good.

I couldn't agree more. I don't know. I guess it's their choice.

They are not coerced to consuming sustenance in this fashion?

Right.

I did not realize humans could get the sustenance they need from simply eating plants. The grass from your world must be truly nourishing.

Ummm, they don't just eat grass. I mean, no one eats grass. Well, there are some vegetables that resemble grass when cooked. That's not the point. Look, the human body can get the protein it needs from other sources besides plants.

Why go to the trouble to find other sources of nourishment when succulent meat is so readily available?

They'd rather not eat animals.

But the animals are there to be consumed, correct?

Er, yes.

And there is an abundance of animals?

We call them grocery stores, but yes.

And if they are there to be consumed, why would they choose to not eat them?

Some people just don't like to eat anything that comes from an animal, that's all.

Have you ever eaten in this fashion?

Hell no. I like meat too much.

Would you ever consider eating in this fashion?

Absolutely not.

Is Sarah a vegetentarian?

You were close that time. It's 'vegetarian'. And no, she isn't. She likes steaks more than I do. Her parents are vegetarians, but I'm convinced they cheat every once in a while.

Your world is a confusing place.

I couldn't agree more.

Sarah stirred against his side.

"Did I fall asleep?"

Steve nodded. "Yep."

"I suppose you're going to tell me that I was snoring?"

"No, but you did drool a little bit on my shirt."

Sarah playfully slapped her husband's shoulder.

"I most certainly did not."

Sarah leaned to her left to look between two of Pryllan's claws.

"Pravara, how are you holding up back there?"

The dragonlet flew close.

"I am fine."

"We've got to be getting close, right?"

Pravara shook her head. "I do not know."

"We're close," Pryllan agreed. "I've been searching for traces of the zweigelan's activities but haven't found any thus far."

"What if it is hiding from us?" Steve asked. "What if this two-headed dragon hates all other dragons? How can we be so certain we'll find him?"

"Kahvel told me the nest is extensive. Moving it and all its contents would be no easy feat, nor would they be able to mask the scents emanating from their collection. For those two reasons alone, I know they are still in the area. I have just picked up its scent."

Steve nodded. "That's right. I forgot that you dragons are just as good as bloodhounds."

"I'm not familiar with that term."

"A bloodhound is a creature from our world that has the uncanny ability to track a scent," Sarah answered.

A distant commotion to the south drew her attention. Zeroing in on the disturbance, she could see a band of humans accosting a creature that was backed up against a rock outcropping. It was long and skinny, almost serpentine in appearance. It was snapping at the encroaching humans and to its credit, wasn't trying to flee. Pryllan realized, with a start, that she was staring at a dragon much smaller than she had ever encountered before. Two long heads were swaying back and forth as it futilely snapped at the humans who were clever enough to keep dodging out of the way. It was the zweigelan!

Pryllan watched as one of the humans aimed a crossbow at the dragon and fired. Thankfully the bolt bounced harmlessly off the dragon's scales, but it was enough of a distraction to get both heads angrily searching for the aggressor. As soon as the zweigelan moved its attention from the group of humans, flanking it from the front, several more darted in and jabbed it with their swords. Sparks flew off the scales as the blows were successfully deflected. Why were the humans crowding so close to the outcast? Weren't they afraid of dragon fire?

Pryllan's eyes widened. That's what was missing from this picture. The zweigelan should have been spitting fire. It wasn't! Had it been stricken by the curse, too? She should inform the others.

We see it, Steve confirmed. *It doesn't make sense, though. Why would the zweigelan curse themselves?*

Unknown. More than anything, it would appear as though it is confused by the absence of its flames. Perhaps it just progressed to stage two?

Sarah suddenly sat up in alarm. "Pryllan, where's Pravara?"

Pryllan's long green neck whipped around to both sides of her body. Her offspring was gone!

Pryllan tucked her wings and dropped to an altitude of about five hundred feet. Frantically she cast her powerful gaze about. A moment ago, Pravara had been by her side. What had happened?

Pryllan detected movement in her peripheral vision. She glanced downward and to her left. What she saw alarmed her so much that she folded her wings and went into a steep nosedive straight toward the earth.

* * *

"We will rid the countryside of you and your accursed exploits once and for all!"

Several men shouted in agreement and renewed their efforts to subdue the freak dragon. While smaller than any other dragon they had ever encountered, they still had to be cautious. One snap from either set of jaws would end a life.

Someone from their group managed to throw a loop of rope around the infernal creature's tail, securing it to a nearby tree. Another coil of rope snagged a foreleg. Then one landed around its left head. A few minutes later the men had managed to completely immobilize the dragon. Only the dangerous jaws still moved.

The leader of the group approached the trussed-up dragon and slowly drew his sword. He hefted his freshly sharpened sword and grinned lecherously. This was going to be fun!

Something small and dark green thumped down to the ground in front of their prisoner. Quickly regaining its feet, it turned to the advancing marauders and growled. What came out was a soft snarl which lacked any ferocity whatsoever. Was this a baby dragon?

"What's the matter with the dragons in these parts?" the leader complained, as he looked back at his friends. "I mean, look at this. We have captured the freak and then we get this wimpy excuse of a wyverian trying to defend it. There must be something in the water around here."

Several of his companions laughed hysterically. All were now brandishing their weapons and were advancing on the growling baby and the trussed-up freak dragon. The tiny green dragonlet was pacing nervously in front of the captive and was trying valiantly, unsuccessfully, to scare the men away.

Something else suddenly fell from the sky. It was large, green, and impacted the ground so hard that all the surrounding trees fell backward. The self-appointed leader felt all the blood drain from his face, staring at what had to be the largest, angriest dragon he had ever encountered.

Pryllan roared her challenge to the humans. Putting the

bulk of her body between Pravara and the marauders, she snarled and crouched low, daring any of them to take a step toward her. Turning to make a run for it, the motley group of attackers was startled to see a man and woman sitting casually on a fallen log, as if they were enjoying watching the scene unfold.

The man slowly got to his feet. He held out a hand. A large fireball appeared in it, then spun about on his middle finger. That was the final straw. Every person there knew full well of the Nohrin. Behind them, advancing slowly, was the huge mother dragon. It was time to cut their losses.

Fed up with the slow-to-act humans, Pryllan issued a second challenge, spitting a huge mass of flames into the air. By the time the blast burned itself out, the only humans left in the glade were Steve and Sarah. Glaring angrily around the surrounding trees to verify that no other humans were lurking about, Pryllan turned around to face her offspring.

Cowed, Pravara hung her head. Pryllan thumped the ground with her tail several times to get her attention.

"Do not hang your head, young one. You performed admirably. You leapt to the defense of another. In the future, either wait to attain your adult size or be certain I am nearby, is that understood?"

Thankful she wasn't in trouble, Pravara eagerly nodded her head.

Steve walked around Pryllan and gave Pravara a friendly pat on her shoulder as he passed by. He looked at the strange dragon with two heads. "You must be this zweigelan we've been searching for."

Neither of the captive dragon's heads did anything.

"You obviously make a lot of friends wherever you go," Steve continued as he sat down on a rock just outside of the zweigelan's reach. "So, are you ready to play nice and listen to what we have to say?"

The zweigelan warily eyed him, but refrained from saying anything.

"I'll take that as a yes. Hold still." Steve took his time as he walked around the still form of the two-headed dragon. Twenty seconds later, he was sitting back on the rock.

"We are still immobilized," one of the heads hissed at him.

"Yes, we are," the other head agreed.

Steve gave the dragon a forced smile. He turned back to look at his wife, who nodded. He then turned to look at Pryllan, who was still shielding Pravara from view.

You ready in case things go bad?

Pryllan's green eyes found his.

Yes.

Here we go.

Focusing his jhorun, he ordered selected points on the ropes to burn. Seconds later the ropes dropped harmlessly to the ground. The zweigelan began struggling to get to its feet as the ropes slackened. Standing upright once more, it studied the four of them.

"Why did you help us?" the right head asked.

"Aye, we would like to know why," the left head added.

Steve briefly turned to Pryllan to mentally ask if he should be the one to address it. Pryllan gave a slight nod of her head.

"You are a dragon."

"We are zweigelan," the right head haughtily informed him.

"Zweigelan, dragon, does it really matter? You're a dragon and part of the Collective, are you not?"

Both heads hissed with annoyance. Apparently, it was still a sore memory.

"Don't hiss at me," Steve scolded. "You asked why we came to your aid. I'm answering. You're a dragon. We are friends to all dragons, regardless of whether or not the feelings are reciprocated."

Sarah stood and shoved her husband out of the way. "Shame on you, you pathetic excuse of a dragon. Pravara came to your aid first. If she hadn't been able to stall your attackers, they probably would have killed you. Do you understand that? You owe Pravara and her mother, Pryllan, your life!"

Both heads turned to study the much larger green dragon who was returning the frank stare. Surprisingly, the twin heads dropped their gaze to the ground.

Sarah looked at the young dragonlet and gestured toward the zweigelan. "Pravara, why did you jump in front of those humans?"

Pravara's glittering golden eyes turned to study the shamed outcast. "He's a dragon."

"Because you're a dragon," Sarah repeated as she turned to face the zweigelan. "You were just ... look at me when I'm talking to you."

When neither head bothered to face her, Sarah used her jhorun to pick up a small rock and toss it at the zweigelan's right flank. Of course, it bounced harmlessly off the protective scales, but it was enough to get the dragon's attention.

"As I was saying," Sarah continued, "you were just defended by a baby dragon."

"I'm not a baby," Pravara grumped, lifting her nose into the air.

"I'm sorry, sweetheart," Sarah told the dragonlet, giving her an affectionate hug. "It's just a figure of speech." She returned her attention to the zweigelan, who was now staring curiously at the dragonlet.

"Why come to the aid of someone who is not a dragon?" the right head asked.

Pravara rapidly blinked her eyes as she stared at the zweigelan, confusion evident on her young face. She turned to her mother.

"Speak your mind, Pravara," Pryllan told her offspring. "Tell him why you did what you did."

"You're a dragon," Pravara simply said as she turned back around. "Dragons watch out for each other."

"We are not —"

"Oh, cut the 'we are not dragon' crap," Steve exclaimed, growing angry. "So, you're not the same species of dragon as they are, but you're still a dragon. You're just a dragon with two heads. There's nothing wrong with that."

"Why didn't you flee?" Sarah asked, before the zweigelan could interrupt with another objection.

"Flee?" the left head said, incredulous. "We never flee. We have never fled before and we have no intention of starting now."

"How's that working for you?" Steve quipped. He looked down at the burnt ropes that had been restraining the zweigelan. "You were about to become a matching set of luggage, dude."

"We need to know what we can call you," Sarah said, drawing everyone's attention. "I don't like addressing you or referencing you in the third person. You must have a name. Some way to set yourself apart from other zweigelans?"

The zweigelan was silent for a few more minutes before it finally responded. It answered so softly that they barely caught what was said.

"I am Syrreth," the left head quietly informed them.

After a few moments the right head also spoke.

"And I am Ferreth."

Sarah smiled. "See? That wasn't so bad, was it?"

Syrreth and Ferreth said nothing.

Steve faced the left head and ignited his hands. "Syrreth, do me a favor and show me your flames."

Syrreth shook his head no. Steve looked at Syrreth's twin. "Ferreth, what about you? Care to show me what you've got?"

Ferreth also shook his head.

"You've become affected by this curse, haven't you?" Sarah informed them. "Stage two, right? But you knew this already, didn't you?"

"You created this curse," Steve added. He sat down on the closest rock again and extinguished his hands with a flick of his wrists. "You created it and have now managed to screw yourselves. Nice going."

"Did this not, I say," Syrreth informed him, directing his gaze at the sitting human.

"Nor did I," Ferreth added with a growl.

Steve scowled at the two heads. "But one of you zweigelans did, didn't you?"

Syrreth and Ferreth fell silent once more.

"And for what? Revenge against the dragons?"

"The dragons deserve everything that's coming to them, they do," Ferreth whispered quietly.

"Aye, they do," Syrreth agreed.

"I hate to point this out to you," Sarah interjected, "but

you're a dragon, too. Looks like whoever created this curse included you."

Silence.

"If you think I'm wrong then prove it. Spit fire. Either of you. Since you can't, then it means you've been cursed."

Neither Syrreth nor Ferreth elected to say anything.

"Two dragons you don't know just saved your life," Sarah added, growing angry herself. "Still think all dragons should be cursed? What has Pryllan or Pravara done to you besides saving you from being hacked into a million little pieces?"

"So, what have you lost?" Steve wanted to know, looking up at Syrreth. "Because the first part of this curse renders you defenseless. You lose the ability to spit fire. The second isolates you from your fellow dragons. That's the loss of the Collective, I'm afraid. And finally, if you become stricken with the third part of this curse, you will become grounded. You lose your ability to fly. Is that what you want? We need to break this curse. *You* need to break this curse. Help us find whoever did this."

"Why should we help you?" Syrreth grumped. "Never wished to join the filthy Collective, did we? Wish to be left alone, we do."

Sarah shook her head with bewilderment. "Do you suffer from short term memory loss? Had you been alone five minutes ago, you would have been killed. Do you not understand that? You ask why you should help? It's because you owe Pryllan and Pravara your life. That's why. Repay your debt. Regain your honor as a dragon."

"Oooh, good one, babe," Steve whispered.

"Very well," Ferreth grumped. "A debt for a debt. The one who did this? Help you find them, we will."

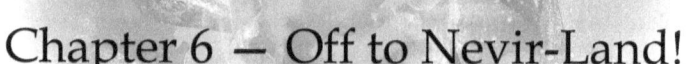

Chapter 6 — Off to Nevir-Land!

We have made contact with the zweigelan, beloved. **W** He hasn't admitted responsibility for this curse, but I do believe he knows more than he's letting on.

Kahvel's powerful thought came back to her almost instantly.

Do whatever it takes to make him talk. Use force if necessary. This curse must be broken if we are to survive as a species.

Pryllan sighed.

Are you suggesting I mistreat the outcast? He is a dragon. I cannot inflict him harm unless he bodily attacks myself or Pravara.

If he mistreats you or Pravara in any fashion, you are to inform me immediately, is that understood?

Pryllan nodded, causing Steve and Sarah to turn and quizzically look up at her.

Understood. I do not believe he will try anything foolish. He has also become infected and has lost his fire.

She felt Kahvel's anger switch to concern. ***Haven't been affected by this curse, have you?***

Pryllan shook her head again. **Not that I'm aware of. How would I know?**

Use the Collective, Kahvel suggested. ***Try to contact someone.***

Very well. A moment, if you please.

Pryllan was silent for a few minutes as she quieted her mind to see if she could hear any other voices. Sadly, she could not. She asked if anyone could hear her but she failed to receive a response.

I asked but did not receive an answer, she informed her mate. **I believe there is no one left to use the Collective.**

Do you still retain your fire?

I did as of an hour ago.

Good. Keep a close watch on Pravara. Do not let her wander off. These are troubling times.

Agreed. Kahvel, where should we go from here? I am not sure what to do next. I have no idea how to break this curse.

What do the humans think you should do?

Just a moment and I'll ask them.

"What do you think we should do now?" Pryllan asked, interrupting the silence and causing Sarah to jump nervously. "We have the zweigelan and he has all but confirmed he knows who is responsible."

"We never said that," Syrreth insisted.

Ferreth nodded his head in agreement.

Steve cleared his throat. "If this was a problem affecting the villagers, and we suddenly had some news to impart, I'd report it to Kri'Entu."

"You're suggesting that we seek out Rinbok Intherer?"

Steve nodded. "He's the Dragon Lord. This curse is affecting the dragons. I'm sure he'd want to know, whether out of curiosity or respect."

Kahvel, Steve suggests we seek out Rinbok Intherer.

Kahvel's voice was silent in her mind. When she didn't hear anything from him for a few minutes she tried again.

Beloved? It was suggested that we...

I heard you the first time, Kahvel's curt response interrupted her. *Rinbok has become … indisposed. To seek him out would be a waste of time.*

He's indisposed? From what?

She felt Kahvel's sigh of impatience. *He still believes he has become infected with some type of ailment and is dying. He has become unresponsive, and if he agrees to see you, which I think he won't, then you will not be able to get a coherent conversation out of him. Believe me, I've tried for hours to get him to listen. I couldn't get any type of response out of him.*

Are you still with him? We have information. It might spur him into action.

I doubt it. Besides, I have since left.

Nevertheless, we have to try. Where is he?

Nevir.

Pryllan growled. Whoever decided the Dragon Lord should live in those caverns must have been mentally unstable.

I know of your aversion to the caverns, beloved, Kahvel thought to her. *Visiting Nevir should only be attempted if you are in the best of health. Trust me.*

Suggesting that I am physically unable to make the journey? I still have my health, Kahvel. I have not fallen victim to this curse. Not yet.

It will be very difficult for you to find, beloved.

Since I already know where it is, I doubt that.

Pryllan's sense of satisfaction deepened as she felt Kahvel's shock of surprise ripple through her.

How do you *know where to find Nevir?*

Because of you, my love.

I never told you, Kahvel insisted.

You didn't have to, my love.

Are my thoughts that transparent?

With me they are, my love.

Very well. You can try to engage Rinbok Intherer, but do not be too disappointed if he chooses not to react to your presence.

Understood.

"What's going on?" a voice interjected just as Pryllan

severed the mental connection to her mate. "What are you doing?"

Pryllan looked down at the only human that she had ever allowed to ride her. Before she could say anything, however, Sarah answered for her.

"Isn't it obvious? She's speaking telepathically to someone. I'd say it was Kahvel. Am I right?"

Pryllan nodded. "You are."

Steve shrugged and slid his hands into his pockets. "Oh, okay. Cool. What does he think we should do?"

"He was trying to dissuade us from speaking with Rinbok Intherer as he has fallen victim to this curse along with everyone else."

"Why wouldn't Rinbok see us?" Sarah demanded. "We're trying to help him!"

"The Dragon Lord is very proud. He wouldn't want our problems to become known to anyone else. It is Kahvel's belief that if it became known Rinbok Intherer had to accept help from the humans then his pride would suffer."

"What a bunch of crap," Steve snapped.

Pravara lifted her head from the ground and regarded him with a querulous look.

"Sorry. I shouldn't have raised my voice."

Mollified, Pravara returned to her impromptu nap.

"I say we go see him anyway," Sarah added. She took Steve's hand. "This is his problem whether he wants to admit it or not. It's time he knows what's going on. You said he thinks he suffers from an ailment? Well, he's going to learn the truth."

Sarah spun on her heel and pointed straight at Syrreth and Ferreth.

"And he's going to hear it from the two of you."

Both of the zweigelan's heads began violently shaking their heads. They both had experienced the unpleasantness that was the gigantic Dragon Lord and neither wished for a repeat performance.

Steve unbuckled Mythrin from his hip and fastened his green-bladed broadsword to his back. "So we're off to see Rinbok, is that right? Where is he?"

"Nevir," Pryllan answered.

"We're never going to see Rinbok? But I thought that was the plan? Why'd you change your mind?"

"We will seek an audience with the Dragon Lord," Pryllan confirmed. The place is called Nevir. N-E-V-I-R."

Satisfied, Sarah turned to Steve. "Vocabulary problem."

"Ah. Got it. So Nevir is the name of the dragon graveyard where all the dragons go to die?"

Surprised, Sarah turned back to Pryllan. "That's right. I forgot about that. That's where we have to go? To a place no dragon can find but a select few?"

"Correct."

Sarah nodded. "This ought to be interesting."

Steve held up a hand. "Wait a minute. I'm confused about something."

Sarah stifled a giggle. Steve shot her a dark glare.

"If hardly any dragon can find this Nevir place, how is it they're supposed to go there to die? How are they able to find it?"

"A dragon will feel the pull once their end is near," Pryllan explained.

Steve nudged his wife to get her attention. "It's like the underworld from Greek mythology, I suppose."

Sarah shook her head. "I don't think that comparison is right. The underworld is essentially hell. I doubt very much Rinbok lives in hell."

Steve looked up at their large green companion. "He doesn't, does he? I mean, living people can go there and still safely return, right?"

Pryllan gave him a pitiful look. "Obviously. Kahvel has journeyed to, and returned from, Nevir many times."

Satisfied, the two humans fell silent.

Pryllan's expression turned neutral as she turned to the much smaller zweigelan.

"We fly north. Keep up. Do not hamper our progress and I will put in a good word for you with the Dragon Lord."

Syrreth and Ferreth studied her a few moments before both heads gave a little bow.

Pryllan nudged Pravara's sleeping form, awakening her.

"Rise, young one. We must return to the valley."

"We're flying back now?"

"We must begin now if we're to return before the sun sets. If you tire, and I expect you will, you must inform me immediately. Do you understand?"

Pravara nodded her head. Unfolding her wings, she took to the air in the same fashion as her mother by leaping as high as she could go and then flapping her wings. Pryllan's huge form sailed past her and continued another fifty or sixty feet into the air before her wings snapped open.

* * *

"Why do you have two heads?" Pravara asked Syrreth, flying just off the zweigelan's left flank.

"You have just the one, you do," Syrreth countered. Ferreth had been trying his best to ignore the dragonlet.

"Do you have any brothers or sisters?"

Syrreth shook his head.

"What happened to your parents? Did something bad happen to them? Were they killed? Were they eaten by a monster?"

Syrreth regarded Pravara with a scornful look. "Knew our parents, we did not."

Pravara's eyes widened in disbelief. "You never knew your mother? What about your father?"

"Ask too many questions, you do," Ferreth snapped. "Listening to us, you are not."

"Play nice over there," Steve warned.

Pravara glanced quickly over at her mother, who was flying nearby, and the two humans safely ensconced within her talons. The fire thrower was pointedly watching the proceedings, no doubt at the request of her mother. Returning her attention to the strange two-headed dragon, Pravara continued her relentless string of questions.

"How old are you? I'm less than a year old. My mother is much older than that. Way older. Way, way older."

Being old isn't a bad thing, young one, her mother's thought interrupted.

"I meant no offense, mother."

I know.

Waiting for an answer, Pravara observed the right head, Ferreth, glance irritably at the left. Syrreth whispered something to its twin before turning to look back at her.

"We do not know how old we are. Much older than you, we do believe."

"Are you as old as my mother?"

"Older," Syrreth assured her.

"Have you always lived in that cave?" Pryllan suddenly asked.

This caused both heads to swivel around to stare at Pravara's mother.

"You know of the existence of our cave? Never showed you where it was. Most alarming, it is."

"You truly haven't had many interactions with other dragons, have you?" Pryllan observed.

"What does that have to do with anything?" Steve's voice asked, as it floated up from underneath her.

Syrreth nodded. "Agreed. The question is sound. Explain?"

"Are your senses not stronger and sharper than everyone you've encountered?"

Ferreth nodded while Syrreth said yes.

"It's a trait common to all dragons. I could see your nest up on the face of the cliff as well as smell it."

"We do not stink," Syrreth argued, as he growled. Ferreth also growled.

Pryllan's return growl, much louder and deeper than both of the heads combined, silenced both of them instantly.

"Do not be so quick to pass judgment," Pryllan scolded Syrreth. "I was not accusing you of being malodorous."

Ferreth blinked his pale green eyes at her. "Insinuating I reek?"

Pryllan started to growl again but was able to stop herself before anyone could hear her. Swallowing her impatience, she tried again.

"Only in close proximity do I detect a scent from either of you. However, the same cannot be said for whatever objects you have in your nest. There is a strong odor of human and dwarf coming from one of the caves high up on the cliff. Therefore, I assume *that* is your cave. Am I correct?"

Syrreth turned to Ferreth and began a heated argument. "I told you that's how they found us. You have become obsessed with finding jewels and gold. Most have been handled by dwarven hands. They are a foul people. Their things stink!"

"Actually, I smelled humans before I smelled dwarves," Pryllan admitted.

Syrreth's smug expression vanished from his face and appeared on Ferreth's. It was the first expression anyone had seen on the zweigelan's right head.

"Did I not tell you that your collection of human artifacts would be our undoing?"

"You are just as guilty as I am."

"Am not."

"Are too. Admit it!"

"Never!"

I am all for open discussions, Pryllan began as she directed her thoughts toward the two humans she currently held, **but I've never encountered someone such as this. Should I break this up?**

She felt Steve's laughter as he answered her.

Naw. Let 'em duke it out.

Duke it out?

Let them work it out on their own, Sarah thought to her. *Listen to them. This certainly isn't the first argument they've had together.*

True.

"Why are you always so angry?" Pravara asked, interrupting the two bickering heads. "Not even my father is that grumpy."

Surprised, Pryllan turned to the dragonlet and hesitated for a few moments. "He's not that grumpy around you, is he?"

"Many times he is," the young dragonlet gloomily informed her. "He doesn't like to go flying with me anymore nor does he take me hunting. All he ever wants to do is worry about the big day."

Surprised, Pryllan turned to her offspring. "Big day?

What big day?"

Pravara approximated a shrug. "I don't know. Father only tells me he's not ready."

If Pravara didn't have her mother's attention before, she certainly had it now. "For what?"

Sensing she had disclosed something that she shouldn't have, Pravara went silent.

"Not ready for what?" Pryllan prompted again.

Pravara fidgeted midair, her tail flicking nervously from the left to the right. She veered off course and crashed into the zweigelan. Syrreth surprised everyone by lowering his long neck and dipping it under Pravara's right wing and holding it steady, stabilizing her.

The young dragon mumbled her thanks and banked to her left so that she could put a little distance between herself and the grumpy dragon, although she was surprised to see the dual-headed dragon had just come to her aid. Well, part of it did. Syrreth seemed to be more approachable than Ferreth, but there was no avoiding the zweigelan's sulky right head if she wished to pursue her conversation with Syrreth. The dragonlet shook her head in frustration. Their strange new companion was just too difficult to figure out.

"Never flick your tail rapidly back and forth," her mother warned her. "We use our tails to help direct the air flowing under our wings. And don't think I've forgotten this secret you're keeping from me. We will return to this discussion at a later date."

Pravara swallowed nervously. She knew her mother hadn't been fooled. She had inadvertently let something slip that her sire had not shared with her mother and now she was being pressured for more information. If only she was old enough to communicate telepathically with her parents! Then at least she could warn her sire of her mistake. Bored by the silence everyone else seemed content with, she again directed her attention to her new friend.

"You never answered my question."

Syrreth sighed, loud enough for everyone to hear him. "Answered many of your questions, I have."

"Why are you always so angry?"

"See anger, you do not."

Pravara noticed her mother's left ear twitch. She was listening intently to the conversation.

"Then what is it?"

"Remorse."

"Remorse? What does that mean?"

Syrreth turned to look back at Pryllan as if to say *your offspring, you tell her.* Steve burst out laughing once he had caught the look of disgust on Syrreth's face.

Pryllan waited a few moments before she answered. "Remorse is a worrisome agony arising from a sense of guilt for past wrongs."

Pravara was silent as she thought about her mother's precise definition. The human female spoke up. "What are you feeling remorseful about?"

Syrreth didn't say anything. Neither did Ferreth.

"It can help you feel better if you get what is troubling you out into the open. We might be able to help you."

Syrreth turned to look at Pryllan's claws. He found Sarah's eyes and held them. "You're a human. It is no business of yours."

"We're all in this together," Sarah reminded him. "You might not appreciate the situation you're presently in, but one of the advantages of having friends is that friends will help you."

"Are you my friend?"

Much to Sarah's credit, she didn't hesitate. "Yes."

Taken aback, Syrreth was silent as he contemplated this turn of events. The two zweigelan heads regarded each other for a few moments before Ferreth resumed responsibility for their navigation, allowing Syrreth to deal with Pravara.

"We were forced to disclose the location of the other two zweigelans."

"I take it you didn't want to?" Steve asked.

Syrreth shook his head no. "We tried to force the Collective from accessing that memory but it was no use. Once our thoughts fused with the Collective, they knew instantly where to find them."

Pravara caught her mother's eye. Pryllan looked straight

at her and winked.

Are you confused about the subject matter in this conversation? Pryllan's thought said to her.

Unable to speak back to her telepathically, Pravara nodded.

Do not concern yourself with Syrreth and Ferreth's affairs. Listen, but do not speak.

Grateful—for once—of the parental guidance, Pravara decided to stay quiet and out of the way, but still close enough to hear what was being said. She might not fully understand but she certainly didn't want to be excluded, either. She had long ago learned that adult matters were significantly more interesting than her own.

"If one of the other zweigelans had been captured in your stead," Sarah began, "your location would have been revealed, too, right?"

Syrreth considered. "Perhaps."

"Are the other two as strong as you?"

Syrreth nodded.

"So if you were unable to keep that information hidden from the Collective, it stands to reason that they wouldn't have had any better luck." Before the zweigelan could find fault with that logic, she added, "You have nothing to be sorry for. Did you willingly tell them where they could find the others?"

Syrreth again shook his head.

"It's a terrible situation," Sarah agreed. "You were forced to give up information and there wasn't anything you could have done about it. There's no remorse there."

Syrreth sighed. "We have been alone for longer than you can ever realize, human. We are accustomed to it."

"We prefer it," Ferreth added darkly.

"You're not alone anymore, Syrreth," Pryllan's soothing voice added. "Dragons prefer their isolation, this is true, but we also have a unique tool that we use in order to help us better ourselves."

"What would that be?" Syrreth asked suspiciously.

Ferreth didn't say anything but everyone could tell his attention was focused on the conversation at hand.

"The Collective."

Syrreth gave a snort of derision and made an elaborate showing of returning his gaze to the passing countryside.

"Would you like to know why?"

Syrreth ignored her.

"I'd like to know why," Sarah announced.

While Pryllan detailed how her fellow dragons keep in contact with one another, and expanded on the many advantages of the wyverian Collective, Steve could see that Syrreth's ears were giving the zweigelan away. Well, half of him, anyway. Syrreth was clearly interested, but Ferreth? The zweigelan's sulky right head remained fixated on a point somewhere in the distance and continued to ignore them.

"You really ought to be paying attention," Steve told Ferreth. "I know you're not happy, but believe it or not, being in contact with the rest of your species really isn't a bad thing. It's not like you have to be in contact at all times, you know. You can always shut it off."

That did it. Ferreth's ear twitched and slowly, ever so slowly, the right head turned to regard him.

"Thought we had to be in full contact, we did."

"It's your choice," Steve said. "Dragons live alone. You guys need to support one another whether you want to or not. If another dragon calls for aid, the honorable thing to do is to come to their aid."

Ferreth turned to look at the human fire thrower.

"What do you know about honor, human?"

Steve took a breath but Pryllan cut him off.

"These two humans are friends to the dragons. All dragons. He has the Dragon Lord's express permission to ride me."

Shocked, both of the zweigelan's heads turned to stare at the male human in Pryllan's claws.

"Dragon riding is forbidden," Syrreth reminded her. "Even we know this."

Steve looked straight at the zweigelan and addressed Ferreth. "Before you joined the Collective, you could pretty much do as you please, right? So, what did it matter whether or not someone hopped up on your back?"

Both heads were silent.

"So that tells us that the ban on dragon riding predates Rinbok. Were you allegiant to his predecessor?"

No answer.

Steve was silent as he mentally addressed Pryllan.

How long has Rinbok been the Dragon Lord?

Nearly a millennia.

Who did he take over for, do you know?

Pryllan thought a moment

Dirgis Drachfyre.

Thanks.

"So, you were okay with Dirgis calling the shots before Rinbok was in charge?"

"How do you know that name?" Ferreth demanded.

Steve patted Pryllan's foreleg. "I don't, but she does. Well, she's heard of him at least."

Sarah nodded. "I see where you're going with this. Ferreth, you were allegiant to Dirgis but you don't want to be with Rinbok, is that right? That suggests Rinbok has done something, besides forcing you to join the Collective, which has caused you not to trust him. Can you tell me what that is?"

Ferreth fell silent.

"Rinbok is going to want to know about this curse," Steve reminded him. "If you hope to make peace with him, you're going to have to come clean."

Both zweigelan's lifted their noses a little higher into the air. "Know nothing of this, we do."

Pryllan growled in response. "My mate, Pravara's sire, has become stricken by this curse. He is at the first stage and lost his fire. Hundreds of dragons have already fallen victim. You must tell us what you know so that this curse can be lifted."

"Responsible for the curse, we are not," Syrreth reiterated to the group.

Both Steve and Sarah felt Pryllan's sigh of frustration. Sarah, however, was looking speculatively at Syrreth.

"You say you don't know who cast it, yet you know it's a curse and that it *was* cast."

Ferreth looked angrily at his twin.

"Keep your mouth closed, you must."

"Aye, we must," Syrreth agreed.

"Aren't you concerned?" Sara continued. "You've lost the ability to use the Collective, which I guess you're happy with."

Both Syrreth and Ferreth grunted in acknowledgement.

"But you've also lost the ability to spit fire. Steve proved that down on the ground. Don't you see? You've fallen victim to this curse, too! Whoever has cast this curse also included you in it. You zweigelans wanted to get your revenge on the dragons, only it's affecting you, too. You need to help us figure this out and I would recommend you do so as quickly as possible or else you're going to lose the ability to fly, too."

"Believe them not," Ferreth warned. "Lying, they are."

"You are the ones lying," Steve countered. "We know you know who created this curse. We know you're involved. Save everyone a massive migraine and just tell us what you know about it."

"Proves we are innocent, it does," Syrreth said matter-of-factly.

"How so?" Steve asked.

"Deliberately sabotage ourselves, we won't. Innocent, we are."

"Dude, you were set up," Steve wryly informed the zweigelan.

"Do you still want to see all dragons suffer?" Sarah demanded. She pointed at the dragonlet. "You want to see her suffer? She who came to your aid?"

Ferreth didn't respond but Syrreth looked over at the young dragon. It even appeared as though his eyes softened somewhat. The zweigelan's left head watched Pravara for a few moments before it turned to look back at the humans. Then his gaze slowly drifted up and settled on the young dragon's mother.

"Please tell us what you know," Sarah implored. "Help us help the dragons. We don't want to see any of them suffer. Not even you."

"Did you know this curse was going to be cast?" Steve asked.

Syrreth nodded. Ferreth, disgusted by Syrreth's willingness

to help, ignored the proceedings.

Steve nodded and smiled. He gave Sarah a brief hug.

"Okay, that's a start. Is this something that all three of you plotted to do together?"

"No." Syrreth gave a loud sigh. Ferreth looked coldly over at him and then resumed ignoring him.

"How did you learn what they were going to do?" Sarah gently prodded.

"Suspected, I did. Another zweigelan joined. Angry, he was."

"Do you know why the other two zweigelans cursed the dragons?" Pryllan asked, trying to keep the anger from her voice. "To what purpose? What do they hope to accomplish? Our downfall?"

"The downfall of the Collective," Ferreth smugly answered. "Free once more, will we be."

Just then the trio of dragons flew over Zylan River and passed over the southernmost edge of Anakash Forest. Pryllan glanced down to see that they were once more flying over trees instead of open prairie. She gazed solemnly over at the smaller zweigelan and caught Syrreth's eyes.

"Ask yourself this. If you had the opportunity to be 'freed' of the Collective that you apparently hate so much, now that you know the benefits that it provides, would you want to be free of it?"

Neither Syrreth nor Ferreth answered her. Both were silent as they considered the question. Ferreth seemed ready to give an instant and resounding 'no', but Syrreth brought his head next to Ferreth's and began a hushed argument that lasted close to an hour.

Several hours later they were approaching the valley most dragons called home. Pravara, much to Pryllan's delight, hadn't tired at all. She could only attribute that to her constant questioning of their new companion. After Syrreth had openly admitted to knowing about the existence of the curse, she had relaxed somewhat. They were on the right course. All they had to do is get one of the two heads to tell them everything they knew about the curse so they could better formulate a plan on how to counteract it. She didn't know if this zweigelan would be willing to talk to the Dragon Lord, nor was she certain Rinbok Intherer would even grant her an audience, but she'd be damned if she wouldn't try. Kahvel's health depended on her and the two humans vanquishing this curse. She hadn't told anyone yet, but she was quite certain she had fallen victim to the curse, too. She could no longer feel the fire in her belly like she did just an hour or two ago.

Pryllan took a deep breath and stoked her internal furnace. She angled her head slightly up and blew a tiny fireball. She wanted something tiny so as to not alarm the others. What came out of her mouth was a small puff of smoke. Pryllan tried again. This time no smoke appeared. No fire, and even though she wasn't at the second stage, she might as well have been as she couldn't use the Collective since no one seemed to be using it any more. At least she could still fly.

I knew it. I knew you had become affected by this curse.

Pryllan visibly jerked, threatening to send her off course. She quickly corrected herself and glanced around to see if anyone had noticed. Thankfully, no one had.

Kahvel? What is it you think you heard?

Think? I don't think, beloved. I know. My thoughts are not the only ones that are easily detectable. Besides, you just confirmed my suspicions.

Pryllan sighed. **I didn't want to worry you.**

I appreciate the sentiment, Kahvel's cross thought came back to her, *but you have failed. I am worried. Do you have any idea how long ago you fell victim?*

Just now. I believe I felt my fires extinguish. I used them to ward off an unruly band of humans from attacking the zweigelan.

And you're certain humans are unaffected by this curse? **What do you mean?**

I do not like knowing you're unable to protect yourself.

I see where you're going with this. You're still worried about me.

I am, true, but I also worry about Pravara.

Fear not. Steve's flames are unaffected. He remains

formidable. Plus, Sarah is also here. I know she can teleport Pravara if necessary.

That is good news. However, that does not allay the fact that you now have a limited amount of time left before you lose the ability to fly. You must hurry, beloved. What can I do to help you?

Pryllan felt her mate's genuine concern and it warmed her heart. Kahvel would do anything for her or else die trying in the process.

Hopefully, it will not come to that, Kahvel's sarcastic thought, *but aye, that's true.*

I used to be better at masking my thoughts.

She felt Kahvel's rumblings of laughter.

If only you knew. How fares Pravara? She's had a long journey today.

Pryllan glanced over to her left and saw that, much to the zweigelan's disgust, Pravara was still firing off question after question.

I think she has been distracted by our newest companion, much to Syrreth's chagrin.

Who is Syrreth?

Syrreth and Ferreth are the names of the zweigelan's heads. Syrreth is the left head while Ferreth is the right.

It has a name?

Plural. Names. They both have names.

I never knew.

I know you didn't, Kahvel. Why was the zweigelan not advised of the nuances of the Collective?

What do you mean?

They were not told that the Collective would lie dormant unless needed. They believed that they had to be connected to the Collective at all times. They didn't know they were allowed to contact other dragons in case they needed help, and finally, no one took the time to instruct them how to use the Collective.

Couldn't you show them? Anger flashed through her mind. Anger at him and sympathy for the zweigelan. *Why direct your anger toward me?*

For the way Syrreth and Ferreth were treated.

Understandable, beloved, but it wasn't my decision. It was Rinbok Intherer's will.

I am aware. I am angry at what's happening to us but I can't help but feel that we brought this upon ourselves.

Pryllan couldn't hear him, or feel him do it, but she knew that Kahvel just grunted.

Have you reached Nevir yet?

No, my love. We are close, though.

Keep me informed.

I will. Be safe, Kahvel.

And you, beloved.

"Is everything alright?" Steve asked.

"I was checking in with Kahvel. All is well. Behold. I believe we are near our destination."

Satisfied with the answer, Pryllan banked right and dropped down below a thin layer of clouds. It was time to start scanning the forest floor. Somewhere nearby were four unremarkable hills. In the center of those four hills, facing north, was a cave entrance cleverly camouflaged by the surrounding forest. One hill swelled higher than the other three, but since the trees covering the fourth hill were shorter than the other three it gave the outward appearance of four mounds of equal height.

Pryllan knew the only way to approach these hills, was through a slight opening in the forest canopy, just south of the western hill. Certain trees had been bitten off in mid trunk to create an aerial pathway through the treetops that led in to the cave itself. Only the most skilled dragons ever navigated the path.

Pryllan hesitated. A comment from earlier in the day flashed through her mind. If it was so difficult to find Nevir, how, then, would a sick or dying dragon hope to find this place? Pryllan decided there must be something else she was missing.

Moments later she spotted the four hills and the canopy opening.

"Pravara, fly around to my back and latch on, like you used to do when you were little."

Pravara looked at her mother, confusion evident on her

face. "Riding is for babies, mother," she haughtily informed her. "I am not a baby."

"It's a dangerous path through the treetops. Get on my back. Hurry! Syrreth, Ferreth, stay on my tail and do not deviate. It would be detrimental to your health."

Syrreth nodded. Ferreth looked more curious than cautious.

Pravara flew over her to her mother and did as she was told. As soon as she hooked her talons into the numerous thick scales on her mother's back, Pryllan tucked her wings close to her sides and dove through the opening. The zweigelan followed.

Faster and faster, she zoomed through the treetops, whizzing by mammoth tree trunks, folding a wing flat against her back and spiraling as the aerial path narrowed inexplicably. Thankfully she was a very good flyer. She dared not check to see if the zweigelan was still following as she ducked through several narrower passages before emerging into a tiny glade. She snapped her wings open to arrest her momentum and settled comfortably to the ground.

Syrreth and Ferreth were two seconds behind her. Pravara started to detach herself from her mother's back but a quick command from Pryllan stopped her.

"Stay there, young one. We must move quickly through the caverns. Steve, Sarah, this is the one time it would be allowed to disobey Rinbok Intherer. Get to my back and sit next to Pravara. Just in case."

Sarah teleported the two of them to Pryllan's back. Pravara clutched her mother's back, her eyes a little fearful.

Steve sat next to Pravara's head and laid a reassuring hand on her.

"Are you ready?" Pryllan stared at the zweigelan, her voice firm. "Again, stay close to me. Syrreth and Ferreth, I want you to remember something. You will be witnessing something very few dragons have ever seen, including myself."

"Then how do you know what to expect?" Steve asked from his perch on her back.

"From Kahvel's experiences. His thoughts have shown me what lies within the cave."

"Good things or bad things?" Sarah's voice asked her.

Pryllan thought for a few moments. "Unknown."

She lifted herself to her feet and headed toward the northern hill. The ground sloped steeply up, and the surrounding greenery grew so as to preserve the appearance that the hill was no larger than the other three. Walking around the base of the northern hill, she found the entrance to the cave covered by several trees leaning in from both the left and the right. She gently parted the trees and waited for the zweigelan to squeeze through. Syrreth surprised her by holding back the left two trees so that she could make it through.

"You have my thanks."

"You're welcome," Syrreth automatically responded before he realized what he said.

Pryllan chuckled to herself. Syrreth seemed genuinely surprised, even a little shocked, that he knew the proper response. She sniffed the air and smelled sulfur. This was the right place.

Following her nose, she headed down the slanted tunnel. She closed her eyes and switched her vision to her parietal eye. Images appeared. Not as sharp as her primary vision but enough to avoid running into a wall or a low-hanging stalactite. Ahead, the zweigelan delicately maneuvered around a particularly large and low-hanging stalactite. Syrreth paused to look behind him.

"I'm here, Syrreth. If you'll step to the side I'll take the lead. Now, in case you were unaware, we are about to pass the Fires of Nevir. Do not look directly at them. Do not venture too close. It is rumored only those who yearn for death can feel the pull, but I'd just as soon not take any chances."

"Feel what pull?" Steve wanted to know.

"To swim with our ancestors," Pryllan replied.

"The only way, this is?" Syrreth asked, growing somewhat fearful.

"According to Kahvel, it is," Pryllan confirmed. "I will lead. Follow me closely."

She passed by Syrreth and Ferreth and stopped as soon as she felt the scales of her chest heat up. While unaffected by the heat she wasn't too sure how fireproof Pravara was, which was why she had Steve sit next to her. She figured the human fire thrower would have an immunity to fire and heat, and since they would soon be approaching a river of lava she needed to be certain it was safe to proceed. She continued on another ten minutes before the tunnel turned sharply to the right. They had reached the beginnings of the great caverns.

"Pravara? Are you well?"

"I am, mother. Why?"

"Steve, Sarah, are you uninjured?"

"All fine up here," Steve answered. "I can see why you wanted Sarah and Pravara close to me. My jhorun is tingling like crazy, so I know it's blocking the heat. I wonder how hot it is out there?"

"It will get worse, I'm afraid. We can't see it yet, but I know the fires are close. I will give you the same warning. Humans should not be affected, but I don't know for certain. I am able to withstand the heat. Syrreth and Ferreth, too. If you two are alright, we will proceed."

"We're good. Go for it."

Proceeding forward, Pryllan and the zweigelan stepped out into the cavern. They all heard loud crunching sounds as they moved. A quick look down confirmed that they were walking across crushed black rocks the size of small pebbles, the results of countless wyverian legs walking over the strange black rock formations over many years. A reddish glow was visible up ahead. Both dragons moved toward it.

"The Fires of Nevir," Pryllan breathed. "Keep your eyes down. Do not look at it."

From his perch on her back, Steve nodded. He took Sarah's hand in his, and with his other, placed a reassuring hand on Pravara's leg.

"New plan, guys. We're going to follow *Raiders of the Lost Ark* rules: keep your eyes shut! Sarah? Pravara? Close your eyes."

"Done," Sarah told him.

"Mine are closed," Pravara said.

Pryllan hesitated as she peered intently at the glowing red river of molten stone.

"What is it?" Steve asked. "I can feel you hesitate. Keep moving. Remember your own advice: don't look at it."

"I haven't," Pryllan said, shaking her head. "But, I'm feeling an odd sensation, like I ..."

Steve thumped his foot to get the dragon's attention.

"No, you don't. Don't finish the thought. Keep moving." Only when he felt Pryllan resume her walking did he let out the breath he'd been holding. "Syrreth? Ferreth? Are you guys all right?

When he didn't get a response from the zweigelan, Steve cracked an eye and risked a glance. What he saw had him cursing. The zweigelan was staring at the slowly moving lava. Both of its necks started to sway back and forth, as though it was getting dizzy. Before Steve could shout a warning, Pryllan hooked her tail around the zweigelan's left leg and gave a violent tug to keep him from falling in.

"What did you do that for?" Ferreth instantly snapped.

"You really want to go swimming in that?" Steve asked, incredulously. "I know dragons are fireproof, but that's stretching it a bit, don't you think? Besides, you heard Pryllan. Something tells me if you went in there, then you wouldn't be coming back."

"Swimming?" Syrreth retorted. "We don't swim."

"Then may I suggest you refrain from getting too close," Pryllan advised as she headed east and followed the lava flow.

"Were you going to jump in?" Syrreth whispered to his twin.

"No," Ferreth answered with a growl. "We wanted ... *I wanted* to see it a little closer."

"Well, I'll be a monkey's uncle," Steve exclaimed.

"What is it?" Sarah asked. "Do you need me to teleport us?"

"No. Syrreth. Ferreth. It's nice to hear you talking like a normal dragon."

"Nothing is wrong with our speech," Syrreth insisted.

"You're right," Sarah agreed. "They're not talking like that little green guy from *Star Wars*."

Steve groaned. "You don't know Master Yoda's name? Oh, I have failed as a husband."

"Ridicule me after we're past the river of death, would you?" Sarah asked.

After she verified Syrreth and Ferreth were following her through the cavern, Pryllan inspected her surroundings as she headed toward the far wall. Everywhere she looked she saw nothing but jagged black rocks, bulky irregular formations, huge broken stalagmites, and the occasional stalactite hanging from the vaulted domed ceiling. As they approached the other side of the cavern, she could see that the ceiling sloped down low enough to blend into the cavern wall. That, in turn, framed an opening that was thirty feet high by about fifty feet wide, more than enough room for the two dragons to pass through.

The river of lava angled north and disappeared through another opening in the wall, whether flowing through another cavern or two Pryllan didn't know. What she did know was that she was thankful they had moved away from the extreme heat and the temptation to visit with her ancestors. She was also extremely grateful Steve had been there to protect her offspring from the dangers of the dreaded River of Fire, but she was relieved when she felt her scales return to a normal temperature.

"Pravara, how do you fare?"

She felt the dragonlet stirring on her back.

"I am well, mother. May I get down?"

Pryllan scanned the new cavern they had just entered.

"Not yet, young one. Be patient."

"Are you able to see where we are?" Steve asked his wife. "Because I can't see a thing."

"No amulet, no night vision," Sarah reminded him.

"We can see everything there is to see," Pryllan assured the two humans. "Which isn't much. I see some light emanating from a tunnel straight ahead of us. Syrreth and Ferreth, do you see it?"

Using their own light-sensitive parietal eyes, the zweigelan nodded.

"Would you like to lead?" Pryllan asked, trying to be cordial.

"We do not know where to go," Syrreth informed her.

"Nor do I," Pryllan admitted. "There's light up ahead. Let's head that way."

Syrreth and Ferreth carefully picked their way through the dark cave, circumventing several large stalagmites that were thrusting up from the ground below. As they entered the third cavern it became bright enough for the dragons to switch back to their primary vision and for the two humans to see what lay before them.

Syrreth's eyes bulged while Ferreth's widened in disbelief.

The entire cavern floor was solidly covered with treasure. Golden coins, jewels, tiaras, crowns, gilded spears, jewel-encrusted shields, everything that could ever be construed as treasure littered the floor and was mounded high against the far wall. It seemed Rinbok had shoved it all into several piles.

"Wow."

Pryllan looked back at the two humans on her back.

"It's just treasure. Every dragon has some. Some more than others it would seem."

Steve stared at her. "Do you?"

"What? Have treasure? Of course. I'm a dragon."

Pryllan's long neck snaked about as she inspected the scattered gold coins, which were the most prolific pieces in the collection.

"Kahvel's description of Rinbok's horde was inaccurate. He said it was organized neatly by category and was his one prized collection. The extent of disarray in here surprises me."

A wave of coins began cascading down one of the mounds of gold. Clinking and rattling, the coins tumbled down the steep slope, picking up speed as the shape of the mound shifted. A green, heavily muscled foreleg covered in jagged black stripes appeared.

The mound shifted again and more of the treasure slid haphazardly to the ground. Most of Rinbok's right side became visible, including his right wing, which lay tattered and limp next to his body. The talons on his front claws lay chipped and flaking from neglect.

"My Lord," Pryllan began. "Please pardon our interruption. We carry news. Important news you need to hear. Will you grant us an audience?"

Two geysers of gold coins erupted from the end of the dragon's body that was still covered by gold. Rinbok Intherer exhaled a second blast through his nostrils before he rose to his feet. The leader of the dragons, easily twice the size of Pryllan, looked right at their group before shuffling uncertainly toward another pile of his extensive riches.

"My Lord, please," Pryllan tried again. "You must hear this."

Rinbok Intherer selected another mound of coins and began pushing his way into it. Pryllan looked helplessly at Steve.

"Don't worry, Pryllan," Steve assured her. "I've got this."

"What are you going to do?" Sarah asked, alarmed.

Steve grinned. "Trust me."

Sarah crossed her arms over her chest. "Every time you say that, the hairs on the back of my neck stand up."

Steve slid down Pryllan's flank and stumbled once his feet hit solid ground. The loot in the cavern was, at its shallowest, several feet deep. When the ground consisted of that many small moving objects, the simple act of walking upright was practically impossible. As he finally regained his balance, he looked up to see that he was face to face with Sarah.

"You could have just let me teleport you down here. It'd have been easier."

"Mm-hmm. Hey Rinbok! It's me, Steve! Do you remember me?"

Rinbok kept burrowing his way into the large golden mound.

"I know you remember me. You granted me permission to ride Pryllan. I'm the only human you've done this for. Ring any bells?"

Rinbok ignored him as he nosed even further into the huge mound of gold.

"It's working like a charm, Ace," Sarah commented from behind him.

"Guess how many dragons I rode since I've been back in Lentari?" Steve challenged.

"Just the one, human," the Dragon Lord finally responded,

not even bothering to look over at him.

"You don't know that for certain!"

"Your provocations are without merit, human."

"Damn," Steve swore softly. He mentally changed gears and tried again. "Alright, point taken. Tell you what. I'll just get right to it and tell you why we're here."

Rinbok refused to acknowledge him. Whether or not he was listening Steve couldn't tell.

"I know you've lost the ability to spit fire and fly."

"Don't forget the second stage," Sarah reminded him, using a loud enough voice so that the irritable Dragon Lord knew she was there.

"Right. The Collective. It must suck to be kicked off of it. In fact, if I was wyverian, and all these things had happened to me, I'd want to know who caused it. Wouldn't you?"

Rinbok hesitated in his burrowing. Was he listening or trying to find a better avenue to conceal himself in his treasure? After a few seconds of silence, his tunneling resumed.

"You might be interested to know that you're not suffering from any type of malady or sickness. You're suffering from a curse, dude."

Rinbok hesitated again. When he didn't resume his noisy progress through his huge pile of gold, Steve pressed on.

"You guys had a little run-in last year, didn't you? With a two-headed dragon called a zweigelan? Is that right?"

There was no answer from the partially concealed dragon. Then again, he wasn't moving, either. Steve took it as a favorable sign.

"This zweigelan was forced to swear allegiance to you. In doing so, he had to join the Collective, and as soon as he did, the locations to the other zweigelans became common knowledge. With me so far?"

A shower of gold coins cascaded down Rinbok's back as he remained standing, motionless except for the heaving of his chest as he breathed. Steve could only hope the recalcitrant dragon was paying attention.

"A second zweigelan was located but the third managed to escape. Still haven't found him, have you?"

More golden coins fell from Rinbok's head as he turned

to look in Steve's direction.

"The zweigelans found a way to curse the dragons, Rinbok."

More of the treasure flowed from Rinbok's massive body as he maneuvered himself out of the pile of gold he had been trying to burrow into.

"How do we know this, you might ask?" Steve turned to point at the nearby zweigelan. "Because he told us."

The final bits of treasure fell off Rinbok's head as his eyes noticed for the first time that a third dragon was present.

"Before you get ready to do something completely drastic…" Steve started, but was shocked to discover how fast the huge striped dragon could actually move.

Rinbok Intherer launched himself at Syrreth and Ferreth. Both of the zweigelan's heads froze with shock as they saw the Dragon Lord hurtle at them. There was no time to react and certainly no time to beat a hasty retreat.

Thankfully Steve was prepared for such a reaction from the stricken Dragon Lord. He stepped directly in Rinbok's path and blasted jets of fire straight up into the air, throwing as much of his jhorun into the blasts as he could. He needed to get the angry dragon's attention and quickly at that.

Rinbok skidded to a halt, creating a colossal wave of golden treasure in the process. He lowered his head and peered angrily at the human.

"Step aside! How dare you protect that renegade! If they are responsible for this malison, they will answer for their actions!"

"They're responsible for what?"

Rinbok stared, unblinking, at Steve.

"Malison."

"What's a malison?"

"Did you not just say the zweigelans are responsible for the curse?"

Steve nodded. "That's right."

"Malison is another word for curse," Sarah whispered in his ear.

Steve extinguished both hands and lowered his arms.

"Oh. Okay. Well, you're right. They will. But they can only

do that if they stay alive. They have agreed to help resolve this. I'd take them up on that offer."

Rinbok's angry gaze fell upon the much smaller form of the zweigelan and pinned it in place.

"If you do not terminate this curse now, I will personally rake my —"

"Oh, cool your jets, you big sourpuss," Steve snapped. He made a sweeping gesture in the air. "This is not helping the situation. What we need is compassion. The zweigelans were angry. Were they right to do this? Absolutely not. But should they have been assimilated in the way it was done? No."

"Wyverians are under *my* rule, human," Rinbok told him. "Not yours. How I administer my subjects is of no concern to you."

"But no one told them how to use the Collective!" Sarah protested, drawing the Dragon Lord's attention.

Rinbok's eyes widened as he stared at her. He faced Steve and growled.

"What is she doing here? There is only one way she could have traveled here, and that was on Pryllan's back! You disobeyed—"

"What's more important?" Steve snapped as he shoved Sarah behind him. "Following your directive that I will be the only dragon rider or coming straight here to tell you about what we've learned? Just for the record, it was my idea to come here. Remember that before you get all snotty with us."

Rinbok looked over at Pryllan, who nodded.

"It's true, my Lord. It is at Steve's insistence that we are here. He felt you should know the nature of your ailment."

Rinbok nodded and looked back at Sarah. "Very well. Your transgression is forgiven. Explain yourself. What is the nature of your objection to the outcast's inclusion into the Collective?"

"Are you aware no one told them how to use it?" Sarah challenged, growing angry. "No one told them they could turn it off. No one told them how to contact someone. No one told them how to access any information should they need it. Explain that!"

Taken aback, Rinbok looked over at Syrreth and Ferreth. "Is this true?"

Syrreth and Ferreth both nodded. "It is," they echoed.

"Then the fault was mine for overlooking that important detail. However," Rinbok's voice dropped so low that it came out as a throaty growl, "it does not justify your actions, zweigelan."

"We understand," Syrreth told him, bowing his head. A moment later Ferreth joined him.

"Are you directly responsible for creating this curse?" the Dragon Lord wanted to know.

Syrreth and Ferreth violently shook their heads.

"Are you indirectly responsible?"

"Knew about this, we did," Syrreth admitted.

"Talk like a normal dragon," Steve told them. "No more of this Yoda crap, okay?"

"W-we knew what was going to h-happen," Syrreth said.

"But we didn't know *how* it would happen," Ferreth hastily added.

Rinbok hadn't stopped growling, not even to take a breath.

"Are one of your brothers responsible for this?"

"We do not have siblings," Syrreth began, perhaps unwisely.

"Do NOT talk to me about semantics, zweigelan!" Rinbok roared, becoming more and more animated with each passing minute. "The other zweigelan that joined the Collective would not have the courage to pull off a stunt like this. If it wasn't you, or him, that only leaves the third."

Trembling beneath the Dragon Lord's dangerous gaze, with the top of his head barely reaching Rinbok's chest, Syrreth looked up. He met Rinbok Intherer's angry glare and bowed.

"We will tell you what we can," Syrreth began.

Ferreth hissed with frustration but did not object.

"But first you must know…"

"What, Syrreth? Speak! What must I know?"

"*You* are the reason this curse was brought about. *You* are the reason all zweigelans hate the dragons."

Chapter 7 — A Grievous Grudge

Watching from her vantage point behind the two humans, Pryllan nervously eyed the wyverian she had sworn her allegiance to. Judging by the Dragon Lord's reaction, he hadn't liked what he had just heard.

Rinbok paced angrily back and forth across his treasure cave. Growling low and deep, the Dragon Lord kept both eyes fixated on Syrreth and Ferreth. A few moments later Rinbok came to a halt. Pryllan's eyes widened. If she didn't know better she would've said that he was ready to... he did. Rinbok had crouched low and had bunched his muscles in preparation of his attack on the zweigelan, but ended up blinking his eyes with surprise. Steve blasted an additional jet of fire as a warning. Pryllan was impressed. She knew from the way Rinbok Intherer paced, that he was going to attack the newest member of the Collective. The only thing she would have done, whether or not she had her fire, was to step aside. It wasn't the wyverian way to involve oneself with another's affairs. Especially the Dragon Lord.

Rinbok eyed the human again, but before he could spew an angry retort, Sarah surprised them all by pushing past her husband and placing herself directly in the Dragon Lord's path. She started venting before Steve could stop her.

"What is it with you dragons, anyway? We're trying to help you! Stop being an ungrateful git and listen to what Syrreth and Ferreth have to say. Ask them why they were loyal to your predecessor and not to you. Ask them why they hate the dragons so much. Go on. You're supposed to be the dragon king."

"Lord," Steve quietly murmured.

Lord, Pryllan mentally corrected.

"Whatever," Sarah said, crossly. She fixed Rinbok with a steely glare. "Start acting like it. They are your people. Your subjects. Protect them. *Help* them. This problem isn't going to go away on its own. Stop hiding like a coward."

Pryllan recoiled in shock. The last person to accuse Rinbok Intherer of being a coward had been silenced on the spot. Permanently.

"Perhaps not the best route you could have taken," Steve whispered.

"I don't care. I'm tired of all this sneaking around. Ooooo, we don't want to upset Rinbok," Sarah mocked. She turned to look up at the leader of all dragons. "Well, I'm sick of it. Rinbok, we have a job to do. There's a curse on the dragons. I plan on doing whatever I can to help break it. For Pryllan and her family. Now are you going to help us or would you prefer we left so you can go back to hiding in your gold? Your call."

Rinbok was so still he could have been mistaken for a statue. He had been preparing to leap at the zweigelan but now he was mired in place, stuck in his gold. He was staring straight at the humans. More specifically, at Sarah.

"No one accuses me of cowardice."

Sarah held her ground. "Prove it."

"I should kill you now," Rinbok growled.

"You could," Sarah agreed. "But you won't. You're the king. As the king you will do the right thing."

"Lord," Steve corrected again.

"Fine, whatever. So, Dragon Lord, what are you going to

do?" Sarah gave a quick glance back at Syrreth and Ferreth. "Are you ready to listen to those two?"

"Your point is taken. Very well. Syrreth. Ferreth. Step forward."

Syrreth cast a worried look down at Sarah while Ferreth looked back at Pryllan, who gave an encouraging nod of her head.

"My Lord," Syrreth began, "we regret our participation in a plan designed to bring about the downfall of every wyverian in this land."

"Including you, too," Steve reminded him.

Both of the zweigelan's heads nodded in agreement.

"Since we have also been stricken by this curse," Ferreth added, "we are not sure whether our inclusion was intentional or accidental."

"Tell me what you know about this curse," Rinbok demanded. His eyes darted from the zweigelan's left head, over to the right, and then back to the left. "Which of you speaks matters not. However, one of you *will* speak."

"We felt his anger," Syrreth told them all. "They were so very angry, even more so than we ever were."

"Who was?" Steve asked.

"The other zweigelan forced to join the Collective."

"Ah."

"More than you?" a small voice piped up.

Rinbok Intherer cocked his head as he stared at Pryllan. His eyes scanned over her back and paused near the juncture of her wings. He approached Pryllan and glanced down. Once he found the owner of the voice, and had noted Pravara's frightened expression on her face, his attitude softened.

"What are you doing down there, young one? Why are you riding your mother's back?"

Pravara hesitantly stood up. Two fearful golden eyes peered up at the much larger adult gazing down at her.

"She made me do it. I tried to tell her I'm not a baby anymore."

"Indeed, you're not." Rinbok stepped away from Pryllan in an effort to allow the dragonlet to calm down. "Are there any other members of your party hiding about?"

"Nope, that's all of us," Steve jovially answered.

"Quiet," Sarah scolded. "Syrreth was telling us his story."

Rinbok shared a brief sympathetic look with Steve, who nodded his appreciation.

"Go on."

"Where were we?" Syrreth asked as he looked at Ferreth. Ferreth looked with disgust at his twin.

"Your memory is terrible."

"Yours is worse," Syrreth accused.

"Guys!" Steve shouted as he waved his arms to get their attention. "Focus! The second zweigelan. He was mad. We get it. What else? Did he ever say anything to you?"

"He spoke to us only once after his assimilation," Ferreth recalled. "Cryptic, it was."

"What did he tell you?" Steve asked.

"That we will be free soon enough."

Sarah looked at Steve. "Does that sound like he was holding a grudge against them?"

Steve shook his head. "Not to me it doesn't. Syrreth and Ferreth getting hit by the curse had to be just an accident."

"Or…"

Six heads, five of them dragon and one human, turned to look at Sarah, who had just sat down on one of Pryllan's talons.

"Before I go into that, let me ask another question. Do we know if the second zweigelan has been hit by the curse?"

Steve shrugged. "What does that have to do with anything?"

"If number two wasn't infected," Sarah explained, "then it would suggest that numbers two and three are getting their revenge against Syrreth and Ferreth for spilling the beans."

Pryllan caught Steve's eye.

I'm not familiar with that phrase. Spilling the beans?

Um, it pertains to Syrreth and Ferreth disclosing their whereabouts to Rinbok.

Oh. Thanks.

You bet.

Rinbok began nodding.

"I understand. If the second is also stricken, that would

indicate a hidden agenda for the third."

"Or else they were double-crossed by whoever cast the spell," Steve added. "Maybe the spellcaster also has a grudge against the dragons. All dragons. Be that as it may, what I want to know is this: why's this curse acting like a virus? Why not just hit all dragons at the same time? Why stretch it out? And why are there still unaffected dragons, like Pryllan? Does this make sense to anyone else?"

"I have become stricken as well," Pryllan quietly informed the group.

Steve cursed loudly while Sarah gasped with alarm.

"Are you sure?" her rider asked, genuinely concerned. "You used your fire earlier today."

"I believe it happened not long after that," Pryllan sadly told him.

Pravara stirred on her back.

"Mother, are you sick?"

Pryllan hesitated, unsure what she should tell her dragonlet.

"For now, yes," Steve confirmed, answering for her. "Don't worry. It's only temporary. She's going to get better soon. Very soon, if I have anything to say about it."

Satisfied with that answer, the young dragon fell silent.

"So we don't know *how* the dragons fall victim," Sarah added, exasperated. "Let it go. The fact of the matter is that they are, and there aren't many more unaffected dragons. For all we know it could be whenever someone tries to use the Collective. You never know."

"The human female is right," Rinbok's deep voice boomed. "How the curse spreads is irrelevant. How to break the curse is top priority. Syrreth, Ferreth, any information, anything at all would be helpful. Have you anything to add?"

"We do not know any of the curse's nuances," Syrreth explained, his voice tightening. "We are affected as well."

Steve and Sarah shared a look with each other.

"He really doesn't like Rinbok," Steve whispered to his wife. "You can see it in his eyes and his body language."

"And also by the fact that he really hasn't stopped glaring at Rinbok ever since arriving here. I've been watching him."

Steve straightened. "Let's get to the bottom of this. Syrreth and Ferreth, what do you have against Rinbok?"

Two reptilian noses lifted into the air. Syrreth looked away while Ferreth dropped his gaze to the ground. Neither head said anything.

"Come on, guys," Steve pressed, "if you ever want to clear the air between the two of you then you need to come clean. Tell him. Tell him why you're angry with him."

Ferreth slowly lifted his gaze from the mass of gold coins on the ground and met Rinbok's eyes.

"Lost our loyalty, you did, many hundreds of years ago."

Pryllan checked to see Rinbok's expression. She sighed. The Dragon Lord hadn't moved a muscle.

"Go on," Rinbok urged.

"Went poorly, it did," Syrreth remembered.

"What did?" Rinbok asked.

"Our first meeting," Ferreth answered.

"What happened on our first meeting?" Rinbok asked, curious.

"Do you remember anything out of the ordinary?" Steve inquired, looking up at Rinbok's enormous head.

Rinbok was silent as he thought back, centuries ago, to the first meeting he had ever had with a zweigelan.

"I was young," the Dragon Lord recalled. "I had just been bequeathed my regency. There was much to learn and little time to learn it. I do not remember much about our first meeting. Will you tell me what happened?"

"We were there at the urging of Dirgis," Syrreth reminded him, citing Rinbok's predecessor.

"We had just introduced ourselves when you said it," Ferreth said with disgust.

Rinbok's interest was piqued, as was everyone else's.

"What was said?"

Both Syrreth and Ferreth gazed impassively at the wyverian ruler.

"Thought you were far enough away, you did," Ferreth spat. "Said it in a loud enough tone, you did."

"Said what?" Rinbok demanded, growing angry.

"You said that zweigelans were freaks and didn't deserve

to call themselves wyverians."

Shocked, Pryllan stared with undisguised disgust at the only wyverian ruler she had ever known. She noticed that everyone else's reaction mirrored her own. In fact, even the Dragon Lord had reacted similarly.

"I do not recall ever saying that."

"We do," Syrreth informed him.

Sarah stepped out from behind Steve and confronted the Dragon Lord.

"Shame on you! Just because Syrreth and Ferreth are a little different doesn't give you the right to disgrace them. They're your cousins. They are *wyverians*. They deserve to be treated with the same respect you extend to every other dragon."

Rinbok growled and brought his nose down so that he was practically face-to-face with Sarah, who inadvertently took a few steps back.

"Are you quite finished?"

Sarah swallowed nervously.

"Yes."

"Good. Now, I said before I don't remember saying that. That being said, Syrreth and Ferreth, I hereby apologize for my disparaging remarks. They were words spoken by an immature and selfish wyverian who had no business judging another creature by their looks alone. Can you forgive me?"

Speechless, Syrreth and Ferreth could only nod.

"I realize now that more tact should have been taken with your inclusion into our Collective," Rinbok continued. He glanced somewhat sheepishly around his cave of treasure. He gave a great sigh and turned to face his guests. "I regret my actions have brought about this curse. Syrreth, Ferreth, will you help me rectify this situation?"

"We will, my Lord," Syrreth instantly agreed.

Ferreth bowed his head before the Dragon Lord and began to speak.

"My Lord, we felt our cousin's rage when he was captured. He tried to resist with every fiber of his being."

Sensing the potential for a long story, Sarah returned herself and Steve to Pryllan's back so they could settle down next to Pravara, who nestled up against Steve's side and fell asleep.

"Don't say it," Steve whispered when Sarah smiled.

"How many zweigelans existed back then?" Pryllan asked. "Did they all know about Rinbok Intherer's remarks?"

The Dragon Lord shuffled uneasily as he shifted his weight from one foot to the other.

"There were five of us then," Syrreth told her. "Two have since passed. One from old age and the other was defeated in an ill-advised move to claim a new cave. The zweigelan's allegiance to wyverian rule was broken that day. We vowed to remain hidden and stay away from other dragons, thus avoiding drawing any attention to ourselves. Over time it worked. We were forgotten."

"No, you weren't," Rinbok assured him. "We knew of your existence."

Ferreth nodded. "Aye, but without a reason to seek us out, we were not worth the effort to locate us. So in this fashion, we lived. For hundreds of years."

"Without anyone to talk to?" Pryllan asked, appalled. "No family to turn to? No support from your brethren? It is a sad way to live."

"We learned to rely on ourselves," Syrreth told them. "Everything we needed we found in each other."

"After the other was forced into the Collective," Ferreth continued, "the third sent the first message we have received from them in centuries. They knew of a human who could help. For the right price, that is."

"How in the world did they ever make contact with a renegade wizard?" Sarah wanted to know. "I would think a two-headed dragon slinking around one of the villages would have been noticed."

"They weren't the ones who made initial contact," Ferreth clarified. "They had recently learned, from a victim, of the wizard's existence and his penchant for gold and jewels. They gave an informant a jewel to give to the wizard in exchange for a meeting."

"So the wizard met with them and not the other way around?" Steve nodded. "Smart. They could then choose when and where to meet." He raised an eyebrow. "Are we *sure* Shardwyn doesn't have any other sons?"

Sarah smiled and shook her head. She elbowed him in the stomach. "Quiet. Listen to what Ferreth is saying."

"Right. Sorry."

Ferreth had paused his narrative while he waited for the humans to fall silent.

"Contact was made," Ferreth continued. "The wizard said he'd be willing to cast the curse."

Syrreth suddenly growled. "For a hefty price."

Ferreth nodded. "Aye. He wanted gold. More gold than the third zweigelan had. The wizard refused to negotiate. If this curse was to be powerful enough to ensnare all dragons, then he wanted to be compensated appropriately. We all contributed."

"My gems," Syrreth moaned. "All of my horde of treasure was confiscated and given to that human."

"Yes, we know!" Ferreth snapped irritably. "You can always get more. Pester us no more with this nonsense!"

"Every last piece of gold..."

Ferreth glanced apologetically up at the humans still on Pryllan's back.

"He still hasn't forgiven them. Moans incessantly about his loss, he does."

"You weren't required to surrender any of your collection as payment," Syrreth angrily reminded him.

"Had it been requested, then I would have."

"Liar!"

"Am not!"

Pryllan stared at the two bickering heads then returned her gaze to Rinbok. The Dragon Lord was staring at the zweigelan with annoyance.

"Where is this wizard?" Rinbok's voice boomed out. "If he cast the curse then he can break it."

"We don't know," Ferreth admitted.

"We really don't," Syrreth confirmed. "We were never told."

"Do either of the other two know where to find him?" Steve asked.

The zweigelan gave the closest approximation of a shrug that they could. "That is unknown. We only know that it was the third zweigelan who brokered the deal."

"Tell me where the third zweigelan is now," Rinbok demanded.

"We would if we could," Ferreth added, eliciting an appreciative look from its twin. "However, we cannot. We do not know."

"Sounds like number two knows where number three is," Steve guessed. "I say we find him. He should be able to help us find the third one."

"What makes you think he will?" Sarah countered. "It sounds like he was madder than Syrreth and Ferreth ever were. I don't think we can count on his help."

"We were against rendering aid," Syrreth reminded her. "Now we give our aid. Freely."

Sarah nodded. "Point taken. So where's the second zweigelan? What's his last known location?"

"Ylani," Rinbok answered. He shook himself to dislodge the last remaining gold coins that were stuck in his thick scales. "In the mountains north of Barod."

Steve sighed and turned to Sarah. "I assume that's a long way away? You can teleport us all there, right?"

"Just because I saw a picture of the castle at Zaran, their capital, doesn't mean I can just randomly teleport to any city up there."

"I know that. Sorry. What I mean is, if you saw a picture of the city, could you get us there?"

Sarah shrugged. "If there's a picture, possibly. The problem is, the picture would have to be so good that I could visualize Barod in my head. Even then it'd be a stretch, and that's just for us. Trying to teleport two dragons that far north would be too taxing on my jhorun. I don't think I could do it."

"I don't think we'd need any wyverian help," Steve argued. "Teleporting just the two of us shouldn't be too bad, should it?"

"Do you really think we'd have a chance? Everyone here knows we're friends of the dragons, but do you think this other zweigelan knows this? The way I see it we're going to need some help."

"We would have to accompany you," Syrreth guessed.

Sarah turned to Syrreth and smiled. "Yes. With you two then we might have a chance to hear what he has to say before they try to kill us."

"So Syrreth and Ferreth are going," Steve decided. He looked up at huge green dragon he had come to know so well. "And I don't want to leave Pryllan behind, either. Especially since Pravara's safety is tied directly with hers. We already know Pryllan's been hit by this curse so the last thing we need is for her to get worse and leave Pravara unprotected. So she stays with us, too."

Pryllan felt an immense wave of gratitude flow through her as moments ago she'd had similar thoughts about not wanting to be left behind. With both herself and Kahvel suffering from the effects of the zweigelan curse, if they were unsuccessful in breaking it, then the duties of raising Pravara would fall to... Well, they would fall to...

We'd be honored to look after her for you if it comes to it, Steve's thought spoke to her. *For the record, you shouldn't be thinking such negative thoughts.*

I specifically made sure my senses weren't being shared, Pryllan thought back to him. **It is becoming increasingly difficult to keep my thoughts private. An effect of the curse?**

Sarah approached and laid a hand on one of her massive forelegs.

We'll beat this yet, Sarah vowed. *We promise. I promise.*

"What will you do now?" Rinbok asked, addressing Pryllan.

"We search for the second zweigelan," Pryllan answered. "He is the key to finding the third and they are the key to finding the wizard."

"Speaking of wizards," Steve said as he held up a hand, "we really need to let Kri'Entu and Shardwyn know there's another wizard somewhere in Lentari."

Rinbok forcefully smacked his tail onto the ground, causing everyone to jump with surprise. Gold coins went flying in all directions.

"You will refrain from telling the humans."

"What for? We need their help."

"*I* don't need their help."

"And if they can help locate this wizard?" Steve countered.

"Irrelevant. The humans must not know."

Sarah's eyes opened wide as she suddenly understood the nature of Rinbok's objections. "You're ashamed, aren't you?"

The Dragon Lord growled with frustration but didn't refute it.

"Tell you what. We will tell Kri'Entu and Shardwyn, but it'll go no further. This was something that you said many years ago. We'll let bygones be bygones."

Rinbok Intherer lowered his enormous head and leaned forward, bringing himself nose-to-nose with Sarah.

"Agreed. I'm trusting everyone here, especially you two," and he looked straight at Steve and Sarah, "to keep what you have heard here private. This is a wyverian problem and it will remain as such. Is that understood?"

"Aye, my Lord," Pryllan agreed as she bowed her head.

"It is," Syrreth and Ferreth said simultaneously. They both bowed their heads a moment later.

"Young Pravara," Rinbok suddenly called as he turned to face Pryllan. "I must have your consent, too."

A nervous exclamation of surprise sounded from Pryllan's back as Pravara jerked to attention.

"Do you agree, young one?"

"I do."

Pravara's reply had been so faint that Pryllan had barely heard it. Had the Dragon Lord heard the dragonlet's response?

"Excellent. I would encourage the five of you to get going. There is much to be done and little time to do it."

"I don't suppose there's an easy way out of here, is there?" Steve asked after he picked up Pryllan's unspoken thought.

"Can you not depart the same way you arrived?" Rinbok asked after casting another disparaging look at the mess his treasure horde had become.

Pryllan nodded. She bent her long neck around to verify Pravara was still clinging to her back. She quickly rose to her feet.

"We will manage, my Lord."

Rinbok comically cocked his head to the left, as though he had heard a faint noise and didn't know the nature of it. "You came through the caverns, did you not?"

Pryllan nodded. "Aye. We entered the caverns through the Four Mounds."

"The Four Mounds? No one has used that entrance for hundreds of years. The aerial path has become much too narrow so no one bothers to use it. Use the caverns instead."

"Are you saying there's another way out?" Sarah asked.

Rinbok Intherer nodded. "Aye. Follow the River of Fire as it flows east. It'll lead to a small subterranean lake. You'll find a tributary flowing north. That will lead you out."

Steve turned to look at Pryllan. "Why would Kahvel tell you to use that path through the trees?"

"He never directly told me how to find this place," Pryllan corrected. "I picked up his thoughts about it."

"Was this after your dragonlet hatched?" Rinbok asked.

Pryllan nodded. "Aye, almost directly after."

"I had discussed maintenance options with him regarding that path and what could be done to restore it to practical usefulness."

"We made it through," Sarah reminded him, "so it can't be that far gone."

"Noted. Now go. I will muster what unaffected dragons are left to check on those that have become stricken."

"Don't forget about Sciathan," Steve added, drawing Rinbok's attention. "He was forgotten for weeks and had practically starved to death. Pryllan hunted for him, so he should be fine for a while but he's going to run out of food sooner or later. I don't want to see him suffer."

Rinbok nodded. "Again, it's noted. I thank you for your concern. Return when there is news to impart."

Steve pointed at Sarah. "That'll be her. She can zip back here at a moment's notice if she needs to. I take it she has your permission to teleport in without notice?"

"She does. If I'm not here then someone will be."

Sarah nodded gratefully. "I'll keep you posted."

Rinbok followed them all the way Topside. Almost as

soon as they emerged, blinking, in the bright sunlight, Rinbok was gone, having disappeared into the forest. Pryllan opened her right claw and lowered it to the ground so Steve and Sarah could climb in.

"How long will it take you to get to R'Tal?" Steve asked, once they were airborne.

Pryllan turned her head to note the position of the sun. She saw that there was only an hour of sunlight left, at best.

"It would be dark before we reached there. Pravara is tired. We all are. I will return to the nest so that we may be refreshed. We will leave tomorrow at first light. Syrreth, Ferreth, our cave is large enough for everyone. You are welcome to stay with us."

Excuse me? What was that?

Kahvel! I, er, invited Syrreth and Ferreth to share our cave. For tonight only. Is that acceptable?

It most certainly is not. You want to share our cave with a zweigelan? I think not.

Anger flared. Pryllan began growling.

If this were any other wyverian you would not hesitate to render assistance. Syrreth and Ferreth are no different. Prove to Pravara that you openly accept all wyverians.

Silence.

Kahvel? Do I have your permission?

Silence.

Well?

As you wish.

Pryllan took a deep breath and turned to her right to see what the zweigelan's reaction would be. Not surprisingly, the two heads were whispering between themselves. Syrreth was apparently open to the invitation but Ferreth was hesitant, as he didn't trust Kahvel.

"We will accept your most gracious offer," Syrreth informed her. He glared at his twin as if daring him to disagree. Ferreth relented and gave a nod of appreciation.

"In that case, we'll meet you at your nest at sunrise tomorrow," Steve told her. Sarah took his hand and they both vanished.

* * *

Early the following morning the two dragons were airborne once more, headed on a direct route straight to the human castle in R'Tal. When Kahvel had learned that he would be responsible for watching Pravara during her absence, he tried to demur, claiming he could be called away again at a moment's notice. One look from Pryllan quelled his objections. Sooner or later, Pryllan angrily thought to herself, she would have to confront her mate and inquire about his absences. Did it have something to do with what Pravara had told her earlier? Was that the reason why Kahvel had been irritable as of late? While sometimes moody, her mate had never been on edge for this long.

"This would be a whole lot easier if I could just transport all of us straight there," Sarah said in a low voice.

Pryllan's keen aural abilities easily heard the whispered conversation between the two humans.

Steve smiled and nodded. "The two of them are just too big. You'd drain all your jhorun and then would use up all of our mimets to replenish it."

"You have plenty of the power crystals. I wouldn't have any problem using up a few. Besides, your jhorun is strong. You can just charge a few more up, am I right? I'm just tired of sitting."

"Now you know how the rest of us feel," her husband told her, with a grin.

"What's that supposed to mean?"

"You can get to wherever you want to go in the blink of an eye. The rest of us have to use the *normal* method of transportation, whether walking, riding, flying, etc."

"How is that my problem?"

Steve sighed and rested his back against one of Pryllan's curved talons. Sarah smiled at her husband then instantly scowled as his eyelids started to droop.

"If you fall asleep on me, I'll personally push you out of Pryllan's hand."

Steve sat up straight and eyed his wife.

"You wouldn't."

"Try me."

Steve glanced down at the passing forest far below them. Detecting movement in his peripheral vision, Steve looked to his left. A small gray dot had appeared out of the nearest cloud and was rapidly approaching.

"Hey, look! Another dragon!"

Caught daydreaming, Pryllan quickly glanced around. There, coming up on her left flank, was a gray dragon. She only knew of a handful of dragons with the unusual hue and the one approaching was one of them. Anghorus, a wyverian long known for his languid lifestyle of sleeping, eating, and sleeping some more, had decided to leave his cave. It was something Pryllan knew he didn't like to do as Anghorus detested physical activity. What was he doing here? Something didn't feel right.

"I don't think I've ever seen a gray dragon before," Steve observed.

"That's Anghorus," Pryllan told the group. "He is a friend. He only ventures out of his cave to hunt. He was also one of the earliest numbers to fall victim to this curse."

"Are you sure?" Sarah squinted her eyes as she watched the gray dragon draw closer. "Looks like he's flying just fine to me."

"I am aware. However, do you see how his right front claw is white? Only Anghorus has that mark, and he hasn't been able to fly for several weeks."

"So how's he flying now?" Steve wondered aloud. "If he found a way to rid himself of the curse, don't you think we ought to ask him about it?"

Pryllan activated her wyverian senses, automatically sharing them with Steve. She zeroed in on Anghorus' madly flapping form and hissed with alarm. Anghorus' normally silver eyes were jet black. Steve felt Pryllan's jolt of alarm and tensed.

Pryllan glanced worriedly at the two humans clutched tightly in her claws. "Steve, Sarah, be ready to teleport to a safe place if you need to."

"You need to get up on her back," Sarah said to Steve. "She doesn't have any fire. You do. You can be of more help up there than down here."

"And leave you by yourself down here?" Steve shook his head. "Nuh-uh. Don't think so."

Steve vanished from Sarah's side and reappeared moments later at the base of Pryllan's long neck.

Steve scowled. "I hate it when she does that."

"Syrreth! Ferreth!"

The zweigelan's twin heads looked over at Pryllan.

"There's a dragon approaching. I don't trust this. Be on your guard."

Both heads turned to look behind them. Sure enough, the gray dragon was getting closer. It was only a couple hundred feet away now. It opened its jaws and...

A blast of fire streaked out of Anghorus' mouth and flew straight at them. Pryllan tucked her wings tight against her body and dropped like a rock. The jet of fire wasn't even close to hitting her. However, it had come dangerously close to hitting Syrreth and Ferreth, who narrowly managed to dive out of the way at the last moment.

"Did it look as though he was trying to hit Syrreth and Ferreth?" Steve asked, suspicion evident in his voice.

Pryllan nodded. "It did."

"Why would he want to ... look out! Here comes another shot!"

The second blast Anghorus let loose streaked toward the zweigelan just as it pulled itself out of its nosedive to avoid the first blast.

"Watch out!" Sarah called from beneath Pryllan's body.

Ferreth twisted his neck around and spied the fireball streaking straight toward them. Syrreth jerked the left wing up while Ferreth snapped the right wing down, causing the zweigelan to do a barrel roll in midair. Anghorus' blast whizzed by them, missing Syrreth's head by a mere six inches.

"What's he doing with fire, anyway?" Steve angrily exclaimed. "I thought that was the first thing to go?"

"Will you worry about that later, please?" Sarah snapped. She was hugging one of Pryllan's talons in an effort to not be tossed around the inside of their makeshift cage like a ping pong ball. She was tempted to teleport out of there but she'd be cut off from the rest of the group. Besides, she wasn't sure if she could teleport back on to a moving target like Pryllan's open claw.

"Anghorus is targeting Syrreth and Ferreth," Pryllan reported. "We need to render aid immediately! However, I do not have any flames!"

Steve ignited his right hand. "I do. Let's see if we can get his attention. Yo! Anghorus! Over here!"

Steve generated a large chaser and flung it at the pursuing gray dragon. His chaser sped toward Anghorus and slammed into his left leg. Chagrined, Steve watched as it bounced harmlessly off the dragon's leg. He rapped his knuckles on Pryllan's scales.

"That didn't slow him down in the slightest. I forgot dragons are fireproof."

"I didn't," Pryllan angrily declared. "I wanted to get his attention. We are fireproof, aye, but we still notice when we are attacked. I was watching. Anghorus didn't even flinch."

Steve cupped his hands around his mouth and shouted down toward Pryllan's belly.

"Sarah! Get up here! We need you!'

Sarah appeared moments later. She hooked her arm through her husband's as Pryllan veered sharply east to keep Anghorus and their zweigelan in sight.

"What is it?"

Another blast of fire narrowly missed Syrreth and Ferreth.

"I'm of no help here," Steve complained. "My fire is ineffective against a dragon!"

"Oh, that's right. I didn't think about that. What do you want me to do?"

Anghorus was near enough now where anyone who didn't have wyverian-enhanced senses could see the attacking dragon's pitch-black eyes.

"What's happened to him? Why are his eyes like that? That's not a normal wyverian trait, is it?"

"It's not," Pryllan confirmed. "He has been bewitched."

"Bewitched?" Sarah thought for a moment. "We are on our way to report the existence of a renegade wizard and now we are attacked by a bewitched dragon. Does anyone else see the correlation here?"

"You think the two events are related?" Pryllan asked.

"You don't?"

Anghorus fired off two more shots at the fleeing zweigelan. Only by spinning through the air, a move Syrreth and Ferreth had recently learned from Pryllan, had they been able to avoid being hit.

"We are unsure how much longer we can keep this up!" Syrreth called out in a panicked voice.

"Whenever you are ready to render assistance, we would be grateful!" Ferreth added.

"Hang in there, guys!" Steve shouted at them. "We're working on it!"

"By talking amongst yourselves?" Ferreth hissed back with exasperation.

Trusting the zweigelan to stay ahead of Anghorus for a few moments longer, Sarah turned back to her husband.

"What do you need me to do?"

Steve hooked a thumb over his shoulder and pointed at Anghorus.

"If he's in a trance of some sort then we need to wake him up. The only way I can think of is to splash him with water."

"Where are we supposed to find water up here?" Sarah demanded.

"We are near the great sea," Pryllan informed them. "There is plenty of water to be found there."

"Can you teleport him over to the water and drop him in it?"

Sarah helplessly held up her hands. "No. Not only is he a huge dragon, but a huge *moving* dragon. I'd barely be able to do it if he were holding still."

"What about bringing the water to him? Can you teleport some water and drop it on his head?"

"If he were holding still, sure. However, he's not. It'd be too hard to hit a target moving that fast."

Syrreth and Ferreth dodged a few more jets of fire.

Steve suddenly smiled. "I have an idea. Syrreth! Ferreth!

Fly straight up! Gain some altitude!"

The zweigelan tipped its wings and flew toward the sun.

"What are you going to do?" Sarah wanted to know.

"Just wait. Watch this. Be ready to lift a bunch of water up. Not far, but enough."

Understanding, Sarah nodded. "Gotcha. I can do that."

"Now, guys! Dive straight down toward the sea!"

Now over the extensive Sea of Koralis, Syrreth and Ferreth tucked their wings tight against their sides and dropped straight toward the water. Their attacker was only seconds behind them.

The gently roiling surface of the sea approached at an alarming rate. Faster and faster the zweigelan hurtled toward it. Just before it seemed they would plunge into the cold blue sea, the zweigelan snapped its wings open and sailed out over the waves.

Intent on pursuing its victim, the gray dragon also extended its wings, but just as it corrected its course, a huge mass of water rose directly up. There was no way to avoid the hundreds of gallons of water.

Pryllan watched as Anghorus flew straight into the column. He spun out of control and crashed into the sea where he floundered for a few moments. Then they all heard a roar of outrage.

"What the ruddy hell am I doing in the water?"

Pryllan circled slowly above him.

"Pryllan? What are you doing up there? Better yet, what am I doing down here?"

"Do you remember anything, my friend?"

Two clear silver eyes regarded her from the water.

"One moment I'm resting comfortably in my cave and the next I'm here. What has happened?"

"You were bewitched by a wizard. You attacked Syrreth and Ferreth, presumably to stop us from telling the human king about the existence of a diabolical wizard."

"What the blazes do I care about a human wizard?" Anghorus spat out. "And how am I supposed to get out of the water? I cannot fly!"

The blue waters of the Koralis churned and splashed

around the partially submerged dragon as an unknown force latched on to Anghorus and dragged him to the closest shore.

"Right about there will do," Sarah decided as she instructed her jhorun to pull Anghorus up onto the rocky beach.

Pryllan made the necessary introductions. She watched, bemused, as one of her oldest friends made a half-hearted attempt to shake the excess water off his hide. Anghorus noticed the two humans and lowered his head for a cursory sniff.

"Would you like some help with that?" Steve asked, never missing the chance to make friends with another dragon.

"How, exactly?" the huge gray dragon inquired.

Steve ignited both hands and generated a chaser to toss back and forth a few times before spinning it on his index finger. Anghorus snorted with surprise.

"I would be grateful," the gray dragon decided.

A few minutes later, after Steve had gently blasted small jets of fire all over Anghorus' body, Pryllan spoke up. "Does this mean that any of us who have fallen victim to this curse could potentially be possessed by this wizard?"

"Anghorus is larger than you," Steve observed, frowning. "If the wizard could overpower him, then I'd have to guess that he probably could. Why try to kill Syrreth and Ferreth? He's already cursed the dragons and obviously it is working. What's he trying to accomplish now?"

"I'd say he's trying to keep his identity secret," Sarah mused. "He's lived in Lentari for who knows how long. I'd say he wants to keep it that way and if we tell the king about him then he'd be exposed. Shardwyn would eventually find him."

"All the more reason to get ourselves to R'Tal," Steve reminded everyone. "The sooner we can let the king know the better."

Pryllan nodded. "Agreed. Anghorus, are you capable of returning back to the valley?"

"That's at least three hours of solid flying," Anghorus grumped. "I'm going to miss my pre-lunch nap. How distressing."

"Nap once you're safe and sound back home," Sarah told the gray dragon. "Don't let your guard down. The wizard may try to overpower you again."

Anghorus nodded. He extended his long, leathery wings and began flapping as hard as he could. No matter how hard his wings beat the air, he was unable to lift off the ground. After a few minutes of the grueling workout, Anghorus gave up.

"It would appear I am still grounded."

Steve was scowling. "So the wizard can temporarily restore your fire and the ability to fly, and yet just as quickly take them away again? That's just great."

"What do I do now?" Fatigue was setting in and threatening to send the grounded dragon into a deep sleep.

"Head toward the castle," Steve told the dragon. "There's a cave north of it that was built specifically for dragons. You can curl up there and wait this curse out."

Satisfied, Anghorus rose to his feet and trudged off toward the distant castle. The two dragons that could still fly took to the air and headed northeast toward the tiny multi-turreted castle they could see in the distance.

"What happens if the wizard takes control again when poor Anghorus is sleeping?" Sarah wanted to know.

Pryllan was silent; she was much more concerned about Kahvel being used as a pawn without his knowledge or consent. She could only hope he was strong enough to resist should the wizard try.

Steve leaned out over Pryllan's huge palm and watched as they flew over Anghorus. The grounded dragon briefly looked up before dropping his gaze back down and continuing to plod on toward the castle.

"Hey, Anghorus!" Steve called back. "Try to stay awake, would you? It'd probably be safer!"

They all heard Anghorus' deep, rumbling response: "I'll risk it."

Chapter 8 — When It Rains, It Pours

Her eyes were closed and the tip of her tail was clamped firmly in her teeth. Pryllan had claimed the far corner of the underground lair and had deliberately positioned herself so that she could keep an eye on the one and only egress to the surface above. The zweigelan was curled up asleep fairly close to her. Clearly the two-headed dragon was enjoying its new-found camaraderie with another dragon and had no intention of being left alone again while another attack was possible.

Pryllan felt her respiration slow as her body relaxed. Activating her wyverian senses, she sought out, and found, her human rider's mind and accessed his senses. She still marveled at the clumsy bipedal locomotion that all humans used as clearly a four-legged gait would be a much more effective and stable means of moving about.

"This is going to require a little bit of finesse," Pryllan

heard Steve tell Sarah. The two humans were now approaching the north gate and eyeing the guards who were speculatively eyeing them back. "We need to explain what we're looking for to the king without really telling him what we're doing. Any ideas?"

Sarah nodded. "Just one. Let me do the talking."

"Excuse me?"

"You said it yourself. We're going to need some finesse. Therefore, I should be the one talking."

"Hmmph."

They didn't notice an elderly gentleman, dressed in black robes from head to toe, come up behind them and start to trail them. Just before husband and wife walked across the heavy wooden drawbridge to enter the vast castle, a wrinkled hand suddenly latched on to each of their shoulders.

Steve bellowed with surprise and whirled around, ready to ignite his hands. Staring back at him was the wrinkled, smiling countenance of the resident castle wizard. Shardwyn was laughing so hard he had tears streaming down his face.

"Good day to you, Sir Steve. Lady Sarah. If only you could see your faces right now. Must have scared ten years of life off of you! If I didn't know better, I'd say you were trying to sneak into the castle. That wouldn't be so, would it?"

Enhance your calm, Pryllan thought to Steve. **There's no need to appear so agitated. You'll only draw unwanted attention to yourselves.**

"Right," Steve quietly mumbled.

Take several deep breaths. Go on, do it.

Steve drew a deep breath and slowly let it out. He forced a smile on his face.

"Hello, Shardwyn. It's good to see you! You know what? Now that I think about it, you're just the person we need to see."

He hooked an arm through the wizard's and guided him deeper into the castle.

Where are you taking him?

I don't know, Steve thought back to the dragon. *Somewhere private. We don't want the king to learn what we're doing here. The Queen's jhorun makes you tell the truth in her presence. It'd be best to avoid both of them. Rinbok's request, remember?*

I do. I appreciate your discretion.

And she did. She was grateful. She could feel Steve's fervent desire to help all dragons. She couldn't have found two humans who were more dedicated than these.

Thanks. I'll be sure to tell Sarah that.

Embarrassment washed through the dragon, startling her. She had forgotten—again—that their linked minds shared everything, including unhindered thoughts. She resolved to tighten her control over her thoughts and emotions. She felt and heard Steve laugh.

Yeah, right. Good luck with that.

"So where are we going?" Shardwyn good-naturedly asked.

"Somewhere we can talk in private," Steve answered, walking past the kitchens and into the main service corridor behind it. "There has to be someplace we can have a private conversation around here."

"You'll find no more secure a locale than that of the Antechamber," Shardwyn told him.

Sarah shook her head. "That's more than likely where the king is."

Shardwyn shrugged.

"We need to keep the king out of this," Steve told him.

"May I inquire why, Sir Steve?" Shardwyn asked, frowning. "Whatever concerns me concerns him."

Steve tried to give the wizard his friendliest, most disarming smile he could come up with. "Will you please just trust us? We need your help."

Shardwyn shrugged again. "As you wish. Oh! Does this have something to do with that mysterious wizard the king has me searching for?"

Steve dropped Shardwyn's arm and clapped a hand over his mouth while Sarah held a finger to her lips and shushed them both.

"Yes, it's about that," she whispered. "We'll tell you what we can but it has to be done in private. Is the Antechamber being used for anything right now?"

"Worried about the king, are you? Then you're in luck.

The Kri'yans left to go horseback riding some time ago. As far as I'm aware, they have yet to return."

Steve nodded. "That's perfect. If we're lucky we can be in and out of there before the king knows anything about it. Come on."

As they approached the king's private study, commonly referred to as the Antechamber, the guards standing on either side of the entrance snapped to attention and held the door open, closing it only after the three of them were safely inside. Steve and Sarah drew up short. The king was sitting at his desk.

"Dude, you said he wouldn't be here," Steve hissed angrily to Shardwyn.

"I didn't see him return. Then again, it isn't surprising. I was running an experiment in my workshop all day and I really wasn't paying attention."

Kri'Entu rose to his feet.

"Sir Steve, Lady Sarah. Is all well?"

Pryllan growled her irritation at the human wizard. Her annoyance rivaled Steve's, who was doing his best not to scowl.

I don't know how, Pryllan, Steve thought to her, *but you and I are going to get even with him for that.*

Agreed.

"Good afternoon, your majesty," Steve began, giving the king a small bow. "We didn't know you'd be in here. We don't want to disturb you so we'll just take our leave."

Kri'Entu looked quizzically at the fire thrower. He glanced over at Sarah, who curtsied. Then the king's eyes fell upon Shardwyn.

"Ah. Don't mind me. I'll just return to my work."

The king promptly sat back down at his desk and pulled a small bundle of fabric from one of his desk drawers. Whistling merrily, the king removed several daggers from his belt and began to rub polishing compounds on them, being careful not to miss any exposed surface on either blade.

"I see what he's doing," Sarah whispered to Steve. Confused, Pryllan listened intently. "He's pretending to be doing something else while he's listening to us. That way he'll be able to know what's going on without us directly telling him."

"You really think he can hear us all the way over there?" Steve whispered back.

Sarah nodded. "Yes, I do. I'll prove it. Watch this." She turned away from the king and angled herself so that she was facing her husband. "If we discuss things in here that aren't meant to be discussed at all since certain parties wish to prevent certain actions from becoming known, could we trust whoever is listening to keep it a secret?"

Steve stared at her as though she was a complete stranger. "What are you doing? Where are you going with this?"

Patience. Let's see what Sarah's intentions are.

"We *all* would like to know what you're doing," Steve told his wife.

Shardwyn held up a hand. "So would I, Sir Steve."

Sarah patted the air and continued in a hushed tone. "Just a moment. I'm proving a point." She raised her voice a little. "So, if those that might be listening would favor me with a small tap, or a knock, we would know whether or not we could discuss our business freely without fear of us breaking our oath to certain individuals who must not be named."

There was a loud clatter as the dagger Kri'Entu was holding slipped out of his hands and fell onto his desk. The king hastily retrieved his knife.

"Oops. How clumsy of me."

Steve turned to give the king a suspicious look. Kri'Entu, meanwhile, had resumed his soft whistling and was continuing to polish his daggers.

Pryllan, I think I see what Sarah is doing. The king wants to know what is going on, but we can't openly tell him. But if he happens to eavesdrop and hears it for himself, then we wouldn't have broken our promise to Rinbok. We can trust the king to keep his mouth shut. Besides, isn't the time for discretion over? We really need to ask them about this renegade wizard.

Very well. Inform the wizard in this manner. No direct communication with the king. That way we will all be protected from Rinbok Intherer's wrath once he learns how the humans learned of our predicament.

You got it.

Steve deliberately turned his back on the king and guided Shardwyn to one of the plush armchairs surrounding a nearby table. Sinking deeper into the heavily cushioned chair than he liked, Steve interlaced his fingers and rested them on the table. Glancing quickly at his wife, he leaned forward and stared at the wizard.

"Okay, Shardwyn, here's the thing. I wasn't sure before if there was an unknown wizard plotting against us, but I sure as hell think there is now."

Shardwyn's brow wrinkled with a frown. "What has happened, Sir Steve?"

"A dragon friend of ours was bewitched and sent to attack us."

The wizard's bushy gray eyebrows shot up. "You don't say? A full-sized dragon was bewitched? How did he do that?"

"Hey, you're the wizard here, remember? I was hoping that you could tell us how that happened."

"It is troublesome that someone with this much power has remained hidden from me for so long." Shardwyn slipped his black felt cap off and scratched the top of his head. "What am I going to tell the king?"

There was another loud clatter as, from across the room, Kri'Entu dropped the dagger again. The king shook his head and retrieved the knife.

"Pardon me. Apparently, I was polishing a little too aggressively."

"Oh, I'd say he knows," Steve continued, giving Shardwyn a patronizing smile. "Anyway, we figured the wizard was trying to stop us from revealing his existence. Since that didn't succeed, we're not too sure what else he might try. So consider this a warning."

Shardwyn smiled and leaned back in his chair.

"Every so often a villager is brought to my attention who possesses a powerful jhorun. Their fellow villagers always say the same thing: they're afraid of them. Almost always it's harmless."

Sarah cleared her throat. "You said *almost* always. What about those times that weren't harmless?"

"An unpleasant confrontation would become necessary," Shardwyn admitted.

"Were any of them strong enough to be considered a wizard?" Steve asked.

Excellent question.

Steve smiled. *Thanks!*

Shardwyn shook his head no.

What does he think we should do next?

"What should we do, Shardwyn? I personally don't like knowing there's a ticked off wizard out there somewhere who's able to do as he pleases. He's going to be angry with us."

"Get him to expend more of his jhorun," the wizard told him matter-of-factly.

Excuse me?

Steve's shock mirrored Pryllan's.

"What was that? It sounded like you wanted him to attack us again."

Observe. The king is not happy with that suggestion.

Steve glanced over at Kri'Entu, who had temporarily paused in his attempts at cleaning the dagger.

Are you sure?

Indubitably. I could hear him scowl with impatience the moment the human wizard suggested it.

How? I can't even hear him. You can hear the same things I can, right?

Perhaps you couldn't hear him above the sounds of your own breathing?

Are you saying I breathe too loud? Spoken like a true smartass! I think I'm starting to rub off on you.

Pryllan fell silent and continued to watch the proceedings through Steve's eyes.

"The more this wizard uses his jhorun," Shardwyn patiently explained, "the more I am able to determine his location. I have many devices and instruments at my disposal, but unless there is jhorun for them to detect, I will never be able to track him down."

Steve looked worriedly at his wife. "Can you believe this?"

Sarah nodded. "I can see the logical sense of what he's

trying to say, only I'm not happy about putting ourselves into danger again."

I concur.

Steve looked at his wife. "We are *all* in agreement."

Catching the emphasis on *all*, Sarah nodded.

"I do have something that might help," Shardwyn told them. He rose to his feet and headed toward the door. "I'll be right back."

"I can only imagine what he might have," Steve mumbled.

"Do you see the flaw with this plan?" Sarah asked her husband.

Steve nodded. "Aside from us becoming the bait to try and lure this guy out into the open?"

"Besides that."

If this wizard assumes that the confirmation of his existence will be shared with the appropriate authorities, what is to prevent the wizard from finding another suitable location to hide?

"Pryllan brings up a good point," Steve said as he turned to his wife and shared the dragon's concerns.

Sarah nodded her head. "Good job, Pryllan. That's the flaw I was talking about."

She has a keen intellect.

"Yes, she does," Steve murmured.

Sarah stared at him. "What was that?"

"Pryllan said you have a keen intellect. I was agreeing."

Sarah beamed her smile at him. "Tell her thank you for me."

You are welcome, Lady Sarah.

"She said you're welcome."

"How about that," they heard the king say.

Husband and wife turned to look over at the king's desk. Entu had finished polishing his blades and was now busy applying a coat of polish to his crown.

"When's the last time this was cleaned?" the king was saying in an exasperated tone. "The matter is simply atrocious. The entire castle will be alerted. They will stand ready to assist, I'm sure."

He is pledging his support to you.

I can see that. Do I thank him?

To do so would be an acknowledgement of his participation.

So what do I do?

Wait for the wizard to return. We have done all we can here. We informed them about the attack. The existence of the unknown sorcerer has been confirmed.

Got it.

A few minutes later Shardwyn returned, carrying a square flat wooden box. Sitting back down in his chair, the canny wizard opened the box to reveal a necklace.

"What do you have there?" Steve asked as he leaned forward.

Sarah leaned forward as well. Shardwyn pulled out a large, gaudy gold pendant off-centered with a huge pink cabochon. He handed it to Steve.

"You're kidding, right?"

Sarah stifled a laugh. Pryllan felt Steve flush with embarrassment. There must be a reason why the necklace was causing Steve to react in that manner.

Of course there is. It's uglier than sin!

I am not familiar with that phrase.

Let's try it this way. Trolls are way more attractive than this.

I see.

Steve held up the medallion and turned it over in his hand so that Pryllan could get a good look.

Wearing that would help determine the location of the renegade wizard?

Apparently.

Why is this a problem?

Gold and pink on a necklace worn by a man? I don't care where you're from. It isn't a good look. Especially for me.

Lady Sarah appears to be enjoying your discomfort.

Of course she is. She's loving every minute of this.

Steve turned to face the wizard and scowled. He slipped the necklace over his head and tucked the emasculating pendant under his tunic. Shardwyn shook his head and pointed at his chest.

"I am sorry, Sir Steve, but the pendant must be worn over

the clothes in order to be the most effective."

Steve sighed. "Of course it does. What do I have to do with it?"

"If you suspect there's been an attack, then return the pendant to me as quickly as you can. I'll analyze it and see what we can learn from it. May I ask a question?"

Steve and Sarah both nodded.

"Can I ask what you plan on doing next?"

"We're going to try and locate the wizard," Steve answered.

Shardwyn rested both elbows on the table and leaned forward. "How?"

"By following the only clue we have," Steve answered.

"Which is?"

"We have to find the second zweigelan. We're hoping he can show us where to look."

"A zweigelan? How remarkable! I've always wanted to see one for myself."

"There's presently one in the dragon cave."

"Oh?"

"That's right. He's a friend of ours. He's helping us track down his elusive relative."

"And you believe the second zweigelan will lead you to this other wizard?"

Steve nodded. "Yes. That's the plan, anyway."

"What are your interests with him?"

"Let's just say he's a person of interest in another matter that desperately needs a resolution."

"With the dragons?"

Steve's mouth dropped open. "Dragons? Who said anything about the dragons?"

"A rare zweigelan is resting in the wyverian lair we created. You're in telepathic contact with a dragon right now. I just assumed that since you've been asking her questions, to which she has been giving her opinions, I deduced the wyverians were somehow involved."

Kri'Entu sprang from his chair. One of his daggers clattered noisily as it fell to the desk. "Shardwyn, do you have the results from your latest scan of Avin?"

"Not yet, Your Majesty. Preliminary scans should be

completed by tomorrow morning."

"Very well. Are you running any experiments right now?"

"I am. You'll be most interested to hear this! I'm conducting a simple test of…"

"Please monitor those experiments closely, Shardwyn. This castle has tolerated enough explosions this month, agreed?"

"I understand completely, Your Majesty. I will take my leave."

The tall lanky wizard rushed from the room. The king bent over his desk to retrieve his knife.

"If I have to assign extra staff to keep an eye on him then I will," Kri'Entu muttered aloud.

The human king is very wise.

Not bad for a human, huh?

Indeed. Where should we search for the second zweigelan?

I figured you'd know the answer to that better than anyone. Isn't he a part of the Collective? I assumed his location, well, his last known location, was common knowledge?

I will consult with Kahvel.

We'll be waiting for you.

Pryllan gently pulled the human's awareness from her own and returned it to him. Quieting her mind, she turned her thoughts to her mate and their offspring hundreds of leagues away in the north. She thought of basking in Kahvel's comforting presence. She thought back to the last time she curled up next to him as they encircled the nest, protecting their offspring. She smiled. There it was. She could feel his heartbeat. Faint at first, the steady beating grew stronger. Almost instantly she felt his irritation and his restlessness. What was going on?

Beloved? Are you well?

Aye.

You appear perturbed. Is all well with Pravara?

Aye.

When no other information was forthcoming Pryllan tried again.

What has you agitated, my love?

She felt Kahvel give a great sigh. ***Our Collective might be presently unavailable, but that hasn't stopped the spread of news. They know.***

They? Are you referring to the other dragons?

Aye.

What have they learned?

They have learned about the existence of this curse, and that it's not a disease.

How many know?

Practically everyone. They are demanding the curse be broken or lifted.

What do they plan to do?

I have spoken with them. They wait for signs of where to direct their anger and their rage.

Pryllan was shocked. They wanted to fight? Together?

Dragons are coming together to help each other. Right now, I am very proud of our wyverian species.

You're trying to dissuade the others from doing anything rash, are you not?

Kahvel was silent.

Beloved, tell me you're trying to defuse the situation.

I am doing what I can.

What would they do?

I do not know, and that is what concerns me.

Pryllan was speechless. Stricken dragons were massing on the valley floor? If that many dragons were truly gathering in the valley, then it could only mean an attack was imminent. They must hurry!

She felt Kahvel's reassuring presence in her mind and relaxed somewhat.

We are hurrying, beloved. We need to find the second zweigelan. The Collective is silent. Do you know where we can find his lair?

I do not want you visiting this rogue without the ability to protect yourself. Do not do this, dear one.

Steve is still here. As I mentioned earlier, his flames are unaffected.

Oh. There was a pause as Kahvel considered. ***I had forgotten. In that case, have your rider with you at all***

times, is that understood?

I will.

Pryllan listened intently as Kahvel explained how to find the second two-headed dragon. Then, before she could thank him for her help, he sent a final thought. Pryllan's growl was immediate.

No. We are going after the second zweigelan. It's too dangerous.

I have no choice, beloved. The Dragon Lord has summoned me.

He'll just have to wait until I can return.

Do you wish to defy Rinbok Intherer's command?

Silence.

Beloved?

No.

I am deeply sorry. You must return to the nest.

Once her mate's presence faded, Pryllan growled again.

What is it? Steve asked. *You're angry. What's happened?*

I have just made contact with Kahvel. He has told me how to find the second zweigelan's lair.

Is it that bad?

Worse. I need to return to the nest and retrieve Pravara. For whatever reason, the Dragon Lord has summoned him again.

He knows what we're doing is dangerous, right?

Aye. He says he has no choice.

Give me a second. Okay, I just told Sarah. She's not happy about it, either. She's promised to help keep an eye on her. I will, too. We'll keep her safe, Pryllan.

Thank you.

Back in the Antechamber, Steve rose to his feet, prompting Sarah to do the same. The king glanced up.

"Sir Steve? Must you go already?"

"Yes. We have things to do up north."

"I want the two of you to remember something. All the castle's personnel stand ready to assist. To help Shardwyn, that is. The task of overseeing Shardwyn's safety is not to be taken lightly, I assure you."

Husband and wife smiled and offered their thanks. Bidding the king farewell, they made their way back to the orchard and descended into the subterranean cavern.

"They really need some more light down here," Sarah informed him. "I can't see a thing."

"I can. I'm looking through Pryllan's eyes. I'm watching her watch us. It's really kind of creepy."

Interesting. Are we ready to depart?

Yes.

Excellent.

Two hours later they were several hundred leagues northwest of the castle. Without Pravara to hamper their progress they were cruising at optimum speeds high amongst the clouds and were making good time. At this velocity, Pryllan decided, they'd be back in the valley in less than an hour and a half. She bent her neck around and checked on her two passengers. Instead of riding in her open palm, as the two of them did on the ride down there, Steve and Sarah had finally agreed to ride on her back after she feigned discomfort from having her claw open and immobile for such an extended period of time. While untrue, she figured it would be much more comfortable for the humans.

There they both were, on her back near the base of her neck. Sarah had volunteered to teleport back to their nest so she wouldn't have to worry about them but Pryllan had persuaded her not to expel any unnecessary jhorun. Besides, the dragon had argued, could the renegade wizard detect her jhorun and act accordingly against them?

Sarah and Steve had agreed and instantly let their objections drop.

"It really is rather peaceful up here," Sarah commented as she snuggled closer to her six-foot-three space heater. "If not for those infernal clouds we keep flying through, I think it'd be downright pleasant."

"The clouds don't seem to bother me as much as they do you," Steve commented as he regarded the passing clouds.

"Feels rather refreshing if you ask me."

Sarah laughed. "Well, I'm not going to. I don't have the ability to generate so much body heat that I'd stay completely dry in a rain storm."

Steve sat up straight.

"Does that mean I'm leaking jhorun?"

"What?"

"If I'm generating heat, more so than I normally do, does that mean I'm using my jhorun?"

"An interesting question," Sarah mused. "We've passed through, what, about five clouds now and you've remained dry the entire time, right? I'd say you're expelling some. Not much, but some."

"Could he track us by that?"

Sarah shrugged. "How would I know that? For all we know this mysterious sorcerer should be referred to as sorceress!"

"Does a human's gender affect how powerful their jhorun is?" Pryllan asked, curious.

Sarah shook her head. "No."

"Of course it does," Steve quipped at the same time.

Sarah slowly turned to stare at her husband, who instantly grinned and began backpedaling.

"Did I say that out loud? What I meant to say was of course not. No way. Out of the question."

"You really want to smell like a girl tonight, don't you?"

Steve looked triumphantly at his wife. "You don't have that smelly, glittery girlie spray here. I think I'm safe."

"I'm sure I can borrow some from the queen. She still has some left over from her trip with Lia and me to the mall."

Steve's smug smile vanished. "Fine, fine, I apologize."

Sarah giggled. "You don't mean it, though."

"Of course not."

She playfully slapped her husband's arm. No one saw a small silvery cloud accelerate across the sky and put itself directly in their path. Having been amused by Steve and Sarah's antics, Pryllan didn't notice and flew right through it. Syrreth and Ferreth, trailing slightly lower, banked left, and missed the cloud altogether.

A split second later, Pryllan and her human passengers were rendered unconscious. They probably would have remained so for longer, only a gust of wind appeared out of nowhere and caused a few seconds of minor turbulence. After a few moments, the winds passed and the skies returned to an eerie calm.

Sarah blinked her eyes in confusion. What happened? Had she fallen asleep? She brought her hands up to rub her eyes and hesitated. Her arms felt leaden, like they now weighed double what they did just a moment ago. Something was wrong.

Right then she realized that someone was sitting in front of her. It was a woman! When had they taken on another passenger?

Curious to see who it was, Sarah reached out to tap the woman on her shoulder when she finally saw her hands. They were big, had scrapes and bruises on them, and totally didn't belong to her! What was going on?

Silently panicking, she rotated her right hand, looking at her open palm. It had three small semi-circular cuts near the base of her thumb. She knew those scars. She had given them to Steve in a fit of playful wrestling the previous night. Those were marks left by three of her nails. Good Lord! She was in Steve's body! Then that meant ... the woman in front of her had to be ... her! Who was in her body? Steve? How could this have happened?

The woman suddenly awoke and lurched violently to her left. Sarah reflexively put a hand on her arm to keep her from falling off Pryllan's back.

"Steve?" Sarah querulously asked. "Tell me that's you." Her eyes opened wide in disbelief. Her voice had deepened, the bass vibrated through her chest. The woman, however, opened her mouth and she let out a shriek of pure agony. Sarah slapped her hands over her ears.

"Is that what I sound like when I scream? Wow. Hey, knock it off. You're Steve, right?"

Her own horrified eyes stared uncomprehendingly back at her. The figure slowly shook her head no.

"No? NO! If you're not Steve, then who *are* you?"

"P-P-Pryllan."

Sarah was speechless. She stared into her own eyes and then slowly turned to look up at the dragon's massive head. Pryllan's eyes were closed. Steve's, she hastily corrected. This was really weird. If her husband was now in Pryllan's body, and since they were still up in the air, then that meant ... The strong winds buffeted them again and they shook uncontrollably for another couple of seconds.

Sarah turned to the zweigelan, who was flying nearby. They had been alerted by Pryllan's scream and had flown closer to see if they could render aid.

"Syrreth, Ferreth, are you two okay?" Sarah called out to them. "Are you still you?"

Both of the zweigelan's heads eyed each other as though they were trying to have a conversation with a dullard.

"I do not know what you're trying to say," Syrreth informed her haughtily.

Sarah looked over at Ferreth. "Ferreth, say something."

"Like?"

Sarah nodded. "That'll do. You guys are still the same."

Both heads were still staring at her.

"Something has happened to us," Sarah told the two-headed dragon. "I'm Sarah. I'm in Steve's body. Pryllan is in mine. I can only assume Steve is in Pryllan's."

"What happened?" Syrreth asked. "Why have you switched bodies?"

"We didn't mean to," Sarah angrily exclaimed. Her awareness suddenly expanded and she automatically looked down at her hands. They had turned red.

"Uh, oh. No, no, no, no, no... This is not good. Calm down, Sarah," she ordered herself. "Just calm down. No fire. A fire up here would be bad."

Thankfully her hands returned to a normal healthy shade of pink. She looked at the terrified woman in front of her.

"Pryllan, is that really you?"

Pryllan had been holding her arms up and staring at them as though she had never seen appendages before in her life. Sarah had to concede the point in this case. Sarah snapped her fingers in front of Pryllan's face.

"Stay with me, Pryllan. We have a much bigger problem to deal with right now."

"There's a bigger problem than being extricated from your own body and given to another?"

Sarah pointed at the inert dragon.

"You, I mean, Steve is unconscious. We are dropping lower and lower. We need to wake you up. Him. We need to wake *him* up. The problem is, how do we do that?"

"I was rendered unconscious once before," Pryllan recalled. She wiggled her fingers. Her brow furrowed as she stared at the writhing appendages on her hand.

"You were? How?"

"By you."

Sarah nodded. "Oh, I get it. Was it when I accidentally teleported you and Steve to Idaho? Did you wake up on your own or did Steve have to wake you up?"

"He woke me up."

"How?"

"I am trying to recall what he did."

"Think faster! We've dropped another hundred feet!" She rose to her feet and kicked the closest scale. Nothing. Steve hadn't twitched. They were in trouble.

"What will he do when he realizes he's no longer human?" Pryllan asked. She tried to rise to her feet but the concept of bipedal locomotion was beyond her.

"Can you try to use your telepathy?" Sarah asked. "Can you mentally contact him?"

Pryllan nodded her human head. "I can try." She tried to quiet her thoughts and focused on her rider's mind. Nothing came. She looked at Sarah and shook her head. Then, it came to her. "He used fire, on my head. That's what woke me up."

Sarah stared incredulously up the long heavily scaled neck and the distant head. She had to climb that? Catching sight of the remote ground far below them, and noticing that they had descended another hundred feet or so, Sarah quickly found handholds on the dragon's neck and began to climb. She found and gripped scales, protuberances, and whatever else she could cling to in her ascent up Pryllan's neck. After a few minutes she was nestled in between the dragon's ears on top of its head.

Sarah eyed her hands and ordered them to light. They didn't. Anger flared.

"Shh…"

Had she really been about to use a vulgar word? Her eyes opened wide. She didn't have time for this. They had been steadily sinking lower; it was definitely time to bring this flight to an end. She had to think like Steve. How did he make his jhorun work?

"Chivalry," Sarah murmured. She smiled. "That should be easy enough."

She thought about the mysterious sorcerer and what she'd like to do to him should they ever meet face to face. Her hands began to tingle and it felt like pressure was building. She looked at her hands. Both had become an ugly shade of red.

Sarah quickly put her hands on Steve's wyverian head and prayed he wouldn't be hurt. Imagining that she was taking aim at the wizard responsible for this predicament, she let both hands spring open. Twin jets of fire blasted out and hit the dragon directly on its head.

The dragon's eyes snapped open.

"What the hell?"

She had heard Pryllan's voice, but it was something her husband would definitely say. Sarah gave a joyous whoop and pumped her fist in the air. It was Steve!

The dragon violently lurched sideways, throwing both human riders off its back. Sarah screamed as both she and Pryllan fell. If she had been in her own body, then she could have simply teleported everyone safely to the ground. However, her teleporting abilities had been rendered useless as Pryllan was now in control of them and had no idea how to use them.

Sarah saw her body, with Pryllan inside, spinning uncontrollably as they fell. Even if she could teach Pryllan how to make her jhorun work, she neither had the time nor the ability to be heard as the roaring wind made communication impossible. Looking straight down she watched as Pryllan kept spreading her arms, as if she were trying to spread her wings, in an attempt to break herself out of this fall.

Out of nowhere the zweigelan appeared and soared past Pryllan's hurtling human body. When the dragon passed, Pryllan was gone, having been plucked out of the air by Syrreth. The right head, Ferreth, twisted around to locate her. Once she had been spotted, the zweigelan's wings snapped open to their fullest potential, pushing the two headed dragon up toward her at a frightening rate. Sarah was wrenched out of the sky as soon as Ferreth was close enough to reach her.

Wings extended, and no longer falling, Syrreth bent his head to check on Pryllan while Ferreth ascertained for himself that Sarah was unharmed. Both of them indicated that they were.

Sarah suddenly gasped with alarm. Steve! What had happened to Steve?

She twisted in Ferreth's grip and saw that her husband, in Pryllan's massive wyverian body, was frantically flapping his wings as he tried to slow his descent. The only thing he accomplished was to send himself into a corkscrew spin. Sarah screamed in terror as Steve plummeted straight toward the ground.

Chapter 9 — And Then There Were Two

Faster and faster he fell, spiraling uncontrollably as he flapped his wings. Wings? What the hell was he doing with wings, anyway? And why the heck was he green?? The answer came a split second later. He was now a dragon.

"I'm in Pryllan's body!" Steve thought excitedly. "I'm not making this up. I'm a dragon! How cool!"

His giddiness evaporated in a flash as he realized his revelation did nothing to solve his present problem. He was falling uncontrollably to the ground and if he didn't do something, and do it quickly, his upcoming date with terra firma was going to be his final one. He glanced irritably at his impotent wings. No matter how hard they flapped, they weren't even marginally slowing his descent. Damn dragons. They made it look so easy!

Spread your wings to their fullest potential.

Steve was taken aback. Who was there?

Do as I say. Extend your wings. Hurry!

I don't know how!

Tuck your forelegs close to your body. Hold them there. Now, extend your wings and keep them extended.

Steve did as he was instructed, only he was still spiraling.

Still your wings. Do not flap. There are plenty of currents to keep you aloft. Open your tail wing.

My what?

Your tail wing. It's the flap of skin on the tip of your tail that resembles a miniature wing. It's used to direct air flow. Your tail and its wing are at an angle which is causing you to spin out of control.

You've got to be kidding me. I have a tail now, too?

Of course. You are a dragon.

What do I have to do?

Pretend you are holding out your human hand and are spreading your fingers as wide as possible.

How is that supposed to help?

I will explain later. Do it! Your time is running short.

Steve did as he was asked. Both sets of his massive talons opened and he spread them as wide as possible. He then felt a similar sensation on another part of his body, but couldn't tell where. He risked a quick glance back at his tail and saw that his tail wing was now fully extended. He said as much to the dragon voice in his mind.

Excellent. You will notice that your spiraling has stopped. Now, angle your wings up, so that air flows under them and is not forced down.

How?

Imagine your second set of appendages is drooping too low and in order to correct your posture, you must raise your shoulders up and push out your chest. Can you do that?

I'll try. Fine, I'm slouching. Let's see if …

Apparently, the subtle request for a shift in body positions was all his dragon body needed. He felt the position of his wings adjust ever so slightly. His front forelegs also shifted slightly as his wyverian shoulders tightened and drew back a few inches.

Steve's rapid descent leveled off and he found that he was able to keep himself aloft by flapping his wings every so often.

I don't know who you are but you saved my life. Thank you.

You do know me. What you are doing inside my mate's body confounds me.

Kahvel! Is that you?

None other.

How did you know I was in trouble?

You may be a human in nature, but right now, you occupy my mate's body. When she's in distress, she calls out to me for help.

You're saying I somehow contacted you?

I felt your distress. Pryllan's memories weren't there, so I knew something was wrong. Can you tell me what happened?

The only thing I can figure is that we must have been attacked by that renegade wizard again. How he managed to get me in Pryllan's body is beyond me. I want to know why he did it. What's his plan?

You are still alive, so I say whatever his plan was, it failed.

You couldn't be more wrong.

Oh? How so?

The wizard's plan worked too perfectly. With Pryllan no longer able to use her flames, it was up to me to handle the protection aspect of this group, which I was more than willing to do. But now? I can barely keep my scaly ass off the ground.

If you're now in Pryllan's body, it stands to reason Pryllan might be in yours. Would you agree?

It makes sense.

Why would this wizard target Pryllan?

She handles our transportation. Now that I'm a dragon, I have every intention of getting my butt safely on the ground and staying put when I do.

But, if Pryllan was your transportation, and since that has now fallen to you, you cannot sit idle on the ground. I am unable to fly, so I cannot render aid. You, as much as you want to deny it, must assume that responsibility.

In your mate's body? Are you serious? Aren't you afraid of me hurting it or something? The last thing I want to do is crash and end up hurting her. Or me, for that matter.

I know that, Steve. You are the only human I have ever encountered that I would trust with my mate's life. Pravara's, too.

That was about the time Steve remembered Sarah had been riding with him, on Pryllan's back. He bent his neck to check his back. His heart sank. No one was there.

Oh, no! I forgot about Sarah! And if I have Pryllan's body, she must have mine. Sarah and I were riding on Pryllan's back before all of this happened. They're gone!

Wait. The two of you were riding on Pryllan's back? At the same time?

Kahvel, focus! My body is gone. Sarah's is gone, too! I have to find them!

Enhance your calm. I sense ...

Dude, stop telling me to enhance my calm. I'm tired of enhancing my calm, okay?

As I was saying, I sense the zweigelan is nearby. There are two humans with him.

Man alive, that is good news. That could have ended badly.

Indeed.

I need to find them. So how do I steer this thing?

Thing? You are referring to my mate's body?

Obviously. How do I turn? I don't want to get into that tailspin again. That wasn't fun.

What you need to remember is that, while you are human, and have human experiences, your body is not. It's wyverian. Do not wonder what muscles have to be used, or how far you should extend your wings. Pryllan has done this many times before. Her body will react instinctively. All you have to do is think about where you want to go and her body should respond accordingly.

You're saying I shouldn't be thinking about what I'm doing but just do it?

Do you have to order each of your human legs to take a step when you walk from one point to another?

Err, no. I do it without thinking.

Precisely. It is the same for us. We all know how to fly. Let the actions come naturally.

Okay, let's see. If I want to turn to the right then I should...

He felt part of his body start to automatically move somewhere on his right side. Deciding against fighting the urge, he let his body's movements play out. Sure enough, his right wing dipped down and he began a gentle turn to his right.

Well done.

Thanks. Couldn't have done it without you, pal.

It has been my pleasure, although I will admit I have a vested interest in keeping you alive.

Steve laughed, which in his dragon form came out as a throaty chuckle. *I stay alive and therefore Pryllan's body stays alive, is that it?*

Exactly. Now, somewhere nearby is the zweigelan. Search for them. Practice your turns. Your body will adjust itself to accommodate your needs.

Got it.

Steve went through a series of wide, careful turns to the left and then to the right. He banked to the right a second time and stayed that way until he had flown in a complete circle and was once again facing north with the sun on his left.

Up ahead, about three hundred feet above you.

Is it the zweigelan?

Aye.

Steve angled his head up and reacted with astonishment as suddenly the tiny figure he had spied in the distance jumped into focus. Syrreth and Ferreth were each holding a human. Looks like Syrreth was holding Sarah and Ferreth was holding his body. A quick check of his body's face indicated that, sure enough, someone was inhabiting it as he could see his face turn from left to right as if he was searching for someone. They must be looking for him!

Suddenly both Sarah and his body were looking straight at him. The zweigelan must have spotted him and announced his presence to the humans. That was odd. It looked like his body was crying. Is that what he looked like when he cried?

No wonder guys don't like crying in public. He looked terrible.

If you don't mind me asking, what did you say to Pryllan earlier?

Why? What did she say?

She was angry about having to put Pravara in danger. I think she said something about you being summoned again, which means you need to leave the nest.

Aye. When Rinbok Intherer calls, you do not ignore.

Are you really planning on leaving once we get there? She's either in my body or Sarah's. I'm sure she'd love your support.

I have already sent a message to the Dragon Lord. An extenuating situation has arisen, and I am hereby unable to leave Pravara unattended.

Have you told her that yet?

No.

Want me to do it?

Would you?

Yes.

Thank you. I will leave you now. Give Pryllan my love.

I will. Thanks again for your help, my friend.

You are most welcome.

Kahvel's strong presence faded from his mind and he was then left to fend for himself. Struggling slightly with a powerful air current, he looked up at the rapidly descending zweigelan and rose to meet them. Syrreth and Ferreth warily watched him as he approached, and they matched his speed. Before Steve could say anything, his body called out to him.

"Steve? Is that you? Are you okay?"

Being addressed by one's own body, in one's own voice, was disconcerting, Steve thought wryly. He'd like to think stranger things have happened, but so far, this one had become the weirdest.

"It's me," Steve confirmed as he tried very hard not to stare at himself. "This is turning out to be a strange day, that's for sure."

"Are you okay? What happened? How did you get out of that nosedive?"

"It wasn't easy. Kahvel was a big help." Steve stared at his body, who was staring back at him with equal fascination.

"Pryllan? Is that you in there?"

Sarah raised an arm.

"I am here."

Steve stared at what he thought was his wife.

"Wait. *You* are Pryllan?"

Sarah's body nodded. Steve stared incredulously at his own body. "Sarah, does that mean you're…"

"You?" She nodded. "Yep. What an experience this is turning out to be."

"What's that supposed to mean?"

Sarah laughed. "Do you really want me to go into that here? What happens if I have to go to the bathroom? You have an entirely different set of plumbing, you know."

Steve burst out laughing, which coming from Pryllan's body sounded like deep resonating growls.

"Laugh it up, Mr. Chuckles," Sarah told him with a frown. "You realize right now you're a girl dragon? So if I told you to go lay an egg, you could. Think about that."

That sobered Steve instantly, causing Sarah to burst out laughing.

"Point taken. So, what do we do now? How do we revert back to ourselves again?"

"Well," Sarah began as she brushed the back of her hand under her nose to give it a good itching, "for all we know, this spell might just wear off on its own."

Pryllan turned to look at Sarah.

"And if it doesn't? What then?"

"We'll get Shardwyn on it. He should be able to break the spell or nullify it."

"Are you sure?" Pryllan let her human hands drop into her lap. "I do not think I can take much more of this human existence."

Sarah turned to her body and put her hands on her hips in a very feminine move. "And what's wrong with my human body?" The sigh Steve let out was loud enough to be heard by all. "What was that for?"

"Don't put your hands on your hips like that. It's not a good look for me."

Sarah stared at the dragon. She slowly folded her arms

over her chest. "I could make it worse. Much, much worse if you catch my meaning."

Steve narrowed his green slitted wyverian eyes and glared at his wife. "Don't you even think about it, lady."

Sarah smiled sweetly at him with his own face. "That's just it. I'm not a lady at the moment, am I? You know, I've always wondered just what —"

Steve let out an irritated breath, which sounded an awful lot like a growl. "Fine, you win. I'll shut up now."

His face smiled back that creepy smile of his.

"So what happened to us?" Steve asked, hoping to change the subject. The last thing he wanted was for Sarah to do something that would embarrass him, and since she was in his body, the possibilities were endless. "How did the wizard switch us around? And why weren't Syrreth and Ferreth affected?"

"Flew around that cloud, we did," Syrreth told them.

Sarah turned to look at the zweigelan's left head. "What cloud?"

"The one that placed itself directly in your path," Ferreth informed her, as though he was doing her a favor. "We suspected you did not notice. Flew around it, we did."

Pryllan glared at Syrreth. "Why would you not warn us?"

"Moved quickly, it did," Syrreth recalled. "Small and wispy, it was. Only because we were flying somewhat lower were we able to avoid it."

"Why would he do this to us?" Sarah asked. "What possible good can come from us being shifted around like this?"

"He's neutralized us," Steve told her as he flew closer to the zweigelan.

"What?"

"Think about it. Pryllan didn't have her fire, but I did. At least I did until I ended up over here. You might be able to produce some flames but not nearly as effectively as I can. Then look at you. Your teleportation is far and away the most useful jhorun we have, only now you're me and can't use it. Pryllan has access to your jhorun but no knowledge of how to use it."

"Why bother with Pryllan?" Sarah countered. "He could have neutralized us by simply switching just the two of us. Why include her?"

Pryllan was watching and listening from her position in Syrreth's talons.

"Because she's a dragon," Steve answered, "and she's responsible for helping us get to our destination. We count on her for protection and transportation and now she cannot provide either. Whoever this wizard is, he knows what he's doing."

"Why not just kill us?" Sarah asked. She noticed that Pryllan was nodding. She must have wondered this, too.

Steve almost shrugged but thought better of it. "I don't know. Maybe he doesn't want any deaths on his hands? Maybe he has a sense of humor? Who can say? All I know is that this is a fine pickle we're in." He briefly glanced down at the passing forest. "What now? Do you really think Shardwyn can fix this?"

"He's a wizard, too. He might be a bit quirky, but I do have faith in him."

Steve lifted his massive head up and turned to look back behind them. "Well, shouldn't we return to R'Tal so we can get switched back?"

Sarah shook her head. "That'll take time. I think that's exactly what the wizard wants us to do. He's trying to stall us without really hurting us. I'm sorry to say he's succeeded. Brilliantly, if you ask me."

Steve scowled. Was that a trace of admiration in her tone? "So we're going to try and continue on like this? What if something happens? What if we need to defend ourselves? We're sitting ducks like this."

"What is a duck?" Pryllan asked.

"It's a bird," Sarah answered. She glanced over at her own body. "Well, it's a kyte to you. Likes to live near the water. It's easy prey for many predators. How are you holding up over there?"

"Are you asking if I am well? No, I am not well. Being this small is uncomfortable."

"And you think being this large isn't?" Steve countered

with a low growl. "We should turn back. I can't even begin to imagine carrying one of you in my hands. Claws. Whatever. I'd be afraid I'd crush you. I'm pretty much useless over here."

Pryllan fixed him with a stare. "You are now a dragon. You may not have your fire but all your other senses should be working just fine. Hearing, sight, and smell are all more advanced than any other creature here in Lentari. Just have a care with my body. I will want it back."

"I'll give it back as soon as the first opportunity presents itself," Steve vowed. "Oh, just to let you know, we don't have to go back to your nest just yet. I spoke with Kahvel. He blew off Rinbok's summons."

Pryllan's eyes widened with surprise. "He didn't."

"He most certainly did. He knows something happened to us, so he'll stick around to help with Pravara."

"Good for him," Sarah praised.

"Now that we don't have to make a detour," Steve said, "how close are we to the second zweigelan's den?"

"Close," Pryllan assured him. "We will be there shortly."

"They don't live too far from you, do they?" Sarah asked.

"I never knew," Pryllan admitted. "I am ashamed to say I don't know much about the zweigelans."

Twenty minutes later, Pryllan raised her left arm and pointed down at the distant ground. "Behold! It appears as though we are approaching our destination."

Steve looked down. A large rectangular glade was visible in the midst of the forest and was occupied by half a dozen dragons. Before any of the dragons on the ground could see that a two-headed dragon was about ready to land in the clearing, Steve and his less-than-stellar landing drew everyone's attention his direction instead. Nearing the ground, he pumped his wings hard to bring himself to a stop. However, as soon as he touched down on the ground, he tripped on an overturned log and stumbled nose first into the tall grass. Embarrassed, he rose to his feet and gave a sheepish smile to the other dragons.

"Wow. That stupid log just jumped right out of the brush, didn't it? I totally meant to do that."

"They are going to think I am a clumsy fool," Pryllan

moaned from somewhere behind Steve's body.

A red dragon with purple flanged wings approached. He was bigger than Steve. In fact, as Steve looked around the small clearing, every dragon there was bigger than he was. They had better be friendly.

"Pryllan? Are you injured? What kind of landing was that?"

The dragon knew him? Well, it knew Pryllan? That was just great.

"Ummm…" Inspiration struck. "Er, could you come with me? It'll be for just a second, I swear."

"Why are you talking like that?" the red dragon inquired, as he followed Steve to the far side of the clearing. "You must have hit your head after that dismal landing."

"Hey, bite me," Steve snapped back, annoyed. "You try to land in a body like this when you have no experience with it."

The red dragon cocked his head to one side and studied him. He stretched his neck over to Steve's head and gave a few sniffs, much like a dog trying to decide whether or not a stranger was to be trusted.

"You sound like Pryllan and you smell like her, but you don't talk like her and you certainly don't fly like her."

"It's because I'm *not* her," Steve confided to the red dragon in a low voice.

"Who are you?" the red dragon demanded. "What have you done to Pryllan?"

"I am here, Rhamalli," a soft voice called out.

Rhamalli blinked his eyes in rapid succession as his eyes scanned the glade. "Who speaks?"

Pryllan appeared by Steve's right rear leg, clutching Sarah's arm tightly as she still hadn't mastered the supremely difficult art of bipedal locomotion on her own.

"I do. Look down. I am Pryllan, but I am in human form now."

Spying the small human female next to the male, Rhamalli lowered his head to the ground and stared at the woman.

"Not possible," Rhamalli decided.

"Is he a friend of yours?" Steve asked, turning to look down at Pryllan. "Can we trust him?"

Pryllan nodded. "He is a friend, aye. We can trust him."

"Good. Rhamalli is it? My name is Steve. As I already mentioned, I am in Pryllan's body. Pryllan is in my wife's body. Sarah, my wife, is in my body."

Rhamalli stared at the three of them as though they had all lost their minds.

"Just forget about that for now, okay?" Sarah looked up at the red dragon. "We'll deal with returning to our rightful bodies after we deal with this curse. Can you tell us what's going on here? Why are there dragons milling about? I thought once you fell victim to this curse then you lose your desire to live and want to just hole up somewhere and die. That's what Rinbok wanted to do."

Rhamalli's eyes opened a little bit wider. "You spoke with the Dragon Lord? What did he say?"

"We told him what we knew about the curse and who's responsible for it."

Rhamalli's huge head nodded eagerly.

"When was this?"

"Several hours ago."

"That coincides with when we learned what was happening to us. The zweigelans are responsible. As it happens, one lives nearby. We are waiting for several more of our brethren so that we can finally drive the abomination away from here."

Syrreth unwisely chose this moment to poke his head out from behind Steve's body. Rhamalli caught sight of the zweigelan and gave a warning growl, so low and dangerous that Steve inadvertently took a step back. Without saying another word, Rhamalli advanced on Syrreth. Ferreth's head appeared moments later. Both zweigelan heads hissed with alarm and retreated behind Steve's body once more.

Steve's first reaction was to raise both arms in an 'easy' gesture, but in wyverian form, all that happened was both wings had snapped open, blocking the zweigelan from sight. Rhamalli instantly changed course and began stomping around Steve's wings to get the two-headed dragon. Steve urgently looked down at Sarah.

"Get his attention. Use my jhorun to stop this. Get mad. Point your arms up and blast your jhorun straight out through your palms. That should send out several jets of fire. Hurry!"

Sarah did as she was instructed, but only managed to generate two rather small spouts of flames that lasted no more than a few seconds. Thankfully, it was more than enough to draw Rhamalli's attention.

"Listen to me, Rhamalli," Steve implored. Once the huge red dragon looked his way, he continued. "Syrreth and Ferreth are helping us deal with this curse. Are they partially responsible? A little. Did you guys bring this upon yourselves by treating them as outcasts? Yes. I heard it myself. 'Drive the abomination out.' So you dragons are not without guilt here."

Rhamalli dropped his eyes to the ground. Steve nodded.

"You clearly know what I'm talking about. You want to drive the other zweigelan out of here? Listen to yourself! He's a dragon. You shouldn't harm or bully other dragons just because they're different. How would you like it?"

A commotion drew everyone's attention from somewhere behind them. Another three dragons had appeared in the clearing and were being heartily greeted by their companions.

Sarah scowled and crossed her arms over her chest. "You need to put a stop to this."

"I don't know if I can," Rhamalli admitted. "They are angry. They are all at stage two or three. Word has spread about the nature of the curse and who is responsible. It seemed the logical thing to do."

"Give us some time," Sarah pleaded, eliciting a low growl from Steve who didn't like to see himself with such an imploring look on his face. "Let us go to him."

"What do you hope to accomplish?" Rhamalli asked in a low tone. "The abom — er, zweigelan is angry and bitter. You will get no help from him."

"Perhaps," Steve told him. "But we still have to try. Where can we find him?"

Rhamalli told them where they could find the second zweigelan's lair. All they had to do was find the large fissure on the northwest face of Rhamalli's mountain, located less than a mile from where they were presently situated, and look for the place where the fissure had naturally widened. From what Rhamalli told them, they should look for this cave about halfway up the mountain.

The group looked east. Everyone could see the craggy peak that Rhamalli called home rising thousands of feet into the air. With a sigh, Steve watched as Syrreth and Ferreth took to the air. Sarah and Pryllan had elected to ride with the more experienced dragon, as Steve was certain his takeoff wasn't going to be pretty.

Desperately flapping his wings in an attempt to correct a dangerous tilt, as he unsteadily rose into the air, Steve tried to ignore the swelling panic in his chest. Why wouldn't his wings cooperate? Thank goodness he didn't have to worry about any passengers. He didn't know how Pryllan managed it. Trying to keep his wings extended and level while tucking his forelegs up tight against his body, and using his tail as a type of rudder were beyond him. Way beyond him.

"Not very elegant," Sarah observed from Ferreth's palm, "but it'll do for now. Good job."

Steve grunted as he fought a burst of wind that threatened to tip him over. Forcing his left wing down, Steve clamped his mouth shut and kept the obscenities to a minimum.

"I thought Rhamalli said the nest was close," Steve complained loudly, fighting to keep up with Syrreth and Ferreth.

"It is." Sarah pointed at the approaching western face of the lone mountain. "The mountain is right there. You can't get any closer than that. We'll start circling it to see if we can spot this fissure we were told about."

"What do you want me to do?"

Sarah looked back at the large green dragon fighting valiantly to stay level and airborne.

"Just circle around up here. We'll find the lair and let you know when we do. Think you can do that?"

"I'll try."

Steve watched the strange two-headed dragon fly off to the north and slowly circle the rugged mountain. If Rhamalli called this home, then his cave had to be there somewhere. Suddenly his head lifted. He had just detected a scent so strong that he could almost see the pheromones in the air, leaving a trail for him to follow. In fact...

Steve blinked a few times. He did see a slight swirling mist dancing through the air like a ribbon in front of a fan. Intrigued, he followed the mist as it twisted and turned, drawing him ever closer to the mountain. Once he was within several hundred feet to the side of the mountain, the mist took an abrupt turn and headed straight down before disappearing into a large crack that extended from the top of the mountain to the base of the cliffs. He saw a ledge just outside of the widened section of the fissure, approximately half way up the mountain. Wait. A fissure? Wasn't this what Rhamalli was talking about? Didn't that mean he was looking at the zweigelan's lair?

Right on cue Syrreth and Ferreth appeared. They flew straight toward the fissure and landed on the ledge. Ferreth noticed Steve flying closer and nodded his head in acknowledgment.

"Is there enough room for me to land, too?" Steve asked as he passed by overhead.

Their two-headed companion jumped off the ledge and soared by him moments later.

"We can do it," Syrreth informed him. "You should be able to as well."

"I should be able to land there," he heard Pryllan say.

"While I appreciate your vote of confidence," Steve told the dragon inhabiting his wife's body, "my landings stink. That ledge looks small."

"Use your wings to slow your descent," Pryllan instructed. "The ledge is much larger than it looks. Once you're close enough, use your talons to grip the rock. Once your talons take hold, fold your wings flat against your back lest you injure them on the side of the mountain. I would prefer you return my body to me in the same condition as when I left it."

"What if I start to fall?"

"Then push off from the mountain and fly away."

"You make it sound so easy," Steve accused.

Pryllan shrugged. "Because it is."

"Uh, huh. Can you walk around yet without falling over?"

Pryllan fell silent.

"I didn't think so," Steve continued. "You take flying for

granted. What seems easy to you is damn near impossible for me. Just like walking is for you."

"I concede the point. Do be careful."

"Yep, I hear you. I think I got this. Hold on, I'm going to give it a try."

Steve's wings wavered as he inched closer and closer to the ledge in front of the widened fissure. Syrreth was right. Up close, it was easily twenty feet wide and perhaps fifty feet long. Dark discolorations were seen scattered all across the ledge.

Pretending he was a small aircraft coming in for a landing, he kept the runway in his sights and dipped his wings to bring himself closer. It took several attempts but Steve finally managed to land on the ledge. He folded his wings as Pryllan had instructed. Proud of his accomplishment, Steve checked the area to see who might have witnessed his heroic feat.

"Nicely done!" Sarah called to him from within Syrreth's clutches.

A grin appeared on Steve's face, which unfortunately looked like a ferocious snarl on Pryllan's. "Thanks!"

Within moments Syrreth and Ferreth had executed a perfect landing and was standing next to him. Sarah covered her nose with her hand.

"What's that smell? It's horrible!"

Steve's gaze darted about the area. The dark splotches he had seen from the air turned out to be decomposing carcasses of dead animals. The grisly piles of matted fur and bones were everywhere: in front of the cave, shoved into crevasses, and, as they all peered into the dark smelly cave, they could see the remains of at least three more animals lying just inside the cave entrance.

Steve snorted. The odor was almost overpowering his keen sense of smell. "Wow. That'll clean out your nasal passages."

Sarah turned to look up at the zweigelan. "Zweigelan number two? What are their names?"

Syrreth shook his head. "Unknown. We were never close."

They all waited and listened. Dead silence. Not even birds

or insects.

"Maybe he's not here," Sarah whispered.

Steve's nostrils flared. Even though the scent of decay was strong and threatening to overpower everything else, he could still detect the unmistakable aroma of another dragon. He didn't know how he knew it, as he hadn't ever smelled this scent before, but he knew this body had. It was time to listen to what Pryllan's body was telling him.

"No, he's in there."

Sarah turned to look up at him. "How do you know?"

"I just do. I can smell him."

"Good Lord, is he dead?"

Steve cast his powerful gaze into the cavern and scanned the interior, seeking out the darkest corners of the cave. There, fearfully crouching in the darkest deepest corner, was the second zweigelan. This one was silver with black stripes running across its chest. It looked like a cornered, frightened cat. There was no way it was going to come out peacefully.

This one, Steve noted, was just as long and sinewy as Syrreth and Ferreth, but had longer, almost stretched out faces. It was the first dragon Steve had ever seen that didn't have some type of twisted, spiraled, or straight-as-a-poker horns protruding from their skull. He watched the left head look nervously toward the entrance of the cave.

"We are not dead," a sinister voice hissed out at them, "but if you do not leave us alone, you *will* be."

"Come on out of there," Sarah called out to the zweigelan. "We're friends. We're not going to hurt you. We need to talk to you."

"You are no friend to us," the voice hissed back with annoyance. "Leave us be!"

"What do we have to do in order to prove we're sincere? We aren't here to hurt you."

"We haven't left the cave in several weeks," the voice angrily responded. "Not safe, it is."

"Why isn't it safe?" Sarah asked, confused. "Do you feel your lives are in danger?"

"The outside is not safe for us."

Sarah looked at the closest rotting carcass. "Because of

all these dead animals? I can't say that I blame you. They smell really nasty. We just figured they were remnants of your meals."

"Left for us to consume, they were," another voice chimed in. "Tainted and unsafe for consumption, they are."

Sarah automatically took several steps away from the rotting remains. "Tainted? Are you sure?"

"They are laced with deadly herbs. Another effort to drive us out, it is. They were dropped here in the hopes we would become drugged. Failed, they did."

Sarah was appalled. "That's horrible! We would never do that! We just want to talk to you."

"No human ever wants to 'just talk'," the second zweigelan informed her.

"How do you know I'm human?"

"Because I can see you."

"Then can you also see that I'm not alone?"

"Traveling with another human is not reassuring," the zweigelan haughtily informed her.

"What about the dragons? What about Syrreth or Ferreth?"

"All the more reason to remain concealed. Go away."

"We must confer with you," Syrreth called out.

The silence was practically deafening. Then they heard movement as the second zweigelan emerged into the daylight.

"What are you doing here?" the zweigelan's left head hissed.

"Trying to break the curse," Syrreth answered.

"What have you told them?"

"All that I know."

The hornless zweigelan began pacing in what little room remained on the ledge. Sarah, Pryllan, and Steve were all ignored as the two zweigelans angrily eyed one another.

"And that's why we don't include you, brother. You're weak."

"Shame on you!" Sarah instantly snapped out. "He's doing what is right!"

The second zweigelan ignored her. That is, until Steve stepped up beside her and cleared his throat. In his dragon body, it was the equivalent of giving a fairly loud roar. Syrreth and Ferreth, who had started to hang their heads, instantly jerked them up and twisted around to watch Steve glare at the second zweigelan.

"Not bad," Pryllan murmured quietly to herself. Sarah immediately smiled but was able to return her face to neutral before anyone could notice.

Their confidence returning, Syrreth raised his head and stared at the other two-headed dragon.

"We want to talk to the wizard who cast this curse."

The zweigelan's right head finally spoke. "I'm sure you do."

"This curse has ramifications that weren't realized," Syrreth continued.

"The Dragon Lord has apologized," Ferreth added.

The second zweigelan focused both of its heads on him.

"Hasn't apologized to us, has he? Even if he did, it doesn't change anything."

"We have pledged ourselves to ridding our dragon brethren of this curse."

The second zweigelan eyed Syrreth and Ferreth dangerously, but elected to say nothing.

"Why did you do this?" Steve finally asked.

"To bring about the downfall of all dragons."

"Well, Mr. Genius, you know you're a dragon, too, right?"

The second zweigelan stared at Steve for a full minute before finally shaking both heads and returning his attention to Syrreth and Ferreth. Steve glanced down at his wife, who shrugged as if to say the staring match between the two zweigelans would have to be resolved by them and them alone. After another minute the hornless one spoke.

"We are *not* dragons. We are zweigelan."

"You may not want to think so, buddy," Steve told the petulant two-headed dragon, "but you are. 'We are zweigelan.' Is that supposed to be some sort of catchphrase? You're a type of dragon. End of story, so let it go. Besides, didn't you say that you hadn't ventured outside in several weeks? You claim it's because you're afraid of these poisoned carcasses. I say it's because you can't fly. You're stage three, aren't you?"

"Am not," the hornless right head snapped back angrily.

"Prove it," Steve challenged. "Try to fly. Take off! Let's see what you can do. Oh! Better yet, try spitting out one blast of fire. Just one! I'm willing to bet all the tea in China that, ummm, that is, I'm willing to wager, er, *anything* that you've fallen victim to this curse. Syrreth and Ferreth here have become stricken, too. They can still fly, obviously, but they can't use their flames. That makes them stage two. You're stage three, aren't you? Just 'fess up."

Sarah let out an exclamation of surprise. She waved her arm to get Steve's attention. "Did you catch that? You mentioned stage three and they didn't ask what that was. They knew what it meant."

Both of the second zweigelan's heads growled angrily. Steve's growl in return instantly silenced everyone.

"You've fallen victim to this curse," Steve told them. "And from the looks of it, it happened a while ago, didn't it?"

"We've been feeling ill," the right head told them. "We haven't had a decent feeding in a while. It is related, we're sure."

"What are your names?" Pryllan asked. "What are you called?"

The hornless silver zweigelan fell silent as the left head returned Pryllan's frank stare while the right head kept an eye on Steve.

"No harm will befall you for just telling us your name," Sarah added as gently as she could. "I'm Sarah. She introduced the others. "

Both of the second zweigelan's heads stared at Sarah for a few moments before turning to look incredulously at the large green dragon, and finally returning back to Sarah to stare at her a few moments longer.

Sarah laughed. "I know what you're thinking. It's a long story."

"I am Dirgath," the left head said uncertainly.

"I am Tirgath," the right head said a few moments later.

Sarah nodded, pleased. "Dirgath, Tirgath, we're pleased to meet you."

"Okay you two," Steve began, drawing Dirgath and

Tirgath's attention, "we know you're at stage three. We know you know it, too. I'm pretty sure it wasn't supposed to happen that way, and judging from your reaction, I'd say that you'd agree. We really need to find this wizard. We have to nullify this curse. Will you help us?"

"We do not know where he is," Dirgath answered.

Steve cleared his throat. "Tirgath, what about you? Do you know where he is?"

Sarah crossed her arms over her chest and looked up at Steve with a look of sheer incredulity on her face. His face. It was still confusing to him. Steve noticed and frowned, causing Pryllan's body to bare her teeth.

"What? What's that look for? Stop looking at me like I'm a complete moron."

"If Dirgath doesn't know where the wizard is, why would Tirgath? I can't believe you'd ask that." Steve was embarrassed; his tail darted between his legs.

"Oh, don't do that," Pryllan pleaded. "I don't ever tuck my tail between my legs. Makes me look silly. Weak."

Steve wiggled his butt in an attempt to get his tail back to where it was supposed to be.

"Sorry. Damn thing did that on its own accord."

"You are a strange group," Dirgath observed.

"You ain't just whistling Dixie," Sarah muttered before her eyes shot open. "Sorry. I didn't mean to say that, either. It just slipped out." Sarah cleared her throat. "Back to the situation at hand. Dirgath, Tirgath, if you don't know where the wizard is, you have to at least know how to break the curse. Can you tell us anything to help us out?"

Tirgath eyed Dirgath with a look that dared him to answer. Both heads were silent. Syrreth and Ferreth let out a small roar of frustration and advanced on Dirgath and Tirgath, who actually retreated a few steps.

"How is this curse lifted?" Syrreth snapped, growing angrier than they'd ever seen him.

"We are not immune to the curse," Ferreth reminded him. "What affects the dragons affects us as well. Agree with my brother, I do. We must lift this curse."

Dirgath and Tirgath finally showed some nerve of their

own. Both heads straightened and their noses lifted high into the air.

"Don't turn on us, brother," Dirgath warned with a vicious growl. "You won't like the consequences."

Anger flared and before Steve knew what was happening, he had given a rumbling growl and was standing beside Syrreth and Ferreth. Pryllan, with Sarah's help, walked over to Syrreth and Ferreth's other side to show her support.

Dirgath's shocked expression mirrored its twin. Tirgath addressed Steve. "Stand beside them, do you?"

Steve nodded. "I do. He is a friend. He saved my wife's life just a little while ago, as well as Pryllan's. For that I will be forever indebted to them. You ask if I stand beside them? You bet your ass I do."

Syrreth was angrily staring at Dirgath, daring him to be the first to look away. Ferreth glanced left and gave Steve an appreciative nod of his head.

"Living like an outcast really stinks, guys," Steve said, consciously making an effort to stop growling. "I will admit there are some advantages to living alone but the disadvantages number more."

Hoping to alleviate some of the heavy tension, Sarah propped Pryllan up against Steve's right foreleg and took a few steps toward Dirgath and Tirgath.

"Let's assume you had no idea you'd be included with the others in the curse. Is it possible the third zweigelan specifically instructed the spellcaster to include you two? Does the third zweigelan hate you that much?"

"It is a theory that fits the facts," Pryllan observed, as she tried to take a few steps. She immediately stumbled and returned to her position against one of her former legs. "Both zweigelans have become affected, which indicates either the third member of their species wanted it that way or else the human wizard engineered the curse to include them."

"If that were so, it would mean the wizard double-crossed everybody." Steve looked down at Sarah. "So either the third zweigelan included them or the wizard did. How do we know which it is?"

Pryllan looked up at Tirgath. "Could the third zweigelan

be angry that you two were forced to join the Collective?"

Dirgath and Tirgath were silent.

"Have you been in contact with the third one?" Sarah asked as gently as she could.

"No," Syrreth answered almost immediately.

"She was asking Dirgath or Tirgath," Steve told Syrreth.

"Oh. My apologies."

Slowly, Dirgath nodded. "Aye. There is no harm in telling."

Sarah gave Pryllan an excited hug and almost knocked her over in the process. "I knew it! What did they say to you?"

"Only to be kept informed what she was doing."

Sarah stared at Dirgath in shock. "She?"

Dirgath and Tirgath both nodded. "Aye. Our third number is female."

Chapter 10 — Quid Pro Quo

A female zweigelan, huh?" Steve snickered loudly. "That explains so much." He detected a drop in the ambient temperature and risked a glance at his wife. "That is to say, it really explains nothing. I mean, what does it matter? Not one damn bit, that's for sure."

Sarah glared at her husband. "Nice save, genius. You're going to pay for that one."

Steve gave her one of his trademark sheepish smiles. "Sorry."

"Uh huh. Can we focus on the problem at hand?"

Steve nodded and looked at the petulant zweigelan. "Right. Dirgath, Tirgath, can you to tell us how to break this thing? You must understand that this is for everyone's sake. You want to be able to fly again? Spit fire? We're going to have to work together, whether you like it or not."

Sarah returned to Pryllan's side and helped her stand back up. "You two know more than you're letting on about this curse. You know how to break it, don't you?"

Tirgath nodded. "Aye."

Dirgath angrily growled at his twin. "Hold your tongue. We mustn't tell them anything!"

"I haven't told them anything," Dirgath insisted, issuing his own growl. "And I won't. They hope to sway me to their cause. It will not work." The left head swung around to stare at Sarah. "Did you hear me? Unlike others, I am not weak. *We* are not weak. We will never be tricked like Syrreth and Ferreth. We are much smarter than you will ever be!"

Sarah felt Steve's growl before she heard it. Deep and rumbling, it reminded her of one of those cars that drive by with the fancy audio systems blasting the bass way too loud. Putting a hand on Steve's foreleg, she turned to look up at Dirgath and Tirgath and gave them her most charming smile.

"You don't want to help, I can understand that. You've been wronged, no doubt about it. Rinbok Intherer is trying to make amends. Can't we compromise? Is there something you want that we might be able to provide which would entice you to help us destroy this curse?"

Dirgath and Tirgath were silent. For several minutes they just stared at Sarah, still as a statue. Was it considering Sarah's proposal?

Sarah knew that she had sparked their interest. When she hadn't been instantly shot down, she knew there was something that they wanted. All she had to do now was get Dirgath, or Tirgath, to tell her what that was.

"Listen, if we get you whatever it is that you want, will you help us break the curse?"

Dirgath shook his head. "No."

Steve scowled. "So much for that."

Sarah held up a reassuring hand and patted Steve's right foreleg again as she looked up at him.

"Hold on. Don't give up on me just yet. Dirgath, you say you won't help us. Will you tell us *how* to break it? Will you tell us what we need to do?"

Dirgath and Tirgath retreated into their cave and began a heated argument. Apparently, the zweigelan was intrigued by Sarah's suggestion of a compromise. Several minutes later the cave fell silent and Dirgath and Tirgath emerged back into the daylight. Before either head could speak, Steve cleared his throat.

"You want to be excluded from the Collective," Steve guessed. "Am I right?"

Both Dirgath and Tirgath gave him a condescending look. "That's a given," Dirgath sneered.

"That is the price for us to even consider this proposal," Tirgath agreed.

"Agreed," Pryllan quickly said.

"Can you speak for Rinbok Intherer?" Sarah asked Pryllan in a hushed tone.

"Since the welfare of my species is at stake, and since he is unable to be here in person, aye, I will speak for him."

"And if he doesn't go along with this?"

Pryllan frowned and bared her teeth, which on Sarah's face looked as though she had just tasted something awful.

"Kahvel will persuade him. And before you can ask, aye, I can and *will* persuade Kahvel if necessary."

Sarah smiled. It worked for her. They both returned their attention to the second zweigelan.

"The price for us to disclose the secret which would break the curse is beyond your power," Dirgath continued.

"If you get whatever it is you want," Sarah interjected, "then will you help us break this curse?"

Both Dirgath and Tirgath shook their heads no.

Undaunted, Sarah pressed on. "If you won't help us, will you at least tell us how to break the curse?"

"We will tell you," Dirgath began, "how to defeat the curse if…"

"And only if," Tirgath continued, "you return what is rightfully ours."

Sarah smiled triumphantly. So they did want something. Perfect. "Something was stolen from you? Well, that's a start. What was it?"

"Our Heart."

Sarah blinked a few times and cocked her head. Of all the things they could have asked for this wasn't anywhere on the list. "I'm sorry?"

"Our Heart," Tirgath repeated.

"Ummm, someone stole your heart? You mean someone broke your heart? Like a potential mate?"

This time it was Dirgath and Tirgath's turn to blink in confusion. Sarah turned to look at Steve. "I think I'm missing something here."

"Someone stole your heart?" Steve asked them, looking first at one head and then the other. "Physically stole it?"

"Aye. We want it back."

"Describe your heart," Pryllan suddenly said. "What does it look like?"

"It's red," Dirgath supplied helpfully.

"You don't say," Steve muttered under his breath.

"It's twisted," Tirgath added.

Steve nodded. "I can believe it."

"It sparkled radiantly in the sun," Dirgath added with a far-off look in his eyes.

"Aye, it did," Tirgath recalled.

Confused, Steve turned to Sarah and Pryllan. "We are on totally different pages here. I thought he meant a physical heart."

Sarah tsked her disapproval. "Of course it's not his physical heart. How would he still be alive if his heart was literally stolen? He must be talking about something else."

Exasperated with the lack of a straight answer, Steve turned to the second zweigelan. "This heart of yours. Describe it."

"It's red, and…"

"Yeah, yeah, we know," Steve snapped. "What else could it be called?"

"A ruby."

Surprised, Sarah glanced up at Steve, who seemed equally shocked. This 'heart' was a ruby? Well, at least rubies were red. But twisted? What was that supposed to mean?

"Did you say that this ruby was twisted?" Steve asked, as if reading her mind. "Literally?"

Dirgath nodded and made a circular motion in the air with one of his talons. "Aye. Twisted."

"How can a ruby be twisted?" Steve wondered aloud.

"Gems come in many forms," Pryllan told them. "While

I have personally never heard of a twisted ruby before it doesn't mean they don't exist. They—Syrreth, Ferreth, have you something to say?"

Their zweigelan, as everyone had started referring to them, was staring straight down at the ground and trying not to attract attention.

"We have nothing to add," Syrreth softly mumbled.

Steve shrugged and returned his attention to Dirgath. "So who stole it? Someone you know?"

"We do not know who took it," Tirgath heatedly exclaimed.

"How long ago was it taken?" Sarah wanted to know.

"Many centuries ago," Dirgath answered. "Our favorite gem, it was."

Tirgath nodded. "Unique and special, it was. We want it back."

Dirgath gazed at their group with a neutral look. "Find our Heart and tell you how to break the curse, we will. Do not bother us again unless you have what rightfully belongs to us."

With that the zweigelan retreated back into their cave with their heads held high.

Steve glanced at his wife and then down at Pryllan. "Well, at least they'll consider helping us. We just have to find this damn gem. How are we supposed to do that? Especially when it was taken several hundred years ago?"

Sarah shrugged. "I'm not sure."

Pryllan tilted her head up to check the sun's position in the sky. The western horizon was slowly fading from blue to orange. There was less than an hour of sunlight left.

"I would like to return to the nest. I would like to see Pravara."

Steve rose to his feet and extended his wings. He hastily turned to the side, accidentally brushing one of the tainted carcasses. It fell from the ledge and clattered noisily down the steep slopes before dropping out of sight. Steve stretched his long neck out over the ledge and looked down at the distant ground. He slowly turned his head and studied the rocky ledge.

"Okay, here's what we're gonna do. As a gesture of goodwill, we are going to get rid of these carcasses. I'm going to—"

"Ew!" Sarah exclaimed. "I'm not touching those things! Gross!"

"What I mean is, I'll get rid of the remains. Syrreth, Ferreth, since you're the only one who can, I need you to go hunting. Find something for Dirgath and Tirgath to eat. You heard them. They haven't eaten anything in a while."

"Why should we?" Ferreth snapped. "No one would do that for us."

"No one would have done that for you *then*," Steve clarified. "Now you'd have all the help you'd need, including Pryllan, Kahvel, myself, Sarah, and even Rinbok Intherer. You have the opportunity to come to their aid. Will you do it?"

Syrreth looked at his twin. "Aye, we will."

Ferreth bristled with annoyance. "I haven't agreed to…"

"Aye, we will," Syrreth reiterated, eyeing his twin. Ferreth wisely withdrew his objections.

Once their zweigelan had left, Steve began flexing his wings. Sarah and Pryllan pointed out carcasses and Steve swept them over the edge until every cranny was free of poisoned remains. Once they were sure they had removed everything, they waited for Syrreth and Ferreth to return.

Fifteen minutes later the zweigelan landed on the ledge with a strange animal dangling from Ferreth's jaws. It had black fur, a really long neck, and short stubby legs. Sarah thought it looked a little like a llama with tiny legs.

Steve inspected the cave's interior with his superior wyverian vision and saw that the second zweigelan was watching them. It had seen the kill and was drooling so much that a small pool of saliva had formed underneath them. It was hungry alright!

"Dirgath! Tirgath! Dinner is served. It's perfectly safe. Bon appetite! We'll be back once we find this ruby of yours."

When it became clear that neither Dirgath nor Tirgath were going to touch the kill until everyone had left, Sarah and Pryllan were scooped back up by their zweigelan. Within moments they had become airborne and were heading southeast. Steve leapt off the ledge and instantly stretched out his wings. He let out a groan of pure ecstasy as a gust of wind caught his open wings and pushed him up. Within moments he was flying next to Syrreth and Ferreth, more confident of his flying abilities.

This was fun! Pryllan was incredibly lucky that she could do this whenever she wanted. Well, any dragon could for that matter.

No, they can't, a small voice corrected in his mind. *Not unless this curse is lifted. The plight of the dragons is hopeless.*

No, it's not, Steve argued to himself. No one should have to give this up. Flying through the air like this was the ultimate thrill! He would be sorry to give it up!

Maybe you wouldn't have to, the small voice persisted. *Maybe you could stay like this forever.*

Steve snorted. As a girl dragon? Never. He didn't care how cool it was. Why would he think that? He wanted to return to his body. He wanted to return to his normal life. He wanted to be with Sarah. That's what mattered. That's what was important.

You could remain a dragon forever, the voice insisted. *It could happen. Just say the word.*

A realization washed over him. That serene sense of calm vanished like a puff of smoke. Steve suddenly realized who the evil source of the small voice was.

You think I want to remain this way? You think I want to give up my life and keep these scales? You're a bigger dumbass than I originally gave you credit for.

He felt a brief flash of anger before it vanished and that calm, peaceful feeling returned to his mind.

Just say the word, my friend, and I will see to it you remain a dragon for the rest of your days. You would like that, wouldn't you? It's your heart's fondest desire!

If you're going to kill me, then kill me, Steve angrily thought back at the wizard. *The problem is, you and I both know you won't do it.*

Really? You have no idea what I'm capable of.

You're capable of a lot of things alright, Steve agreed, *but murder isn't one of them.*

How can you be so certain?

Because you would have done so already. Be a royal pain and nuisance? Sure. You have that down pat. But to kill someone in cold blood? No. You won't do it. You've got the power to do it but you won't. So for that, I'm grateful.

Irritation flittered through his mind. For now, the wizard was at a loss for words.

Back to the problem at hand. Yes, being able to fly is great, Steve reluctantly admitted. A brief victorious sensation washed through him. But then anger once more coursed through his veins. *You want me to say the word? Okay, I will. In fact, I'll give you three: Kiss. My. Ass.*

Clearly the renegade wizard had exploited his lack of attention and slipped inside his mind. How could he stop it? Then his mind took the guesswork out and his mental senses were turned off, like the flip of a switch. The anger he felt from the wizard vanished immediately.

Steve growled. If the wizard was able to get into his mind when he was daydreaming then he'd have to warn the others.

"Guys, no daydreaming. Don't let your minds drift."

Sarah looked over at him from Ferreth's claw. "What? Why?"

"Because I heard a little voice in my head encourage me to stay as a dragon forever."

Sarah stared at him. "Okay."

"It's because I was thinking how cool it was to fly." Steve related the mental conversation he'd experienced.

"You said that? To a wizard who has already done this to us? Are you crazy? What if he retaliates? What if he tries to kill us?"

"He has had ample opportunity." Steve shook his head. "I don't think he wants to kill anyone. Seriously mess them up, sure. But kill? Apparently not."

Sarah was furious. "How many times have I told you NOT to provoke a wizard? You never know what he's capable of doing."

"Sorry. If I talk to him again, I'll try and keep it cordial. Would that suffice?"

"Is he going to talk to you again?"

"Not if I can help it. So that's why you need to stay in control of your senses at all times. Apparently if you start to zone out, like I did, then it makes you more susceptible to him."

"What does 'zone out' mean?" Pryllan asked.

"Well, it means if you're just alone with your thoughts and you're not really paying attention to what you're doing."

"We dragons meditate all the time."

"Can you sense when someone else invades your mind?"

"I know when I'm sharing senses with you. Is that what you mean?"

Steve suppressed a chuckle. "Umm, not exactly. You initiate the connection. What if someone else initiated it for you? Would you be able to tell if someone came in? Uninvited?"

"I would like to think so."

"Just remember Anghorus," Steve reminded her. "He somehow lost control and was taken over by that wizard."

"Your point is taken," Pryllan admitted.

A short flight later, they were nearing the mouth of Pryllan's cave. Pravara flew up to greet them. She instantly sought Steve out and nuzzled against his dragon body. The problem, however, was that he still hadn't come in for a landing. It was all Steve could do to keep from tipping over so that he didn't knock Pravara over the head with his wings.

"Mother! I am so glad to see you!"

"Now wait just a second," Steve cautioned, as he pumped his wings to slow his descent. "I'm not your mother. She's over there, riding with Sarah."

Confused, Pravara turned to watch the zweigelan touch down just outside the cave entrance. She saw that each of the zweigelan's hands held a human. Pravara turned back to Steve, who executed his best landing yet.

"What are you saying, mother? I do not understand."

"Your mom is over there," Steve explained. "See the person getting out of Syrreth's hand? That's your mother."

Twin golden orbs stared at him for several long seconds.

"It's true, young one," a deep voice spoke. Kahvel emerged

from the cave and approached. "Thanks to the mischief of a human wizard, your mother is now inside Sarah's body, Sarah is inside of Steve's body, and Steve is inside of your mother's."

Dumbfounded, Pravara stared at Steve in shock.

"You're not my mother?"

"Sorry, squirt."

"My mother certainly doesn't talk like that."

"Nor will I ever," Pryllan agreed as she approached her offspring, standing on shaky legs.

Dragon and human stared at each other. Pravara gently sniffed Pryllan's human arm.

"You don't smell like Mother."

"You are more intelligent than this," Pryllan scolded. "If I tell you that I'm in human form, and you then attempt to prove it, you're going to be disappointed."

"How do you get back over there?" Pravara asked as she swung her head around to look at Steve.

"We need to go back to R'Tal," Pryllan informed the dragonlet. "The human wizard at the castle can restore us."

Kahvel snorted decisively. "Again? How many times will you be forced to go there?"

"About as many times as you sneak off to Nevir, I'm sure," Pryllan countered.

Kahvel instantly dropped his objections and wisely changed the subject.

"Was the other zweigelan cooperative?"

Steve shrugged. "If we get him some ruby that was stolen from him a long time ago, then yes, he was. If you're thinking that this is a serious long shot, like I do, then no, he wasn't."

"A ruby? That's all?"

"Not just any ruby," Sarah added as she frowned. "One that is apparently twisted. I don't even know what that means. Does it mean this ruby has been enchanted?"

Kahvel gave a slight jerk of recognition. Sarah was instantly at his side. "Wait! You know this jewel?"

"It seems to me that I have heard something about a spiraled ruby. Something recent. I'm trying to think."

Steve sat down on his haunches directly in front of Kahvel and cleared his throat. Kahvel looked up.

"I just wanted to say thanks again. You saved my life. I won't forget it."

Kahvel nodded. "As I told you then, you're welcome. I didn't want any harm to befall Pryllan or her body."

"He was the one who helped you learn how to fly?" Sarah asked. She gazed up at the huge golden dragon. "You have my thanks, too. That may be your mate's body but that's my husband in there. Thank you very much."

"Aye," Pryllan added. "As always, you have my thanks, too, my love."

"You're thankful, he's thankful, everyone's thankful," Kahvel grumbled, uncomfortable with the praise everyone was heaping on him. "Please let the matter drop. I am trying to concentrate. I am certain it will come to me."

Steve shook his head and chuckled. "Boy, that was really weird to see Sarah's body call Kahvel 'my love'. We seriously need to get straightened out before we all end up needing psychiatric help."

Pryllan looked at him. "I'm not familiar with…"

Steve held up a talon. "Yeah, we know. It's just a saying."

Sarah gave Pravara an affectionate pat before turning to Kahvel.

"Anyway, we'll head back to our house and leave you guys in peace. We'll be back in the morning."

Steve dropped his wyverian head and rested it on the ground as he stared at his wife.

"Dearest love of my life, pray tell, how willest thou accomplish such a feat if thine own jhorun does not answer to thee?"

Sarah swatted Steve directly on his snout. "Why are you talking like that? Dork. And what do you mean I don't have control over my jhorun? Sh–" Sarah managed to slap a hand over her mouth before she could finish the vulgar word. She glared at her husband. "Why do I get the feeling I would start swearing like a sailor if I didn't censor myself? You and I are going to talk about that filthy mouth of yours."

Steve laughed so hard he almost wet himself.

"So I guess we're staying here tonight? Kahvel, is that okay?"

Kahvel nodded. "You and Sarah may use the far corner of the cave. Do try to be quiet. If Pravara cannot sleep because of you, then you get to keep her entertained."

"Does she have a problem staying asleep?"

"Not if she isn't disturbed."

"Ah, got it. We'll be quiet."

"Thank you. Please perform your, shall we say, *personal* ablutions outside."

"My what?"

"Ablutions. Bodily functions."

"Oh. Right."

"Thank you."

* * *

"What was that?"

Sarah bolted straight up from her position on Steve's wing, warily eyeing the sleeping dragon her husband had become. She glanced around the quiet cave. Judging from the increasing levels of light streaming in from the front of the cave, sunrise was only moments away.

Sarah yawned and stretched her back. It had been her husband's idea for her to sleep on his wing as the springy leather turned out to be an excellent hammock. Kahvel, following Steve's suggestion, invited Pryllan to do the same, which she gladly accepted. Sitting upright and gently rocking back and forth, Sarah wondered if she should try and get some more sleep. She sighed. The analytical part of her brain had been awakened and once that happened, she'd never be able to get back to sleep. So what had awakened her? She thought she had heard an animal growling. Was it Kahvel? Maybe it was Steve's snoring? Who knows what a dragon sounds like when it snores. *If* it snores. Sarah giggled to herself. There was a question to ponder.

A loud rumble reverberated through her as Steve's body trembled with the noise. Steve was causing this? Had he eaten something that was disagreeing with him? Wait. Has he eaten anything? That's it! That was Steve's stomach. Her husband was hungry! Why hadn't he said anything?

Sarah paused. He hadn't said anything because if he had then that would mean he would have had to eat like a dragon. Dragons ate raw meat. Steve hated raw meat. He must be trying to wait until they were all able to switch back before he would eat a meal. What if he couldn't make it back to R'Tal? Would he have to hunt? Would he be able to kill an animal and consume it?

She shuddered. She wouldn't have been able to, that's for sure. She gently poked Steve's wing. "Psst."

Poke. "Psst, you awake?"

Silence.

Poke. "Are you sleeping?"

Silence.

"Don't ignore me. That's rude."

Steve cracked an eye open and stared at her. "Yes?"

"And good morning to you, too, Mr. Sunshine."

"Keep it down. Kahvel, Pryllan, and Pravara are still asleep."

"No, we're not," came Kahvel's deep voice. "We were just wondering how loud your snores would become. It was quite impressive, actually, seeing how Pryllan has never snored in her life."

"If I'm in her body then how is it that I snore?" Steve complained. "That's not fair."

Sarah flashed him a smug smile. "I told you it was all psychological."

"Zip it, lady."

"Make me, Dragon Boy."

"That's Mr. Dragon Boy to you, snot."

Sarah giggled. "Actually, it'd be Ms. Dragon Boy. Girl. Hmm, we'd better let that one go."

She put a hand on Steve's abdomen and felt his scales tremble for a few seconds. "Are you hungry?"

Steve nodded. "Yes, and that freaks me out."

Kahvel rose from his position on the ground and ambled over. He looked down at Steve's prone form, much like a scientist would do when inspecting an experiment.

"Why does being hungry concern you? If you hunger, then you eat. It's not a difficult concept."

"It's *what* he'd have to eat," Sarah clarified. "He doesn't like raw meat."

"That would present a problem," Kahvel agreed.

Steve looked over at Pryllan who was sporting Sarah's typical morning-hair.

"Pryllan, how long can you go without eating?"

"A week if necessary."

Steve exhaled loudly. "Whew, that's a relief."

"However…"

Steve's sense of relief evaporated. He looked worriedly at Pryllan. "What?"

"If you expend energy flying, which you have been doing, then you will consume your resources much faster. I predict if you choose to not eat until we arrive at the castle, then you will need to feed as soon as the switch is made."

Sarah held up a hand. "Actually, it will be you, Pryllan, who will need to eat. Once Steve is back in his own body then he'll be fine, provided you eat. You're going to be starving when you're returned to your body."

Kahvel nodded. "That's a very good point. Steve must eat."

Steve paled. He hadn't thought about what this would do to Pryllan's body; let alone what it would do to her once she regained possession of it. "Can't we have food waiting for her once everyone is back to being themselves?

"Can you guarantee sustenance will be made available?" Kahvel asked.

Both Steve and Sarah nodded. Kahvel appeared mollified.

"Very well. There is no time to lose. You must start your journey now."

Pryllan looked up at her mate then over at her offspring. "Will you two be alright until I return? What will you do if Rinbok summons you again?"

Kahvel shrugged. "I will decline a second time. My family comes first. Go. Do not concern yourself with us. See this human wizard and return to us in your natural form."

Pryllan nodded, and with Sarah's help, stumbled toward Syrreth.

Several hours later Sarah hopped down from Ferreth's open claw and stretched her back. She looked down at the steeply angled tunnel entrance and watched her husband and the zweigelan disappear down into the darkness. Once she was sure the two of them were settled in the large underground cavern provided by Kri'Entu, she took Pryllan's arm and helped her navigate the steep tunnel. At the mouth of the cavern, she paused.

"Wow, it's dark. Can someone light a torch?"

"That would be you, Hot Stuff," Steve's voice called out of the darkness.

"Oh, that's right. Hold on a sec. I should be able to do this."

Sarah felt along the walls just inside the cavern and found one of the many torches and its holder. She generated a small bout of flames and lit the torch. Taking the lit torch down from its holder, Sarah walked around the perimeter of the cavern and lit the others. Replacing the torch back onto the wall, she faced her group of friends. Even though Steve was on the far side of the cavern, she could still hear his stomach rumbling with hunger.

"Okay, wait here. I'll go get some help. Pryllan, Syrreth and Ferreth, I'll be right back."

Sarah ran back up the tunnel and emerged into the daylight. Blinking, she set off toward the castle at a healthy jog. The guards manning the northern gate waved her across without so much as exchanging a word of greeting. Continuing into the castle, Sarah navigated her way toward the Great Hall, where the king's and queen's thrones were situated. Luck was on her side, as both the king and the queen were there listening to a group of villagers petition for the right to hold a festival in Donlari.

Ny'Callé caught sight of her first. While the villagers conversed amongst themselves to haggle out the details of the Kri'yans' offer, the queen nudged the king and looked pointedly at her. Kri'Entu caught Sarah's eyes and nodded his head. He returned his attention to the villagers. The queen, however, sensing something amiss, kept watching Sarah.

Sarah mouthed *I need the king* to the queen. Ny'Callé

nodded and nudged her husband again. She bent forward and whispered something in the king's ear. This time Kri'Entu's head snapped up and looked over at her with a look of concern. Sarah nodded. She adopted what she hoped was an urgent look and maintained eye contact.

Kri'Entu nodded. He politely excused himself and told the villagers that the queen would continue to listen to their petition. He pointed back toward the heart of the castle and mouthed *Antechamber*, to which Sarah nodded. Once the Antechamber's door was closed, the king turned to Sarah.

"Sir Steve, is all well?"

Sarah took a deep breath. "Where do I start? Let's see. For starters, I'm not Steve, I'm Sarah."

"Excuse me?"

"Pryllan is in my body, and Steve is in hers."

"Are you serious?"

"I'm afraid so, your majesty."

"How did this happen?"

"Ummm, remember the task you have Shardwyn working on right now?"

The king nodded. "To locate and identify the... Is the wizard responsible?"

Sarah nodded. "Yes. We need to be returned back to our own bodies as quickly as possible. Steve is hungry. And, being a dragon, he really doesn't want to eat like one."

Kri'Entu nodded. "Understood."

The king walked over to his desk and pulled out a gold device from one of the drawers. He tapped on the surface a few times and waited. Within moments Shardwyn's wrinkled face was peering back at him.

"I'm sorry, your majesty," Shardwyn instantly began, "but I'm having difficulty locating him. You have to give me more time. Just as soon as I find something then I'll let you know, I promise."

Kri'Entu looked up at Sarah. "Are they in the cavern?"

Sarah nodded.

"Shardwyn, report to the dragon cavern at once. Bring everything you need in order to nullify a spell which has switched several people around to different bodies."

"What was that, your majesty? Did I hear that correctly?"

"You did. Be there in five minutes."

The king snapped the device closed and returned it to his desk.

"We do have one additional favor, Your Majesty."

"Of course. What is it?"

"Steve is hungry, which is why he won't eat. As soon as Pryllan is returned to her body then she's going to face the same dilemma."

The king pressed something on his desk. The Antechamber's main doors opened. A guard poked his head in.

"Your majesty?"

"Notify the kitchens. We have a hungry dragon we need to feed. Take as many men as needed. Gather as much meat as you can and head to the northern orchards. Is that understood?"

Not showing the slightest bit of surprise at the unusual request, the guard bowed and closed the door.

"Have you made any progress?" the king inquired.

Sarah fidgeted. She really wasn't supposed to confide in the king in any way. So far they had skirted the edges of truthfulness, and if she wasn't careful, she'd end up breaking her promise to the Dragon Lord.

Kri'Entu smiled. "They say that the *right* way to do things is always the exact opposite of the *left*."

Sarah was confused. "I'm sorry?"

The king picked up a bottle of ink with his right hand. "I am the king, you know."

More confused than ever, Sarah nodded.

The king switched the ink bottle to his left. "Just as I am when I visit different villages on the back of my dragon steed."

Sarah's brow furrowed. "No, you don't."

The ink bottle switched to his right hand. "You're right, I don't." The ink bottle passed to his left hand. "I didn't know your husband had ridden the zweigelan. You never told me."

Comprehension dawned. Sarah took the ink bottle and held it in her right hand. Whenever the king had said anything while the bottle was held in his right hand, he spoke the truth. While in the left, a false statement.

"I understand."

She passed the bottle to her left hand. "Yes, of course, Steve loves riding that two-headed dragon. He said it is his favorite thing to do in the whole wide world."

Smiling, the king nodded. "Have you made much progress?"

Sarah tossed the bottle to her right hand.

Kri'Entu nodded.

"Do you know what will resolve the situation our allies are facing?"

Sarah tossed the ink bottle up into the air but caught it with her right hand.

"Is there something you must do?"

Another toss, caught by Sarah's right hand.

"Is there something we can do to help?"

Sarah hesitated, then tossed the bottle into the air again and caught it with her right hand.

The king thought a moment. "There is something to be done but you're not sure what that is."

Another right-handed toss.

"You have to find the wizard."

Sarah tossed the ink bottle to her left hand. Kri'Entu's eyes widened. "That surprises me. Let me try again. The wizard is involved but you're not looking for him at the moment."

The bottle was tossed back to the right hand.

"I see. Is there an object you're looking for?"

The bottle was gently tossed up into the air and caught right-handedly.

"Seeing how you haven't said anything of what you're doing, if you were to describe what you were looking for, I would simply pass it off as fanciful rambling."

Sarah thought a moment. This was seriously pushing the limits of the oath she swore to Rinbok Intherer, but since their time was running out, she had no choice. She took a deep breath.

"How many rubies does this castle have in its treasury?"

Surprised, the king hesitated. "Rubies? Quite a few. Would

you like a ruby, Lady Sarah?"

Sarah smiled and nodded. "You know what? I would. I'd love to make a big pendant. The thing is, I'd love it if the ruby could be twisted."

"Twisted? A twisted ruby? Wait. Wasn't there something about … Of course! The hammer!"

It was Sarah's turn to be confused. "The hammer? What hammer?"

The king took Sarah's arm and guided her out of the Antechamber. Walking through the castle, the king guided Sarah back to the orchards north of the castle. Several squadrons fell into step behind them.

"What hammer?" Sarah asked again, lowering her voice. "What does a hammer have to do with a ruby?"

"The Narian power hammer," Kri'Entu answered. "It was discovered last year. I had a chance to study it when Master Breslin of the Kla Guur visited the castle. The hammer, you see, is powered by a ruby helix. This ruby is spiraled."

They reached the dragon cavern and immediately descended. The king signaled for his men to wait on the surface.

Shardwyn was already there and had set up several complicated devices. He was holding something that whirred and clicked next to Pryllan while simultaneously jotting notes in a small leather book. He looked up and smiled as both Sarah and the king entered the cavern.

"Lady Sarah! You appear to be a bit off today."

"Aren't you full of it?" Sarah automatically responded. She cursed silently to herself and gave Steve another dark look. She looked back at the wizard. "Sorry. I didn't mean that to come out as harsh as it did. That was Steve's fault, not mine."

"No harm done, I assure you. Now, let's see what we have here."

Leaving Shardwyn to his work, Sarah returned her attention to the king. "Now what can you tell us about this hammer?"

"The Narian power hammer is an ancient tool that was assembled last year when the dwarves went searching for Nar."

Sitting back on his haunches, Steve raised a taloned claw into the air. "What is Nar?"

"An ancient dwarven city," Kri'Entu answered. He hesitated as he suppressed the urge to smile at the comical figure the sitting dragon presented. "The hammer was assembled from various components that were found scattered across the kingdom. As it turns out, the helix, if I remember correctly, was found in the possession of a zweigelan."

Sarah turned to study Syrreth and Ferreth. "Do you know anything about this?"

Syrreth quickly shook his head no while Ferreth looked away.

The corners of the king's mouth turned upward into a smile. "Would you all excuse me? I will return as soon as I am able."

Kri'Entu walked back through the tunnel and disappeared from sight. Pryllan gave Sarah an inquisitive look, who shrugged in response.

Twenty minutes later the king was back, this time accompanied by the queen. Kri'Entu made the appropriate introductions and then stepped aside to join Pryllan at the side of the cavern. The queen walked up to the zweigelan and smiled.

"Hello. There seems to be some type of dispute about a ruby that may or may not be missing. What can you tell us about it?"

Syrreth answered first. "It belonged to us."

Ferreth's response followed immediately afterward. "Wrongfully acquired it, we did."

Sarah crossed her arms over her chest. "O-ho! Is that so? You neglected to mention that little fact, didn't you?"

Both zweigelan heads kept their gazes fixed on the ground. Steve was staring at their zweigelan.

"Wait a minute. I'm confused. Didn't Dirgath and Tirgath say it was stolen from them?"

"By Syrreth and Ferreth, I presume," Pryllan added.

"Is this true?" Sarah demanded as she walked directly under Syrreth's downturned face and looked up at him.

Syrreth was silent. Remembering that the queen's jhorun forced anyone in her presence to speak the truth, no matter how much they wanted the truth concealed, Sarah looked at Ny'Callé and smiled. "Perhaps you'd like to ask him."

Clasping her hands behind her back, the queen approached Syrreth and gazed up at him. While Syrreth looked back at Sarah with a tinge of defiance in his eyes, Ferreth avoided the queen's gaze as though her look alone would be poisonous.

"Syrreth is it?" the queen began, using calm, soothing tones. "Did you take this gem without permission?"

Syrreth hissed with frustration as he fought the urge to answer the question. He took a breath but before he could stop himself the answer slipped out. "Aye."

"Is this the gem that, I'm sorry, what were their names again?"

"Syrreth and Ferreth," Steve answered from his place against the cavern wall.

"Dirgath and Tirgath," Sarah corrected. "She wants the names of the other zweigelan."

"Oh."

"So," the queen continued, "is this what Dirgath and Tirgath want returned to them?"

Ten seconds went by as Syrreth valiantly fought the desire to reveal the truth. "Yes."

"Why did you steal it?"

Another pause.

"Because we wanted it."

"This creates a dilemma," Kri'Entu commented. "That ruby is part of the Narian power hammer. It's a priceless artifact. The dwarves are not going to want that hammer disassembled."

Sarah spread her hands. "What choice do we have? We need that ruby."

There was a sudden shimmer in the air. Sarah and Pryllan collapsed to the ground; with a huge thud, Steve also fell heavily to the floor.

Alarmed, both the king and queen looked worriedly over at Shardwyn, whose smile stretched from ear to ear. "Got it."

Steve got to his feet first. He held out his arms and gave them a quick shake. He wiggled his fingers. Moments later he held out his right hand and ignited a chaser. "I'm back! Nice job, Shardwyn!" He pulled Sarah to her feet and looked into her eyes. "Are you back in there, hon?"

Sarah nodded. She ran her hands down her body and sighed contently. "No offense to you, but I'm very glad to be back in my own body."

Steve grinned. "Trust me, no offense is taken."

"I need to feed." Everyone turned to look at Pryllan, who was just regaining her feet.

"They should be ready for you," Kri'Entu told her. "Please help yourself."

Pryllan rushed by them and practically flew up the tunnel to reach the surface. Within moments, they could hear the disquieting confirmation that Pryllan had found the large pile of meat just outside the tunnel entrance.

"I have a question," Ny'Callé began.

The king turned to her. "Go ahead, my love."

"If the hammer has the ruby you need and therefore must be disassembled in order to return the ruby to its rightful owner, can you not find a replacement?"

Kri'Entu was silent as he contemplated his wife's suggestion. Steve turned to Sarah. "Is that possible? Can we get another one?"

"I'm led to believe that it was most difficult to come by," the king finally answered. "I don't think that's a viable alternative."

"Who found it the first time?" Steve wanted to know.

"It's a long story," the king said with a smile. "A map of sorts appeared on a boy's back. This map led to the hammer's components, which in turn was used to find Nar."

"Who made the map to find the components?" Sarah asked.

Finished stowing his equipment back into their respective holders, Shardwyn approached the group. "That would be Kasnar, Master Maelnar's father."

Steve whistled. "Maelnar is already old. His father is still alive? Wow. How did Kasnar know where to find it?"

"That's part of the same story," Shardwyn explained once the king nodded his permission to continue. "Kasnar was held captive for centuries. In order to escape he learned to become a spellcaster and became quite good at it. He found the hammer parts and guided others to find them."

"Couldn't he do that again?" Sarah asked. "Could we ask him to see if he can find another ruby?"

Everyone turned to look at the king, who smiled. "That is an excellent question, Lady Sarah. Let us investigate the matter in a more comfortable setting. Perhaps the Antechamber?"

Steve glanced up at the domed cavern and then over at Syrreth and Ferreth.

"No offense, Your Majesty, but if we could do it here that'd be great. Two members of our party won't fit in the Antechamber."

Syrreth and Ferreth raised their heads to look at Steve. Once Syrreth was looking at him, Steve approached. "We won't tell Dirgath and Tirgath you two are the ones who stole their gem."

"In exchange for what?" Ferreth asked hesitantly.

"No exchange," Steve told them as he looked over at Ferreth. "The only stipulation is that you promise to tell them yourselves. Soon."

Thirty seconds later neither Syrreth nor Ferreth had responded. Steve cleared his throat. "Unless you'd like us to tell them now."

"Very well. We have an accord."

Steve pulled Mythrin from its holder and gripped it tightly in both hands. It was time to call in some favors.

Breslin? Are you there?

Several minutes of silence ensued.

Breslin? We need to talk to you.

Sir Steve? I am here. What is it?

Do you have some type of magical hammer?

The power hammer? Aye, I have it here. Why?

Does the hammer have a spiraled ruby on it?

Aye. What's going on?

We have a situation developing here. The rightful owner of that ruby wants it back.

The zweigelan?

Right, only not the one you're thinking of. That zweigelan stole it from another zweigelan and now that one wants it back.

That is most unfortunate. The ruby is now part of a power hammer, for which it was originally intended.

I know that, and you know that, but… Hmmm… Any way I can get you to come here so we can talk about this?

You are serious? You need the helix?

No, we need the ruby.

The ruby is *the helix.*

Oh. Then yes, we need the helix.

Is Lady Sarah there? Please have her come get me.

Where are you?

I'm on my way to the Borahgg Council Chamber. I'll meet her there.

Thanks, my friend.

Of course.

Steve turned to Sarah. "Could you go get Breslin? We need to tell him what's going on."

"We're not supposed to tell anyone else," Sarah reminded him.

"I know that. You know that. However, the ruby has been located and the present owner is a friend of ours. If there's any hope the ruby will be returned to Dirgath and Tirgath then we have to tell Breslin what's going on."

"We should ask Pryllan what she'd like us to do."

"Bring the dwarf," Pryllan's voice spoke, echoing loudly through the cavern. "We must negotiate for the ruby's return. That much is clear."

"Damn, you have good ears," Steve commented as he glanced up at the domed ceiling above their heads. "Are you almost done up there?"

"I just finished. I'll rejoin you shortly."

Sarah shrugged. "Once Rinbok throws a temper tantrum after he learns everyone has discovered their predicament, don't go pointing the finger at me. I'll be right back."

Once Sarah vanished, Steve turned to Shardwyn. "So how'd you fix us? Was it easy?"

Shardwyn smiled, which caused his wrinkles to deepen in his face. "It was just a matter of knowing which enchantments he used. Ultimately it was a combination of three spells. The first was … Would you like to know which spells they were?"

Steve shook his head. "Not really. You learned what they were and nullified them, which returned us to the right bodies. For that, you have my thanks, although I will miss flying."

"I will NOT miss trying to move around on only two appendages," Pryllan quipped as she emerged from the tunnel. "How someone is supposed to maintain their balance for an indefinite amount of time without four legs on the ground is beyond me."

Steve looked up at the huge emerald dragon and grinned. "Your biggest complaint about being human was the walking? Please. You had it easy."

Pryllan's nose lifted in the air. "I challenge any other dragon to inhabit a human body and do better than I."

Sarah appeared, along with three other dwarves. Pryllan recognized Breslin, the dwarf she had spoken to before. The other two were older than Breslin, and one looked so old it appeared as though he could collapse at any moment.

Breslin, Maelnar, and Kasnar introduced themselves to those they didn't know, be it human or dragon. Only one person refrained from approaching Syrreth and Ferreth, and that was Breslin. He frowned as he glared at the zweigelan.

"I remember you, dragon. We've met before, under less-than-ideal circumstances."

Surprised by the vehemence in Breslin's voice, everyone turned to stare at the dwarf.

"He tried to kill me," Breslin explained to his father. "Myself and several others, including an underling."

Ashamed, Syrreth stared at the ground. Ferreth looked pointedly at Breslin and bowed his head.

"Regret our actions, we do."

Syrreth looked up. "We would never have harmed you."

"You could have fooled me," Breslin muttered under his breath.

"Will you accept our apology, friend dwarf?"

"Trust is earned," Breslin responded flatly. "Not bestowed. I will accept your apology but do not think for one second that all is forgotten, because it isn't."

Both zweigelan heads nodded. "We understand," Syrreth replied.

"Hope to earn your trust as we have earned the others," Ferreth added.

"Perhaps," Breslin told the two-headed dragon. "For what it's worth, I should tell you that our actions during our last encounter were done by necessity, not by desire. Do you see my grandfather there? Kasnar was held against his will. I needed this hammer in order to free him from his confinement. The only way to do that was to retrieve the jewel in your possession."

Both of the zweigelan's heads stared at the youngest dwarf and didn't say a word. Breslin finally smiled and looked over at his father. "I think they are still mad at me."

Maelnar's curiosity was piqued. "Why?"

"I solved their riddle."

"It was a lucky guess," Ferreth grumped.

"Zweigelans love to ask riddles," Breslin explained as he caught his grandfather's confused expression. "Either you answer the riddle or they rob you of all your things." He turned back around and looked up at the two-headed dragon. "You two should select a more difficult question. I first heard that riddle when I was a wee lad."

Once more Syrreth and Ferreth lifted their noses into the air. Giving the zweigelan a speculative look, Maelnar strolled over to Steve and Sarah and gave them each a hug.

"Sir Steve! Lady Sarah! I am glad to see the two of you again. I don't suppose that you, or someone else, can tell us what's going on?"

Steve pointed down at the unique hammer on Breslin's belt. He had noticed the handle was carved with various designs and had spotted a flash of red from the head of the hammer. Seeing his interest, Breslin pulled the hammer from his belt and rotated the head so everyone could see the ruby embedded within. Steve walked over to get a closer look. He tentatively held out a hand to see whether Breslin would let him inspect the hammer up close. Breslin surprised everyone by placing it down, head first, on the stony floor. Breslin eyed the group and winked.

"Trust me."

Steve bent to pick up the hammer, shocked to discover it

weighed over fifty pounds.

"Oomph, what's this thing made of? How are you supposed to wield this thing?"

Breslin easily took the hammer from Steve's hand and spun the handle in his grip, as though it weighed no more than a claw hammer from back home. He handed it to Maelnar, who did the same thing. Maelnar then handed it to Kasnar, his father. The ancient and fragile dwarf took the hammer in his hands and easily held it up to his eye level and looked hard at the ruby. Then he grasped the hammer by the head and held it out, handle first, to Steve.

Thinking someone was playing a trick on him, Steve quickly took the hammer and grunted with surprise as his arm was forcefully yanked down.

"Okay, I'll bite. What's with this thing? How are you guys able to hold it?"

"What if they're just stronger than you?" Sarah asked in all seriousness.

Steve spun in place and frowned at his wife. "Really. Even Kasnar?"

All three dwarves burst out laughing.

"I'm sorry, Sir Steve," Maelnar said as he wiped his eyes, "the hammer can only be wielded by one with Narian blood in their veins. We are all of Narian descent, so the hammer is active for us but inert for anyone else."

Kri'Entu approached Kasnar and bowed. Kasnar returned the bow.

"Master Kasnar. You found the components to this hammer, including the ruby, correct?"

Kasnar nodded. "Aye."

"Do you think you can find another one?"

"Not without a spell. The spell necessary to find all the pieces took me several years to write."

"What if you're searching for just one piece?" the queen asked. "Like another ruby? Is that possible?"

"You really intend on returning the ruby to this wretched dragon?" Kasnar exclaimed. "How do you know he didn't steal it from someone else?"

"We don't," Steve told him. "Where he got it or how he

got it is irrelevant. The fact that he wants it in exchange for helping us is what is important."

"What's going on?" Maelnar demanded as he turned to look at the king. "What's with all this secrecy? Can you not tell us? Are we not allies?"

"Very well," Pryllan's voice spoke, startling everyone into silence. "I will tell you. Do not blame the humans. This is our problem and Rinbok Intherer wants it to remain that way; however, that is no longer possible. A solution to break the curse is now available."

Maelnar looked at his son, who shrugged. "Curse? What curse?"

"The wyverians have been struck down by a curse brought on by someone we have wronged. We can no longer spit fire. We have lost our Collective. Many of us have lost the ability of flight."

Kri'Entu snapped to attention. "This is the dilemma that the dragons are facing? Why did you not say something before? We are allies! We are willing to help!"

"Rinbok Intherer knows this," Pryllan explained. "He is proud. Too proud, if you ask me. He doesn't want our problems becoming known, so he swore us to secrecy."

"What does the ruby have to do with it?" Breslin asked as he stared at his hammer.

"This curse came into being through the direct actions of those we wronged: the zweigelans."

Everyone turned to stare at Syrreth and Ferreth, who once again decided to count the many bumps on the floor.

"There are three zweigelan," Pryllan continued. "Syrreth and Ferreth have already accepted responsibility for their role and are now helping us rectify this atrocity. The second zweigelan has informed us they know more about the curse and will reveal what they know if, and only if, a certain gem is returned to them. As you might have guessed, it's a spiraled ruby.

"We have also learned that the ruby in your power hammer was stolen from the second zweigelan by Syrreth and Ferreth a long time ago. It must be returned to Dirgath and Tirgath or the dragons are doomed."

Silence ensued as everyone, including Maelnar and Kasnar, looked at Breslin then down at the hammer still resting on the floor. Breslin retrieved the hammer and turned to face his father.

"How do we get this thing apart? We have to give the ruby back."

Maelnar laid a hand on his son's shoulder. "You're talking about the only Narian power hammer in existence, my son. Are you sure you want to do this?"

"The dragons are our allies, too. This hammer is just a thing, Father. The dragons need our help. I will not turn my back on them."

Gratitude swelled within Pryllan's chest as she listened to Breslin speak about upholding the pact between dragons and dwarves. He was willing to sacrifice his priceless relic in order to return Dirgath and Tirgath's prized jewel. She didn't know how, but she vowed she would repay Breslin and the dwarves for their kindness and generosity.

As she sat silently in the dark, contemplating how to adequately express her gratitude, she saw Sarah tap Kasnar on the shoulder. When the ancient fellow turned, Sarah squatted down low and smiled at him. Kasnar returned the smile.

"Ah. Lady Sarah, is it? What can I do for you?"

Sarah looked over at Breslin, Maelnar, Steve, and the king, who were huddled together to see about disassembling the hammer. The queen, not wanting to be left out, joined Sarah just as she looked back at the dwarf's wrinkled face.

"How difficult would it be to find another one?"

Kasnar blinked with surprise. "Another hammer? Incredibly difficult."

"No, not the entire hammer. Just the jewel."

"The spell itself wouldn't be too terribly difficult, my dear, as I have long ago memorized the spell I wrote to locate an inanimate object. I don't have a suitable map to reference, however. I cannot ask the spell to pinpoint the location of another ruby without having a point of reference to draw upon."

"We have many maps," Kri'Entu hastily added as he looked up. "You are more than welcome to use any of them."

"Do you have a quiet place where I can work?"

The king smiled. "I do, indeed. Please follow me."

Shardwyn suddenly held up a hand. "Master Kasnar?"

Kasnar and the king stopped to turn and look at the wizard.

"My apologies, Your Majesty," Shardwyn began, "but I was wondering if I might be able to watch Master Kasnar at work. I am fascinated by layered spells and would love to watch an expert at work."

A huge smile split Maelnar's face. "Never once have I heard him call anyone expert, Father. You should let him tag along."

"An audience matters not," Kasnar told them. "If I allow you to remain by my side, you must promise to keep silent unless spoken to, is that understood?"

Shardwyn refused to look at Maelnar. "Perfectly."

"Why don't we call it a night here?" Steve suggested. He took Sarah's hand in his own and pulled her close. "I think we could all do with a rest."

Pryllan shook her head and clicked her fangs angrily. "I cannot. Kahvel has informed me that Rinbok has summoned him yet again. I know not why he is always called away. I assure you, I will find out why the Dragon Lord has taken such an interest in him."

Steve's eyes traveled up Pryllan's long curved neck and he studied her reptilian face. She looked exhausted.

"So you need to take care of Pravara, is that it? That's a long flight. You wouldn't make it back until the middle of the night."

Pryllan sighed and looked down at her rider. "Agreed; however, there is no alternative. The journey must be made."

Pryllan watched Steve pull his baldric around until he could reach his sword's scabbard and the many small pouches sewn onto the leather surface. He pulled two crystal discs from separate pockets and handed them to Sarah.

"I should've thought of this sooner. Think you can do it?"

Sarah took the proffered disks. "Yes. I'll go get her. Wait for me."

Steve nodded. "I'm not going anywhere."

Sarah vanished. Kri'Entu stared at him. "Where did she go?"

"To bring Pravara here."

Surprised, Pryllan looked down at Steve. "Sarah is bringing Pravara here? That would … That means…"

"That means it'll save you a trip north," Steve finished for her.

For the second time that night a strong sense of gratitude washed through her. Pryllan felt her already tired wing muscles go limp as parts of her overtaxed body began to shut down.

Moments later Sarah and Pravara appeared. Sarah had wrapped her arms around Pravara's abdomen, something she had been wanting to do for a while now, and was gently whispering words of encouragement to the young dragon. Pravara's golden eyes were closed.

"You can open your eyes now," she gently told the dragonlet. "We're here."

Pravara cracked an eye open and scanned the area. She saw her mother nearby and rushed to her side. "Mother! I was just teleported!"

Pryllan smiled down at her offspring. "Aye, you were, young one. Did you find the experience agreeable?"

Pravara nodded her head enthusiastically. She sniffed the air as several unknown scents were detected. She saw Steve and Sarah, and then saw three more humans standing nearby.

"More humans!"

Pravara bounded over to the king and brought her nose to within inches of his face. She inhaled his scent and then moved to the queen, followed shortly thereafter by an inspection of Shardwyn.

Pryllan was mortified. "Pravara! Respect the humans' privacy! You don't need to get so close. You could detect their scent from where you were."

Crestfallen, Pravara slunk back toward her mother.

"No harm done, I'm sure," Shardwyn assured the mother dragon. "I am quite sure young Pravara will find many different scents on me."

"As for us," Kri'Entu added, "you shouldn't find any scents at all."

"Speak for yourself," Ny'Callé chided, eliciting snickers and giggles from the others present.

Kri'Entu's face colored in a rare bout of embarrassment. He cleared his throat. "That is not what I meant. I mean…"

The queen put a finger on his lips. "We are all tired, Entu. Let us do as Sir Steve suggests and retire for the day. We will reconvene tomorrow morning."

Shardwyn bowed. "By your leave, Your Majesty, I will accompany Master Kasnar and see if I can be of any help."

"I doubt it," Maelnar muttered.

"I heard that, dwarf," Shardwyn accused.

"As you were meant to, wizard," the dwarf returned.

"I will have provisions sent down here for everyone," Kri'Entu assured the dragons. "Be comfortable. Let us know if there's anything you require."

"How?" the queen asked, turning to her husband.

Kri'Entu nodded. "As I was saying, if there's anything you need, inform Sir Steve and he can inform us."

"Would you like me to take the two of you back?" Sarah asked Maelnar and Breslin.

Maelnar shook his head. "If my father stays, then I will stay, too."

Breslin nodded. "That goes for me, too."

The queen smiled at the two dwarves. "We will assign guest quarters for each of you. Come with us. Lady Sarah, I assume you and Steve will return to your house?"

Husband and wife nodded.

King and queen started walking toward the mouth of the cavern.

"Until tomorrow."

When the following morning came, Sarah returned the two of them to the cave to check on the dragons. Pryllan was curled up, still asleep. Syrreth and Ferreth were also asleep. Pravara, of course, wasn't. Her head perked up at the appearance of the two humans and she came bounding over to them. Steve chuckled. He wasn't sure a dragon could hop like a gazelle but Pravara certainly gave it a good try. The dragonlet had apparently been awake for some time and was eager for some company.

"Hello!"

Sarah smiled at the little dragon. "Good morning, Pravara. How are you today?"

Pravara's tail swished noisily back and forth over the rough surface of the stony floor. "I am well. And you?"

Pryllan cracked an eye and pinned her offspring with her gaze. Pravara froze as she looked up at the still form of her mother. Thankfully for Pravara, Sarah came to her aid.

"Pryllan, try to get some more sleep. We'll watch Pravara for you."

I am grateful.

Pryllan's eye closed and she went still.

Steve tapped her shoulder. "She said she was —"

"Grateful, I know. I heard her, too. Come on, let's let her sleep."

Walking up the steep slope of the tunnel, followed closely by the strikingly dark green dragonlet, Steve and Sarah emerged into the bright sunshine. A gentle breeze blew from the northwest, causing the nearby fruit trees to rustle lightly. Steve looked at the nearby castle.

"What do we do now?"

"Let's go check on Kasnar," Sarah suggested. "I'd like to get an idea how long this is going to take."

Steve nodded. "Sounds good."

They headed toward the castle, with the young dragon in tow. They had just stepped foot onto the drawbridge leading through the north gate and into the main part of R'Tal when half a dozen guards burst through a nearby door and blocked their progress. Several of the guards were still scrambling to put on their armor.

Steve ignited a hand and held it up. "Relax guys. Pravara is with us."

"You will vouch for this dragon, Sir Steve?"

"Yep. She's harmless. We're keeping an eye on her."

The guards hastily stepped aside, but watched, thunderstruck, as the small procession walked by. None of them had ever been this close to a live dragon. Too tempting to resist, one guard reached out to gently touch the passing dragonlet.

Navigating their way through the labyrinth of passages and corridors inside the castle and drawing gaping stares from everyone they passed, they finally approached the Antechamber. Two sets of eyes bulged as the guards standing on either side of the Antechamber's door snapped to attention. They nervously eyed each other and then pulled the doors open. However, there wasn't any way Pravara was going to fit through those doors.

Sarah glanced inside and saw Shardwyn and Kasnar sitting in plush armchairs laughing and smoking. Both had long elaborate pipes packed full of tobacco and were lazily puffing away. Kasnar was blowing perfect smoke rings while Shardwyn's were slightly elliptical in shape and appearance. Seeing no one else in the room, Sarah teleported Pravara to the other side of the door.

Shardwyn squawked with surprise at the sudden appearance of the dragon and jerked backward so violently that he tipped over his armchair with a loud thunk. Kasnar stared at the young dragon and held out a hand, to which Pravara inched closer to sniff.

"Greetings, young one," Kasnar said with a smile. "What are you doing in here?"

Sarah and Steve walked through the open doors. "She's with us," Sarah informed the dwarf. "Sorry, we should have given a warning or something."

"Nonsense," Kasnar told her. "I love dragons! I said this to my son last night and will do so again: this has to be one of the prettiest dragons I have ever seen!"

Pravara perked up and gazed adoringly at the ancient little dwarf.

"Looks like you just made a friend," Steve commented.

He walked over and held out his hand to help Shardwyn to his feet. "You okay there, buddy?"

"*What* is a *dragon* doing in here?" the wizard sputtered, staring disbelievingly at Pravara.

"We're babysitting. We wanted to see how Kasnar was doing, so we stopped by for a visit. Is there a problem?"

There was a commotion at the door as Kri'Entu strode into the room. "Good morning to all. Pravara, it is nice to see you again. Have you and your mother breakfasted?"

Pravara nodded her head. "Aye. Mother awoke once the meat was delivered. It was good! Mother went back to sleep, but I didn't. I wanted to explore, but she told me I had to stay in the cavern. That's when Steve and Sarah arrived."

Smiling, the king gave Pravara a friendly pat on her head and then turned to Kasnar. "I have news, my friend."

Kasnar, and everyone else in the room, turned their full attention on the king.

"The Kla Guur have located the vein of silver that contains the first gem and are rapidly closing in on it. The Kla Chanus are searching for the second but with no luck so far. However, they are close and should have it by the end of the day."

Steve stared incredulously at the king and then back at Kasnar. "You found another gem? Already?"

Kasnar smiled. "I remembered a great deal more than I thought I had. The difficulty was modifying the spell to use a different map. Thankfully that didn't take long, either. As it turns out, three more rubies exist. Two are subterranean. As you have just heard, one is in Kla Guur territory, and they are actively tunneling toward it as we speak. The second is somewhere within Kla Chanus territory and while progress there is slow, it is progress."

"And the third?" Steve prompted.

"The third is Topside," Kasnar told him. "It's near the human village of Verdayn."

"Verdayn's constable is searching for it now with a team of men," Kri'Entu reported. "All we have to do is wait to see who finds it first."

Sarah smiled at Kasnar. "You've been busy. Did you work all night?"

Smiling profusely, Kasnar nodded.

"You poor thing. You must be exhausted."

"On the contrary, Lady Sarah," Kasnar contradicted, "the satisfaction of knowing I have been useful again is all the energy I need to stay awake."

Maelnar and Breslin appeared and joined Kasnar. Each of the two dwarves selected a chair and jumped up onto it.

"Good morning!" Sarah said, brightly. "Did you sleep well?"

"We never went to sleep," Maelnar told her. "We kept my father company."

"He wanted to make certain I didn't mistreat Master Kasnar," Shardwyn informed them with a frown. "Which I didn't."

"Because we were there to chaperone," Maelnar fired back.

Shardwyn muttered something else but then fell silent as the king shot him a dark look.

Two hours later, not one but two glittering spiraled rubies sat on the table before them. The Kla Chanus were still searching for theirs, but the other two had been located relatively easily once they knew where to look. Breslin set the power hammer down on the table and gently turned it on its side so that everyone could see the face of the hammer with the ruby embedded in it. Steve joined him and stared at the magical tool.

"Does anyone know how this thing comes apart?"

Chapter 11 — A Crafty Curse

I don't see why you just don't give him one of those," Steve suggested again, pointing at one of the other two ruby helixes. "You guys have been trying to get that hammer apart for close to an hour now."

Maelnar looked up from his position by Kri'Entu's desk. "From what you have told me, lad, that dragon specifically requested this jewel. How do you think it will appear if you attempt to return the wrong gem?"

"Do you really think Dirgath or Tirgath could tell the difference?" Steve argued. "Because I sure can't."

"Do you want to take that chance, Sir Steve?" Breslin asked, without looking up.

"Twist that there," they heard Kasnar say, "and try pressing that right there."

"Nothing," Maelnar reported.

"What if all three of you touched the helix at the same time?" Shardwyn suggested.

"It only took one of us to assemble the hammer in

the first place," Breslin pointed out. He gripped the square counterweight and tried pulling it away from the main hammer head. "It stands to reason that it would only require one of us to take the blasted thing apart."

Kasnar let out an exclamation of surprise and held the ruby helix up into the air. "Hah! Got it!"

Without the centralized power source to keep the components of the hammer together, the heavy counterweight slid off the tang and landed with a solid thud on Kri'Entu's desk. Breslin hurriedly pulled the weight up off the wooden surface, but not before everyone could hear the telltale scraping of heavy metal across delicate wood.

Horrified, Kasnar and Maelnar leaned over to inspect the damage. There, marring the pristine surface of Kri'Entu's rare shadow oak desk, was a nasty inch-long gouge. As one, they turned to look at Breslin, who swallowed nervously. The youngest dwarf looked up at the king.

"I can fix that. Fear not."

"I will take you at your word, Master Breslin," Kri'Entu answered, trying desperately to keep a neutral expression on his face.

Kasnar handed his son the recently extracted ruby and reached for one of the others on the king's desk. He handed the second ruby to Breslin, who hastily reassembled the hammer and then touched the point of the spiraled ruby to the tiny divot that had appeared on the hammer's surface. The helix rotated on its own and embedded itself deep into the hammer.

Breslin plucked the hammer up off the king's desk and experimentally swung it through the air a few times. Grunting with satisfaction, and detecting no differences from the last time the hammer had been assembled, Breslin slid the ancient tool back into its place on his belt. Breslin ran a fingertip over the gash on the desk and cringed. While he and Kasnar inspected the damage, Maelnar approached Kri'Entu and bowed. He held out the spiraled ruby.

"I believe this should be returned to its rightful owner."

The king reverently took the jewel and studied it. The ruby sparkled radiantly, as though a sunbeam was shining on it. Kri'Entu nodded. With its unique corkscrew shape and its many facets covering the jewel's surface, he could see why the zweigelan coveted it so much. He stretched out an arm and handed the gem to Steve, who took it and repeated the king's inspection.

"It's magnificent," Kri'Entu announced.

Maelnar retrieved the last unused helix from the desktop and handed it to the king. "Here. You hang on to this."

Kri'Entu's eyes widened. "This is a priceless artifact from a dwarven civilization that has been gone for many centuries. It belongs to the dwarves."

"Your constable found it," Maelnar reminded him. "It was within an hour of your village. I'd say that makes it yours. Take it as a sign of goodwill between our two people."

"Well played, dwarf," the king murmured, unable to hide his smile.

"Thought you might like that," Maelnar whispered back. "The only way we'd ask for this back is if we found enough components to assemble another power hammer. Seeing how I don't think that will happen, you shouldn't worry about it."

"What if the Council doesn't approve of this gift?" Kri'Entu asked, as he was well aware of dwarven laws.

Maelnar hesitated and then stroked his beard. "You may be on to something. You're right. That kind of gift can only be authorized if sanctioned by another member of the Council. Let's hear it. All in favor?"

Both Kasnar and Breslin, still inspecting the damage to the king's desk, raised their right arms and spoke at the same time. "Aye."

Satisfied, Maelnar turned back to the king. "There you have it. Now let us worry about repairing your desk."

The sounds of distant barking echoed through the halls, followed shortly by the rapid clicking of doggie toenails on marbled floors. Mikal, Crown Prince of Lentari, only son of the king and queen, and former charge of Steve and Sarah, bolted inside the Antechamber with a victorious whoop. Peanut, the Pembroke Welsh Corgi he had acquired while staying at Steve and Sarah's house for a number of years, barreled inside and slid to a halt as the feisty canine detected a myriad of new scents.

Mikal threw on the brakes and slid the remaining few feet over to his father's desk as soon as he saw that they weren't alone. He looked at his father and was instantly embarrassed. "Father. I apologize. I did not know you had company."

Kri'Entu leveled a serious gaze at his son before his complexion softened. He turned toward the dwarves and held out an arm in his son's direction.

"Kasnar, this is my son, Kre'Mikal. Maelnar, Breslin, I believe the two of you have already met?"

Maelnar nodded and smiled at Mikal. Breslin approached the tall youth and they each grasped forearms. "Master Mikal! A pleasure to see you again, lad! You are growing faster than a patch of albino lichen."

"Growing faster than what?" Steve wanted to know.

"It's a lichen from our caves. Can double its size in just about a day's time."

"Oh."

Mikal turned to Steve. "What are you two doing here? I didn't know you were coming for a visit. You should have told me!"

"It was a spur-of-the-moment decision," Sarah told him after he gave her a hug.

Mikal then noticed the far corner of the room where several chairs had been pushed aside and something large and green was curled up, sleeping.

"What's that?"

"Peanut is about to find out," Steve said with a smile as he watched the curious corgi inch closer to the sleeping form of the dragonlet.

Pravara's tail suddenly twitched. Peanut let out several soft warning woofs. The corgi was clearly still undecided about the strange form.

A golden eye cracked open. It spotted the inquisitive dog and opened wider. Pravara uncurled her body and stretched, keeping her front torso down and elongating her rear legs as high as she could go. With her muscles loosened, and her curiosity awakening, Pravara looked down at Peanut, who stared up at the young dragon with equal fascination. Peanut yipped a greeting and adopted the same pose: head low and rear high in the air.

She may have been a dragon and Peanut may have been a dog, but Pravara knew when another young creature wanted to play. She mimicked the small animal and wiggled her hind end as a signal she was a willing playmate.

That was all Peanut needed.

With a joyful bark, the corgi darted to the far side of the Antechamber and found a suitable place to hide in the narrow space between the wall and the pedestal a suit of armor was standing on.

Mikal snapped his fingers in an attempt to get the dog's attention. "Peanut! Get out from there! You're going to get me into trouble!"

Pravara followed the dog and the inevitable happened. With a mighty crash, the armor hit the ground and fell apart, sending gauntlets and greaves in opposite directions.

Steve was horrified. What was Pryllan going to say? "Pravara! Come on out of there. Now!"

Her hiding place discovered, Peanut headed for the next nearest hiding place, beneath one of the plush armchairs. With her short stubby legs she was able to wiggle under the chair and disappear from sight. Moments later, Pravara dove headfirst under the chair. It flipped as though it weighed no more than a feather. Unfortunately, the chair's occupant catapulted through the air and flew almost as far as the chair did. Through tears of laughter Sarah was able to catch Shardwyn with her jhorun before he could hit the ground.

"Your timing is impeccable, milady," Shardwyn told her once solid ground was under his feet. "That could have ended badly."

Smiling, Steve turned to Pravara. "Okay, before someone gets hurt, we should…"

Peanut bolted again, this time heading straight for the door. Even though a corgi's legs were some of the shortest in comparison to other species of dogs, she could really move when she wanted to. Peanut was out the door and running down the corridor before Steve could open his mouth.

In a flash, Pravara was in pursuit. However, the dragonlet

had forgotten she could not fit through the door. A loud crunch emanated from the Antechamber as the door frames, wooden they may be, refused to grant passage to the much larger dragon.

Intent on chasing down the small animal, Pravara tried to back out of the mangled door frames but only proceeded to wedge herself in even tighter.

"Stop wiggling," Sarah told the dragon. "I'll get you out. Just a second."

Pravara vanished from the open door and appeared moments later on the other side. She was free! Once more she was off like a shot, tearing across the hall in a mad dash to catch up with Peanut. The corgi glanced behind her, saw the rapidly approaching dragon, and yipped with excitement. She loved to be chased.

The ruckus echoed noisily through the hallways as those people unlucky enough to be in their way were bowled over. Servants, suits of armor, a few tapestries, and even a squadron of palace guards were knocked out of the way as corgi and dragon came barreling out of nowhere and vanished just as quickly.

Back in the Antechamber, Steve's horrified face slowly swiveled to look at the king's. "I am so sorry, Your Majesty."

Mikal grinned. "Suddenly I do not feel so bad."

The king eyed his son before turning to Steve. He waved him off. "No apologies. It's not often we can say we entertained a dragon *inside* the castle. Not that we would want to do it that often, but if you could direct them outside, it would be much appreciated."

Sarah grabbed her husband's arm. "We'll head them off at the pass. Thanks again for all of your help, Your Majesty."

Kri'Entu nodded. "Think nothing of it. Say nothing of it, either."

Sarah teleported the two of them to the Great Hall. All was quiet. No signs of destruction there, so either they had got there first or else the two playmates had deviated course and were causing chaos somewhere else.

"Do you see them?" Sarah asked as she looked around the vast chamber.

Steve shook his head. "No. I don't hear anything, either, which is odd. We should be able to..."

Steve paused as he heard the familiar clicking of a dog's toenails scrambling madly over a hard surface. Then he heard Peanut let out a few more playful barks. They still couldn't see her. People in the Great Hall had ceased their activities and were beginning to stare around the room in search of the noise.

Peanut zipped between Steve's legs and ran for the huge double doors leading out into the castle's keep.

"That little booger!" Steve exclaimed. "Where was she hiding? Where's Pravara?"

Sarah looked across the hall at Peanut, who was almost to the doors.

"If she's there, then Pravara should be ... Look out!"

Sarah teleported the two of them to the far corner of the room just as Pravara appeared. The little dragonlet was galloping across the floor just as fast as she could. Her large golden eyes were open wide with delight, clearly loving every minute of it. From across the Great Hall, Peanut slid to a stop and sniffed the air. She looked back at Pravara and faced the doors again. She shook her collar a few times before she finally lowered her rump into a sitting position.

Pravara slid to a halt right beside her. Mimicking her new friend, Pravara also sniffed the air.

What is going on in there?

Pravara paled. "Mother! I can explain!"

Steve and Sarah appeared beside them. Steve nodded. He had heard Pryllan's question as well.

Do you remember me telling you that we would try to arrange an introduction with Pravara and Peanut?

The little creature from your world. I do remember.

Consider them acquainted.

Is everything alright? I detect elevated levels of emotion from Pravara.

Let's just say she's enjoying her new playmate.

Understood. Do you have what we need?

Yep, I have it right here.

Excellent. We should go.

Would you like to say hello to Peanut?
I would. Can you bring it with you?
Her. I'll bring her with us.

Gathering up the squirming dog in his arms, Steve guided the strange group outside and to the northern orchards. Mikal, having finally caught up to the frolicking canine and wyverian, decided to tag along as he was intent on watching the reunion between Pryllan and Peanut. Pryllan had indicated she was coming Topside so they all waited at the mouth of the tunnel.

"Is mother upset with me?" Pravara whispered to Steve. "I know I should not have acted the way I did. I couldn't help myself. There aren't many creatures that would play with a dragon."

"She's not angry with you," Steve assured the little dragon. "She felt your excitement and wanted to make sure you were okay."

He gently set the dog down on the ground to give his tiring arms a break, but before he could hook a couple of fingers through her collar, Peanut bolted.

Cursing silently, Steve sprinted down the steep tunnel and emerged into the cavern just as Peanut slid to a stop in front of Pryllan. The corgi inched closer and waited for Pryllan to lean down and touch noses with her. Satisfied that an absentee member had rejoined her pack, Peanut yipped and proceeded to roll over on the ground.

"I do remember you, little one," Pryllan remarked, as she lowered her neck to the ground and sniffed the playful creature.

Pryllan kept her head at ground level and let the little creature sniff her body as Peanut familiarized herself with the peculiar scent of dragon once more. It was during this longer inspection of her former packmate when Peanut detected a second strange scent in the air.

The corgi's ears perked up. Her nose lifted. She slowly turned and saw another large creature watching her. Curious, Peanut ambled over for a cursory sniff but stopped as a second head lifted from the ground. Peanut blinked her eyes a few times as she studied the creature with two heads. What was it? Was it friend or foe? Two heads could only mean two potential packmates!

Barking excitedly, Peanut bounded toward the strange being and adopted her trademark playful dog pose. Her short stump of a tail wiggled back and forth as she waited for a response from the two-headed creature.

"She wants to play," Steve told Syrreth and Ferreth. "That's her way of inviting you to play a game."

"Play?" Ferreth repeated, as if unfamiliar with the word. "We haven't played for many centuries."

"There's a shocker," Steve muttered quietly to himself. "Well, here's your chance to have a little fun again. Go ahead, give it a try! Just don't take too long. We've got to be going soon."

Syrreth took a hesitant step toward the corgi. The sudden movement set the playful canine off. Peanut bolted. The mischievous canine darted forward a few feet, gave a few encouraging barks, and then turned tail and ran all the way back to Pryllan. Noticing that she hadn't been followed, Peanut repeated the invitation.

The zweigelan took a few more steps. Ten seconds later Syrreth was doing his best to keep an eye on the small dog as Peanut was now running laps around the zweigelan's long, sinewy body.

"I don't see it anymore," Syrreth reported as he twisted his neck as far as he could go. The dog had vanished from sight. "Where did it go?"

"That's why I'm asking you," Ferreth angrily responded. "I don't want to step on it."

"Neither do I."

Enjoying the impromptu game of hide and seek, Peanut peeked out from behind the zweigelan's tail and as Syrreth was bending around to check their hind end, Peanut darted out and ran toward the front of the creature.

"There it is," Ferreth exclaimed swinging around from the left.

"Where?" Syrreth asked, as he swung around to the right.

Peanut darted straight forward and ran between the zweigelan's front legs. Both intent on watching the dog, neither head saw the other coming.

WHAM!

"I can't believe we just fell for that," Syrreth complained as he gave his head a violent shake.

"Clumsy oaf!" Ferreth angrily exclaimed. "Watch what you're doing!"

"You two both hit each other at the same time," Steve nonchalantly pointed out.

Ferreth gave an exasperated glance at his twin and then straightened.

"We are done playing this 'game'. We should be off."

Steve nodded. "You're right. Let's go. Mikal, can you get Peanut for me?"

Mikal, who had been standing at the mouth of the cavern, was silently doubled over with laughter.

Steve approached and leaned toward the teenager.

"Pull it together. How am I supposed to keep a straight face when you can't? Get the dog, Mr. Chuckles."

Wiping tears from his eyes, Mikal called for Peanut, who sprang from her hiding place and reared up on her hind legs once she was in front of Mikal.

"That's a pretty girl. You showed those dragons who's boss, isn't that so?"

Peanut's enthusiastic barks echoed noisily throughout the cavern.

"They're waiting for you up top," Steve reminded Pryllan.

"Very well. Syrreth, Ferreth, let us be off."

The two dragons exited the cavern and headed to the surface. Steve and Sarah bid Mikal and Peanut farewell and clambered up Pryllan's back.

Several hours later, Pryllan flying northwest with Pravara and their zweigelan in tow, approached the far western shore of Lake Raehón. Rhamalli's peak was just ahead. Pryllan turned her long neck to her right and once more verified Pravara was alright. Her offspring had flown almost the entire distance on her own before tiring just south of their valley. Pravara had joined the two humans on her back and appeared content there.

Now, sensing the end of their journey, Pravara had leapt off her mother's back and was now flying alongside Syrreth and Ferreth, no doubt asking them more questions. The interesting thing, Pryllan noted, was that neither Syrreth nor Ferreth appeared to be objecting.

She turned her head even farther to check on Steve and Sarah. Both were sitting motionless with their eyes closed. "Steve? We approach Dirgath and Tirgath's lair."

Both humans' eyes snapped open. Steve yawned and stretched his back. "That was quick."

Sarah turned around to face him. "Were you asleep the entire time?"

"Hmmph. Of course not."

"Yeah, right."

The dragons landed on the small ledge outside the second zweigelan's cave without preamble. Steve and Sarah climbed down and faced the narrow cave opening.

"Dirgath! Tirgath! Want to come on out? We've got something you might be interested in!"

They could hear movement from within the cave. A few moments later the second zweigelan emerged. They stared at the group, barely noticing the dragonlet standing by Pryllan's side. Disinterested, Dirgath and Tirgath approached Steve. Both heads slowly lowered until they were less than ten feet away from him.

"Do you have our Heart?" Dirgath asked.

Tirgath, saying nothing, stared, unblinking, at Steve.

Steve reached into his right front trouser pocket and pulled out the glittering jewel. "Oh, you mean this?"

Dirgath and Tirgath looked excitedly at each other. "How do we know it is the right jewel?" Dirgath asked.

"It must be inspected," Tirgath answered. "Studied, it should be."

Steve walked brazenly right up to the second zweigelan and held out the jewel. "Here. You want to study it? Fine. There it is."

Steve tossed the jewel toward the two heads, hoping they'd be able to catch it. Tirgath deftly plucked the ruby helix from the air as it neared his head. He looked down at his open claw and studied the spiraled ruby as it gently rolled back and forth against his scales.

"This is the one!" Tirgath said excitedly. "Brother, look! You can feel its beat!"

Dirgath held out his claw and waited for Tirgath to pass it over. Once he did, the claw closed. Dirgath closed his eyes and waited. A few seconds later he opened them and smiled maliciously down at the humans.

"We expected so much more from you humans. You have given us our Heart back. Why should we tell you about the curse now? What leverage have you?"

Sarah stepped forward and smiled. She opened her hand to reveal … a sparkling ruby helix. Dirgath was silent as he stared at the gem in her hand.

"You didn't think we'd give you our only bargaining chip, did you? Not without a way to get it back. Now, let's talk about that curse."

Dirgath's claw sprang open. He checked his palm. It was empty. No gem!

"How did you get it back?" Dirgath wanted to know.

"Devilishly sneaky, it was," Tirgath agreed. "You are nothing more than swindlers!"

"No more than you!" Sarah hotly contested. "You speak of trust, yet you try to double-cross us the first chance you get! You want to know how I got it back? I'm a teleporter. You don't stand a chance in getting this from me."

Dirgath and Tirgath growled angrily and advanced on Sarah. Steve stepped forward, ignited his hands, and blasted two powerful jets of fire straight up into the air. It had the desired effect, stopping Dirgath and Tirgath in their tracks.

"By the way, my fire still works," Steve reminded them. "Try to remember that."

"As I was saying," Sarah continued, "let's talk about that curse. Since it's clear you two aren't to be trusted, let's begin with what you know about this curse."

"You return our Heart to us or we will tell you nothing!" Dirgath screeched.

Sarah turned to her husband. "We're getting nowhere. Let's go. We'll give this back to the dwarves."

"No, wait!" Tirgath frantically called. Dirgath growled with frustration. "We will tell you what we know. We will trust you to honor the deal."

"Why should we?" Sarah countered. "You obviously weren't planning on it."

"A foolish ploy," Tirgath admitted. "We haven't seen our Heart in many years. Desperate, we were."

"You'll get it back," Sarah promised, "but only when you tell us what we have to do to break the curse. Are you ready to talk?"

Tirgath nodded while Dirgath said nothing.

"We need both of your cooperation," Steve informed them. He flicked his burning hands out. "What's it going to be, Dirgath?"

The second zweigelan's left head came as close to pouting as any of them had ever seen.

"Very well," Dirgath reluctantly agreed.

"Before you begin," Pryllan interrupted, "there is something I need to tell both of you."

Dirgath and Tirgath looked over at the huge green dragon.

"Syrreth, Ferreth, this goes for you, too."

Surprised, Syrreth and Ferreth glanced at each other before also looking over at Pryllan.

"You will not be forced to join the Collective."

"That was already part of our accord," Dirgath sneered.

"And it will be upheld," Pryllan assured them. "Being invited to join the Collective is an honor. It should never be forced upon anyone. With that being said, you have our deepest apologies for forcing you to accept our culture as your own. Every dragon should be free to live as they see fit."

Dirgath eyed Tirgath, who in turned eyed Pryllan.

"Why do you say this?" Dirgath asked suspiciously. "Think you speak for Rinbok Intherer? You don't. You cannot say such things."

"This is what Rinbok Intherer told Syrreth and Ferreth, to make peace. The benefits of the Collective far outweigh the disadvantages, but it should be the dragon's choice whether or not to accept the honor. As such, our offer is withdrawn."

"What's she doing?" Sarah whispered to Steve. "Rinbok never said any of those things."

"Maybe she's communicating with Kahvel," Steve whispered back. "He could be telling her what to say."

"Since when does he speak for the Dragon Lord?" Sarah asked.

"He hangs out with Rinbok. If anyone would know what Rinbok Intherer would say, or how he'd behave in certain situations, it'd be Kahvel."

Just as Pryllan had expected, Tirgath began to complain. Bitterly. "You have no right to withdraw the offer."

"You said it yourself," Pryllan reminded him. "You don't want anything to do with the Collective or with any other dragons. You'll be allowed to live your life. In peace. Completely alone."

"We choose to remain," Syrreth announced. Ferreth nodded in agreement.

"Good for you two," Steve said, as he gave a thumbs-up to the dragon. Syrreth and Ferreth stared uncomprehendingly back at him.

"Why would you choose to remain?" Tirgath asked, both heads twisting to look over at Syrreth and Ferreth. "Once the curse is broken and the Collective restored, you'd be free to return to the life you had before."

"We don't want the life we had before," Ferreth said, in a voice so soft it almost went unheard.

Dirgath stared at Ferreth as though he was a mutinous traitor. "Why? Why would you stay?"

"Tired of being alone, we are."

"Have friends now, we do," Syrreth added.

"Friends? Pah! Zweigelans don't have friends. We don't need friends."

"They are my friends," Pravara announced.

The little dragon had been crouching low to the ground next to Steve for the entire time they had been talking with the second zweigelan.

"And mine," Pryllan added.

"Ours, too," Steve said. Sarah took his hand and nodded.

Dirgath and Tirgath fell silent as they contemplated this

sudden turn of events.

Sarah waved her arms to get Tirgath's attention. "Look, we're all friends now, okay? Let's move on. We have a curse to break. Here, Tirgath, open your claw."

Tirgath shifted his weight off of his front foreleg and then opened his claw. The ruby materialized on his open palm a few moments later.

"There, you have it back," Sarah told him. "Help us break this curse. What do we have to do?"

The smaller zweigelan fell silent. After a few minutes of awkward silence, Dirgath finally spoke. "We will tell you what we can."

Steve raised a hand. Sarah noticed and shook her head while mentally rolling her eyes. "Steve? What is it?"

"I have a question." Steve looked up at Dirgath. "If we hadn't found this ruby or been able to return it to you, would you have really not helped us? Even if it meant you'd never fly or spit fire again?"

"We would have helped," Tirgath admitted.

Steve looked over at the other head. "What? Really?"

Dirgath and Tirgath both nodded their heads. "We would have, aye."

"So why did you make us go through all that trouble to find that damn ruby?"

Dirgath gave him a wicked smile. "It is our favorite ruby, isn't it?"

Tirgath nodded. "It is. We wanted it back."

Steve sighed and rubbed his temples. Dragons. None of the fantasy books he had ever read made one mention of how stubborn or finicky certain dragons could be.

"Just tell us what you know. The third zweigelan. Did she come up with this curse on her own or did she ask this wizard fellow to come up with some type of dastardly deed?"

"Entirely of her doing, it is," Dirgath admitted.

"Did she know the curse would affect the other zweigelans?" Sarah asked.

Dirgath shook his head. "We do not believe she knew we would be stricken like the dragons."

Steve coughed a few times and cleared his throat. "Do you

think the zweigelan's inclusion with this curse is the wizard's doing or is this just some type of unplanned side effect?"

Sarah raised her hand. "I'd like to weigh in here."

Steve smiled. "Yes! The fetching young lady there has an opinion. You have the floor, milady."

Sarah curtsied. "Well thank you, kind sir. Dirgath, Tirgath, I have something I'd like to run by you."

The second zweigelan stared at her but didn't say anything.

"I think this wizard is smart. I think he's responsible for your involvement."

"How could you possibly know that?" Steve asked.

"Think about it," Sarah persisted. "No dragon has died."

"That we know of," Steve added.

Sarah looked over at the huge green dragon. "Pryllan? Has any dragon died as a direct result from this curse?"

Pryllan shook her head.

"Steve, you told me earlier that when the wizard tried to convince you to remain a dragon that you confronted him about having a conscience. Not a very ethical conscience, mind you, but a conscience nonetheless."

"So you're saying the third zweigelan should be affected, too?"

Sarah nodded. "Right, otherwise she set up this curse that way on purpose."

"So she can't fly or spit fire," Steve mused. "Finding her shouldn't be too difficult."

"She has remained concealed for centuries," Tirgath informed them. "If she wishes to remain concealed, you will never find her."

Steve scratched his head. "Refresh my memory, would you? If you know all about this curse, and what we need to do to break it, why do we need to find the third zweigelan?"

"Because she carries the wizard's talisman," Tirgath explained. He looked lovingly down at the ruby helix and then back at Steve. "All curses exist only because they are called into existence and linked to an inanimate object. Destroy the object and you destroy the curse."

"You know for certain she has this talisman? Did you see it? What does it look like?"

"We have not seen it," Tirgath replied. "We cannot tell you what it looks like."

"She said she had to keep it on her at all times," Dirgath added. He opened his claw and looked at his twin. "It's my turn to hold it."

Tirgath reluctantly passed the jewel over.

"As long as the talisman exists, the curse will be active."

Steve turned to Sarah. "That would suggest that if something happens to the female zweigelan then the curse could keep going, couldn't it?"

Sarah turned to look back at Pryllan, who shrugged. She approached Syrreth and Ferreth and slowly walked around them. The two zweigelan heads tracked her the entire time.

"What are you doing?" Syrreth asked, curious.

"You don't have any pockets," Sarah observed. "There's nowhere to hide this talisman thingamajig that I can see. So, if you had something precious you needed to keep concealed, would you risk hiding it on the ground?"

Dirgath snorted derisively. "She's too cunning and too intelligent to think that if she hid the talisman somewhere, it couldn't be found."

"Then she'd have to have it on her," Steve surmised. "But where?"

"Where would you hide something, Syrreth?" Sarah asked.

Syrreth considered. Then he considered some more.

"It must be on her," Ferreth finally answered once it became clear that Syrreth didn't have any ideas.

Sarah held up her hands in frustration. "Where? Somewhere on her person? What, maybe under a loose scale or something?"

Tirgath shook his head. "Unlikely. She'd be afraid of it falling out."

Steve started to pace. "I don't know, how about under her tongue?"

Dirgath answered him this time. "Too risky. She wouldn't risk accidentally swallowing it and then passing it out."

Steve stopped pacing and stared at Dirgath. "Ew. I was joking."

Dirgath stared at him, unblinking. "That wasn't funny."

"You need to lighten up."

Sarah turned to Pryllan. "Where would you hide something?"

The green dragon considered.

"And you didn't want it to be stolen?" Steve added.

Pryllan considered some more.

"Provided this talisman is small enough, I would find a way to attach it to the underside of a loose scale, or perhaps find a missing scale and have the talisman made to resemble that scale."

Steve sighed. "That means it would look like any other scale and you'd never know what you were looking at even if you happened to be looking straight at it."

Sarah turned to him. "What? That doesn't make any sense."

"Let's just agree that it makes our lives more difficult."

Sarah shook her head. "That's just one plausible scenario. We don't know if that's what she ended up doing. We need to find out what she did with it, whether she hid it..."

"She wouldn't have," Tirgath interjected.

"...or disguised it as something else and is hiding it in plain sight."

"How do we find out?" Steve asked.

Pryllan growled low and deep.

"We must find her. As soon as possible. I will lose my ability to fly at any time now."

"Where is she?" Steve asked as he turned to Dirgath and Tirgath. "Where can we find her?"

"She never told us," Dirgath answered.

"We'll find her," Sarah vowed. "Even if I have to teleport all over this kingdom, we'll find her."

Tirgath shook his head. "Impossible. She is way too cunning and clever. An expert at staying hidden, she is."

"She's been practicing for many centuries," Dirgath added.

"If she doesn't want to be found, she won't be," Tirgath assured them.

Sarah suddenly turned to face the second zweigelan and

smiled. "Then we must make her come to us."

Everyone looked over at her. Steve cleared his throat. "Umm, how?"

"We're going to set a trap."

"Dare I ask what we're going to use for bait?"

Sarah smiled. "I have an idea. We're going to need a little help on this one."

Chapter 12 — The Game is Afoot

Pryllan dozed lightly, resting comfortably in the cool shade of the warm summer day. She and Pravara had followed Steve, Sarah, and the two zweigelans from Dirgath and Tirgath's lair back to the valley floor and were now at the southern tip of the valley, bordering Anakash forest. While the humans and zweigelans conversed, mother and daughter decided to get some rest.

It had taken a little longer than she liked, as everyone had to wait while the second zweigelan carefully climbed down from their cave. They could have made arrangements to meet later in the day but Sarah had discreetly suggested that they all travel as a group and therefore just travel on foot. The silver zweigelan hadn't said anything, but Pryllan could tell it had been the appropriate thing to do as she could see Dirgath and Tirgath appreciated being included in the group.

The tall majestic pine trees cast plenty of shade, which the two dragons were taking full advantage of. Rustling leaves and a slight disturbance in the wind attracted her attention.

Pryllan gently sniffed the air. Myriad scents assailed her senses.

Pryllan cracked an eye open. A human had just appeared out of thin air. Ever since she had announced she had a plan to lure the female zweigelan out of hiding, Sarah had been mostly absent. Pryllan watched Steve approach the human female. They embraced. Sarah started gesturing toward the trees, then off to the east at more trees, and finally, straight at her.

Both of Pryllan's eyes opened. Yes, she saw that correctly. Both humans now appeared to be talking about her as even Steve had looked her way a few times. She activated her heightened senses but unfortunately, she had tuned in at the tail end of their conversation and hadn't been able to hear anything.

Pravara stirred and stretched. The dragonlet noticed Steve nearby and gamboled over to him. Sarah vanished just as Steve turned to see Pravara approach. He generated three fireballs and juggled them, much to Pravara's delight.

Several minutes later Sarah reappeared next to Steve. She looked over at Pryllan and vanished once more, only to appear directly in front of her. Sarah looked up at her, expectantly.

"Yes?" the large dragon inquired.

"I'm going to need your help, too, Pryllan."

"I fathomed as much. What would you like me to do?"

"I need you to bring Rinbok Intherer here."

Pryllan's full and undivided attention fell upon Sarah. "You want the Dragon Lord here? Why?"

"His role is crucial to this," Sarah explained. "We need him here. Better yet, get him here as fast as you can. Get him riled up. We need him to leave Nevir in a complete huff. The louder and angrier you can get him, the better."

Pryllan paled. "Is there anything else I can do that would be considered useful? Angering the Dragon Lord is not generally considered a wise course of action."

"I know that, Pryllan, but we need the female zweigelan to see him all agitated and anxious."

"You believe she's in the area?"

Sarah nodded. "Yes, I do."

"Why?"

"To keep an eye on Rinbok. Where I come from, there is a saying: keep your friends close but keep your enemies closer."

"Why would you want your enemies closer?" Pryllan asked, confused.

"It's because ... no, never mind. It's not important. If you can get Rinbok to go rushing out of his lair then the third zweigelan's interest should be piqued. She will follow."

"And if she doesn't?"

"We have a backup plan that's also in the works. If one plan fails then the other is sure to lure her here."

"What is the backup plan?" Pryllan asked.

"I need to keep that one secret," Sarah told her in hushed tones.

"You think she may be listening," Pryllan guessed.

"It's a possibility," Sarah confessed. "If she can hear us half as well as you do, we need to make sure we don't disclose anything that would give our plans away."

Pryllan looked over at Pravara before letting her gaze drop back down on Sarah. "What could I possibly tell the Dragon Lord that would make him leave his nest in that state of mind?"

Sarah shrugged. "Couldn't you make something up?"

Pryllan stared incredulously down at the human. "Like what?"

Sarah smiled and held out her hands. "I'm sure you can come up with something, Pryllan. You are a dragon. He's a dragon. There must be something you can say that will get him to follow you."

"You want him to follow me? To where?"

"Right here will do."

"I am confused."

"Trust me, Pryllan. This will draw her out into the open."

Pryllan looked at the young dragonlet sitting complacently by Steve's side. "What about Pravara?"

Sarah waved off her concerns. She turned to look back at Steve.

"Look at them. Pravara will be fine. Steve will keep an eye

on her for you."

Her list of objections exhausted, Pryllan reluctantly took to the air and headed northeast. What type of story could she possibly fabricate that would not only fool the Dragon Lord but incite him enough to warrant following her out of his cave? Could she lie convincingly enough to deceive the leader of all dragons? Just then she felt another presence in her mind.

What troubles you, My Love?

Kahvel! I face a dilemma.

Please elaborate. Are you in danger?

Not yet, but I will be if things do not go as planned.

What is going on?

I need to convince the Dragon Lord to follow me from Nevir in such a way that he appears completely agitated and reckless.

You're unable to tell me why?

I can tell you what I personally know, but you will find the explanation severely lacking.

Very well. What ideas do you have?

What about reporting a false invasion?

She felt her mate chuckle.

That is unlikely to succeed.

What about telling him we are being besieged by malwerns? They are despised. It could work.

Malwerns are despised, aye, but they are quite delectable. They are also winged. He cannot fly. You'd anger him, but it wouldn't incite a desire to leave the caverns.

Perhaps a new development for those stricken with the curse?

Such as?

I have no idea, Pryllan confessed.

Hmm, what else?

What about telling him more wyverians have become bewitched by the renegade human wizard?

Bewitched to do what?

Er, well, to do his bidding?

You must have your story thought out if your delivery is to be believed. Any hesitation would arouse suspicion.

What do you suggest?
I believe I can help.

A sense of gratitude toward her mate and his unquestioning desire to help overwhelmed her.

I appreciate your willingness to help, beloved, but unless you can think of a better story, I do not believe you can help me this time.

I know what will get him moving. What I am about to impart must be kept secret from all others, is that understood? That includes Steve.

Surprised, confused, and insanely curious, Pryllan agreed.

Very well, My Love. Listen carefully to what I am about to tell you …

* * *

Pryllan burst into Rinbok Intherer's treasure cave, deliberately out of breath. She scanned the immense piles of gold coins, jewels, and open chests in the cavern-sized treasure chamber. However, there were no massive green dragons with black striped wings in the immediate vicinity. She eyed the two largest mounds of treasure against the cavern's back wall. Each was large enough to conceal the Dragon Lord.

"My Lord! Are you in there?"

The deep rumbling voice of the wyverian leader echoed loudly around the cavern. "What is it?"

Pryllan flinched. Rinbok Intherer had appeared behind her.

"I have news, my Lord."

"Unless you can tell me the curse has been broken, then I am not interested."

Pryllan swallowed nervously. She never should have agreed to do this. "I believe you will want to hear this, my Lord."

"I have been listening to a myriad of complaints against the zweigelans and their involvement with this curse for hours. Unless you have something pertinent to contribute then don't bother me with trivial matters."

Rinbok Intherer turned to look longingly at his golden horde. His gaze lingered on one of the large piles of gold.

Pryllan held her breath. It looked as though the Dragon Lord wanted to hide inside his treasure again. Rinbok took a few tentative steps away from her, toward the far wall. Pryllan steeled herself and said precisely what her mate had instructed her to say.

"Valkira is in danger, my Lord."

Rinbok froze in mid step.

She didn't know who Valkira was. Kahvel obviously did but had refused to tell her. When the Dragon Lord turned to face her, she realized right then that Kahvel had been right. This bit of news, whatever it was, was not something Rinbok wanted to hear. A look of sheer incredulity came over his features.

"How do you know that name?"

Rinbok Intherer's body resembled a tightly coiled spring, which looked as though it would snap under the strain at any moment. Pryllan slowly backed away.

"No one knows that name," Rinbok continued. He stepped forward and deliberately stomped on the ground with each step. Whatever semblance of order the Dragon Lord had restored to his horde collapsed under the vibrations. "I haven't ever spoken that name aloud. To anyone!"

At last, the rage boiled over and Rinbok roared his anger. Pryllan was properly cowed. She dropped her head and refused to make eye contact.

"How could she be in danger? No one even knows she exists!"

Pryllan's curiosity got the better of her. "My Lord, I offer my sincerest apologies for asking this, but who is Valkira?"

Rinbok towered directly over her, fangs bared. It looked as though he was going to attack her!

"Valkira is my offspring," Rinbok told her in a frighteningly calm voice. "My one and only offspring. Her existence has been kept a secret ever since she hatched. No one knows she is even alive. So I ask you, how could she be in danger?"

Pryllan was ready with her answer. "I'm told it was the trolls. They—"

"Trolls? How did those detestable walking dung heaps find her?"

Pryllan couldn't help it. She panicked.

"Kahvel told me, my Lord. He is unable to use the Collective, as I am. He knows I still retain flight so he asked if I would deliver the message. He didn't tell me who Valkira was. I asked. He refused to say."

"How did Kahvel learn of her existence?" Rinbok demanded. He scoffed loudly. "I will determine that later. Where is Valkira now?"

Pryllan, intent on trying to contact Kahvel to warn him things weren't going as planned, missed the question. Rinbok smashed the ground before her with both forelegs.

"I *said*, where is Valkira now? Has she been driven away from the nest?"

Thinking quickly, Pryllan nodded.

"Do you know where she was taken?"

Pryllan nodded again.

"Then we must go to her. Now!"

"Of course, my Lord. Follow me!"

Pryllan turned tail and fled the cavern. Rinbok Intherer's thunderous steps sounded directly behind her, so close that he was practically stepping on her tail. She hastened forward, but the much larger dragon easily paced her. He was following!

Pryllan swallowed nervously. The humans had better know what they were doing.

* * *

"Why are you so angry?"

"We do not like the dragons."

"Why?"

Dirgath sighed. "They force us to do things their way. Always their way. Tired of it, we are."

Pravara looked up at the shiny silver dragon with jagged black stripes running across its chest. She had become fascinated by the strange two-headed dragons ever since she met Syrreth and Ferreth and wanted to learn all about them. This zweigelan, however, was just as grumpy as the first one.

Had been, Pravara corrected. Syrreth and Ferreth were much more pleasant to be around now. Hopefully this one would become nicer as time went on, too. Determined to be friends, Pravara followed the second zweigelan wherever it went, even if it appeared to reverse direction to try and evade her.

"Do you think all dragons are bad?"

Tirgath ignored the question but Dirgath gave an affirmative shake of his head.

"I'm not bad," Pravara insisted.

"You're young," Dirgath told her. "You'll get there."

"Why?"

Tirgath growled. "It's considered rude to ask too many questions."

"It is?"

Tirgath nodded. "Aye."

"Are you sure?"

"I am positive."

"My father says only fools are positive," Pravara helpfully informed him.

Dirgath eyed the young dragonlet. For the first time, he smiled. "Are you sure, young one?"

Pravara nodded. "I'm positive. Oh. That's not fair! You tricked me!"

Amazed she had fallen for Dirgath's clever ploy, Pravara was silent as she considered how to best the zweigelan at his own game. The human male she was fond of wandered close. Steve winked at her.

"Is everything alright over here?"

Pravara nodded. She met Dirgath's eyes and silently vowed to win the next battle of wits with him. Steve looked up at Dirgath and Tirgath. "Remember, you wanted to tag along. We let you. Play nice or go home."

Dirgath and Tirgath lifted their noses high in the air. In unison. Steve looked over at Syrreth. "Are you sure you're not related? I've seen you do that move a few times."

Syrreth gave him a scornful look. "Hmmph."

"My parents," Pravara continued, "always tell me what to do, too. They constantly order me around."

Tirgath gave the young dragon a sidelong glance. "Does that not irritate you? Do you not wish they would leave you alone?"

Pravara nodded. "Aye, I do."

"Then tell them, you should."

"I have."

"And?"

"They laugh at me. They tell me I'm young and wouldn't survive on my own."

"You wouldn't," Dirgath assured her.

The young dragon frowned. "Are you siding with my parents?"

"If you feel you can survive on your own then what's stopping you?" Dirgath asked as he looked down his nose at the young wyverian.

"I couldn't leave my home. I'd miss my parents. They just want what's best for me. Just like your parents do for you."

Both heads scoffed loudly. Pravara looked at them with sadness. "I'm sorry. Were your parents called to Nevir? As long as you're part of the Collective, you're never alone. I wish I was old enough to join."

Tirgath scoffed loudly. "Whatever for?"

Pravara gave Tirgath such an uncomprehending look that the silver zweigelan's right head was taken aback.

"It's what all dragons strive for," Pravara finally answered. "I want to be like them. I want to fit in. I want to hear the song of my brethren."

"Did your parents force you to recite that?" Tirgath bitterly asked. "Typical wyverian hypocrisy."

Properly confused, Pravara turned to Steve. "What does that mean?"

Steve laid a reassuring hand on her side. "Don't listen to them. He's just a grouch. Ignore them."

Pravara nodded once then looked back over at the silver zweigelan. "Mother tells me the Collective will return soon."

"The Collective is not for us," Dirgath quietly responded.

"It is so," Syrreth corrected.

Dirgath and Tirgath turned to see Syrreth and Ferreth join Pravara and begin to walk alongside her.

"Heard the songs she speaks of, we have," Syrreth told them.

"Not as bad as we had originally thought," Ferreth added.

The silver zweigelan faced off against its green counterpart.

"Have you grown to enjoy being their puppet?" Tirgath sneered.

Ferreth bared his teeth and growled. Worried that he might actually try to snap at Tirgath, Syrreth deliberately swung his head in front of his twin's.

"We hated being included in their Collective at first," Syrreth admitted, "but have since discovered something we hate even more."

Curious, both Dirgath and Tirgath cocked their heads to the side, as if they had heard a high-pitched noise.

"And what would that be?" Dirgath wanted to know.

Syrreth met their gaze. "Returning to solitary life."

"Zweigelans do not need the support of others," Tirgath spat out. "Not now and not ever."

"Aye, we do," Syrreth countered. "Try it sometime, you should. Wait until you are fully accepted by the wyverians. Then, if you prefer, you may leave. The Dragon Lord says it is up to us now whether we wish to remain in the Collective. An honor, it is. We have accepted that honor. You should as well."

Dirgath snorted. "Do you believe that?"

The green zweigelan nodded both of its heads.

Dirgath eyed Tirgath and stepped off to the side and started a hushed argument between themselves. Syrreth and Ferreth moved off to the side as well.

"Why did you come?" Ferreth asked them, genuinely curious. "You told us what you know. You don't have to be here. Why bother in the affairs of the dragons?"

"We want to see her outwitted," Tirgath answered as he and his twin smiled lecherously.

"Why?" Steve asked as the dragons were loud enough he could still hear them. "You don't owe her any allegiance."

"Arrogant, she is," Tirgath told him.

"Believes herself superior, she does," Dirgath agreed.

Understanding, Steve smiled. "She thinks she's better than you. That must be annoying."

Neither of the silver zweigelan's heads responded.

"So you're just waiting, *hoping*, that she'll be defeated. Humiliated. Am I right?"

Dirgath shrugged and tried to act indifferent. "Whether successful or not, it should be interesting to watch."

Steve suddenly straightened. He reached an arm up behind his back to grasp the hilt of his sword. A knowing look passed over his face. He glanced at Sarah and nodded. "It's showtime."

"Already?"

"They're ready, so yeah. We're up."

Sarah looked at him. "Okay, let's do this. Dirgath, Tirgath, make yourself scarce. Be watching and be ready. If you want to see the female zweigelan defeated, then we're going to need your cooperation."

Dirgath and Tirgath nodded silently. They disappeared into the densely wooded forest. Steve waited a few moments before he cracked his knuckles and took a few deep breaths. He then allowed his posture to slump. He became fidgety, restless.

As he nervously glanced around the surroundings, he briefly locked eyes on their zweigelan.

"Remember," he quietly whispered to them. "No matter what you're about to hear, just play along. Understand?"

Syrreth nodded while Ferreth began glancing nervously around, as instructed. Steve smiled and gave them a thumbs-up, but the meaning was lost on the two-headed dragon. Steve looked at Sarah and leaned forward. Wanting to be included, Syrreth and Ferreth stretched out their necks so they could hear what was being said. Little Pravara squeezed past their zweigelan so that she could be next to Sarah. Steve spoke loudly so everyone could hear him.

"So do you think they'll agree to the trade or do you think they'll want something else in exchange for it?"

"In exchange for what?" Pravara automatically asked.

Sarah placed a hand on her nose and smiled.

"Don't say anything," she quietly told the young dragon. "Just listen and play along, okay?"

Pravara fell silent.

Sarah nodded. "I'm certain they will. They really didn't

like giving up their helix. Personally, I think they're getting the worst part of this deal. A firestone. Can you believe it? Even the Kri'yans don't have one of those."

"I assume you are Lady Sarah and Sir Steve?" a gruff voice suddenly announced.

Everyone turned to look back at the forest. Three dwarves dressed in full leather armor, complete with black dual-headed battleaxes strapped across their backs, had appeared. They bowed so low that the tips of their beards brushed the ground.

"I have a package for you from Master Breslin," the lead dwarf announced.

"Louder," Sarah whispered.

Caught off guard, the dwarf blinked at her. "What?"

"Say that louder."

"Very well."

The dwarf cleared his throat a few times. "Ahem, ahem. I have a package for you from Master Breslin," the dwarf said again, this time projecting his voice almost to the point of a shout.

There were a few seconds of silence as the three dwarves eyed the humans, who in turn, eyed them back. Sarah nudged her husband. Steve snapped his fingers.

"That's right. I have lines." He straightened and then said in a much louder voice, "You've kept your promise. So shall we. We'll get you your ruby helix back. The last thing we want to do is return this rare firestone."

"How is it the stone hasn't incinerated the package?" Sarah asked as she took the tightly wrapped bundle. She looked at the lead dwarf and waited for an answer.

"How is *what* not burning the package?" one of the other dwarves asked, bewildered.

"You were told to play along," Steve whispered to the dwarves. "No matter how absurd. Now, you were saying?"

Recovering first, the lead dwarf chuckled. "Right. That's a good question. The wrappings haven't burnt because the fabric is composed of, um, er, dragon fibers."

Startled, both zweigelans began growling at the dwarves, who hastily started backing away.

"How hot can the firestone get?" Steve asked as he began warming up to the game.

"Hot enough to melt the strongest armor," the third dwarf added. "I've heard it will even melt Narian armor."

"Impossible," the lead dwarf instantly snapped out. "Um, er, I mean, really? How remarkable!"

Sarah started to unwrap the bundle when Steve let out a concerned shout.

"Sarah! What are you doing? If you unwrap that thing, then you'll burn! You'd better let me."

"Darn it, I want to see it," Sarah softly muttered.

"You will, but I have to be first," Steve whispered back.

He took the tightly wrapped bundle from Sarah and began peeling back thick layers of leather.

"That's some mighty fine dragon fibers you have there," Steve commented as he tried to keep a straight face.

"There's a reason you've never heard of a dwarf storyteller," the first dwarf grumbled in a quiet voice but loud enough for Steve to hear.

Peeling back the last layer of fabric, the firestone was revealed. On cue, the stone began to blaze brightly as soon as everyone could see it.

"Ooooo, that's pretty!" Sarah exclaimed as she looked at the exotic jewel.

What she was looking at was a simple fire opal, but thanks to Steve's impressive jhorun, anything would look like it was burning in his hands and still remain undamaged if he so chose. Therefore, this stone gave off the appearance of being covered with flames, yet it wasn't showing any signs of damage.

"Want to hold it?" Steve asked as he offered it to his wife.

Sarah hesitated. "Are you sure?"

"It's perfectly safe," Steve quietly assured her. "It won't burn you unless I want it to, and trust me, I don't want to end up in the doghouse for an entire month."

Sarah giggled quietly. "If you burned me, it'd be longer than that, dear."

Steve smiled and handed her the jewel. He watched, fascinated, as Sarah studied the flaming stone. The fire opal was the size of a baseball, perfectly spherical, and was a grayish white in color. What made the stone even more striking were the bright streaks of vibrant color running through the heart of the opaque gem. Dazzling ribbons of gold were interwoven with stunning cobalt blues and blazing reds. Holding the gem up to the sunlight caused it to sparkle even more. Adding the pyrotechnical effects of Steve's jhorun, the firestone became the prettiest gem anyone had ever seen.

"This is lovely," Sarah decided. "I'm sure Dirgath and Tirgath would gladly exchange their Heart for this firestone."

"Well, let's find out. They said they'd meet us at the edge of the forest. Well, the border is right over there. Let's go find them."

"They better not have wandered off," Sarah muttered under her breath.

"Do you trust this other zweigelan?" Steve asked, remembering that he had more lines to recite out loud.

"No," Sarah admitted as she shook her head, "I don't."

"Well, before she puts in an appearance, maybe you should hide the firestone. Just in case."

"Hide it where?"

"How about that tree?" Steve suggested.

He was pointing to a fallen log that looked as though it had been hollowed out on one end, no doubt by some burrowing creature. There was more than enough room to stash a jewel. Sarah got down on her hands and knees and rewrapped the firestone. She reverently placed the leather bundle inside the log and then pulled some dried shrubbery in front of the log's open end. She hastily returned to her husband's side. Together they hurried away from the log, but kept the fallen tree within their line of sight.

"This damn female zweigelan had better be around here," Steve grumbled. "This is an awful lot of work to go through if it isn't."

Sarah smiled. She put a finger to her lips.

Right on cue, the silver zweigelan appeared. It hooked the tip of its tail around the closest tree and leaned forward, all without completely leaving the safety of the trees. It fixed Steve and Sarah in its sights.

"Have you brought the stone?"

Steve nodded. "We have. Show us your Heart first."

"Our Heart is here," Dirgath assured him. "It is safe. Give us the firestone."

"You can have the stone once we're holding the ruby helix," Steve gravely told the zweigelan. "And not a moment sooner. We trust you about as much as you trust us."

"We will not show our Heart until we see the stone."

Sarah laid a hand on Steve's outstretched arm and gently pushed his arm down to his side.

"Fair's fair. Let's show him."

Sarah teleported the bundle to her arms. She unwrapped the fire opal and held it up as soon as the last layer of packing had been removed. The jewel burned brightly. It was the first time the second zweigelan had seen the firestone.

"We would exchange it," Dirgath decided, using a low voice.

"Gladly," Tirgath agreed.

Steve looked up at the silver zweigelan, who only had eyes for the firestone.

"It's a fake, you guys," Steve whispered to them. "It's only burning 'cause I'm making it burn."

"We'd still exchange our Heart for your firestone."

The group began walking toward the nearby forest. Dirgath and Tirgath were gazing at the firestone with such rapt fascination that Steve halfway expected the dragon's tail to start wagging like a dog's.

"Aren't you forgetting something, human?" the first dwarf asked.

Startled, everyone turned back to the previous owners of the firestone. They had forgotten that the dwarves were still present and had been watching the proceedings. The first dwarf had his hand out, palm up.

"I'll have that ruby now."

Steve hesitated. He looked worriedly at Sarah.

"Umm, we don't have it at the moment," Sarah admitted. "We'll get it to you, okay?" In a much quieter tone she added, "You weren't supposed to say anything else. Maelnar assured me himself!"

"If you want this to be believable then an exchange must be made," the lead dwarf insisted. "Just hand me anything."

"Thanks to you and your big mouth now we have to give you something that looks like a ruby," Steve complained as he scowled at the dwarf.

"Do you promise to return our Heart to us if we were to give it to you?"

Steve turned to look up at Dirgath.

"We do."

"We were asking the female."

Sarah suppressed a giggle as she caught sight of Steve's darkening expression. She nodded. "We do."

One moment the silver zweigelan's claws were empty. A second later the twisted ruby had appeared in the zweigelan's right claw. Dirgath held it out to Sarah, who gingerly plucked it out of the dragon's claw. Sarah, in turn, faced the dwarf and dropped the ruby onto his palm.

"We'll need this back."

The dwarf studied the ruby whorl. Then he turned to Sarah and bowed. "This is the jewel that has caused so much fuss. Milady, I am Vardos. You have my word I will keep this safe."

Sarah curtsied. "I know you will. Better get going."

Vardos nodded. "Right. Until we meet again."

The three dwarves stepped back into the heavily wooded forest and disappeared.

Tirgath spoke up. "We were serious. We will exchange our Heart for the firestone. May we see it?"

"This is just for show," Steve reminded them, as he took the jewel from Sarah and showed it to Tirgath.

Since the jewel had been uncovered, Steve ordered his jhorun to keep the gem nestled in a bed of flames. *No burning,* he told his jhorun. *Put on a show, sure, but the jewel needs to remain unharmed.*

The firestone blazed brightly as tongues of red flames danced through Steve's fingers and across the glassy surface. Steve raised the jewel high into the air and at the same time blasted his jhorun up through his hand, making it look like the firestone had just emitted a jet of fire.

Facing away from the forest, Steve waved the stone through the air. A snaking tentacle of fire shot out and hovered in the air for a few moments before eventually fading away. No matter how he waved the jewel through the air he instructed his jhorun to create a burning strand of fire in the same shape so that it looked as though the gem had created the streaks of fire.

Dirgath and Tirgath only had eyes for the firestone. Slowly, one of the zweigelan's claws stretched out and remained open, palm facing up. He wanted the firestone.

Steve shook his head. "Nuh-uh. No way. I think our firestone is worth more than your helix. I think we need to renegotiate."

He handed the gem back to Sarah, who wrapped the pieces of leather back around it and teleported it back to its hiding place within the log. Sarah suddenly looked at him. Goosebumps had appeared on her arms. Steve returned her gaze and stiffened. The hairs on the back of his neck were standing up.

"Are you feeling this?" Steve quietly asked Sarah. "It feels like we're being watched."

"I feel it, too," Sarah agreed. "Think it's her?"

Husband and wife turned around just in time to see a sleek red and black shape bolt out of the nearby forest, rip apart the hollow log, and raise the bundle triumphantly up into the air. Twin black heads on thin serpentine necks grinned maliciously at the two humans before the leather wrappings were ripped off the jewel. It held the firestone up in its left claw and hesitated as it was expecting bolts of flame to come erupting from its hand.

Nothing happened.

The gem sat harmlessly, glittering in the sunlight, in the red dragon's hand. It wasn't burning. Confused, the female zweigelan looked up at the approaching humans and growled dangerously. It again tried to use the non-existent powers of the gem before finally giving up and streaking back to the forest.

It happened so fast that the third zweigelan vanished into the trees before any of them could move. The black tip of its tail was the only visible part of it, and even that was rapidly disappearing, much like a coil of rope would be pulled into the water if it was attached to a sinking anchor. The tail suddenly froze in place and at the same time everyone heard twin bellows of outrage. Without warning, the tail was yanked backward, dragging the struggling zweigelan with it.

Trees were uprooted and deep gouges appeared in the soft earth as the red zweigelan, with black wings and dual black heads, was dragged out of the forest by its tail. Sarah pulled the struggling creature a full fifty feet away from the forest's edge before she finally ordered her jhorun to stop. The female zweigelan shrieked with rage and lunged at them.

Sarah jumped backward in alarm as twin jets of fire blasted from Steve's outstretched palms, hitting the black-winged red dragon full in the chest. Unaffected by the blast the third zweigelan readied another lunge, but was suddenly lifted up off the ground. It writhed and flopped around in the air as though someone had electrified its tail. Cursing, growling, groaning, hissing--the zweigelan went through the entire gamut of emotions while trying to find some way to pull itself back to the ground.

"I'm going to have to lower her," Sarah gasped. As strong as her jhorun was, it wasn't enough to keep a creature the size of a dragon in the air very long.

"How much longer can you hold her?" Steve asked as he pulled several of the power crystals from his sword's scabbard. He handed the mimets to Sarah.

"It's hard to say. It feels like I'm depleting my jhorun faster than I can replenish it. Twenty seconds maybe. I'm sorry!"

Steve faced the angry glares from the twin black dragon heads.

"You must be this female zweigelan that we've heard so much about."

Chapter 13 — The Gang's All Here

"How dare you!" the female zweigelan's left head screeched in an abrasive, high pitched voice. "Release us at once! You have no right to restrain us!"

"And who do we have the pleasure of addressing?" Steve asked in his most condescending tone. "What are your names?" He pulled out two more of the crystal power discs and handed them to Sarah, who was showing definite signs of strain. Beads of sweat were starting to trickle down her forehead. "You should set them down. Just don't let go of them."

Sarah gratefully lowered the female to the ground with a solid thump. As soon as contact was made with the ground, the red zweigelan frantically scrambled toward the safety of the trees. Black wings flapped uselessly as neither wing nor claw could make any purchase.

Growing angry, Steve blasted several jets of fire up into

the air. When he saw that his flames were being ignored, he directed a jet to one of their black wings. Roaring in pain, the zweigelan snapped both her wings closed and twisted about until she found the person responsible for her singed wing.

Steve smirked. "That got your attention, didn't it? Dragon scales may be some of the toughest materials I have ever encountered, and quite fireproof, but your wings don't have those scales. Remember that. Now, why don't you sit down, zip your lips, and listen to what we have to say, okay?"

The female's left head eyed Steve with more malice than he would have thought possible. The right head was directing its own evil glare at Dirgath and Tirgath. Then it noticed another of its kind watching quietly just behind the silver zweigelan.

"What are you two doing here?" the left head screeched. "Stop acting like the sniveling little worms I know you are and do something useful! Destroy them! Now!"

Steve glanced worriedly at Syrreth and Ferreth. The last thing he needed to worry about was whether the green zweigelan would switch loyalties. One look at the firm resolve that had appeared on both Syrreth and Ferreth's faces confirmed he didn't have anything to worry about. The look of disgust on Syrreth's face spoke volumes.

"We need to break this curse," Sarah said after she snapped her fingers a few times to get the female's attention. "You have grievances with the dragons. That's understandable. However, this curse is targeting not only the dragons but you zweigelans, too."

Two sets of sunken eyes in pitch black faces swiveled to stare at Sarah. "Impossible!" the right head screeched.

"Liars!" the left head accused.

Steve and Sarah shared a glance.

"I'd say that proves Ms. Congeniality here wasn't trying to double cross the other two," Steve commented.

Right Head briefly glanced at Steve before refocusing its attention back on Sarah.

"The filthy wyverian population must be punished. Every dragon should be made to suffer as much as we have."

"What suffering?" Steve sputtered. "So the Dragon Lord

called you guys a name. While I agree he shouldn't have done that, it doesn't mean all dragons should suffer. Besides, Brainiac, you three are suffering the same fate as them."

"Believe that, we do not," the red zweigelan's left head snapped.

"What are your names?" Steve asked, as he deliberately walked away from where Pravara was still lying, crouched in the tall grass.

After a few moments the left head finally answered. "Yamira."

"And your cohort?" Steve prompted.

"Lamira."

"We're not your enemies, Yamira," Sarah pointed out. She let out a little gasp and sat down on the closest rock.

"You okay?" Steve asked her in a hushed voice.

His wife nodded and patted his hand reassuringly.

"I'm burning through the mimets like crazy," Sarah whispered to him. "Hand me some more. I'm out. These crystals may be restoring my jhorun, but not my stamina. I'm feeling beat, as though I've used all my reserves. I don't know how else to explain it."

"Stay seated," Steve told her. He handed her several more charged crystals. "Conserve your energy." He turned to look back up at Yamira and resumed his questioning. "Aren't you curious why you can't spit fire anymore?"

"We *can* spit fire," Yamira insisted.

Bewildered, Steve looked at Sarah, who shrugged. "That doesn't make any sense. If you could've burned me to a crisp then you would have done so by now."

"We have no need to," Lamira told them as she looked down her nose at the humans.

Steve smiled. "Prove it. Spit fire. Give me a single flame and I'll believe you."

"If we spit fire now," Lamira snidely told him, "then you would not survive."

Steve ignited both hands and generated a chaser. Tossing the fireball back and forth between his hands, he smiled.

"Don't let that stop you. Go on, do it. Try to light me on fire. You can't do it, can you? You know you can't. We know you can't. Stop pretending otherwise."

"We choose not to," Yamira told him condescendingly.

Steve wasn't fooled. "Yeah, sure you do. How about flying? Let's see how well you take to the air."

The third zweigelan kept their noses skyward.

"We don't like flying," Yamira informed them.

"Prefer the ground, we do," Lamira confirmed.

"Are you that pig-headed?" Steve asked, incredulous. "Look around you. Look at the other two. Syrreth and Ferreth are at the second stage. They can't spit fire or use the Collective. Poor Dirgath and Tirgath are at stage three. No more flying for them. If you can still spit fire and fly that means you haven't been affected by this curse and more than likely you're trying to make sure you are the last zweigelan in existence. Are you trying to drive your species into extinction? Is that what you want?"

A soft squeak sounded from Dirgath and Tirgath's direction. Nearly a dozen set of eyes, wyverian and human alike, turned to look down at the young dragonlet, who had just poked her head up and over the tall grass. Even Lamira had turned to look at the dragonlet.

"What is it, Pravara?" Steve asked as he cast a worried look over at the young dragon. "Are you okay? Your mother should be here shortly. I hope."

Steve watched Pravara edge away from her hiding place in the grass and hesitate. It looked as though the young dragon was truly afraid of Yamira and Lamira. Steve grunted quietly. He couldn't blame her. This zweigelan was easily the angriest and meanest of the three. Both heads were now staring at the dragonlet with such hatred that Pravara retreated to Syrreth and Ferreth's side. Both of the green zweigelan heads noticed how frightened she'd become and instantly adopted a protective stance. Syrreth bared his fangs and added his growl to that of Ferreth's, eliciting a flinch from the red and black zweigelan, who quickly tried to cover it up. Steve caught Ferreth's eye.

He gave Syrreth a look, as if to say, *is Pravara okay?*

Syrreth returned his gaze and shrugged.

"What's on your mind, Pravara?" Steve asked the

dragonlet. "Why did you make that sound?"

"Why are you being so mean to them?" Pravara timidly asked as she looked over at him.

Yamira and Lamira's eyes widened with disbelief.

"We are not being mean to her," Sarah patiently explained. "We are trying to figure out why she has brought about this curse."

"Out of curiosity, what made you say that?" Steve asked the dragonlet.

"Father says that we should never force anyone to do something against their will."

Yamira grunted while Lamira scoffed loudly.

Sarah laid a comforting hand on Pravara's shoulder. "Honey, we aren't hurting her. We're just talking to her."

"You are holding me against my will!" Lamira snapped out. She was quivering with rage.

"Only because you hold the key to breaking this curse," Sarah reminded her. "Just calm down and give us the talisman and you'll be free to go."

"We do not know what you're referring to," Yamira told her, albeit a little too quickly. She, too, seemed to be trembling uncontrollably.

Sarah looked up with alarm. She held out a hand to Steve. "I need a mimet. Quick! I don't know how she's doing it, but she's fighting my jhorun. She's breaking free! That must be why they're shaking. Hurry!"

Steve's hands flew to his sword's scabbard, where he kept the surplus power crystals. He unsnapped one of the pockets and pulled out a mimet, but before he could get it to Sarah the last ounce of her jhorun was gone. Wordlessly she tipped over backward on the rock she had been sitting on and landed in the soft grass.

Roaring triumphantly, the red zweigelan rose to her full height and lunged at Sarah's still form. Steve ignited both hands and blasted twin jets of fire, hoping to slow the zweigelan. His stomach sank as he realized he wasn't going to make it.

"Over here, you creep!" Steve called out as he waved his lit hands, trying frantically to get Yamira and Lamira's attention.

The problem, Steve realized, was that the female dragon was aware that only one person was capable of immobilizing her and that was Sarah. They could not let that happen again. Generating a chaser in each hand, Steve cocked an arm and prepared to throw one of the fireballs. Just as he was swinging his arm forward, a green blur swished by him and snatched Sarah from the ground.

It was Syrreth and Ferreth. They withdrew a fair distance and gently placed Sarah's unconscious form down into the tall grass. Steve nodded appreciatively. Ferreth nodded back. A loud commotion from behind caused him to spin around. With both hands still blazing, Steve saw that the female zweigelan had chosen to attack Dirgath and Tirgath. What should have been an even fight between the two zweigelans was turning out to be anything but.

Dirgath and Tirgath clawed and bit at the female whenever she got close, but the red and black zweigelan proved to be too cunning. Yamira and Lamira were quicker, stronger, and more motivated to win this fight. It would be over in moments.

Steve herded Pravara to the edge of the forest, for safety. The battle went eerily quiet and he saw that each of the zweigelans had completely coiled themselves around the other, like a snake trying to overpower its prey. The red zweigelan was wrapped so tightly around the silver that they resembled a huge candy cane, one that continued to writhe in anger, each attempting to bite into the other.

Pravara stared at the battling dragons with wide, unblinking eyes. The little dragon kept trying to say something to Syrreth but her small voice was lost over the roars from each combatant. Suddenly, she darted around Steve and raced toward Dirgath and Tirgath. Steve yelled a warning, but couldn't make his voice heard over the ruckus. Syrreth and Ferreth, unfortunately, had chosen that exact moment to glance over to make sure Sarah was still alright.

This isn't going to end well, Steve thought with alarm as he raced toward Pravara and the fighting zweigelans. Where was Pryllan? Why hadn't she arrived yet? If she didn't get here soon then they were going to wind up with a casualty. There was no way he could prevent Pravara from reaching the zweigelans.

Desperate, and with no other recourse, Steve pressed a finger to each of his temples, in the proper telepathic manner, and tried to get Pryllan's attention.

Pryllan! HELP! We have a problem!

A speck appeared in the sky and rapidly increased in size. Steve stared with relief as Pryllan's familiar green form descended from the sky. There were no attempts at stealthiness. She hit the ground so hard that nearby pine trees lost most of their needles.

What is going on?

Steve mutely pointed toward the two fighting zweigelans. Pryllan's jaws opened in shock. Her precious baby, her one and only offspring, had just rushed to a friend's defense and was now circling the tightly coiled zweigelans growling as loudly as she could. Pryllan leapt forward.

Little Pravara, trying to help, darted in to bite the tip of Yamira and Lamira's black tail. She knew the tip of her own tail was incredibly sensitive and could only hope other wyverian tails were the same.

They were.

Yamira and Lamira roared in pain. Within seconds the two zweigelans had ceased their wrestling match. Dirgath and Tirgath limped away as fast as they could. Yamira spun toward the young dragon. Pravara bared her short fangs and growled another warning at the angry female zweigelan.

Yamira and Lamira bunched their muscles and prepared to lunge. Two blasts of fire snaked through the air and headed straight toward the female zweigelan's leathery wings. Steve was on the run toward them.

Yamira saw the fire and folded both wings flat against its back. Lamira smiled maliciously as the twin heads watched the fire jets miss their targets. However, Yamira's smile vanished as she saw that the twin jets of fire had just curved unexpectedly and were now circling around for another attempt. Nudging its twin, Yamira tried to dodge again, but this time the jets dipped low and slammed into both wings.

Both black heads roared in pain. In her fury, Lamira saw that Pravara was still within range. She again tried to attack the young dragon. A silver wing with jet black stripes whipped in, viciously swept the ground, knocking everything before it violently backward.

Pravara was knocked off her feet and went tumbling into the tall grass. The third zweigelan refocused its efforts on Dirgath and Tirgath, who was now standing directly in front of Pravara's patch of grass. The injured silver zweigelan was trying to slowly back away from the advancing female while keeping Pravara shielded from sight. Fortunately for Dirgath and Tirgath, Yamira and Lamira's luck turned for the worse.

Pryllan.

The huge green dragon finally made it to her offspring's side. In the blink of an eye, she had located her baby in the grass and coiled her long tail around her, lifting her up and out of harm's way. She stretched out her tail and dropped her child as far away as she could. Once Pravara was safe, Pryllan turned back to the red and black zweigelan and roared her challenge.

For a few seconds it looked as though Yamira and Lamira might back down, as Pryllan easily out massed the two headed dragon. With her claws ripping into the grass-covered valley floor as she crouched low, Pryllan readied herself to attack. She surged forward and the red and black zweigelan vanished right under her nose.

"Watch out!" Steve shouted. "She's right behind you!"

Pryllan whipped her head around to check her flank. There was a loud scraping sound and a brief flash of pain as Yamira and Lamira darted in for a quick bite, damaging several scales in the process. A split second later the female zweigelan was gone.

"You need to be on your guard!" Steve called out. "She's moving way faster than you are!"

Pryllan growled ominously, jerking her head left and right, as she tried to locate her foe. Another clang sounded; the enemy took another bite and damaged several more of her scales. Catching sight of a black-tipped red tail disappearing into the nearby trees, Pryllan rushed to the forest edge. She tried to grab the rapidly receding tail but it vanished.

Twenty feet away a black head poked back through the trees and leered. Pryllan reacted astonishingly fast. She lunged, bit down hard, and heard bones snap. However, instead of tasting blood, Pryllan tasted bark. The zweigelan managed to pull its head to safety at the last second and Pryllan had instead bitten the closest tree.

The majestic pine, rising well over a hundred feet into the air, toppled with a crash. Pryllan's bite sheared it off at the trunk. Steve and Pryllan both looked up hearing loud hissing.

Yamira and Lamira appeared in the midst of the trees nearly thirty feet away this time and were regarding Pryllan with speculative eyes. Lamira turned to look at the thickness of the fallen tree trunk while Yamira kept an eye on Pryllan's location.

"You might be smaller and quicker than she is," Steve quipped, correctly guessing what the female zweigelan was thinking, "but she only needs one bite to take you out. Do us both a favor and stop this nonsense!"

Both heads vanished. They saw a fleeting glimpse of the long, sinewy tail before it, too, vanished into the woods. Hisses and snarls erupted as the female zweigelan was once again pulled from the trees by its tail. Steve turned and saw that Sarah had awakened, had found the mimet Steve had thrown to her, and had replenished her jhorun. While still physically tired, Sarah's jhorun was more than up to the task of pulling Yamira and Lamira back out into the open.

"Nice timing, babe!" Steve called out to her. "Welcome back! How long can you hold her?"

Sarah shook her head. "I don't know. Not for long. Groggy. Honey, whatever you're going to do, you'd better do it *quick*."

The red zweigelan attempted its old trick to break free. Once more Steve watched Sarah shudder with pain as the female zweigelan fought like a demon. Hissing and snarling, Yamira and Lamira tore up the ground, grabbed hold of nearby trees and anything else to escape the iron grip of Sarah's jhorun.

The strain was taking its toll on Sarah. How many times

could someone recharge their jhorun before their body finally became too exhausted?

A quick check of his sword's scabbard revealed he only had four charged mimets left. That meant Sarah had to have used at least fifteen! No wonder she was so tired!

Sarah stumbled and almost fell to the ground. Steve sprinted over to her and caught her as she stumbled again. He gently lowered her to a sitting position.

"I hate to say this but you're going to need to let Tweedle Dee and Tweedle Dum there go."

"Can't," Sarah murmured. Her eyes were heavy, practically closed.

"Sit here and rest. Get your strength back. Pryllan, we have to let them go. Sarah can't hold her anymore. Are you ready?"

Pryllan nodded. Yamira and Lamira roared in unison. Unfortunately, they were ready, too.

With a quiet sigh, Sarah relinquished her hold on their captive. She leaned back in the grass and practically disappeared from sight. And then, all hell broke loose.

Yamira and Lamira surged forward, heading straight toward Sarah. Before Steve could bring his hands up to retaliate, Syrreth and Ferreth placed themselves directly in front of Sarah and added their own roars to Pryllan's.

"Stand back," Pryllan growled as she cautiously circled the glade. "Syrreth, Ferreth, you are no match for her."

Syrreth shook his head. "Faster than you, she is."

"More experienced at fighting, she is," Ferreth added.

Syrreth and Ferreth barely had time to jump out of the way as the female zweigelan lunged toward Pryllan, who bellowed with rage, lurching forward.

Amazed, and a little frightened at the brutal savagery, Steve squatted low in the grass next to Sarah. Catching sight of a tarnished silver chain around Sarah's neck, Steve gently pulled on the chain at the nape of her neck, but was hampered by Sarah's tunic. Steve gently untied the leather cord and pulled again on the chain. A tarnished silver medallion with a slightly misshapen purple crystal emerged from beneath Sarah's shirt.

It was the gift from Shardwyn all those years ago when

the two of them had set out in search of Maelnar, Breslin's father. This medallion, Steve knew, was enchanted to repel physical attacks, but was useless against jhorun. He gripped the medallion and gently twisted, activating a hidden compartment. Steve pulled the tiny crystal vial of elixir he knew was concealed. Wetting his finger with a drop of the clear potion he gently touched his finger to Sarah's lips. Seconds later her eyes opened. She looked down at the open medallion sitting on her chest, noted that the top of her shirt had been untied, and then looked up at her husband.

"What do you think you're doing?"

"Helping you. What did you think I was doing?"

Sarah raised an eyebrow. Steve's ears turned red. He shook his head in exasperation.

"Get your mind out of the gutter. I was just getting this stuff ready. Others will need help sooner or later."

Sitting up, Sarah retied her shirt, watching the battling dragons. Yamira and Lamira were clearly quicker, but Pryllan had more power. Both appeared to be evenly matched. She caught sight of Dirgath's head, leaning against a tree just inside the forest. She couldn't see Tirgath. She tapped Steve on his shoulder and pointed at the forest.

"Go help them. They took a nasty beating. I'm sure they could use a drop of kaormac elixir right about now."

Steve ran over to the silver zweigelan and applied a drop of liquid to each head. Tirgath's head lifted off the ground. Broken scales healed. The torn skin on their wings sealed itself right before their eyes. Twin silver heads regarded him for a few moments before each bowed low.

"Why did you do that?" Dirgath asked. "That elixir must be extremely valuable."

"It is," Steve confirmed, "and it's what friends do for each other. Thank you for saving Pravara. Where is she, anyway?"

"She is unconscious," Tirgath informed him. "She landed badly when her mother dropped her here."

"And you're watching over her?" Steve asked. He was both impressed and extremely grateful at the same time.

Dirgath nodded. "Aye. We have been guarding her, and will continue to do so."

The intensity of the roars increased. As Steve turned to see how the battle was faring, he saw Lamira rear back with her fangs bared. Pryllan's left wing had drooped down and had made a target of itself. Lamira was going to bite Pryllan's wing! He had to warn her!

The left wing snapped back against Pryllan's abdomen. She twisted her torso around, pulling her left wing away from the zweigelan. What Lamira, and Yamira for that matter, weren't expecting was that the exposed wing had been a ploy to get the female to venture closer.

It worked.

As Lamira had been readying herself for a bone-crunching bite to Pryllan's wing, Pryllan twisted to her left. There before her was a prime opportunity. She took it.

Pryllan curled her right claw into a fist. In its clenched state her fist was easily the size of a Clydesdale horse. She lashed out at Lamira with a tremendous right hook. Lamira's head snapped back so hard that several fangs were knocked out of her mouth and her jaws slammed closed. All four of the red zweigelan's feet cleared the ground and she landed on her back.

Yamira hissed with annoyance, trying to regain her feet, while Lamira blinked several times rapidly, attempting to regain her senses. She ran her forked tongue over her broken teeth and growled.

Standing thirty feet away, Sarah slowly rose to her feet. She had just watched Pryllan clobber Lamira, but it wasn't the blow that had caught her attention. It was the zweigelan's mouth. With her jaws wide open, Sarah had seen a flash of metal amongst her fangs. Could she be hiding the talisman inside her mouth?

"Nice punch, Pryllan!" Steve shouted. He glanced over at the female zweigelan who was slowly rising to her feet. "Where'd you learn to do that? I can't imagine all dragons fight that way."

"I have no idea," Pryllan admitted as she slowly unclenched her claw. "I think I picked it up from Sarah's mind."

Sarah suddenly materialized in front of Steve. She excitedly took his hand and looked over at Pryllan. She tapped the side of her head.

Pryllan, can you hear me?

Aye.

There's something metal in Lamira's mouth. I think it's the talisman!

Steve pumped a fist into the air. *Now we're talking. We need to take a look inside her mouth. The question is, how?*

Yamira and Lamira were back on their feet but weren't moving too well.

We need to see inside Lamira's mouth, Sarah explained. *I think she has the talisman concealed in there. We need to spread out and make her mad. If she gets mad then she'll start roaring, or possibly try to bite.*

Steve was incredulous. *That's it? That's the plan? Make her mad? What if she attacks one of us? Pryllan is the only one that stands a chance against her.*

Circle around her, Pryllan instructed. **Keep her in the center. Do not be caught unaware. She will worry more about me than anyone else. We can use that to our advantage. We must hurry, though. Observe. She becomes steadier with each passing moment.**

For the past minute or two Yamira and Lamira remained motionless, taking huge gulps of air. Pryllan was sure once their disorientation had passed, they would disappear into the forest. That mustn't happen. They needed that talisman! If Sarah wanted to peer inside Lamira's mouth, then she would personally pin that skinny red neck to the ground and pry her jaws apart with her own talons.

Pryllan placed herself directly in Yamira and Lamira's path. Steve was on her left. Syrreth and Ferreth were directly across from her, and after they informed Dirgath and Tirgath what they were doing, the silver zweigelan was on her right.

Keeping the female zweigelan in the center of their circle, Pryllan spread her wings and snapped them closed. A loud thunderclap echoed noisily through the valley. Yamira's head jerked up and their eyes met. The black head growled a warning. Pryllan returned the growl. Lamira, finally shrugging off the last effects of Pryllan's right hook, looked over at her and growled. Unfortunately, she kept her jaws firmly closed.

A section of a fallen tree suddenly lifted from the ground

and flung itself straight toward Lamira's head. Yamira caught the trunk in her jaws and crunched down, snapping the trunk in half. Both of the black heads turned to see Sarah wave at them.

"A gift from me to you!" Sarah called out. "I have plenty more. Want another?"

A second log rose from the ground and sped toward Lamira's head. The female zweigelan's right head ducked, but not before Yamira caught this log in her jaws, too, and reduced it to splinters. The left head roared in frustration.

Steve blasted a jet of fire above Lamira's head, deliberately missing by a few inches as what Pravara had said earlier was still fresh on his mind. Is that what they were doing? Tormenting a dragon just as a bully would torment a small defenseless child? Steve frowned. He didn't like this at all.

Lamira bared her fangs at him and growled. However, her jaws remained closed.

"You are a disgrace to zweigelans," Syrreth accused, as he and Ferreth circled slowly from the right. "Act alone, you do."

"You are pathetic and weak!" Yamira countered. "Unable to stand up to the tyranny of the Dragon Lord, you are. It is we who are ashamed. Ashamed to know you!"

Two more growls joined the cacophony of grunts, hisses, and snarls.

"They are not weak," Dirgath snapped. He bared his teeth. "Nor are *we*. We do not choose to live as you do."

"We are male," Tirgath smugly told her. "We are superior to you."

Pryllan stopped her circling and turned to glare at the silver zweigelan. She began emitting a deep, low growl. Sarah, who had been popping in and out of existence all around the fight as she desperately sought to see the insides of Lamira's mouth, didn't appear to take notice of the taunt.

Dirgath looked at his twin. "A curious thing to say," he whispered.

"We must be insulting," Tirgath whispered back. "Trying to enrage her, I am."

Dirgath grinned. He looked back at the female of his species. "No female has ever beaten the male of the same species," he haughtily informed them. "Especially the zweigelans."

Yamira scoffed while Lamira growled.

Steve appeared next to Dirgath. "I think you hit a nerve! She thinks she's better than you males. Now's your chance to tell her what you think of her."

Having overheard Steve's comment to Dirgath, Syrreth decided to take a turn. "Belong in the cave, you do," he said, with as much of a sneer in his voice as he could muster.

Lamira finally gave them a roar, but her head angled upward and no one could tell if there was something in her mouth other than fangs.

"Have the intelligence of an immature youngling, you do," Ferreth added with a malicious smile. "We would look to Pravara before we would look to you."

"We should have left you in that hillside cave!" Yamira screeched. "Scavenging for food! Almost called to Nevir, you were! This is how you thank us? By turning against us?"

Lamira looked down her long snout and roared her anger. Sarah materialized directly in her path. Before either Yamira or Lamira could notice, Sarah smiled and vanished again, this time reappearing next to her husband. She was hopping up and down in her excitement.

"What is it?" Steve asked. "Did you see something?"

Sarah closed her eyes and visualized the inside of Lamira's mouth, as she had seen it. One of the small incisors, on her lower jaw, had clearly been metal! What better way for a dragon to hide a talisman than to disguise it as one of their fangs. It had been a perfect plan!

Sarah focused on the artificial fang and asked her jhorun to teleport the fake tooth to her hand. A wet, heavy metallic object appeared in her outstretched hand. Sarah recoiled with shock. It was covered with saliva and still warm! Gross! And what was with that smell? She grimaced and held the slightly curved foot-long phony fang away from her. Her jhorun tingled. It could apparently sense the power emanating from the talisman.

This was it, Sarah thought excitedly. This was the thing they had been searching for! This was the source of the curse!

All they had to do now to break the wyverian curse was to destroy it. For that, she needed her husband.

Sarah tossed the slimy metal fang to Steve, who reflexively caught it. He frowned at the saliva and whiff of Lamira's halitosis.

"Yuck!"

"Honey, it's the talisman!"

Steve blinked with surprise. "What do you want me to do?"

"What else? Destroy it!"

Steve stepped backward a few steps and ignited both hands. Clutching both of his hands tightly around the talisman, Steve blasted his jhorun through his hands and watched the fang slowly turn red. Within moments the fang was glowing brightly, as though it was nestled in the heart of a forge.

Sarah was ecstatic. The talisman was on the verge of melting! Would the curse be instantaneously abolished? How quickly would Pryllan get her flames back?

There was a loud crack, like a firecracker. The talisman ruptured, then it melted. The remnants of the fang dripped through Steve's fingers and dropped to the ground. Grass sizzled and burned as the metal rapidly cooled. Steve looked up at her.

"Now what? Is there something else we have to do?"

Sarah shook her head. "I don't think so. Let Pryllan know the talisman has been destroyed."

"Hey Pryllan!" Steve called out in his loudest voice. "We destroyed it! See if you can use your fire now!"

Both battling dragons paused, turning to look at him. Lamira ran her forked tongue over her teeth while Pryllan took several deep breaths of air. Lamira roared in anger as she realized a certain fang was missing. Yamira also roared as she realized their plan had been foiled.

My flames have returned! Pryllan confirmed. **My blood has begun to warm. Why couldn't you have waited?**

Excuse me? Wasn't the plan to abolish the curse? That's what we did. We destroyed it! You have your flames back!

So do they! Pryllan countered as she suddenly dropped to the ground. Twin jets of fire narrowly missed her as they passed overhead.

Oh, whoops. My bad.

Pryllan wasn't the only one angry with him.

"What in the world did you do that for?" Sarah exclaimed. She punched him on the arm. "Why wouldn't you mentally tell her we destroyed the curse?"

"I was caught up in the moment, alright? Give me a break!"

With fire and flight restored, both dragons took to the skies. The female zweigelan hadn't been exaggerating when it had told them it preferred the ground, as it wasn't that graceful in the air. Pryllan was easily outmaneuvering the red zweigelan at every turn, but since Yamira and Lamira were smaller, she was having difficulty bringing the two-headed dragon down.

Syrreth and Ferreth had just spread their wings in an effort to help Pryllan when the ground began shaking. They nervously eyed each other as the vibrations increased in intensity. Both of the humans had been thrown off their feet. Nearby trees were snapped off at the trunk as something large rapidly approached.

Three trees broke in half as the Dragon Lord finally arrived on the scene. Spying their group, Rinbok Intherer rushed over to demand answers. Then he noticed the battling dragons in the air. His massive head slowly turned to stare at the two humans. Both smiled and nodded. The Dragon Lord returned his attention to the fight above. He gave the tiniest of coughs and watched with satisfaction as a small jet of fire escaped up into the air.

Rinbok exploded upward in a massive flapping of wings. Neither Pryllan nor the zweigelan knew what hit them. Suddenly a third combatant had entered the melee and had easily taken control. A swipe of Rinbok's enormous striped wing pushed Pryllan out of harm's way when Lamira tried to rake her claws down Pryllan's chest. Then he knocked the female zweigelan senseless.

All three dragons landed heavily on the ground. A split second later, the female zweigelan had her wings pinned behind her back and both necks held against the ground. Pryllan slowly regained her feet and approached the Dragon Lord.

"My Lord, I…"

"Your transgression is forgiven," Rinbok told her. He looked down at the struggling zweigelan in his claws and growled once. The red zweigelan instantly fell silent. "I see now why you lured me here. All is forgiven, I assure you. However, I wish to speak to Kahvel. I must ascertain how he learned of that particular subject."

"If you must punish someone, let it be me," Pryllan pleaded as she dropped her gaze to the ground. "He was only helping me."

Another green dragon dropped from the sky and landed nearby with a loud thud. This one was almost as large as Rinbok and looked as surly. However, it remained motionless as it waited to see what would happen. Then a female red dragon landed. Then a maroon one. Suddenly it was raining dragons. Rinbok must have called for reinforcements once he realized the Collective had been restored.

What happened next shocked everyone. Rinbok released his grip on the female zweigelan and moved back a few steps. Yamira and Lamira shakily rose to their feet and they both glared at the Dragon Lord.

"This fight is over," Rinbok declared in a loud voice. His thick green neck muscles rippled as he turned to look at each dragon present, including Pravara, who squeaked with alarm. "There will be no more violence today. Yamira, Lamira, you are free to go."

Yamira and Lamira nervously eyed each other. Lamira turned to look at the safety of the nearby forest.

"Why would you release us?" Lamira asked suspiciously. "What game are you playing now?"

Rinbok shook his head. "No games. I am rectifying a situation that happened long ago. It has been brought to my attention that I referred to you zweigelans as freaks of nature and that you didn't deserve to be called dragons. I offer my sincerest apologies. Dirgath, Tirgath, this is directed toward you as well."

The silver zweigelan joined Pryllan. They gave a small nod of their heads. Rinbok turned back to the female zweigelan, who was slowly trying to slink away to the forest. However, three dragons had blocked their path and were now growling at them.

"Move aside," Rinbok ordered. The three dragons looked surprised, but did as instructed. "As I said, you are free to go. The Collective is a privilege. It's an honor for all dragons to be included. I will never again try to force someone to join that doesn't wish it. Syrreth, Ferreth, that goes for you, too. Dirgath and Tirgath, you may also go about your business. If you wish to stay, I will welcome you as full-fledged members of the wyverian Collective."

"We choose to stay," Syrreth instantly responded. Ferreth nodded in agreement.

Rinbok bowed his head once, causing the other dragons to follow suit. "We welcome you, brothers."

Syrreth turned to Dirgath.

"What say you? Will you stay?"

Dirgath eyed his twin. Then they turned to look at the small group that had become their friends.

"We will stay," Tirgath told the Dragon Lord. "By your leave, my Lord."

Rinbok nodded. "Welcome, brothers."

Everyone turned to look at Yamira and Lamira. Both black heads were staring straight at Rinbok, and everyone could see that neither looked happy.

"You dare try to make amends after so many centuries have passed?" Yamira accused.

"You cannot disregard what was said that easily!" Lamira continued.

"Trust you, we do not!" Yamira added.

"Wouldn't follow you even if you —"

The female zweigelan trailed off as they noticed the Dragon Lord had a very uncharacteristic smile on his face. He looked at both Yamira and Lamira and inclined his head, toward the lake.

"Walk with me. There is much to be said."

The female zweigelan surprised everyone by turning to follow Rinbok west toward the setting sun.

Chapter 14 — It's Good to be the King

How long did it finally take? Neither of us has ever seen a dragon that angry. We could hear her complaining long after the two of you disappeared from sight. That's assuming you managed to convince her to join the Collective."

The Dragon Lord turned to look down at the tiny humans walking beside him. "Are you that certain she joined?"

Both husband and wife nodded.

Rinbok Intherer gave a mighty sigh.

"Three days. Three days of incessant venting."

Steve whistled. "She didn't have anything nice to say about any dragon?"

Rinbok grunted. "She didn't have anything nice to say about *me*. I cannot fault her. I deserved it."

"I'm impressed," Sarah admitted. She looked up at the green dragon towering over the two of them. "You've accepted responsibility. The Dragon Lord I thought I knew would never have done that."

Rinbok elected to remain silent. The three of them, all alone, resumed walking east. The Dragon Lord had reduced his normal gait to a fraction of what it was so that he wouldn't outdistance the two humans walking alongside him.

"How many times did you end up apologizing?" Steve asked good-naturedly.

Rinbok didn't bother looking down. "Once."

Steve grinned. "Only once, huh? How'd that work out for you?"

"Three days, human. She carried on for *three days*."

Sarah cleared her throat. "At least it all worked out for the best, right?"

Rinbok paused in mid step. He dropped his neck down to the ground and eyed Sarah and then Steve.

"Before the event starts I wanted to personally thank you and Sarah. For everything. Pryllan tells me your help was instrumental to lifting the curse. You have performed a great service to me and to all wyverians everywhere. You have my thanks."

Steve stared, open-mouthed, at the enormous reptilian head that was less than a dozen feet in front of him. There was a time, Steve recalled, when the temperamental Dragon Lord wanted nothing more than to put an end to any human involvement in wyverian affairs. Rinbok had barely tolerated the presence of humans, had grudgingly allowed Steve to ride Pryllan and, he was certain, hated every minute of it.

However, now the Dragon Lord not only was taking the time to talk to the two of them, privately, but had actually thanked them for their involvement in this whole situation. Steve had to admit he had been worried about how Rinbok was going to respond after everything quieted down. Being personally thanked by the Dragon Lord was nowhere on the list of possible outcomes.

"Where is everyone?" Sarah asked after they had walked companionably in silence for several minutes. "You made it sound as though everyone is waiting for us."

"They are waiting for *you*," Rinbok confirmed as he turned his great head to look down at her.

Steve looked around the valley floor. Nothing but grassland could be seen straight ahead, but if they looked to the left, they could see the calm blue waters of Lake Raehón. The forest's northern border was slightly to their right. The more they walked, the farther the trees receded from them.

"There's no one out here but us," Steve observed. He looked straight ahead at the leagues of open grassland comprising the majority of the dragons' valley. "Do we really have to walk across that? Just tell us where to go and Sarah can teleport us there."

Rinbok's thick neck turned to look at the nearby tree line. "Right about here will do."

Steve and Sarah eyed each other. Steve slowly spun in place. He still couldn't see anyone else.

"So what exactly are we supposed to be doing here? Is this where your event is being held?"

Rinbok shook his head no.

"What type of event is it?" Sarah asked.

"An event that hardly any humans have ever witnessed," the Dragon Lord told them. He went stock still as though he was using the Collective.

"Are we early?"

"No," Rinbok's deep voice rumbled.

"Is everyone still waiting on us?"

"Aye."

"Are they coming to us or are we going to them?" Sarah wanted to know.

"We are going to them," Rinbok answered.

"You're being awfully damn cryptic," Steve grumped. "Out with it, dragon. What's going on?"

Rinbok's stoic countenance finally cracked. A smile appeared. Moving with the speed only a dragon could muster, Rinbok snatched husband and wife up off the ground and leapt into the air. In the blink of an eye, they were airborne.

"I'm sure Pryllan informed you that I was ready to give up."

Steve nodded. Thankfully Rinbok was flying at a normal velocity, for a dragon, and therefore communication was possible. Had he elected to accelerate to the dizzying speeds

Steve knew the wyverians were capable of, then the air would have been rushing by so fast that conversation would be impossible, with the howling wind.

"She did, yes."

"I truly thought the time of the wyverians was over. I never dreamed that my own folly had caused this."

Ascending through the light, misty clouds Rinbok dipped his left wing and turned until he was facing north.

"Words cannot express how grateful I am that Pryllan asked you two for help," Rinbok continued.

"*Can you believe this?*" Steve whispered to Sarah. "*I've never heard him talk like this before.*"

Sarah put a finger to her lips and shushed her husband.

"Pryllan's actions saved the life of every wyverian."

"You have yourself a very dedicated dragon," Sarah told the Dragon Lord. "Every dragon I've ever seen has been the same way. They are loyal to you. You're obviously doing something right."

"Hmmm."

Steve met Sarah's questioning glance and both craned their necks to look up at the Dragon Lord's distant head.

The southeastern shore of Lake Raehón appeared. Rinbok appeared to be angling for the extreme northeastern edge of the valley, right where the prolific grasslands merged with the heavily concentrated Anakash forest. Both Steve and Sarah gasped with surprise.

There were dragons everywhere.

Reds, blues, greens, yellows, golds, blacks and whites. Every possible color combination they could think of was represented in the huge gathering of wyverians. At least several hundred long serpentine necks lifted skyward to watch the Dragon Lord approach.

Sarah sighed and gently inhaled. Steve sniffed the air and turned to his wife.

"Do you smell that?"

Sarah nodded. She leaned out over Rinbok's claw and gazed at the ground below. From this altitude it looked to Sarah as though there was a purple line separating the edge of the forest from the grasslands of the valley. The purple line stretched south for at least a mile or two. Sarah sighed wistfully.

"It smells like sweet roses with a touch of vanilla. Honey, they're lilacs! It's one of my favorite flowers!"

Steve joined his wife by leaning out over Rinbok's palm, too. As they neared the ground, he could see that the flowers were growing big and tall, looking like large pine cones with the outermost layers being a light purple and the inner petals becoming progressively darker. Having bought Sarah many varieties of flowers, lilacs included, he knew Sarah's expert knowledge of flowers had again served her well.

"We could just teleport down there," Sarah announced. "It'd save you the trouble to…"

"No," Rinbok interrupted. "I am capable of delivering you two safely to the ground."

Rinbok Intherer landed near the edge of the forest and, much to Sarah's chagrin, away from the lilacs. A small group of humans were standing together uncertainly. They recognized Kri'Entu and Ny'Callé from R'Tal, along with their former charge, Mikal. Also present was a tall, thin figure dressed entirely in maroon robes, from the tip of his tall conical hat all the way down to the slippers on his feet. Tufts of steel gray hair were visible under the hat just above his ears.

"Shardwyn looks uncomfortable, doesn't he?" Steve quipped with a smile.

Sarah nodded and then grabbed Steve's arm. "Look over there! Do you see who's standing next to him? And enjoying every minute of it by the looks of it? It's Maelnar! I see Breslin, too."

"I see a bunch more dwarves standing off to the side," Steve told her as he hopped down from Rinbok's open claw. "They really blend in with the trees, don't they?"

Even though they were much shorter than the human King and Queen and farther away, Maelnar, Breslin, and the rest of the dwarves, made it to them first.

"Sir Steve! Lady Sarah! A pleasure as always!"

Steve bowed while Sarah curtsied. He grasped Maelnar's forearm and gave a friendly shake. Breslin caught him by his arm and pulled him in for a hug.

"Sir Steve!" the boisterous dwarf exclaimed. "It's good to see you, lad! And you, Lady Sarah! How have you been?"

Sarah smiled warmly at the dwarf. "We've been really good, Breslin. And you?"

"I just welcomed the birth of my first daughter!" Breslin proudly proclaimed. "Eloise Malanar. She was born just last night!"

Sarah clapped her hands with delight. She darted forward to pull Breslin in for a hug. "Congratulations, Breslin! I'm so happy for you!"

Steve slapped a hand on the dwarf's back. "Couldn't have happened to a finer person, my friend!"

Introductions were made as each of the other dwarves wanted to meet the famous humans responsible for eradicating the dreaded guur during the legendary battle that took place years ago. Steve knew, with absolute certainty, that after the third dwarf had bowed and introduced himself, he'd never be able to remember any of their names.

Rinbok waited patiently for the humans and dwarves to become acquainted. After the Dragon Lord was certain the introductions were finished, he cleared his throat. To any non-wyverians, it sounded like a low growl.

Steve nudged Sarah and leaned down to her ear. "I don't see Pryllan or Kahvel, do you?"

Sarah shook her head no. "I wonder why. Maybe —"

"The last time we gathered like this," Rinbok began, raising his voice to deliberately drown out Steve, "was over a thousand years ago. It was on that fateful day I inadvertently set into motion that which nearly caused our downfall."

It was so still and quiet that husband and wife held their breath.

"I was brash. I was stupid."

The sounds of crickets chirping would have been deafening.

"I called several wyverians, several of our *brothers,* freaks."

Several dozen muted conversations broke out all around them.

"Be silent," Rinbok snapped.

The valley returned to utter silence.

"As I was saying, I insulted another dragon. Three other dragons. In an act of retaliation, they exacted their revenge. I am ashamed to say that they targeted not only me but all of you as well. I accept full responsibility for my actions. I have already apologized and made amends with all three zweigelans. Now, without further ado, let me introduce the newest members to our Collective. Syrreth and Ferreth are standing next to Kemxandra."

Steve looked over at the familiar black female dragon and saw the green zweigelan staring at Kemxandra's luxurious black scales with envy.

"On Rhamalli's right are Dirgath and Tirgath."

Everyone looked over at the silver zweigelan with the jagged black stripes.

"And finally, on my right you've no doubt noticed Yamira and Lamira."

The female zweigelan wordlessly bowed each of their heads.

"They are now our brothers. Treat them as such."

Lamira turned to look at Rinbok and gave him a neutral stare. The Dragon Lord noticed and again cleared his throat.

"*And* sisters. You have also noticed the presence of our allies, the humans and the dwarves," Rinbok continued. "Their help has been invaluable to the abolishment of the curse and will not be forgotten. We owe our allies our thanks."

"Where's Pryllan?" Steve asked, once Rinbok had paused long enough for the multitude of dragons to stare awkwardly at the group of humans. "If there's someone you should be thanking, it's her."

Rinbok smiled a big toothy grin. "That's not for me to decide."

That one statement silenced the entire mass of dragons.

"If not you, then who?" Steve demanded. "You're the Dragon Lord, aren't you? I'd say this falls under your jurisdiction, wouldn't you think?"

"Not anymore, human."

"Come again?"

"Effective immediately, I am abdicating my position as ruler of all wyverians."

No one said a thing. Everyone--dragons, humans, and dwarves included--stared at Rinbok Intherer with expressions of utter disbelief.

"The purpose of this gathering," Rinbok continued, as he looked around at the hundreds of dragons staring back at him, "was to announce the name of my successor. You know him well. Behold! The new Dragon Lord approaches!"

Rinbok pointed a talon toward the nearby forest. Over three hundred wyverian heads turned. There was a collective gasp of astonishment. The dragons formed two lines, standing shoulder to shoulder. Walking slowly through the newly created rows was a golden dragon. As he passed, each dragon bowed low.

Holding her head high, Pryllan followed close behind. A dark green nose inserted itself between Steve and Sarah and nudged them both aside. Once there was enough room for her, Pravara settled down into the soft grass to watch the proceedings with her two favorite humans standing on either side of her.

Kahvel's golden scales sparkled radiantly in the sunlight. Each scale had been polished to a mirror shine. Rinbok, noticing that Kahvel had paused to make eye contact with his two human friends, thumped his tail and indicated his successor should take his place at the front of the procession. Once Kahvel reached the front he turned and looked at Rinbok, who nodded once and stepped aside. Kahvel turned to face the mass of dragons who were jostling amongst themselves to get as close as they could to the new Dragon Lord.

"And *that* is why Rinbok kept summoning Kahvel," Sarah whispered. "Rinbok was probably preparing him for this day."

Steve nodded. "Makes sense."

"Brothers! Sisters! Let us honor my predecessor, Rinbok Intherer!"

Hundreds of dragons raised their heads and roared.

"Never has there been a wiser ruler. I can only hope to lead you half as well as he did."

The ground shook as dozens of dragons thumped their tails.

"What's the deal with the tails?" Steve asked Pravara as he watched the nearest dragon, a white one with streaks of red on its wings, smack its tail repeatedly on the ground.

"I have no idea," Pravara confessed.

"It's to signal agreement," Kri'Entu whispered to him.

"How long are we supposed to hang around here?" Steve asked the king in a low tone.

"Until it's over," Kri'Entu told him with a smile. "It is extremely rare for a dragon to assume the mantle of Dragon Lord while the previous Dragon Lord still lives. I wish I knew why he was doing this."

"Because of Valkira," a low, deep voice said.

Everyone turned to see Rinbok resting comfortably in the grass a dozen feet behind them. The former Dragon Lord glanced around the assembled dragons to try and judge how well Kahvel was doing in his first address as the wyverian monarch. Kahvel, he decided, was doing an admirable job in enlightening the wyverian population about his plans, his thoughts, and some proposed changes to wyverian law.

"You made an excellent choice," Kri'Entu told Rinbok. "He has captured his brethren's attention and is holding it. He is making them think."

Rinbok grunted and the corners of his mouth turned upwards in a smile. "Be that good or bad?"

"Good, of course," Maelnar assured him as he and Breslin joined them.

"Who, or what, is Valkira?" Ny'Callé asked.

"Valkira is my daughter," Rinbok answered. He leveled a gaze at the human monarchs. "She hatched last year. I knew if it became known that the Dragon Lord sired an offspring then that dragonlet would be in mortal danger from the moment she cracked her shell. So her existence was kept hidden."

Rinbok paused; apparently Kahvel had said something else which the dragons agreed on as they all roared in unison. Once he could be heard again, Rinbok continued.

"As I sat in my cave, bereft of fire, shunned from the Collective, and unable to fly, I started to think about Valkira. What type of life could she live as a dragon? Who would be there to care for her? Her mother abandoned the egg once it had been laid. I spent many days searching for her, but no trace could be found. I can only presume she was killed."

"So you're a single father, trying to do what's right," Steve surmised. "Trust me, dude, what you're doing is commendable."

"Is Valkira safe now?" Sarah asked. "Can we do anything to help?"

Kri'Entu was nodding at this. He and the queen were more than ready to help if necessary.

Rinbok shook his massive head. "Thank you, but no. At the moment she is with a trusted friend. Now that Kahvel is Dragon Lord, I am free to protect my daughter as only a father can."

"What about Pravara?" Steve suddenly asked. "If it's that dangerous for a Dragon Lord to have kids then does that mean she's in danger?"

Rinbok looked down at the tiny dragonlet and chuckled. "Ordinarily, I'd say yes, but in this case, Kahvel has more friends than I do. I do not think anyone would risk harming young Pravara as long as you two are nearby."

"She also has us," Shardwyn reminded them. "Kahvel has but to ask."

"That goes for us, too," Maelnar added, jumping up to stand next to the wizard. "Besides, we live closer. Our response time would be faster."

"We have portals," Shardwyn reminded everyone. "It takes time to climb all those stairs from Borahgg. I'm sorry, Master Maelnar, but you're not an underling anymore."

Maelnar crossed his arms over his chest. "Says one geriatric to the other. Your portals don't lead to anywhere around here. We can still get here faster. If young Pravara here needs any help, I'm sure the new Dragon Lord will be contacting us first."

"I'm sure either of us would be more than happy to help," Kri'Entu said as he frowned at the wizard. "This is not a competition, Shardwyn."

"Tell that to him, Your Majesty."

"I think that's wonderful," Sarah interjected, before

wizard or dwarf could think of something else to argue over. "To think that one little dragon has so many protectors. That's amazing!"

"To which I say you have my eternal thanks," Kahvel's voice rang out. "All of you."

Steve, Sarah, Kri'Entu, Ny'Callé, Shardwyn and Maelnar all turned to look at Kahvel, who was staring right at the group of them. Apparently, the new Dragon Lord had heard them arguing.

Kahvel thumped his tail once. "Steve, Sarah, would you please approach?"

The dragons parted once more, forming a narrow aisle from the group of humans and dwarves to the front of the procession. Taking his wife's hand in his, the two of them made their way toward the water's edge and the shiny golden dragon waiting for them there.

"Pryllan asked for help. You two answered when you didn't have to. You left your world behind to come to our aid when we needed it most. You protected my family. I will be forever in your debt."

Kahvel bowed low. One by one, the rest of the dragons copied him. After ten uncomfortable seconds of silence Kahvel reared his head once more and waited for his fellow dragons to follow suit.

"The question is how I should repay you for your kindness?"

"You don't really need to—" Steve began, but was cut off by a nudge from Sarah.

"He already has something in mind," she whispered to her husband. "Accept whatever he offers."

"From this day forward, the two of you hereby have my permission to ride any dragon you'd like."

Wyverian jaws gaped open in surprise. The valley fell silent once more.

"With their permission of course," Kahvel added. "You will never ride a dragon without their full consent. Agreed?"

Steve and Sarah both nodded. "We agree."

The angry murmurings that had started instantly ceased. The dragons were mollified as each knew they'd never grant permission to be ridden. By anyone.

Kahvel moved off as he began to address the individuals who were waiting to be seen. The Kri'yans approached. Mikal, who noticed Pravara had approached and had lowered her head to sniff his outstretched hand, patted her on the head before he turned to his former bodyguards.

"Are you returning home now?" the prince asked.

Sarah nodded. "Yes. There isn't anything else we can do here."

"Well, there's nothing more to be done ..." Steve added as he draped an arm over Sarah's shoulders, "...except to maybe find that damn wizard."

The king sighed heavily at this. Both Steve and Sarah turned to the king.

"Is everything okay?" Steve hesitantly asked.

"About that wizard..." Kri'Entu began.

"What about him?" Sarah asked. "Did you find him?"

The king shook his head no. "On the contrary, Shardwyn has completed the preliminary census of jhorun in the kingdom."

"And? What did you learn?"

"That we have seriously underestimated him," Kri'Entu softly told them as he glanced over at the wizard. "Shardwyn was unsuccessful. We had thought him to be in Avin."

"So what happened?" Sarah wanted to know.

Kri'Entu spread out his hands in a 'who knows?' gesture.

"It was either a false reading or a false trail. Shardwyn insists his jhorun detector is foolproof and therefore sound, so I am forced to believe we were led astray."

Steve raised a hand to ask a question but Sarah instantly pulled it back down. "Put your hand down, dear. You're not in school."

Steve shrugged. "I have a question. You said the renegade wizard led you astray? To where? What did you find?"

The king shook his head. "Nothing significant. We were led to a cottage in Avin. A young family was, and still is, living there. We detected only average jhorun. Why we were led there remains a mystery."

"Is there a more methodical way of checking everyone's

jhorun?" Sarah asked. "He has to be here somewhere."

Kri'Entu nodded. "I would agree. This person appears to take great pleasure in knowing he continues to successfully elude us. Shardwyn is working on additional methods to register jhorun, so I am confident it will only be a matter of time before this wizard's location, and identity, is known."

Ny'Callé tapped the king's shoulder. "We should be going, my love. We are expected in Capily by sundown."

"What do you have going on in Capily?" Steve asked, curious.

"There are a growing number of unexplained phenomena happening in that village," the king explained. "I'd like to believe it's related to that renegade wizard, but I think that would be too obvious of an answer."

"I'm sure everything will turn out fine," Sarah assured the king.

"I hope so." The king held out his right arm and waited until the queen slipped hers through his. "There's nothing quite as disturbing as hearing reports of missing villagers."

"Missing villagers?" Steve repeated, frowning. "How long has that been going on?"

The king's expression turned grim.

"That's what I want to find out."

The adventure continues in
A Portal For Your Thoughts

Craving more adventures in Lentari? Read about Steve and Sarah's first foray to Lentari in
The Prophecy (Bakkian Chronicles #1)!

Author's Note

I hope everyone enjoyed the story. I've wanted to write a story featuring dragons as protagonists for quite some time. And, since everyone asked me to bring them back, our favorite husband & wife team also made an appearance. It was a lot of fun writing about Steve and Sarah again. It was even more fun to introduce some new characters, especially Pravara. I was thinking to myself that it was time for Kahvel and Pryllan to start a family!

Now that the lives of the dragons have been put back in order, what's next for Lentari? Well, I can tell you that there are some strange things happening in Capily and the king has just now learned about it. It's time for the Kri'yans to figure out what's going on! The last thing I'll tell you about Tales of Lentari #3 will be in the form of a question: have you ever wondered how or why our world was chosen to be the one forever linked to Lentari?

Mwahahaha! That was for you, Brett!

Is ToL#3 a prequel? Technically, no. But could it be classified that way? Perhaps.

As always, if you liked the story, I would encourage you to leave me a review wherever you bought the book. Reviews can help authors like myself become more visible on retailers' websites. Reviews, word of mouth, and recommendations. They're all best friends to an author! Thank you for taking the time to read mine.

If you'd like to learn more about Lentari, or else maybe ask me a question or two, feel free to look me up online. I usually have contests running on my blog for print copies or possibly some Lentarian themed merchandise, so check back often. And, thanks to my sister, I'm also on Facebook, so if you'd like to friend an author, I won't turn you down!

Here are the links to use:

Blog: www.AuthorJMPoole.com
Facebook: /BakkianChronicles

Have you submitted a name for a fictional character? A list of the names I used is on the next page. If you submitted a name but didn't see it used, fear not! Keep an eye on the blog. I'm always asking for character names, whether human, dragon, dwarf, or?

To all you fans of the books, you can consider yourselves honorary citizens of Lentari! These books wouldn't be here without your support, so thank you very much! Your friendly notes and messages mean the world to me and I appreciate each and every one of them.

If you'd like to follow the progress on the latest book, I'm working on then I would encourage you to sign up for my newsletter so you'll never miss another book release, or contest, or any other bit of news that I pass along to the readers. You'll even get a free short story for signing up!

The Daily Scroll: Sign Up Today!

J.
April, 2014

Fan Submissions

The following is a list of submitted names from fans of the series which made it into the book. If your name is on here then you have my eternal thanks! Sometimes it is a pain to come up with names for characters. Thankfully I know I can call upon my fans for support! Here we go!

Pravara, Loken, Argus, & Xaj — Giliane
Sciathan — Heather Green
Syrreth & Ferreth — Christine Carr
Lamira (& Yamira) — Mel Henderson
Anghorus — Clawra
Dirgath & Tirgath — Angela Jones
Valkira — Tamara Newman

Thank you very much, guys (& girls)! I appreciate the help!

ABOUT THE AUTHOR

Jeffrey M. Poole is a professional writer who writes in both the fantasy and mystery genres. His series are listed below. Jeffrey lives in picturesque Southern Oregon, with his wife, Giliane, and their Welsh Corgi, Kinsey. His interests include archery, astronomy, archaeology, scuba diving, collecting movies, collecting swords, and tinkering with any electronic gadget he can get his hands on.

In March, 2015, Jeffrey became a proud member of SFWA, the Science Fiction & Fantasy Writers of America! Jeffrey encourages readers to connect with him on Facebook (facebook.com/bakkianchronicles). Fans can also follow him online at: www.AuthorJMPoole.com.

BOOKS BY JEFFREY POOLE

Epic Fantasy
BAKKIAN CHRONICLES
The Prophecy
Insurrection
Amulet of Aria
Disneyland Debacle (short story)
Winter Wonderland (short story)

Epic Fantasy
TALES OF LENTARI
Lost City
Something Wyverian This Way Comes
A Portal for Your Thoughts
Thoughts for a Portal
Wizard in the Woods
Close Encounters of the Magical Kind
The Hunt for Red Oskorlisk (short story)
May the Fang be With You (Pirates trilogy #1)
The Hammer is Strong with This One (Pirates #2)
These are Not the Stones You're Looking For (Pirates #3)
Blast from the Past

DRAGONS OF ANDELA
Harness the Fire
Strike the Spark
Clear the Water*

Mystery
CORGI CASE FILES
Case of the One-Eyed Tiger
Case of the Fleet-Footed Mummy
Case of the Holiday Hijinks
Case of the Pilfered Pooches
Case of the Muffin Murders
Case of the Chatty Roadrunner
Case of the Highland House Haunting
Case of the Ostentatious Otters
Case of the Dysfunctional Daredevils
Case of the Abandoned Bones
Case of the Great Cranberry Caper
Case of the Shady Shamrock
Case of the Ragin' Cajun
Case of the Missing Marine
Case of the Stuttering Parrot
Case of the Rusty Sword
Case of the Secret Staircase (short story)
Case of the Unlucky Emperor
Case of the Ice Cream Crime

www.ingramcontent.com/pod-product-compliance
Lightning Source LLC
Chambersburg PA
CBHW050142120726
47903CB00002B/455